D0484241

A Genuine Vireo Book | Rare Bird Books
Los Angeles, Calif.

RONALD COLBY

A Vireo Book | Rare Bird Books
453 South Spring Street, Suite 302
Los Angeles, CA 90013
rarebirdbooks.com

FIRST HARDCOVER EDITION

Set in Warnock
Printed in the United States.

10 9 8 7 6 5 4 3 2 1

Cover, Title Page, and Prologue Art by Curtiss Calleo.
Interior Images by Alex Tavoularis.

Publisher's Cataloging-in-Publication data
Names: Colby, Ronald, author.
Title: Night driver / Ronald Colby.
Description: First Hardcover Edition | Genuine Vireo Book | New York, NY; Los Angeles, CA: Rare Bird Books, 2018.
Identifiers: ISBN 9781945572654
Subjects: LCSH Taxicab drivers—Fiction. | Revenge—Fiction. | Grief—Fiction. | Murder—Fiction. | Los Angeles (Calif.)—Fiction. | BISAC FICTION / Thrillers / General
Classification: LCC PS3603.O4195 N54 2018 | DDC 813.6—dc23

With deep appreciation and gratitude to my late wife, Patricia van Ryker, for her encouragement, critical abilities, kind understanding, and love.

PROLOGUE

IN THE EARLY MORNING light, retired detective Jim Pearson lumbered from the small, rustic lodge toward the outhouse. In the distance, mist rose off the Nakina River. Pearson looked around and noted with relief the sky was a clear blue. The weather had been abysmal since the small seaplane dropped them off from Juneau four days earlier. At seventy-nine, he acknowledged he might be getting too old for this sort of primitive pleasure.

In the years since his retirement from the Los Angeles Police Department, he had made the annual pilgrimage to hook into huge salmon throughout the Pacific Northwest. But every year, even in the remote regions he frequented, the salmon runs were thinner. So was his blood. *It's too cold, I'm too old, and I'm also not a very good fisherman,* Pearson mused as he sat down on the frosty seat in the outhouse. The ventilation slats let in rays of welcome morning sun. He picked up a magazine from the well-thumbed pile on the wooden plank, put on his glasses, and started browsing.

It was a copy of *TIME*, six months out of date. Pearson flipped his way toward the back of the magazine and quickly scanned the old news when his eyes suddenly fell upon the review of a book by a contemporary photographer. Uncharacteristically, the magazine had given strong praise and printed several pictures from the book. One was of Haitian refugees struggling in deep water near their capsized boat. They reached toward the camera as though the lens might pluck them away from their flimsy sinking craft. Another was of a man staring into the camera from a blackened landscape as the oil fires of Kuwait raged in the background. Exhaustion had left the firefighter's face slack and his eyes glazed, and smoke from the conflagration had coated his face to match the ruined background. There were recent pictures of the revolutions in Libya and Egypt. But the photograph that captured Pearson's attention the most was a poignant shot of three children in Rwanda standing in the doorway of their home. Their bellies were distended from malnutrition. Their eyes bulged from gaunt faces as they stared down at their machete-slain parents lying before them. The photograph told a massive story of the ruination of an entire country. Pearson began to close the magazine out of compassion, when suddenly his eyes caught the name of the photographer. He struggled with the distantly familiar name. Minuscule sparks in his aging brain fired around until they finally hit the right nerve and ignited a memory almost forty years old. Involuntarily, a little puff of air blew from his nose and a tight smile pulled at the corners of his mouth.

CHAPTER ONE

NICK CULLEN COULDN'T BELIEVE he was there. It was 3:30 a.m. on November 3, 1976, and even LA could boast of cold at that hour. The weather forecast promised the arrival of unseasonably hot Santa Ana winds during the day, but now there was only damp cold. Nick wandered around the yard looking for his numbered cab. Inside the long, narrow-fenced lot, cabs were wedged together with little apparent order. The taxis were covered with heavy dew that crawled greedily onto the fabric of his clothes as he brushed against their frigid bodies.

Finally, he found his cab. It was jammed in by two other cold, wet taxis he'd have to move. He was a logical man and reasoned he should immediately try and start his own to make sure it would run. He would then shuttle the others around in the cramped space until he got his free.

Climbing inside, he set about checking the meter numbers as instructed when he abruptly found himself surprised by his surroundings. He stopped and sat back against the seat. Before him, the windshield, wet with mist, reflected the distant yard lights with splays of brightness against the gray glow. The image reminded him of an illuminated television screen with no program. Suddenly, flashed against the windshield was a momentary but graphic detail of the horrible evening that had altered his life forever.

He saw his hand unlock the door to his apartment. Pushing the door open, his eyes quickly took in the scene, and the shock of what he was seeing kept him rooted to the spot. The sound of a metal case hitting the floor snapped him from total paralysis, and for a moment his eyes moved and focused on a man's hand as it reached for a pistol under a sheepskin vest. Nick caught sight of a black panther tattoo on the man's forearm, which moved as his muscles flexed. Suddenly, the arm extended toward him. Nick stood transfixed as he watched the man's finger pull the trigger.

Inside the cab, Nick tensed as he often did when the memory unexpectedly leapt back upon him. He violently shook his head in an effort to throw off the compelling images. When his mind completely returned to his dank surroundings, he noticed the seat was damp and the steering wheel felt like ice. *Next time, I'll wear gloves,* he thought. When he turned the ignition, the engine groaned but refused to start. He tried pumping the accelerator, tried waiting, tried not pumping, but still the worn engine declined his invitations.

Sitting back against the brittle plastic, Nick glanced at the cars surrounding him. Maybe he should forget the whole idea. Just get out, walk from the lot, and go home. But, he had to admit to himself, there was to be no walking away. Getting the cab going was a necessity. It was the only immediate hope he had for his financial survival and planned revenge.

He rapidly pumped the accelerator a few more times, floored it, snapped on the ignition, and heard the engine heave to life with a rod-clattering, tappet-tapping surprise, like a skeleton shaken on a spring. As he maintained the rapid idle, he placed his hands under his armpits to keep them from the cold. He stared again at the dew-covered windshield. Fearful of another disturbing image, he switched on the wipers and looked down as he eased back on the pedal. The engine now ran without the accelerator depressed. Leaving the cab idling, he got out and, in a determined manner, set about starting and moving the other cabs. It took him twenty minutes to get them shifted around, but finally, he pulled his cab up to the service area.

He checked the oil in the engine. Though it was black and thick as paste, it registered full. The oil-breather cap was missing. Reluctantly, he went over to ask the Mexican mechanic if he had one. The answer came back in a lilting accent, "No, amigo, they get lost. It's OK, you don't need one."

Nick knew the car would run without the cap, but he didn't like the idea of inhaling smoking oil vapor all day.

A taxi whipped into the yard and came to an abrupt stop at the opposite pump. The headlights immediately went out and a tall, gaunt young man emerged from the cab. His eyes were glazed and long, stringy hair hung to his shoulders. Snapping the gas cap off and throwing it onto the trunk, he walked purposefully to the pump, grabbed the hose, threw the switch, and plunged the nozzle into the neck of the gas tank as though stabbing a beast with a dagger. Nick watched the night driver and realized, starting tomorrow night, that's what he'd be doing. As he regarded the man's exhausted, spaced-out countenance, he also thought, in time, that's how he'd be looking.

Back in the cab, he turned on the wipers and wondered what his day would be like but recognized there was no way to predict what could happen. The company insisted he drive one day to get familiar with procedures before starting nights, but day or night, he knew driving a cab was, by its very nature, unpredictable.

The uneven wipers finally wore the moisture from the glass and began to shriek in protest. Watching their performance and observing the smoke-crusted insides of the windows, Nick thought the cab was a joke, but he didn't have to remind himself that though the cab *was* a joke, he had nothing to laugh about. He turned on the CB radio, pulled out of the yard, and called the dispatcher as he had been instructed. "One-o-two," he called into the mike uncertainly.

"One-o-two," the nasal voice of the dispatcher shot back immediately.

"I'm clear outside the yard," Nick informed him.

"One-o-two, take it to seven-nine-one Walgrove, apartment seven."

Nick was taken by surprise. He hadn't expected an order right off and fumbled for his pen. By the time he found it, the dispatcher's voice shot at him, "Did you copy, one-o-two?" Nick groped for the microphone, which he had sat down while looking for his pen. "One-o-two, I'm asking you, did you copy?" The voice, insistent, nasal, ate into him.

Nick retrieved the mike and called back, "One-o-two going to seven-one-nine Walgrove, check."

"Seven-nine-one Walgrove," the voice lashed back, "and make it snappy—time order, due right now, regular rider."

Nick resented how intimidated he felt during their little exchange and determined not to let it happen again. Next time, his pen would be ready, the overhead light would be on so he could see, and he'd stay loose about remembering the number and name of the street. He reasoned to himself he wasn't going to be intimidated by a little radio and some character on the other end. He was a man who had mastered many things far more complicated. Turning on the overhead light, he picked up the *Thomas Brothers Street Atlas* and began to look up Walgrove.

The yard where the cabs were kept was tucked away on a short backstreet near the old Hughes Airport between Marina Del Rey and Culver City. Walgrove, he discovered, ran across the middle of Venice. The book gave him little indication of exactly where number 791 would be, so he drove to the nearest place he could intersect.

As he listened to the dispatcher give an occasional order, he came to Walgrove and noticed he was still quite a distance from the number he needed. He was startled to hear his cab number called, "One-o-two, what happened to you? I got the lady on the phone."

"One-o-two, I'll be there in just a minute. I'm on the street right now."

"Check."

It was difficult to see the numbers on the houses and apartment buildings, but he finally made out the house and rather than sounding the horn at that early hour, he got out of the cab and walked toward the door. As he approached, he saw the light within the house go out and a heavyset woman of about sixty emerge.

"Where were you?" she demanded. "This is the third time you've been late this week."

"Ma'am, this is my first day and you're my first fare," Nick retorted, holding the door open for the woman.

"I hate it," she continued, sliding into the seat with difficulty. "Every morning I have to rush my breakfast, or I'll be late for work."

Nick dropped in behind the wheel. "Where you off to?"

"Zucky's on Wilshire and Fifth. I go there every morning for breakfast with my friend. I work at the telephone company on Ocean, but they don't like it when I'm late."

"No one likes it when people are late," Nick offered. "Not even you."

The woman agreed and lapsed into early morning silence until the old cab rumbled up in front of Zucky's. She had the fare ready and handed it to Nick. "Next time, be prompt," she admonished and got out of the cab.

Nick watched her walk into the restaurant, then looked at the fare in his hand. The meter said $3.20. The fare had given him $3.75. He figured his 40 percent of the meter came to $1.28. With tip, he made $1.83. He sadly acknowledged it was the most money he had made in a year. He radioed the dispatcher.

"One-o-two," dispatcher returned.

"I'm clear at Fifth and Wilshire."

"One-o-two, I have a couple of cabs on stands in that area, take it up to Westwood or to the Century Plaza Hotel. Clear up there, I should have orders coming."

Nick congratulated himself on negotiating the exchange. He wrote down the fare on his trip ticket, turned the cab around, and headed up Wilshire Boulevard. He didn't get far when he was startled by a click from the meter. He looked over and saw it registered $3.35. He had forgotten to clear it.

It was still dark when he pulled into the taxi area near the front of Century Plaza Hotel. Not a soul was in sight. He got out of the cab and, leaning against the front fender, fished out a joint from the shirt pocket beneath his sweater, and lit up. Taking a deep drag, he felt the strong Colombian weed sink into his lungs. He wanted to cough, but he fought the feeling and held it down.

So this is it, he thought. He had his first fare and was now officially a cab driver. He shook his head as he exhaled the smoke into the morning cold. Well, he'd use the taxi time just as he had promised himself. He would figure things out, get a hold on himself, keep a little money coming in, and find the men who murdered his wife. It was a simple-enough plan that nonetheless required luck, constant vigilance, and determination—characteristics of which he was currently almost completely devoid of.

His thoughts drifted to his daughter, Melissa. She would be having her second birthday in the beginning of February. The wave of guilt came over him as it had since he had brought his wife's body to Macon, Georgia, to be buried in the Thombridge family plot. After the interment, he had reluctantly let go of Melissa's tiny hand, given her a long hug, and then made his way to the car waiting to take him to the airport. Melissa had cried uncontrollably; the beautiful features of her face contorted into grief. She had her mother's thick brown mane of hair, and strands stuck to her face as they drank up her tears. Lillian Thombridge, Melissa's maternal grandmother, stared after Nick with a look of condemnation. It was condemnation for her daughter's death, for leaving his daughter, and for his lifestyle. Nick shuddered under the memory. Possibly he should have stayed for a while, but he couldn't bear the looks from Lillian and their old family friends. Once on the plane, he had his first drink of hard liquor in over three years. When he got off the plane, he made his way back to Venice. He bought a quart of tequila and managed to score some marijuana. It was with difficulty he refrained from going for something stronger.

Nick was startled by the high, melancholy sound of a London Bobby's whistle and noticed the doorman, liveried like an English Beefeater Guard, facing his direction. Nick regarded the marijuana roach held between his thumb and forefinger, then wedged the resin-stained remains in the back of a matchbook. He put the matchbook in his pocket as the doorman impatiently blew the whistle, again. As soon as he pulled to the front of the hotel, a well-dressed man around Nick's age of thirty-two came through the revolving door. Tipping the doorman, the man got into the crumbling taxi. "Christ, what an hour," the man groaned. "I'm going to the Atlantic Richfield Building, downtown. Do you know where that is?"

"I think so," Nick offered.

"It's that big sucker down around Fifth and Flower."

"I know the place," Nick said. He remembered to throw the flag about the time they emerged from the hotel's driveway onto Avenue of the Stars. The sun was beginning to declare itself from across the flattened landscape of West Los Angeles. *It's going to be strange working only nights*, Nick thought.

"I have to be there by six thirty. Think we can make it?"

"Yes."

The man fell back against the seat with his briefcase in his lap. "I'll tell you," he said, "the next time I come out here, I'm going to bring my wife. Everyone says LA is great for the women, but it sure hasn't been for me."

"Depends how you hit it."

"Well, I hit it like a soft grounder to first. Friends of mine and I had a little election party with some women from the company. Can you believe Jimmy Carter won? We're going to have a peanut farmer in the White House. Jesus!"

"A lot of our founding fathers were farmers," Nick said, remembering his grammar school history.

"Yeah, but peanuts?"

"He also commanded a nuclear submarine," Nick offered.

"Yeah, then he got all peacenik-y."

"Want a little more war?" Nick asked.

The man ignored the question. "I had this party—admittedly, it was a little stupid of me—and the women weren't too impressed with Carter or the setup, so they went home early. Finally, at two in the morning, I snuck some black hooker up to my room. Cost me a hundred bucks and I couldn't even get a hard-on. I couldn't get one because she wanted to blow me with a rubber on. Did you ever hear of such a thing?"

"Seldom," Nick said.

"Well, I never heard of it," the man protested. "Cost me a hundred dollars to let her put a rubber on a limp cock. Now that's an obscenity if I ever heard one. Next time, I'm bringing my wife. At least with her, I can get laid without a rubber and when we get away from home, our sex gets pretty good." The man fell silent for a moment and then asked, "You ever been married?"

"Yes,"

"Got any kids?"

"I have a daughter who is almost two."

"I'm trying to get my wife to move out here, but she thinks she's got everything she needs right there in little old Scarsdale."

"Probably right."

"What's your wife think? Does she like it here?"

"My wife is dead."

"Oh, jeez, I'm sorry." The man wanted to end the conversation right there but clearly felt obliged to say something else. "God, with a kid so young, it must have happened just a little while ago."

"Two months."

"Gee, I'm sorry. It must be hard on you with the kid and all."

"She's in Macon, Georgia, with her grandmother."

"I see. Well, I guess that's a good idea."

Impulsively, the man snapped open the latches on his briefcase and began rummaging inside. "I've got to meet my West Coast partner so we can go over some stuff. We've got a presentation at nine o'clock and we haven't seen one another in three months."

Nick glanced in the mirror and watched as the man began to read some typewritten material. He'd have to be careful to keep conversation and questions where he wanted them. Better yet, maybe he shouldn't talk at all. Before he began driving, he had contemplated the idea of exchanging information with customers to learn possible facts about who and where the killers could be. Since his wife's murder, idle chitchat had become strange, even difficult and threatening. Now, on his second fare, he had discussed his wife and child with a complete stranger. He didn't like the feeling because there was so much more and he wasn't ready to share.

He hadn't been sure which route to the downtown area would be the shortest and fastest at that hour. He decided on Olympic. As he neared Western Avenue, he noticed for the first time what a sizable Korean community there was. There would be a side benefit to driving, he realized, as he would learn many things about the city and what neighborhood's held what secrets.

He dropped the man at the Atlantic Richfield Building and received a good tip. As he drove away and passed vendors opening steel gates to the diamond marts, he thought of Julianne's stolen jewelry and, in particular, her ruby ring. The ring, with the large perfect ruby, had been a strong presence during their brief marriage. Originally, it had belonged to Julianne's great-great-grandmother. As a young woman, she had received it from her father on her sixteenth birthday. For a brief time before the Civil War, Mr. Thombridge had been quite well-off. Regardless, it had been an indulgence to purchase the ring at Tiffany's during a rare trip to New York in 1859. It demonstrated how much he adored his beautiful daughter with rich brown hair that flowed down to her waist. Subsequently, the ring had been hidden from Yankee soldiers and passed down through good times and bad. More than a hundred years after the original purchase, Julianne's grandmother relayed the ring's history as she presented it to Julianne once she graduated from college. Julianne loved the story her grandmother told and she treasured the ring. She wore it often. Despite her love for the ring and its history, she had offered to sell it rather than see Nick sell his cameras and lenses. Nick refused the offer and told her he would never allow the ring to be sold. It would belong to Melissa or to their daughter when the time came. Nick left the memory behind and drove on.

As the morning progressed, he quickly felt at home with the meter, writing out the trip ticket, and using the *Thomas Guide*, which revealed the whereabouts of every street in Los Angeles. But one thing gnawed at him way out of proportion to what he anticipated. It was the cab's radio, or, closer to the point, the personality behind the radio. The business of having to constantly interact with and listen to an individual over the air was not something he had anticipated. He found the voice a nagging presence in his sanctuary. Clearly, the dispatcher's attitude was that Nick was a tool with which to make the company money. Nick understood persons getting into his cab would be people he didn't know, new personalities to deal with, forced meetings in a sense. But the rides would end and the personalities would get out and disappear. However, as the morning's rush picked up, the dispatcher's voice seldom left the air. It was like listening to a bad disc jockey who never played a tune and you couldn't turn him off.

◆◆◆

JESSE CARMODY SCRATCHED AT his sheepskin vest as though it had an itch. He was listening to Victor Koss proclaim he could see at a glance the ring with the large ruby wasn't worth as much as Jesse had estimated. Vic was the fence Jesse and his partner Cal used for all the goods they stole. Victor Koss operated out of the "Totally Used Furniture" store in El Monte, a drab eastern township of greater Los Angeles, known primarily for used car lots and sweatshops. In the back room of the store, Vic carefully examined the ring that had belonged to Julianne Thombridge-Cullen. Julianne had been wearing it the day Carmody stabbed her six times then ripped it off her ring finger. Standing near Jesse was his reluctant partner, Cal Santiso. Cal hunched his powerful shoulders, ran his hand through his long black hair, and tried to concentrate on the bad news the fence was telling them.

Koss explained the ring's setting was antique and the cut of the large ruby old-fashioned, so the price would be greatly compromised. Jesse and Cal had held onto the ring at great possible risk because they thought they might be able to sell it for a larger sum if presented separately. They had taken the stolen goods from Cullen's apartment to Vic weeks earlier and gotten modest money for the cameras, jewelry, and electronics. But they held back the cherished ring and came around to sell it later, when things were slow. Cal didn't like Vic Koss and thought they should go to another fence, but they didn't know one. As Koss bent over the ring for a final inspection, Cal felt himself getting angry as he studied Vic's fat, soft white arms and dangling wisps of thin gray hair. Carefully concealing his glee over the ring's possibilities, Vic peered intently through the magnifying loop held against his thick glasses. The purity and color of the jewel were intoxicating. Carmody and Santiso shuffled in place, waiting.

Finally, Victor Koss put on his best poker face, looked up, and said, "Four fifty."

By ELEVEN O'CLOCK IN the morning, Nick sat grimly behind the wheel in Culver City, a plain uninspired community that played host to a couple of motion picture studios. He had just dropped a

New York costume designer at the gate of Metro Goldwyn Mayer. The thought of turning the CB radio back on was repugnant. He decided to drive to the airport and try to find a fare on his own.

✦✦✦

WITHIN THE HORSESHOE-SHAPED LOS Angeles International Airport, the heated air sat stagnant and thick with the smell of car and jet exhaust, but there was also a feeling of energy. Nick drove past the first terminal and pulled in behind some cabs parked at TWA. Getting out of the cab, he entered the terminal. It was cool inside, and he watched as the arrival information board shuffled itself with the latest arrival/departure news. A plane wasn't due in for a few minutes, so he walked the short distance to the men's room, washed his hands, and wet and dried his face. Leaving the men's room, he took one last glance at the arrival board and left the building. Thinking the line of cabs wouldn't move for some time as patrons had to wait for their luggage, he began to walk around. He avoided the other drivers. He wasn't ready to deal with them. Studying the area, he discovered steps to the roof of the terminal. Climbing the stairs, he saw the door to the roof was locked, but the steps were shaded and comparatively cool. From that position, he could view the line of taxis and people entering and exiting the terminal. He sat on the steps and stared out at the passing humanity.

He was reminded of his flight to Macon just weeks earlier. His mother-in-law, Lillian, had begged him to remain in Georgia with her and Melissa. It was agony leaving Melissa, but he knew he had to return to LA rather than remain powerless and injured in Lillian's home. He had to return and face the horror and failures in order to drive those demons away. Regardless, he couldn't have been comfortable living with his mother-in-law in her environment. Having been raised in the Hell's Kitchen part of Manhattan, the notion of living in Macon, Georgia, was more alien to him than

Marrakech. But could he actually complete the murderous task he had set for himself?

As he posed the question, the awful tableau came forcibly to mind. Again, he saw himself opening the door to his Venice apartment. Julianne was lying on the living room floor, bleeding and near death. From her crib, Melissa stared wide-eyed. Poised in the room like startled hyenas were three young men. One was a tall, thin black man around eighteen. Over his shoulders were slung the last of Nick's still cameras—a Nikon F.2, two Nikon F's, and a pocket-sized thirty-five-millimeter Olympus. Just hours before Nick had sold his Leica and Hasselblad to help with bills and rent. Seeing his remaining cameras, Nick was hit with the bizarre thought he should have sold those as well since they were now being stolen. Nick's gaze shifted. Next to the young black man was a short, very muscular Hispanic of about twenty-three. He had been wiping Julianne's blood from his knife with a clean diaper. He had thick, shoulder-length black hair and wore black leather gloves. Nick's small television and portable stereo were at his feet. Another man, about twenty-five, carried the Halliburton cases filled with Nick's camera lenses and a fistful of Julianne's jewelry. He had dirty blond hair, wore a sheepskin vest, and stared with speed-fed blue eyes at Nick, struck dumb in the doorway. The whole encounter took less than two seconds. Suddenly, the tableau animated as the young black man shrank back, whispering, "Jesus." The man wearing the sheepskin vest dropped the Halliburton cases, pulled a large caliber revolver from his belt, rapidly extended his left arm, and fired a shot at Nick's head. The sound of the gun was unbelievably loud.

"Hey you!" a voice shouted. "You, driving one-o-two, move your fucking cab up."

Nick snapped back to reality and saw a burly driver in his fifties standing near the bottom of the stairs. Looking over at the taxi zone, he noticed two cabs had quickly loaded and left and a third was pulling away. He bolted down the stairs and passed the driver returning to the cab behind Nick's. As Nick jumped into 102, the driver yelled, "I should have fucking gone around you."

The sun-scorched seat burned into Nick's back as he pulled the car up to first position; he thought to himself how nice it would be to drive at night and not have the heat.

A porter wheeled a cart to the trunk as a young family, bleary with travel fatigue, lagged behind. As Nick packed the bags into the trunk, the father who was holding a quarrelsome daughter in his arms asked, "How much does it cost to go to Newport Beach?"

Nick didn't know but he knew it was a good long fare. From the way the man looked, Nick could tell there wouldn't be any debate over the price. Nick only worried as to whether the old clunker would make a sustained round trip of almost eighty miles without breaking down. "Why don't you sit down, we'll get going, and I'll call the dispatcher and get the price."

The man was suspicious, yet uncomplaining.

A new dispatcher informed Nick the fare was about twenty-five dollars on the meter and an eight-dollar surcharge. On that trip, Nick learned the benefits of the long fare. The meter cheerfully kept clicking up charges as they drove along the freeway and Nick felt relief from the stress of not having to search and wait for fares.

The drive to Newport was pleasant though warm as the old Ford ran hot and smoky. The little girl slept deeply in the arms of her mother and the husband and wife chatted, just enough to make the ride interesting. He was a doctor and they had just returned from a three-week vacation in Europe. They were returning to move into their new house, which had been readied during their absence. When they arrived at the large Spanish-inspired house, the man tipped Nick ten dollars. As he drove away from the home high on a hill overlooking the Pacific, he mused that the small family was the perfect enactment of the American Dream. It had been Nick's dream as well to make a nice living and provide for his wife and daughter, but the Golden State hadn't been all that receptive.

As he drove into the yard, he felt a sense of relief. He concentrated on getting his trip ticket and cash envelope filled out correctly. He had booked $85.30. Of that amount, before taxes, $34.12 was his. In addition, he had made $21 in tips. He knew as time went on, he could do much better. He could live. He could send some support money to Georgia and pay his bills and in time maybe even begin to purchase camera equipment. He felt weary but gratified, enjoying the feeling of having freshly earned money in his pocket. It was long overdue.

As he walked out of the yard, he noticed men standing around waiting for cabs. They were night drivers. He studied them as they restlessly shuffled about. Whether it was the hour, shift, or their personalities, they looked different than day drivers. In the slanting sunlight, their long shadows reached out across the oily blacktop, beckoning Nick to join.

CHAPTER TWO

THE NEXT MORNING, NICK drove his gray '68 Camaro to the Venice Police Station. After being kept waiting twenty minutes, he was told to go back and see Detective Jim Pearson. Pearson was one of the detectives working on the case and from Nick's point of view had been the most promising. The other officers just took notes and asked perfunctory questions. Pearson seemed to peer into the horror. Nick had requested a meeting with him to learn what was happening with the investigation and Pearson in turn asked Nick to come in and go through some new mug shots.

Pearson had the look of a Marine sergeant gone to pot. He was young for a detective and that was one of the things Nick liked about him. If he was a detective at a comparatively young age, that could mean he knew what he was doing. Pearson had a buzz cut and a large, flat, tough-looking face. Beneath his pressed shirt and slacks, his body swelled out to an almost-hard 240 pounds. Depending on how the fish were biting, he could do two to three six-packs of beer on a long Sunday trip. He was intimidating, but if you looked long enough, you could see remnants of kindness and humanity. Fourteen years with homicide hadn't erased it all.

Nick walked into the office and quickly noticed, with satisfaction, the three collages he had created spread out on Pearson's desk. With cuttings from newspapers, magazine photographs, and illustrations, Nick had assembled the likeness of the three individual killers. On each creation, Nick had drawn or written things that were pertinent to the killers. The result was not anything like police sketches, those sort of simple line drawings, but rather they were works of art that took creative liberties and, in style, were closer to abstract impressionism. Nick had drawn tattoos on random bare arms, put earrings in disembodied ears, and with advertisements he'd shown the kinds of pants the men had been wearing. There were cutouts of shirts, pictures of cowboy boots, a sheepskin vest similar to the one the blond-haired man had been wearing. Many different images graced those pages of grim remembrances. All in all, Pearson thought they were quite ingenious. If only they had something to go on besides Nick's description, they might even be useful. Pearson looked over at Nick and felt compelled to say something. "So, how you doing?"

"All right, I guess."

"These composites, or collages as you call them, are something else."

"Well, I'd like to keep working on them because every once in a while I remember some other little detail."

"I'll get them copied. In the meantime, take a look at these."

Pearson handed Nick two loose-leaf binders of mug shots and left the office to have the secretary make photocopies of Nick's work. Pearson had read that color-copying machines had been invented and would soon be available. *That would be useful,* he thought, *if the city would pay for them.* Returning to his desk with the originals and one copy for himself, Pearson complimented Nick. "No wonder you were a good photographer. These assemblages show some real imagination."

"I don't have a camera, so I'm not much of a photographer anymore."

As Nick continued looking at mug shots, Pearson studied him from across the desk. Nick was well built, weighed somewhere around 175 pounds, maybe more, and he moved with a kind of athletic grace. Pearson critically examined the pale red-gray scar on Nick's forehead as it tunneled its way into his bushy reddish-brown hair. A fraction of an inch lower, he thought, and the bullet would have smashed into Nick's head and killed him instantly. Instead, it had bounced off his skull, sending him falling backward where he struck his head on the cement stairs. Pearson also wondered about Nick's slightly bent and flattened nose, like a guy that had had several rough fights.

As Nick neared the end of the second mug book, the detective decided it was time to exchange some final information. It didn't take him long to explain his end. "There hasn't been anything new in the last month," he said. "There hasn't been one single lead, but I think a couple of the guys in there come close to answering the description. What do you think?"

Nick finished looking at the pictures, folded the binders shut, and carefully put them on the detective's desk. He spoke slowly, calmly, and directly to Pearson. "I don't think it was any of the guys in these books." He paused for a second and then continued in an uncharacteristic monotone. "I understand you and the other officers have been trying your best and I should just relax and let you go about your business, but something horrible happened to my wife and child..."

"It happened to all of you," Pearson interjected.

"I want to know the details, Lieutenant Pearson. If she was raped, how, how many times she was raped, how many men raped her. I want to know the details same as you. As a citizen and husband, I'm entitled to that. I want to read the report and then I want you to interpret the report for me in those areas I don't understand."

"Listen, Nick. I can't let you do that. Just forget it."

"I can't forget it. They could have just taken my cameras and stuff but they didn't, instead, they...they did it all in front of my daughter."

"We don't know that. We think your wife was raped in the bedroom and then somehow she got into the living room, and..."

"You're saying they only stabbed my wife to death in front of our child? Very sensitive of them to rape my wife in the bedroom before they stabbed her to death in front of our daughter."

"Listen, Nick..."

"I want to see those guys put away. I want them dead."

"I know how you feel, and we want the same thing," Pearson offered.

"Let me see the reports, Lieutenant."

It was against his better judgment, but Pearson tossed Nick the file. Nick picked it up and read it carefully. It took a while, and then Nick handed it back to Pearson. 'Is that all there is?"

Pearson nodded and lied. "That's it." He was glad he hadn't put the coroner's report into the folder. Once in a while, sloppy filing has its advantages.

Nick continued as though Pearson hadn't spoken. "I know how busy you guys are and what happened to Julianne is happening all the time, all over the city, and there's only so much time you can devote to any one case..."

"We're working on this one full time. The items taken were well described by you and we've had a very active Pawn Shop Detail out there looking," Pearson said, defensively.

"Anyway," Nick continued, "I thought it might be possible for me to lend a hand." Pearson started to say something but Nick cut him off. "I've taken a job as a cab driver with a company that services most of the city but in particular they handle Venice and West LA. I thought maybe, during the time I'm driving around at night, six nights a week, I might see them."

Pearson jumped in, "I know you come from New York City, but you were from a small neighborhood within the city. Out here, it's not the same. Things of this kind spread around a lot more."

"I'm going to find them, so—" Again Pearson started to interrupt but Nick pressed his final point home. "And so, I'd like a permit to carry a gun. Just driving a cab at night in this city is dangerous and reason enough to have one. I'm sure considering the circumstances, you could have that arranged. A gun would..."

Pearson finally waved his hand and interrupted. "I'll tell you, you'll never get a permit for that, especially in a vehicle licensed by the city for the transportation of the public. You can try but they'll never let you. The city doesn't want that kind of potential trouble and, frankly, neither do we. Now, if you're driving around at night and see them, just call us and we'll have them picked up. But that's all you should do. Understand?"

Nick understood, but he didn't like it. He had known all along they wouldn't go for him carrying a gun, but he thought he'd try anyway. The least his request could do was to wake Pearson up to the fact Nick meant business. He got up and started to leave, then turned to Pearson. "I'm not playing at this, Lieutenant."

Nick walked out the door. Pearson sat sucking on his lower lip and drumming his fingers on the cover of the murder file of Julianne Thombridge-Cullen. He knew the chances of finding the killers were practically nil. There were no fingerprints except a couple of questionable partials. There was forcible rape but no semen, and with two or three guys, things get dicey. To make that work, you had to find all three guys with their balls intact and there were no other clues. Nick, who was the only witness, had been knocked unconscious by a bullet careening off his skull the moment he spotted the assailants. The Pawn Shop Detail had not discovered the stolen merchandise. The Detail primarily worked the Westside, and by this time, the goods had probably gone out into the void, out to where people snatch up a bargain camera or jewel and don't ask questions of origin. The killers had possibly fled to some other city and maybe in different directions. *The big hope*, Pearson thought, *was they would get lucky and catch the killers on some other offense.* Then, through pictures and other information, they could put the killers together with Nick's case. He stood up and walked to the battered filing cabinet, and as he stuffed the folder in, he muttered to himself, "Nah, this has all the smell of an unsolved murder."

Pearson walked back to his desk and sat down. Putting his right hand behind his head and left hand under his jaw, he pushed and pulled until he heard a couple loud cracks in his neck. Relieved, he began to deal with the problem that was beginning to bother him most. This Nick Cullen guy reminded him of a former case. Some years earlier, Pearson had taken into custody, a good-looking young man accused of murder. The young man's name was Reginald Post and he was suspected of killing the father of his former fiancée. After questioning Reginald for some time, Pearson concluded Reginald didn't seem to be the killer. He had a good alibi and a good family name, and Pearson found the guy very amusing and personable. He let the man go. A few days later, Reginald Post shot his former fiancée and her lover to death. Then, he did himself. Pearson had never gotten over his lack of instinct and poor judgment. Officers around the station house didn't forget about it either. Now, a man who had just left his office had asked to get a permit to legally carry a concealed gun so he could kill three criminals if he saw them. City law can see that kind of trouble coming and doesn't give gun permits for that kind of mayhem. But would Nick do anything illegally? Pearson thought about the possibilities and concluded he'd better keep an eye on Nick. He didn't need any more Reginald Posts in his life.

DETECTIVE LOU STABILE WAS bench-pressing 180 pounds for three reps of ten. Once he had been able to do a lot more, but that was then. When he finished his second set, he saw Mose come into the gym and look around until they made eye contact. Mose was huge and could have easily pressed Stabile, the bench, and the 180 pounds of barbells all at the same time. Mose worked for Big TC, and in a way, so did Stabile. Two minutes later, Stabile still in his gym clothes was taking a back seat ride with Big TC in the man's Cadillac, with Mose behind the wheel.

"So, what's this shit all about?" Big TC asked, slowly running his index finger over his lips. The finger sported a large gold ring with his initials.

"We should have met somewhere else. I shouldn't be seen riding around with you," Stabile said morosely.

"Man, you said you had to speak to me right away, so I cruised by where you hang."

Stabile looked out the back window to see if they were being followed.

"Shit, man." Big TC laughed, slapping his skinny thigh and flashing a row of bright white teeth, "You can always say you were investigatin' my ass. What am I gonna say?" Big TC tossed an envelope onto Stabile's lap; Stabile didn't respond to the question or the envelope. Big TC suddenly turned serious and stared at Stabile with dead black eyes. "Man, you called me. Said you had important news. I'm here. What's up?"

"They're going to transfer me to Venice."

Big TC stared hard at Stabile, then lit a cigarette and thought for a moment. "So, who am I going to do business with now? Not that raggedy-assed partner of yours."

"No."

"Well, who then, motherfucker?" TC shouted.

"Don't 'motherfucker' me," Stabile countered.

Big TC reached over and snatched back the envelope from Stabile's lap. "Man, I'm paying you good money, you don't do shit, and now you tell me you're gonna be gone?"

Stabile didn't make a move for the envelope but turned and faced Big TC. "Can't you understand? They're not shipping me to Venice because they think I could use some time by the beach. They're sending me because I haven't been doing my job busting shithead dealers like you. They're suspicious of me but they don't want any investigation in their own station."

Big TC looked to the back of the head of his bodyguard. "Hey, Mose. How long a drive is it to Venice?"

"No traffic, about twenty minutes straight down Washington Boulevard."

Big TC turned back to Stabile. "See that? Only twenty minutes. I've got some new brothers working for me and I'm going to send them down there and get some of that good Venice biz. We'll let you know what's happening, but before they ship your ass out, get me some motherfucker in your division who will give me cooperation. You can do that, right?"

Stabile didn't have to think about it. He knew someone because he'd personally trained him. He was also gratified to know the arrangement with Big TC would be ongoing in his new Venice location. He didn't want to give up the envelopes. "Sure, this is all going to work out," he said. 'But if I'm going to oversee a new territory and supervise my associate in the old one, start putting a bigger taste in those envelopes."

"Now you're going greedy on me, motherfucker. We see how I do in Venice and then we see how you do." Big TC tossed the envelope back on Stabile's lap and turned to Mose. "Take this smelly-assed white man back to his gym." He snuffed out his cigarette and turned back to Stabile. "You got to wash them gym clothes, man. You reek like some old mule's pussy." He and Mose shared a big laugh and Stabile quietly put the envelope inside his sweat-stained shorts.

CHAPTER THREE

THE LAST BLUE LIGHT was being snuffed by night when Nick walked into the yard. There were cars at the pumps and a dozen drivers milling about. He wondered why so many guys were standing around.

Inside the dispatcher's room, two overweight women in their late thirties sat taking orders and passing the dispatcher small paper forms illustrating the pickup information. At the open window stood a tall, slim black man with a pockmarked face who kept the drivers from annoying the dispatchers when things were busy. Nick walked up to him. "My name is Nick Cullen. I'm starting nights and was told to come in at five sharp." The clock showed ten minutes of five.

"They gonna be a little wait," the tall man said.

"About how long?"

Immediately, Nick knew he'd hit upon an often-abused sore spot with the man because his expression turned to one of indignant pain and he hesitated a long time before answering. "Well, there about twelve guys waitin," he cracked. "A few cars is shopped but there a lot of day drivers due in."

Nick decided to press it one last time. "Well, could you give me an estimate as to how long it's going to be?"

The man lit up a Marlboro before he answered, "Forty-five, plus."

"Thanks," Nick said and walked off in search of a quiet spot away from the other drivers to wait things out. He found a secluded area, leaned against the sagging perimeter hurricane fence, and placed one foot to rest against the bumper of a shopped cab. He turned and gazed across the yard at drivers shuffling restlessly about and wondered what he had in common with them. He answered his own question. "For one reason or another, we're all driving cabs."

Settling in, he flashed back to his meeting with Pearson. It had not been at all satisfying, but there was more to it. Pearson had called attention to Nick's failing career as a photographer. It shouldn't have bothered Nick, but the acknowledgment of how long it had been since he'd had an assignment or sold anything rankled him. Admitting to Pearson he was now driving a cab was another problem. Pearson was the first person he had told, and Nick felt an unexpected impact in his head. A failed career and subsequent cab-driving gig didn't sound good, regardless of circumstances. He had rationalized being a cabbie fit with his impending search for the killers, but how committed would he be to his notion of driving and searching for killers if he suddenly got some good assignments? Emotions swirled around and Nick reflected on the fact he had gotten into photography only by the most odd happenstance. Driving a cab was probably closer to where his life had been drifting. Coming from a lower-middle-class working family, he always had a little guilt that his life had so quickly become interesting and successful. He thought, with a trace of irony, that's possibly why he felt the need to mess it up. He let his head fall back against the interlaced wires of the fence and it bounced with decreasing pulses until it remained still.

Nick's distinctive looks, his draft deferment, and his career all stemmed from one incident. Growing up as a Scotch-Irish kid in the west side of Manhattan known as Hell's Kitchen, gave him a distinct and special status. It wasn't readily apparent to someone passing through, any more than a person would pay much mind to a hundred-acre farm in Illinois. But Nick's neighborhood was often laced with violence. He had heard of violent things, seen them, and even done a couple, but he never thought of himself as a particularly tough kid. That was for the few who had the special calling, which in some ways was similar to the calling for the priesthood. You had to know that was the life for you and then go for it. Nick was a loner and may not have had the calling, but he didn't like to be pushed around either. He just tried to play things by local rules. That particular west-side neighborhood carried with it an expected code of behavior. One minded one's own business, stuck with one's own kind, and didn't inform on anyone. Unlike most of the other kids in the neighborhood, Nick was an only child. His mother had suffered with a long illness and had passed away when he was twelve, leaving him to be raised by his longshoreman father, Sean. He'd been drifting along without any particular plan other than possibly following his father to the docks. But Nick's background and code caused things to happen, and while the thought never occurred to him, some people would have said it was fate.

It happened one day as Nick was on his way to high school during his senior year. Angelo, a twenty-two-year-old hotheaded punk who worked for Joey "The Loop," was standing outside a storefront with drawn curtains and a small sign proclaiming "social club." Seeing Nick walking along, head down, deep in thought, Angelo impulsively loosed a hocker onto Nick's pants cuff. Nick heard the sound and felt it hit him. He couldn't tell if it had been accidental or intentional as he only heard the guttural sound of Angelo clearing his throat and spitting, and felt the heavy phlegm pelt his leg. Nick turned back to look questioningly at Angelo. In turn, Angelo bored back into Nick with his enforcer's eyes and asked, "What's the problem, Mick? You don't like the rain in this part of town?"

Nick was momentarily confused by the uncalled-for hostility. Nick had lived two blocks away since he was two. He had been walking along, thinking of Ruthie Ackerman and her large soft breasts. In the split second it took Nick to fully comprehend the insult, Angelo laughed and went back into the "social club," which, as any Irish kid knew, was not a place you entered without an invitation if your name was Cullen.

Nick walked off, stopped by a fireplug, put his foot up, tore a back page from his history book, and wiped the sticky yellow-green phlegm off his cuff. He couldn't believe what an asshole thing the guy had done, but more importantly he was ashamed of how he had behaved. *So fucking sappy*, Nick thought.

He was trembling when he walked into algebra class. He sat down and mentally coiled into himself, a trick he'd perfect as time and troubles wore on. He never glanced over at Ruthie Ackerman's breasts, even though she was doing her best to give him a good angle. Instead, he locked in on the anger within himself.

Three days later, Nick was walking by Louie's candy store. At the same time, Angelo came out tapping a cigarette loose from a fresh pack. Angelo stopped to light up near the entrance, which was atop three worn steps bracketed by cast-iron railings. Seeing Nick passing by, he gleefully and loudly cleared his throat as though once more preparing to spit another horrible gob the size of Riker's Island. Nick eyeballed him, but the tall thin punk just grinned as though nothing was going on. When Nick turned to go, he heard a sound like a blowgun as Angelo spat. He felt the wad hit his pants leg just behind his knee. Without thinking, Nick turned and ran the twelve feet back to the punk. Angelo thought of jumping off the steps, or going back into the store, or kicking Nick in the face as he charged in wide open, but finally decided on the wrong move and went for his gun. He tossed his cigarettes away and lost a crucial second. Just as Angelo's hand slipped inside his jacket, Nick was on him. Nick's left hand grabbed his arm before he could pull his gun, and with his right fist, he slammed three uppercuts into the punk's balls. The first caught him almost square, the second deflected off the involuntary and momentary contraction of his thighs, and as his thighs bounced back open, the third punch mashed his jewels perfectly. Angelo fell off the stoop like a dropped mailbag. His gun slipped from his hand and fell out from under his jacket, clattering onto the sidewalk. "Don't ever do that to me again!" Nick hissed and walked away.

It was then Nick completely understood what fear was. He knew the altercation would never be forgotten. It would only sit there, until Angelo or his friends decided their revenge. He felt like a lone soldier in a city filled with enemy snipers. Nick's father tried to smooth things over and talked to some of the men "connected" in the neighborhood. The word came back that it was personal between Nick and Angelo. The Italians who hung out in the social club didn't want to get involved. Angelo had a habit of behaving like a jerk and they weren't going to step into something that could escalate. Their power was shrinking as the neighborhood was rapidly changing. As the local Italian residents moved away to the suburbs of Long Island and New Jersey, they were being replaced by Puerto Ricans and immigrants from Iran and Poland. Nick tried to rationalize the situation by asserting that, as far as he was concerned, the score was even. He had been insulted and he squared it. However, deep down, Nick knew Angelo and his pals were out there waiting for him. They had something to prove.

It took almost seven weeks. It happened right after he left a party in the basement apartment of one of the neighborhood girls. Nick had lost the first flush of searching fear and begun to relax a little. He began to think things were possibly going to settle back to normal.

He had drunk too many seven-sevens and staggered from the apartment unnoticed. Even though he was drunk, he would have instinctively been aware and sharp enough on the way home to smell trouble waiting, except he'd also been rebuffed by a new girl he had a crush on. She didn't like horny, drunk boys and told him so. At the time, he didn't know how to approach a girl without being high and a little out there, unless it was with Ruthie Ackerman, who would do you no matter what condition you were in. With the new girl, it was a doomed introduction, so, after the direct rejection, Nick plunged out into the night, alone.

Staggering along, he negotiated the four blocks toward home with a growing determination to not show his father how loaded he was. It wasn't until he reached the alley near the front of his building he sensed a problem and felt the rush of fear return. A half second later, a sawed-off shovel handle cracked across his nose, flattening it. He was blinded by the hit, which in stickball would have been a hard grounder, good for three bases, but for Nick it was a smashed nose and cracked bones around his left eye. Nick didn't go down but he was gone anyway. He staggered backward and after a moment instinctively started punching. He felt the shovel handle crack down on his skull and he dropped to his knees. Suddenly, blows from fists and feet were raining down on him. One thing Nick knew before he sank to the sidewalk and into a weird form of semiconsciousness—there were more than two of them.

Suddenly and inexplicably, the blows stopped. He could make out the sounds of men panting from exertion. Then, through the reddish haze of his mind, Nick heard Angelo say, "Give me back the handle." There was some rustling of clothing and the sound of wood slapping against a hand. "Hold his legs open. I'm gonna whack his nuts into jam."

In his delirious state, Nick felt no fear; he wondered how it would feel when he got hit. Suddenly, another sound rang out, a large hollow sound somewhere between a firecracker and a base drum. Then he heard his father's voice. "Get out of here, you fucks, or I'll kill all of ya."

Suddenly, Nick heard the scrape of shoe leather and footsteps retreating rapidly down the alley. Moments later, he felt the comforting sensation of his face being lightly touched and was aware of his limp body being lifted and shifted once in his father's strong arms. He felt a soft jostling as his father set off at something between a rapid walk and forward stagger. It was an odd feeling being carried by his father. Nick chuckled at the idea and left his body for a better look. As he floated above, he saw his father carrying him in his arms down Ninth Avenue trying to get a cab and get closer to the hospital all at the same time. Several cabs passed by without stopping, but abruptly a Russian guy in a gypsy cab pulled up. Nick watched from above as his father laid his body across his lap in the back seat. The cab started to pull away and Nick decided he might as well go along. He swooped down inside the cab just as he had seen Casper the Friendly Ghost do so many times on TV when he was a kid. That was the last thing he remembered for three days and nights.

When he came off the critical list, some of the boys from the neighborhood visited and were duly impressed with his battered appearance. Claiming an inability to see in the darkness, Nick and his father refused to identify the assailants. Wild stories swirled around the high school, but the tales weren't great enough to get any of the girls to visit, not even Ruthie Ackerman. His father came every day. On the sixth day, Nick could begin to speak through his swollen lips. "What happened?" he asked his father.

Sean pushed his Mets cap back on his head and pulled at his right ear, an old habit. He began speaking as if embarrassed to relate the story. "I switched off the Carson Show when it was over and went to crack open the window and have a beer and smoke before bed. I look out the window and next thing, I see my kid staggering home like some Bowery bum." Sean stared at Nick to see how he was taking it. Nick waited him out. Since he didn't rise to that one, Sean continued. "Then, some guy steps out of the alley and like DiMaggio swings a long skinny bat at your face. Two other guys come out of the alley and start wailing on you. They were fucking serious. I go and grab my gun and run down the four flights of stairs. I come outside and see DiMaggio with the club ready to tee off on your balls. I drop down behind the stoop and pop off a shot. I shoot high because I'm afraid with that snub nose I can't hit anything. I figured they also had guns, so I wasn't going to be a jerk and get into a firefight and get us both shot. If I had a rifle, I could have done them all in three seconds, but anyway, I got their attention, they got the message and ran."

Nick looked at his father in wonder. His father had done it all so coolly. He studied his father seated near the foot of the bed, in his worn windbreaker and Mets cap, and Nick stirred inside with the question his father had never answered. From time to time Nick had asked his father about the war, in which he had fought his way across the Pacific with the Marine Corps. He'd been in Iwo Jima and other island assaults. He had a pile of medals and ribbons in a coffee can on a shelf in the closet. As a kid, Nick had taken the can off the shelf and examined the medals, dozens of times. But his father would never talk about any of it. A couple years had passed since the last rejection so, probably for the last time, Nick asked the question every boy wants to know: "Dad, you ever kill anyone during the war?"

His father sighed, got out of the chair, started toward the door, turned to Nick, and stared him in his eyes. "Son, they give you a gun and put you right in front of the enemy and the enemy tries to kill you. I'm here, they're not. Don't ask me that again." His father walked the rest of the way to the door, opened it, then closed it, turned, and said, "If you're thinking about killing somebody like that punk Angelo, forget about it." Nick just stared at his father. He raised a gnarled finger and pointed it at Nick. "They proved their point, so forget about it. You hear me?' His father was not going to leave until Nick nodded, which he did. "It was bad business all around, but now it's over. For our little family's sake, I'm glad you've still got your balls." He turned and walked out the door.

THEY TOOK EVIDENCE PHOTOGRAPHS of his injuries at Roosevelt Hospital. Though the overworked doctors on the night shift tried their best to fix it, Nick's nose still looked bad. The doctor's congratulated themselves on saving his eye. Nick asked for a photograph to be sent to his high school principal, with a note saying he wouldn't be showing his face around school for some time.

When he was finally discharged from the hospital, his face invited stares and pitying looks. His aunt Celia was going to be taking care of him for two weeks or so while his father worked. She had a small rent-controlled apartment off Houston Street in Greenwich

Village. Nick was happy not to have to go back to his neighborhood right away. He was ashamed of how he looked. He would have stayed inside for the two weeks but he got restless and Aunt Celia refused to buy him cigarettes. When Celia left to visit with her friend Rita and go grocery shopping, Nick decided to go out and buy some smokes. He painfully slipped into some clothes and went for the door.

He stepped out of Celia's apartment building and limped up to Houston to find a store. He stood on the street corner for about five seconds waiting for the light to change when a new Chevrolet van passed close by and he heard someone begin to yell hysterically, in a high pitched voice, "Stop, stop!"

The van halted and began to back up against honking traffic. When the van braked in front of him, Nick wondered if he should start running. Immediately, a heavyset, slightly effeminate-looking man slid out the passenger side and approached Nick. "Oh, you're perfect, just too perfect. Just what I need."

Nick studied the guy. He certainly didn't look threatening, a pushover. Still, the man brazenly came closer and peered intently at Nick's battered face, which Nick didn't like at all. "My poor boy, what have they done to you?"

"What's up?" Nick asked. He didn't like being called "boy" by a guy who was in his early thirties, looking a little too fucking bizarre and coming so completely into his space. Nick was about to tell the guy to push off when at that moment, a tall beautiful young woman with long slender legs stepped from the van. She was very thin but had impossibly full lips. She shoved a cigarette between her fat red lips and lit up. Nick was enchanted.

The man studying Nick gushed on in a near breathless way. "I'm looking for someone to pose with my girls for a shot I have to do right away. I was suffering terribly, trying to come up with something new. I needed inspiration and suddenly, there you were." The man glowed at Nick, but Nick eyed the girl. She couldn't have been more than nineteen but was as unattainable as the Statue of Liberty. "You'll be paid, of course."

"How much?" Nick asked, his interest shifting from the girl to money.

Nick noticed the guy had to think about it. "Fifty dollars." The money sounded fine, but Nick hesitated. It was all a little new and fast. The man's impatience escalated, "All right, seventy-five but for as long as it takes," the man said. The girl with the great lips laughed lightly at the negotiation, flipped the scarcely smoked cigarette away, and climbed back into the van. The man watched Nick's eyes follow the girl. "Coming?" he asked.

Three hours later, Nick found himself in Chinatown in the center of Mott Street, standing between two beautiful women in mink coats. He was now dressed all in black leather. With his battered face, the models' stunning beauty, and the sinful richness of the fur coats, they made an extraordinary shot.

When it was over, the man handed Nick a card and said, "Come by my studio tomorrow and get your check."

The girl he had first seen leaned over to Nick and whispered, "Just make sure the only thing he gives you is the check. And when he gives it to you, take it and run before he grabs you."

"Personally, I'd like to make a grab for you, that's for sure."

The girl gave him a mock slap on his hand and followed with a light soft kiss on his cheek with her ripe lips. "Goodbye," she said in an affected manner. "We'll never see one another again."

As it turned out, that wasn't true. The next day, Nick showed up at the studio. The man, whose name was Arnie, was going through the proofs of the previous days work. "These are absolutely fantastic, fan-fucking-tastic." Nick walked over and took a peek. Arnie called over his shoulder to a very plain-looking woman. "Terri, cut this nice boy a check for seventy-five dollars."

"I don't want a check," Nick said.

"You don't want a check?" Arnie paused a minute and then smiled shrewdly. "Then, what do you want?"

"I want a job."

"My dear boy, photographing that face was a one-shot deal, believe me. Once your face gets mended, your modeling days are over, except possibly for *Ring* magazine."

"I know. I want a job so I can learn to do this, to do what you do. I like it."

"Oh, my God, future competition, competition, competition." Arnie moaned and looked Nick up and down. "You're not a gay basher are you?" Nick just looked at Arnie. "What can you do?"

"Not much. I learn fast though and I could do some straight guy bashing if you needed it." Nick grinned at him through his cracked lips.

Arnie giggled for a full minute. "All right, you want a job, you got it. I could use a little butch protection around this city."

"What is it?"

"What is what?"

"What's the job?"

"You have to ask? Look at this place. There's a dust mop in the cabinet, start mopping and go on from there. I'll hire you for a week with a look."

"What's that?"

"At the end of the week, if you look like you might work out to be a good second assistant, I'll keep you around. Pays a hundred fifty a week to start."

Nick limped off to where the dust mop was.

He stayed with the job for almost three years. Arnie had been badly beaten a couple of times and his reference to being a "gay basher" was not an idle one. If Nick was going to "watch his back" as part of his job, Arnie wanted Nick to study marital arts. At first, Nick resented it because he felt he was tough enough, but after a while he was seduced by the rituals and training and continued for years. To his credit, Arnie took Nick's apprenticeship to heart and insisted he also study art, photographic techniques, and any related subjects. Arnie was a good teacher and during that time Nick picked up a lot of photographic knowledge and what Arnie always referred to as *savoir-faire*. After a couple of years, he also picked up the beginnings of a solid cocaine habit and a string of pretty ladies. The girls for the most part were beautiful, liked to do a lot of coke, and, unless you were established or rich, were prone to very short-term relationships—usually a night or two. Nick didn't care. He was having a ball and learning by the handful. Gradually, though, he began to realize he didn't really have what it took to be a fashion photographer. He had a problem dealing comfortably with clients and agency people, he didn't have a great flair for design or artificial posing, and he didn't have the entrepreneurial business sense Arnie possessed. There was another and more profound reason as well. It was that Nick often found himself pointing his camera at something he instinctively found far more interesting than posing models—like Helios "the Hippo" after he'd been shot five times getting out of his Cadillac, or the homeless man he discovered seated on a park bench one fierce winter morning. The man was frozen solid but staring out at the Hudson River as though watching the passing tug push its way against the tide. Gradually, Nick moved away from Arnie and his coterie by finding a niche for himself, freelancing, shooting crime, homicide, and other unfortunate happenings such as fires, suicides, and wrecks. From there, it was a logical step to move on to wars, famines, and disasters.

THE SOUND OF A driver repeatedly slamming down a loose-fitting car hood brought Nick back from his remembrances. Darkness had fallen and the damp evening chill had set in. As the list of waiting drivers barely contracted, conversations got less and less elaborate. After an hour, Nick found himself edging near the dispatcher's window with the other drivers. "Who wants one without a radio?" the dispatcher called out.

Nick was surprised when no one immediately called out, and he heard himself say, "I'll take it."

"You gonna take one without a radio?" A short black man asked. "Shit, you can't make no money that way."

"I just want to get sprung," Nick said. There were still several men before him waiting for cabs, but more than that, Nick welcomed the chance to be on his own his first night in the city.

As Nick drove the hulking Ford out of the yard, the disturbing thought came to him that while he would not have to contend with the probable irritation of dealing with a dispatcher, he would now have to find orders himself, and there would be no direct communication if he broke down, had an accident, or worse.

Instinctively, he drove down Lincoln Boulevard through Marina Del Rey and into the Venice area. It was here he felt he should begin to look for the killers. He reasoned Venice was where the crime had been committed and that was where the killers might still be. They probably thought Nick was dead, for there was only one little story about Julianne's murder in the *Evening Outlook*. Unless they had read the six-inch, single-column article on page ten of the local paper, they had no way of knowing whether he had survived, apart from the very dangerous method of looking or asking. If they had thought Nick was alive at the time of the assault, they would have finished him off then and there. By that reasoning, Nick calculated there was a good chance the killers were still around.

He began to slowly cruise the Venice area, starting with the pier at Washington Boulevard. He parked briefly and looked at the transients huddled nearby, then checked out the local bars that capped the pier. No one was close to his recollection. Back in his cab, he traveled north along Ocean Avenue to the Santa Monica amusement area. He drove slowly out onto the wharf, turned at the end, and headed back, scanning the bumper cars and shooting galleries for some sign of the young men. He moved back along Main Street checking out pedestrians.

Two hours of driving and searching had produced not one fare or character worth watching. He was surprised no one had flagged him down. This certainly was not like New York City where everyone rode a cab, bus, or subway. Here, almost everyone had a car, and if they wanted a cab, apparently, they called for one from a telephone. With no radio in the car, Nick thought it was time to get out of there if he wanted to make some money. He knew he wouldn't be a driver long if he didn't make minimum book, and that was sixty-nine dollars a night on the meter. It was also a rule of the cab company that your unpaid miles could not exceed your paid miles, and Nick had gone almost twenty-five miles and not made a nickel. Though they might be somewhat understanding because he was driving a cab without a radio, he knew he'd better get a fare. He didn't want to lose his job, for he could think of nothing else where he would be so unrestricted. He turned his cab toward the airport.

He didn't know where the killers were, so hunting anywhere in the city could prove fruitful. There should be no off time. He would have to learn to do it instinctively. He could hunt while he was driving a fare and hunt during the day when he ventured from his apartment. He remembered while he was at Fort Benning, Georgia, photographing advanced infantry training, the Ranger instructor saying, "When you're walking through the forest, no matter what is going on around you, be hunting. Look through the forest, not at the forest. Hunt through the forest all day long and step around a snake without looking down."

Entering the airport, he was surprised to notice only one or two cabs on the International and TWA stands. He decided to circle the rest of the terminals and observe the situation. By the time he looped around to the far end of the airport, he was astounded to see over a dozen people waving to him from the taxi stand.

As he pulled up, he noticed, with a sense of alarm, how the people swarmed in his direction, demanding of him. He got out of the cab and an enormously fat woman yelled, "Taxi, taxi, I'm first, I've been standing here."

"Hey, fella, we're going downtown to the Hilton, how about it?" a man yelled.

"I'm going there, too," a small thin man wearing a gray felt hat called out.

An elderly man, called from the curb, "That woman isn't first, there's a line here, I'm at the head of the line."

"Where are you going?" Nick asked the man.

"I'm going to the Wilshire Hyatt, on Wilshire Boulevard."

He wasn't sure where the Wilshire Hyatt was, but if it was on Wilshire Boulevard, he reasoned he could also take Wilshire the rest of the way downtown to the Hilton. "I'll take you and I'll also take these three gentlemen going to the Hilton."

"But how about me?" the fat lady demanded. "I was here first."

"You were not here first," the elderly man snapped.

Nick began putting the men's luggage into the trunk when the huge woman advanced upon him again. "Where are you going?" Nick asked defensively.

"I'm going to Third Street, not far from Fairfax," she fretted. "If you're going to the Wilshire Hyatt, you can drop me off and then go there."

As she spoke, another cab whipped in behind Nick at a perilously fast speed. When the woman saw the fresh cab break hard to an abrupt stop, she rolled away from Nick and went in pursuit of the new driver, calling to him that she was first. The driver sprang from his cab and immediately began walking toward his trunk. He was a tall jiving, young, black man, and as the woman ran up to him yelling, he abruptly and aggressively turned toward her and said, "Shit, lady, what you talkin' 'bout? There ain't no first and there ain't no last to this line until I find out where everybody's going. And I know you ain't goin' far, otherwise that dude up there would have took you." Turning to the rest of the line, he asked, "Now who's lookin' to go somewhere?"

"I'm going to the City of Commerce," a man offered.

"I'm going to Beverly Hills," said another.

"We're going to Anaheim, Disneyland," offered a father with his two children.

"Well, I'm taking Mr. Disneyland and Mr. City of Commerce," the young man announced.

The chosen few eagerly pressed toward the taxi, while those not chosen grumbled and shifted uneasily on the curb. Nick snapped his trunk shut on the luggage just as the enormous woman, having been defeated by the other cabby, turned again toward Nick. He saw her coming and as the men piled into his cab, Nick leapt into the driver's seat, pulled his door closed, started the car, and was pulling away by the time she neared his door. "Slow down, for Christ's sake. At least let a guy get in the door," a man in the back seat exclaimed.

Looking back, Nick saw the man's leg was still partly out the door. Nick slowed down and the man pulled his leg inside and closed the door. "I mean, I didn't want to ride with her either, but you didn't have to almost take my leg off."

The other men laughed in mutual relief and, momentarily, Nick cracked his first grin in a long time. "Sorry about that."

"What's going on here with the cabs, anyway?" the small thin man in the front seat asked, adjusting his hat.

"They're out on strike. Yellow Cab is out on strike," the elderly man in the back seat going to the Wilshire Hyatt offered.

"Is that right?" the man in the front seat asked Nick.

Nick didn't enjoy being called upon. He was trying to work out in his head the best way to the Wilshire Hyatt and then downtown. "Well, as far as I know, they're not out on strike, they're out of business," Nick said.

"Out of business? No kidding? How could Yellow Cab go out of business?" the man in the front seat asked incredulously. "I always thought Yellow Cab was indestructible, like ITT."

"I always thought it belonged to the boys. You know the kind of boys I'm talking about?" the man in the middle of the back seat asked, pushing his nose to one side with his forefinger and grinning.

"Well, it doesn't belong to anyone now, except maybe the courts. They went bankrupt," Nick said.

Nick had read about the company's financial problems in the papers and had followed it closely since his return from Georgia. He thought with Yellow Cab out of the picture, the remaining small companies should be able to do great business. Nick's theory was right, but he was just beginning to catch on to how to make it work for himself.

"So, if you're not Yellow Cab, then who the hell are you?" asked the man in the front seat. He didn't like Nick. There was something about Nick's attitude; he was too distant, aloof.

Nick could sense the man's disapproval, for he noticed the man's critical gaze take in how he was dressed and the objects he kept on the front seat. He decided not to answer the man's questions and instead, made believe the traffic along Century Boulevard was more intense and required more concentration than it did.

The man continued to stare at Nick, observing the hiking boots he wore, and noticed, though they were well used, they had obviously been very expensive upon purchase, top of the line, the man reasoned. The rest of Nick's wardrobe followed as being worn but of very good quality. Nick wore dark brown corduroy slacks, a light brown cotton turtleneck, and a dark green V-neck wool sweater. There was an air of casualness about it, but the man knew it had been carefully selected. Added to that was a distracting scar that sank its way into Nick's thick half-wild hair. The man studied it intently. *What could have made such a scar?* the man puzzled. It was as if someone had taken a hot poker and laid it where a part should be. *Yes*, the man thought, as he studied Nick's almost six-foot, well-formed body, *the guy looks in pretty good shape, probably played ball in college, if he went to college.* He took a final glance at Nick, and though the wardrobe and wristwatch he saw were tasteful, there was something about Nick that irritated him. Maybe it was that Nick didn't fit his image of a cab driver. "So, answer me this," the man asked, "if Yellow is out of business, who's servicing the city, scab cabs?"

Nick pulled from the access road onto the freeway doing sixty and remembered his longshoreman father's brief explanation of scabs: "Scumbags!"

Nick kept his mounting irritation with the man in check and gave a civilized explanation to the men in the cab. "A scab is someone who crosses a picket line to take the job of a regular worker who is on strike. I work for a taxi company where no one is on strike. Yellow Cab is out of business, bankrupt, therefore, there is no strike and there are no scabs."

The man in the front seat looked at the meter facing his chest as it clicked over and then back at Nick. There was something about the way Nick answered the question; it was too succinct, too accurate, and the accent, what sort of an accent was that? "Where are you from?" the man asked, his voice tinged with a note of sarcasm.

"I'm originally from New York City and I've lived in England and other places."

"I'll bet you've been to college, too, haven't you?" a man in the back seat asked.

"Yes" Nick gave the short answer. He never graduated high school, as he went to work for Arnie. Yes, he had attended college at The New School and NYU, but had primarily taken classes in advanced photographic techniques, film printing, art, and journalism. But that was none of their business. He was weary of the men and their questions, but he was inexperienced on how to stop it, so he let them talk on.

"Didn't I tell you, Merv, last week when we took that cab from the Americana that a lot of these cab drivers are college PhDs and artists and stuff like that?"

"How much college have you had?" the man in the front seat demanded.

"What did you do before you were a cab driver?" Merv in the back seat asked.

Nick cringed again at the attention and the questions. Not having dealt with people on a close active basis for a long time, he found this direct line of questioning intolerable. He searched for a way out, as he said simply, "I'm just a cab driver." Nick turned to the man in the front seat and, in an effort to get the light off himself, followed immediately with the question, "How about you, what do you do?"

The reaction of the small man was surprising. He turned a little pale, and when he finally spoke his voice was thick with stifled emotion. "I work in the men's retail clothing business."

"As a buyer or what?" Merv in the back seat asked.

"No, I'm an accounts manager," came a subdued reply.

"Take a look at this shirt; what do you think it's worth? I might have to hock it to pay for this trip," Merv said.

The men forced a laugh at the bad joke and the effort killed conversation. They lapsed into silence and sullenly peered out into the night. The old cab steadily chugged along the San Diego Freeway. As unobtrusively as possible, Nick looked up in his Thomas Guide where the Hyatt was on Wilshire Boulevard. As he did so, he thought of the young black man who had taken the fares to the City of Commerce and Anaheim. Nick wasn't sure how much they would run, but he knew the fares would probably double his and he had been on the spot first. He promised himself he wouldn't make that mistake again. He dropped the elderly man off at the Wilshire Hyatt. The man tipped him and paid full fare.

When he dropped the men at the downtown Hilton, there was a discussion about the fare. They wanted to just pay half because the elderly man had paid as well. Nick turned to them and said in a straightforward manner, "Listen, I'll take a dollar off for the stop at the Hyatt but the two of you guys are together and this man in the front seat is separate. You guys can all share what's on the meter but don't ask me to cut the fare any more."

Merv said, "That's fair." He produced some bills, paid his half, and gave a three-dollar tip.

The retail accounts manager grudgingly settled up his part of the fare, giving Nick a fifty-cent tip. "See ya, college boy," he said and cracked a tight grin for the small tip and a hundred other reasons he'd never acknowledge.

CHAPTER FOUR

CAL Santiso slowly woke in the claustrophobic motel room and stared across at Jesse lying on his back snoring loudly. Getting up, he walked to the door, pulled it open, and stared out at the midmorning glare kicking off surrounding cars. He had been dreaming of his mother. He loved his mother and she had a definite affection for him, but that was buffeted by her constant disappointment of the way he lived his life. His younger brother George had learned from his mistakes as he watched Cal move from reformatories, to jails. George had graduated grammar school, high school, and got an AA degree from the community college. George was now an X-ray technician, making good money, and living in Sacramento. He sent money to his mother every month. It had been almost a year since Cal sent anything. Cal looked over his shoulder at Jesse and then to the Nova parked outside. He could get dressed, get in the Nova, and drive to New Mexico and see his mother. Jesse would never find him or even have much reason to. Maybe he could get a job as a mechanic at a garage. Dressed only in his underpants and standing in the sun-warmed doorway, Cal considered it for a brief moment. Then he turned, went into the bathroom, and sat on the toilet. Someday, he was going to do that. Leave Jesse and go back home.

◀◆▶◀◆▶◀◆▶

NICK HAD BEEN DRIVING for two weeks when a catastrophic earthquake struck Turkey. An internal eagerness grabbed hold. Before he had fallen out of favor, that was the sort of event he would have been sent to cover. Nick looked around at the sad interior of the taxi and impulsively pulled to the curb. It was exactly six o'clock in the morning in Venice, nine o'clock in the east. Nick impulsively walked to a pay phone outside a liquor store and started dumping his night's tips to call New York. He knew getting sent from Los Angeles was a long shot. When he got back to his apartment at 7:15 a.m., he continued his efforts.

He called for three hours. No one in authority took his calls and no one called back. He tried to fight off the depression of not getting an immediate response. *Maybe that's it*, he thought. *End of career.* Then he took brief comfort in the fact he had been offered an assignment less than two months earlier. While living with Julianne, his sobriety and attempts at repairing business relationships had actually begun to pay off. He had been offered a job going to Alaska for six weeks with possible follow-up assignments shooting construction of the oil pipeline. He had sold the Hasselblad to leave money for Julianne because he wouldn't get paid for some time. Then, the murder happened and he blew off the assignment. Employers and friends had already distanced themselves from him, and with the killing they moved even further away. People liked to stay with winners, and Nick was now known as a loser.

How would he have felt if he had been in Alaska when Julianne was raped, murdered, and his daughter traumatized? Who would have discovered Melissa? They knew no one in Los Angeles who would be checking in. Nick was suddenly stricken with the question, *How would he feel now if he were visually recording the misery in Turkey while he had abandoned what he had sworn to do?* Nick opened a beer, stared around his apartment, and was abruptly and completely ashamed. He had panicked and so easily abandoned his quest. Half the world could go up in flames, but he was going to find those men. Once justice was done, he could look ahead. Then he could see what his life might be. For now, no one was going to hire him except to go to the airport or a bar.

◀❙▶

JIM PEARSON PUT THE key in the lock and admitted himself to his five-room house in Westchester. In the near distance, a 707 took off from LAX, filling the house with its rumblings.

He stoically accepted the screams of landing planes and roars of those incessantly taking off. Occasionally, when a thick blanket of fog shut down the runways, he welcomed the damp silence, but that night the planes bounced in and roared out. Pearson walked around, shedding jacket, tie, and gun. He poured himself an Irish whiskey and walked to the mantel above his fireplace. It was a routine he did every night, to say "hello" to the photographs of his life. Prominent among them was his ex-wife. He had knocked her up and married her when they were just nineteen. He had been in the Marines at the time and learned he was not alone as a teenage father. Ten years later, his wife left him for the owner of a trucking company in Arizona. Their two children, Wayne and Diane, had gone along.

That was ten years ago and Pearson still hadn't gotten over it. Jim now saw his son every two weeks at Chino State Penitentiary. Wayne was in jail for vehicular manslaughter. On President's Weekend, Wayne was on a rare visit to his dad. With three friends in his car and driving under the influence, Wayne had run over and killed a twelve-year-old skateboarder, panicked, and kept on going. For a while, Pearson had shifted the blame to his ex-wife and her husband, but he realized it was he who should have taken charge of Wayne and developed his character. Even though he visited him in jail, he could not comprehend what Wayne would be like in three years when he finished his sentence. His other child, Diane, was beginning college at Washington State. She declined his attempts at affection but needed more money and shoes than Imelda Marcos.

Moving his eyes down the mantelpiece, he stared at pictures of him holding fish he'd caught. There were several different shots: the tarpon from Florida, the marlin from Cabo San Lucas, the salmon from Oregon, and the yellowtail from Catalina Island. It was one of the few things gave him pleasure, even though he constantly acknowledged that, compared to expert anglers, he wasn't very good. The pictures all whispered the same thing: "In sixteen years, you'll have worked thirty and can retire with a full pension. Why hang around after?" Often, he wondered if he could go the distance. He spent a lot of time looking at bad happenings and chasing bad people. Still, there were some interesting cases he'd like to crack, and he'd like to get his daughter out of college, help put Wayne back on track, and pay off the mortgage—the usual middle-class catastrophes. The longer he kept on going, the higher his pension. Yeah, he acknowledged, he was stuck. As he drained the rest of his whiskey, for some reason he thought of Nick Cullen. That Cullen guy was like Wayne and a lot of other young men he came across. You could look at their faces and see trouble coming. It was as clear as an eighteen-wheeler coming down a sidewalk. Pearson made up his mind—if that fucking Cullen guy got into anything he shouldn't, he'd slap cuffs on him and teach him a lesson.

THE NIGHTS BLURRED ON, and Nick quickly became a more seasoned night driver. He was out there driving hard, and it suited his temperament and mood like an old jacket turned up against the cold. He was comfortable in its fit, but it didn't keep away the deep chill.

He would leave the yard in a cab with the setting sun, have some hits off a joint on the way to the airport, and plunge into the long night. He would stay out all night, driving, looking, booking, and then return to the yard around six thirty as the sun was beginning to show in the east. He put in thirteen- and fourteen-hour shifts six nights a week and he quickly began to catch on to the intricacies of being a high booker.

Weeks rolled by, and the Christmas holiday came upon him like a dark cloud. He bought a pretty and expensive dress from a children's shop on Montana Avenue in Santa Monica and sent it to Melissa. On Christmas Day, he called but Lillian picked up. She was furious. "We don't hear from you for over a month. You don't call to see how your daughter is when she misses her daddy so badly? You ought to be ashamed of yourself."

"I know," Nick said. "But..."

"I understand you're sad, but I lost my daughter. You killed my daughter with your moving, strange life, and wastefulness."

"Granny, I loved Julianne and I love Melissa. I'm sorry if I've..."

"Melissa wants to hear from her daddy all the time. Not every month or two. Now, don't call again. I'm so upset I can't talk anymore."

Nick heard the line go dead but Lillian's harsh words, graced only by the Southern accent, continued to ring and spin in his head. It was only 8:00 a.m. but 11:00 a.m. in Macon, Georgia. He'd been out driving all night and called as soon as he got in, but Lillian didn't understand, or possibly didn't care.

Walking into the kitchen, he pulled a bottle of tequila off the counter and crossed into the bedroom. Since Julianne's murder, he had developed a nagging knot of tension in his stomach, but he had learned how to deal with it. He kicked off his shoes, sat on the bed, unscrewed the cap on the bottle, and took a deep slug. The pain in his stomach began to diminish. Setting the bottle on the nightstand, he stared at three framed pictures. The first was of Melissa at her first birthday. The second was of Melissa and Julianne at the merry-go-round in Central Park. It was the third picture that brought all his attention into focus. Nick lifted the framed picture he had shot when he and Julianne were at Montauk Point, Long Island. It was a head-and-shoulders shot, in black and white. Her dark hair was blowing and backlit, so there was a fashionable style and professionalism to the photo, but, more importantly, Julianne stared into the camera with a look of such womanly understanding, compassion, and intelligence, one could see at a glance she was a person of depth and soul. Nick pulled a small package from the nightstand drawer. "Here, I'll open this for you," he said to Julianne's image.

The little gift was neatly wrapped and Nick carefully opened it to reveal a small metal replica of a taxicab. "I bought this for you so we could feel closer to one another. You can look at it and laugh in that ironic way you had and think of me out there."

He kissed the picture and felt the impersonal chill of the glass touch his lips. He placed the photograph back on the nightstand and cruised the little cab to a stop in front of it. "Julianne, you were the only truly good thing ever happened to me. Merry Christmas, honey." Tears sprang to Nick's eyes and for a while he wept. "Oh, baby, I'm sorry, I'm so very sorry."

After a time, Nick fought back his tears bringing them to a watery pool around his lids. He stood up and took one more long pull from the tequila bottle. Taking off all his clothes, he thought, *Granny was right. I haven't been paying attention to what's important.*

Nick pulled down the covers and crawled into bed. A vision of his daughter in her crib staring at her mother on the floor drifted into his consciousness. Someone in the building had gotten up and was now loudly playing tapes of Christmas carols. Nick fought the image of his frightened little girl from his mind and tried to reflect on the Christmas Eve fares he had.

It took a while, but thirteen hours in the cab and tequila blasts finally caught up with him. The neighbor's tape segued into "God Rest Ye Merry Gentlemen." Nick's mind acknowledged the ridicule and reluctantly relaxed into sleep. As he drifted down, the mental snapshot of the three killers developed in his mind and the last thing he saw was an extreme close-up of the muzzle flash from the killer's gun.

CHAPTER FIVE

WHEN HE GOT UP on Christmas evening to go to the yard, he called Lillian again. No answer. *She's punishing me*, he thought. He was still thinking about it when he walked into the yard and got his trip ticket and cab assignment. It was true he had handed over his daughter to Julianne's mother partially out of guilt and the thought it would help Granny with the loss. But if Melissa was going to be used as a weapon and the woman didn't have her emotions together, then it could be a bad scene. He possibly should have sent Melissa to his father. Sean would have protected Melissa with his life and the situation would have brought joy to him. On the other hand, growing up in a tenement on the west side of Manhattan with only a working longshoreman for company didn't have many selling points.

The widowed Mrs. Thombridge had a large and comfortable house with a manicured yard hosting peach and pecan trees. Nick had handed Melissa to her because he thought the girl needed safe and maternal care. But he realized with suddenness, he had also done it selfishly, to have time to track the killers and bring himself back together. Someday, he hoped it would all change and he'd have Melissa back again. He wondered what it would be like living with his daughter without Julianne. He couldn't picture it. Hopefully, he'd get a chance to experience it, but for now, he knew he wasn't ready for anything except running the cab through the streets of Los Angeles. Turning on the ignition, Nick had one of those frequent moments where he questioned if he was doing the right thing. A second later he stepped on the gas, and drove into the night, leaving behind both the question and comfort he and Melissa could have shared.

♦ ♦ ♦

IN ROOM ELEVEN OF Ruth's Motel outside Bakersfield, Jesse Carmody and Cal Santiso were partying for the Christmas holiday. They had enough tequila, beer, cocaine, and heroin to keep them going until New Year's. Life was good. Sprawled on the bed was a nineteen-year-old Hispanic girl they had picked up outside a 7-Eleven in Pacoima. She had a small suitcase and a knapsack when they spotted her, so they knew she was on the move. It took some sweet-talking, but finally she went with them, mainly because she had nowhere else to go and they promised her some really fine drugs. She soon discovered they were right about the drugs. She was flopped on one of the twin beds in an unflattering way, arms and legs akimbo. Her worn denim pants were thrown carelessly in a corner and her brief-cut underwear was hanging from the light fixture over the nightstand. She was totally whacked from doing speedballs for three days, a new experience for her.

Cal wasn't too happy with the speedballs. It wasn't his thing, but he did like snorting a little coke, drinking beer and tequila, and having sex with the girl. She'd let him do pretty much what he wanted with her and seemed to like it. Well, maybe she didn't exactly enjoy what Cal wanted to do, it was more like she expected it. Cal was happy when women liked what he was doing or didn't complain. He got irritated in a dark way when they protested or screamed, like the woman they had done in the apartment a couple months earlier, the one with the little girl. That was a bad scene. Now that it was over and he'd had time to think about it, it wrenched at his mind. Cal instinctively crossed himself. Getting off on beating and raping women was more Jesse's thing. Cal switched his gaze from the girl's crotch to his companion. Jesse was coming off his last dose and getting restless. Jesse got up and paced around the room, which contained some fiberboard dressers, a chipped Formica table, plastic-covered furniture, twin beds, and a dirty green shag rug. Jesse was dressed only in his cowboy boots, underpants, and sheepskin vest. "You look goofy dressed like that," Cal volunteered and snickered. Jesse continued to pace like an animal in a cage. "When are you going to get rid of that vest? You ought to throw that dead animal out. It's like roadkill."

"I'll get rid of it when there's no more fur on this fucker, or it rots on my sorry-assed corpse. This is my suit of armor against the world. It keeps me warm, protects me, and feeds the mind. It all feeds the mind," Jesse said obsessively.

"Well, there's people all over this country that are either hurtin' or huntin' that vest. I'd toss the fucker."

"This is my lucky vest, so drop it."

"With all the shit you done, it ain't gonna be so lucky if somebody remembers it."

Jesse didn't pay any attention to Cal's last statement but rather increased the speed with which he paced the room, clomping heavily in his boots and beginning to smack his fist into the palm of his hand.

Through his fogged mind, Cal instinctively knew Jesse was going to do something harsh. He just hoped it wouldn't be to the girl who was sprawled on the bed. He might want some more of that when she came around a little. To his surprise, Jesse suddenly moved to the telephone and placed a long-distance call. Someone answered and Jesse listened for a quiet moment while he lit a cigarette. He took a drag and then suddenly screamed into the telephone, "It's Christmas Day, Pop, and I just wanted to say, fuck you! Fuck you where you breathe."

Jesse ripped the telephone from the jack and threw it across the room where it bounced off a cheap cardboard landscape picture hanging crookedly on the wall. He broke out into a forced high-pitched laugh and fell down backward on top of the prostrate girl. She moved imperceptibly. Jesse sat up, flipped the girl over, and smacked her on the ass five or six times, hard. The girl groaned but hardly moved. He then got up and walked to the Formica table where their stash was laid out. He built himself a gonzo speedball and shot it. Cal looked at him from across the room. Jesse grinned back at him and, just before the rush hit, he said, "Merry Christmas, motherfucker. We're out of this shit-hole tomorrow. We got work to do."

NEW YEAR'S PASSED, JANUARY began drifting by, and Nick found a kind of peace in the long nights. He learned he could easily become preoccupied with the demands of night driving. In the morning, he would return to his apartment, have a few drinks, go to bed, and rise around three in the afternoon. He would shower, fix himself something to eat, have a couple of beers or some wine, make a sandwich for the night, run an errand or two, and then return to the yard around 4:30 p.m. to wait for a cab. It was an all-consuming, exhausting schedule, and, as such, Nick found sanctuary in its numbing effect on his tortured memories and failed career. Driving incessantly, he began arriving back at the yard as late as he could. Fourteen- and fifteen-hour shifts became common. Business was extraordinary, and Los Angeles was such an expansive city he found at times he was driving over two hundred miles a night. He learned high mileage was synonymous with high bookings. From the airport alone, with Yellow Cab out of the way, little companies found themselves with more business than they could handle. The companies prospered and, to a degree, so did the drivers. Double loading, triple loading, and even quadruple loading was not unheard of in the airport and at some hotels. Nick discovered the business of picking up people was a game of chance with an infinite variety of possibilities. As many as two hundred people would sit in his cab during the week, and all the time, Nick hunted.

He found people often would want to talk and gradually he became more willing to communicate with them as well. Since the passengers knew nothing of his condition, sorrow, anger, history, or hunt, he was able to exchange thoughts, feelings, and, if he felt like it, become totally involved with them for the duration of the ride. As each person or group entered the taxi and closed the door, they immediately filled the small space with their karma. Increasingly stoned, Nick would sit behind the wheel and become immediately desensitized to what was flowing from the back seat. With each fare, he was less and less emotionally threatened and with each pass along the dark streets he became more and more familiar with the City of Angels. He began to know and understand it.

AT 12:18 A.M., NICK answered a call to pick up at the Airport Marina Hotel. A young woman was standing off to the side of the entrance. She looked to be about twenty-five and was demurely dressed in a small print Laura Ashley, brown pumps, and a cardigan sweater. As she got into the cab, her shoulder-length brown hair moved freely about her face, which seemed to be makeup free. She was pretty in a girl-next-door manner and Nick was pleased she was his fare. "I'm going to the Cornell Motel on Santa Monica Boulevard in West Los Angeles," she requested. Nick started the meter and drove toward the destination. He thought it odd the woman would be leaving one hotel and going to another at that hour of the morning. In addition, she had no luggage, but Nick didn't question her. He felt she was studying him from her vantage point in the back seat. About halfway to her destination, Nick's mind calculated the improbable but accurate answer to the situation. Even though she had the appearance of a young librarian, she was a prostitute. "Do you drive many nights?" he heard her ask.

"Yes, I drive six nights a week."

"I've never seen you before," she said.

"I don't know what to say about that. I'm out here."

"I ride back every night about this time, or a little later. Most of the drivers I don't like."

"Why is that?"

"I don't know, they just worry me a little. Could I ask for your cab number and if you're around you could pick me up?"

"Well, I'm driving a different cab every night, so that wouldn't work, but you could ask for Nick and if I'm near the area, I could swing by."

"All right, Nick. I'll try that. You seem like a nice man."

"Do you mind if I ask your name?"

"Irene."

"Well, just ask for Nick and say, 'Pick up Irene,' and I'll know what to do." Possibly, he was wrong about her, but he didn't think so. He decided to gently check it out. "This has to be rough for you, just going from hotel to motel."

"I have my reasons. It wasn't what I had in mind but it's what happened."

"What did you have in mind?"

"I was interested in history, ancient history."

"That sounds like something you could follow up on."

"I still read a lot."

"You should try for a degree or something."

"Well, I did. I was in college."

"So what didn't work?"

"I got into trouble."

Nick didn't say anything more. They were straying into territory he didn't feel he could ask about but, after a moment, Irene continued. "I was going steady with a boy I met there. We were both sophomores. Our families were poor and couldn't contribute much, so we never had any money to do anything fun. We worked in the college cafeteria every day to make some cash and get some free food."

"What was your boyfriend's name?" Nick asked and then wondered why he had.

"Jimmy. One day, he told me of a plan he had to rob the cafeteria of the day's receipts. It was all cash, in small bills, and would probably be over a thousand dollars. I didn't want to do it, but Jimmy said we couldn't get caught. He had gotten a duplicate key made to the office. All we had to do was steal the lock box, take it to his apartment, and crack it open. I was to be the lookout and he was going to go in and get the box."

"Did you do it?"

"Yes," she murmured. "Somehow they suspected him. The police went to his apartment the next day and found the lock box."

"Don't tell me this guy Jimmy implicated you."

"Yes." Irene pulled her purse closer to her stomach and looked out the window. "I didn't know what to do. I was suspended from school, my parents were scandalized, especially my father. None of my friends wanted to have anything to do with me."

"So, you came down here?"

"I went to San Francisco first but then I came here."

So there it was, Nick thought, *as easy as that*. He dropped her off at the two-story motel and watched her walk toward the stairs. He sat for some minutes as Irene's presence lingered inside the cab. It was near 1:00 a.m., so Nick decided to cruise the bars in Venice. Soon they would begin to send drinkers out into the street. He'd go see who came out.

Detective Jim Pearson walked down Windward Avenue toward Ocean Front Walk. He had tried variations on his walks around the streets of Cullen's neighborhood ever since the murder. He thought, *Cullen's out there driving and looking for the killers*

*and I'm here walking his neighborhood. I like my chances better and
who wants to sit in a car all the time?*

He spent an hour a day, usually his lunch hour, walking, asking
questions, and looking. He never brought along Nick's collage
of the killers. Carting the artwork and showing it around would
have made him feel foolish and maybe direct things in the wrong
direction. He'd save those for later after the people he questioned
thought about it. He congratulated himself on his occasional
subtlety. If the killers had any subtlety at all, they wouldn't walk
around very far together. That combination of rough-looking guys
might attract some attention, even in Venice. Pearson theorized
the killers most likely had made a rendezvous in the area near the
apartment and then gone over to Nick's to commit the crime. They
could have met at the apartment's entrance, or staggered their
entry; if he could identify one he might get the trio. If the men
thought they had gotten away clean, they could still be hanging out.
Countless things bothered Pearson about the case. Did the killers
know beforehand of the valuables the Cullen's possessed? If so,
how? There was also the puzzlement of the unlikely combination
Nick had described: one white, one Latino, and one black. That
didn't seem probable but it's what he had to go on. They were
not musicians or athletes, where it would be easy to visualize the
combination. No, it was business, and these guys make their living
the old-fashion way—murder and theft.

Jim was having no luck with his inquiries, but at least he was
out of the office. Times like this, he actually liked his work. It was
more like a game and a warm midday sun made the promenade
pleasurable. Arriving at Ocean Front Walk, Pearson strolled along,
casually dodging skateboarders, bicyclists, and tourists. He paid
little attention to the vendors selling bad food, T-shirts, and caps
beneath the portable tents that made Venice Beach similar to a
Middle Eastern bazaar. Rather, he concentrated on the moving
crowd, people on benches, and those huddled by the apartment
buildings that marked the end of the beach and the beginnings of

the massive sprawl that becomes Los Angeles. Then it was decision time: Which vendor to visit for lunch? The choices were great if you wanted to grab something and keep walking—pizza, gyros, burgers, sausages, fish tacos. He decided on tacos with extra hot sauce. When finished, he walked over and plucked some extra napkins from the stand to clean up after the messy, runny, incredibly fresh, and delicious tacos. As he was wiping his face, he spotted a fully clothed man sleeping on the sand. There was nothing unusual about that in Venice, especially on a warm late-winter's day. But there was something about the way the man was dressed that made Pearson linger. He tossed the napkins in the trash and, trying not to get sand inside his black street shoes, carefully stepped across thirty feet of the soft sand. Stopping, he turned his back to the sun and studied the man. The warm sun was a luxury today and he reached up and cracked his neck. The vertebra made a loud rapid snapping noise as the tension was released. Four pops. Sometimes he got more, sometimes less, but it was always satisfying. He needlessly worried the four pops might wake the man. It was then that Pearson put the description he had heard in briefings with the creature at his feet. "Faded orange high-top canvas sneakers, black pants, white shirt, dirty gray nylon jacket..."

Pearson leaned forward for a closer look. Everything fit except the man's T-shirt wasn't white, it was dark blue, but that didn't matter; there was one other identifying characteristic that could not easily be changed. Pearson bent down and peered at the man's face half buried under his arm and noticed the scar that ran from the man's top lip down to his chin. Reaching back, Pearson, pulled his gun and flicked off the safety. With his other hand, he pulled out his wallet and flipped it open to reveal the badge. Pearson carefully reflected the sun's glare off his badge at the man's eyes. Groggy and annoyed the man shifted shielding his eyes and peered up at Pearson. Sand clung to one side of the man's face and his eyes went wide as the sun glinting off Pearson's badge made the significance of the moment register. The man's feet spun in the sand as he tried to jump. "If you move, I'll shoot you through your eye. I know who you are, Mister. I know what you did. Now, put your hands behind your back, slowly."

As Pearson cuffed the man and read him his rights, a crowd slowly began to gather. A young German tourist couple stopped and took pictures of the event. Pearson resisted the silly impulse to put his foot on the rapist's back and grin at the cameras but he did make a show of reading the suspect his rights in front of two vendors. He knew they would be around in the months to come in case some defense lawyer should question if he had. The tall Iranian sunglasses vendor and the Rasta man who sold incense knew Pearson for what he was. They'd testify honestly as to what had taken place, how the defendant had not been harmed in any way, and had been read his rights before their very eyes. The vendors valued their tent space on the Promenade.

NICK EMERGED FROM THE American Airlines terminal clutching a wad of hand towels he had pulled from the dispenser in the men's room. From inside the cab, he took out the bottle of Windex he now carried and began to clean the windows. He did them all, very carefully, inside and out. It was difficult for him to understand how some drivers could live with their filthy windshields, especially at night when vision was so important and the glare off a dirty windshield so intense. Yet, he noticed most cab windshields were filthy. In what was probably a carryover from his photography days, every night, he would methodically clean the front windshield inside and out before he left the yard. He cleaned it as though it were a lens, a wide-angle lens through which he viewed the night and its creatures. He thought of the windshield in that manner, and even referred to it in his thoughts as "the lens." If time permitted, he would do the rest of the windows and clean the front windshield as often as three times a night. He had discovered the evening mist in LA carried the additional components of smog, dirt, and salt spray. The combination conspired to dull the glass, which was unacceptable for someone on the hunt.

Peering through the clean window, Nick spotted a tall elderly lady stiffly following behind a porter's brisk walk. She caught Nick's eye and moved toward his taxi. *A straggler from the last flight,* Nick thought as he got out of the cab.

The porter pulled the dolly across the sidewalk, swung it around, and pushed it rapidly toward Nick's cab. The suitcases on the dolly were thin and old, yet in impeccable condition. Nick knew instantly this was a woman who had never had much money, for the purchase price of the bags could not have been expensive, nor could she have traveled often, for the condition of her bags was better than the years should have allowed. He opened the trunk as the porter snapped the dolly into an upright position. Nick neatly snagged the first bag and lowered it carefully into the left side of the deep trunk well. The larger bag he placed in the center of the well, and then, taking the last two small bags, he wedged them snugly into a compact unit. He had come to take some pleasure in properly packing a trunk. Closing the lid, he watched as the elderly woman tipped the porter a dollar.

As she turned to get into the car, Nick got a full look at the woman and was startled by her face. In the shadows, it seemed slightly misshapen but was also tender and fragile. White powder makeup made it seen even more delicate and striking. Her eyes and lips were made-up a little too heavily, the colors contrasting darkly with her white face, so that she looked like a mime. The face stood out mask-like under a large-brimmed, dark blue hat. A thin, finely woven veil fell before her face. Nick couldn't remember the last time he had seen a woman wear a veil during anything other than old movies and photo shoots. Her dark blue suit was simple and nicely cut, without being elegant. The material, however, was getting old and soft and struggled to maintain its original shape.

Nick opened the back door and she stepped carefully off the curb and into the taxi. The slowness of her movements irritated Nick and he slapped the door shut and walked around the back of the cab, keeping an ever-wary eye at the erratic oncoming traffic. He got into the cab and drove off.

He reached over, grabbed the flag, and pulled it around and down to the six o'clock position. It made the sweet grinding sound of small gears becoming engaged and money beginning to flow, like the sound of a slot machine that always paid off. Turning toward the back seat, Nick looked once more at the woman and wondered where she could be headed. It was a game some drivers played. Try and guess the person's final destination by the way they looked and what airline they'd come from. This woman was difficult to judge. Nick thought of Westchester, a small community near the airport, but then dismissed the idea. He ruled out the Valley immediately and thought of the Westwood area. That was a possibility, but it didn't feel right to him. *Possibly Santa Monica*, he speculated. That sounded right. She might be a widow, living in a small rent-controlled apartment, scraping to make ends meet but living in frugal, quiet dignity along a breeze-blown street of western Santa Monica. "Where are you off to, ma'am?" Nick asked.

When she answered, her voice was high, brittle, having a certain class but not an imperious quality; fragile, like her face. "I'm going to Hollywood," she said.

"Are you an actress?" Nick asked, again observing her theatrical-looking hat and makeup in the rearview mirror.

"No. I work for the city of Los Angeles as a bookkeeper."

"Where in Hollywood are we going?"

"A little street near Franklin and Gower. There's an all-night market there and I'd like you to wait while I go in and get something."

Nick said he didn't mind. He suspected the "something" was a pint of gin.

"I wouldn't ask you to wait, but I'm afraid to walk from there myself and I have the luggage. I was robbed in that parking lot, twice."

"I hope you weren't hurt."

"Well, one time they ripped the bag from my hand before I knew what happened and the other time, one man bumped me and another one yanked the bag from my shoulder so powerfully, I was knocked down very hard and had my arm wrenched almost out of the socket. I would have given them anything they wanted because I knew it was senseless for me to fight. I was attacked once and struggled. I'll never do that again."

"I'd be interested to hear about it." Nick was astounded at himself for asking her, but the request had come out in an impulsive and uncharacteristic manner.

What was more surprising was the woman was quite willing to tell the story. "All right," he heard her say. It took a moment but then she began. "It was years ago. I was living at a boarding house. I had graduated high school and was working during the day but in the evening I was taking classes at the university."

"Where was this?" Nick asked.

"I was living in Silver Lake. I would have to take the trolley home from USC." She waited as though expecting Nick to ask something. Nick said nothing as the cab swooped off the long ramp that ran adjacent to the freeway and onto La Cienega Boulevard. He dropped the pace to a speed slower than usual. He didn't want to terrify the brittle woman and also wanted to carefully listen to the story she was beginning to tell.

"It was quite late when I came home, almost midnight. After classes I had stopped to get something to eat with my girlfriend, Ingrid. We waited for the last trolley. You see, we didn't have enough time to eat before we went to school. When I arrived at Mrs. Taylor's house, I found the front door unlocked. I was surprised because Mrs. Taylor always kept the door locked after dinner hour. I didn't know it but there was a prowler in the house."

"How many other people lived in the house with you?" Nick asked as the cab barely made the light across La Tijera Boulevard and began the lonely drive over Baldwin Hills.

"There were two girls who lived on the second floor. Mrs. Taylor lived in the back on the first floor and I lived on the third floor. I climbed the stairs and it seemed everyone was asleep but as I entered my room, I felt something was wrong. I stood in my room for several moments listening and while I didn't hear a thing, I sensed something. I went to the nightstand to turn on the light but decided against it. There was a neighborhood boy who used to climb a tree and peek into the windows at us girls. I got undressed in the dark and went to the closet to get my nightgown. I noticed the door slightly ajar but I didn't think much of it. I opened the door all the way, and suddenly I saw a big man standing in my closet."

There was something about the way she said "big man" that startled Nick. The image came to him of a naked, delicate young woman opening her closet and confronting a huge, dark apparition. *Apparition, no,* Nick corrected himself, *for an apparition is not real.* "The man quickly reached out and pulled me toward him with one hand and then punched me with the other. The force was incredible and I flew, I mean I was actually sent through the air across the room and landed half on the bed. His punch had hit me in exactly the middle of my face, and as I tried to sit up I felt blood flow down from my nose and into my mouth. I knew my nose was smashed. I should have laid still. I tried to sit up and see who and what was happening to me. He quickly took a couple of strides and sprang upon me with both of his knees hitting me here."

Nick glanced in the rearview mirror and saw the woman cupping her small breasts in her hands. She was staring wide-eyed, looking out at the oil pumps working in the murky night. Nick looked back to the road and drove easily down the curving boulevard as it made the long descent from Stocker into the basin containing much of Los Angeles. The smell of oil fumes leaked into the drafty cab.

"My breath was knocked from me and he grabbed my throat with one hand and with the other he began punching me. He broke my jaw and cheekbones in several places and split open the skin around my cheeks and lips and eyes. He just ruined my whole face," she said in a distant manner. "As though from far away, I heard Mrs. Taylor calling my name from the bottom of the stairs. 'Doris, Doris.' The man leapt off me and listened at the door. I tried to sit up and call to Mrs. Taylor because I was afraid she would come up and the man would attack her as well. He saw me attempting to sit up and speak and he turned toward me in such a way, I knew he was going to kill me. He jumped at my throat and as he did so, I involuntarily took a deep breath. His fingers crushed my throat so fiercely and painfully I almost couldn't bear it. I knew I must hold my breath and remain conscious, yet make him believe I was dead. But he didn't stop there. He lifted me up by my throat and shook me up and down. I thought he would break my neck. I was losing consciousness when, finally, he let me fall to the bed and went back to the door to listen." The woman paused momentarily in her remembrance before continuing. "He remained by the door for what seemed a long time. I lay still, breathing as quietly and shallowly as possible. I had seen his face and I knew what he would do if he discovered I was still alive." She fell silent with the memory.

Nick had to stop for the light at Jefferson Boulevard and as he sat there, the shrieking memory of his wife's bloody form and his child's terror was projected from the red stoplight against his mind's eye.

The light turned green and to escape the memory, Nick floored the accelerator and the old cab roared off as fast as its half-million miles would allow. Easing off the pedal, the car bounced over railroad tracks and Nick asked, "How long were you on the bed before they found you?"

"Apparently, it wasn't very long because Mrs. Taylor and the girls heard the man dash down the stairs and out the front door. As soon as the man left the room, I lost consciousness. It was then that Mrs. Taylor and one of the girls came to see if I was all right."

"That's a devastating thing to happen. I don't know what to say."

The woman said nothing and they drove in silence for a while. It wasn't until they crossed Wilshire Boulevard Nick asked the question he had wanted to ask almost from the beginning. "Did they ever catch the man?"

The woman had drifted into her own thoughts and she asked Nick to repeat the question. After a moment, she answered, "No, they came to the hospital several times to have me look at pictures. After I got out of the hospital, they would bring me down to headquarters for lineups, I believe that is what they are called, but I never could be certain. It had been dark and I never heard him speak." After a moment, she added, "And I was terribly afraid. I was terrified he would see me."

"I can understand," Nick said. But deep in his mind, he rumbled over the question of what ever happened to the brutal man. What fate did he encounter for brutalizing and shattering the woman in the back seat? Was he alive and well and living as a fry cook in Tucson, a car mechanic in Barstow, or had his dark-sinned blood flowed out onto the floor in the blue neon light of a cheap saloon after losing a fight? Nick's mind sloshed with possibilities until he wondered, "When did it happen?"

"Oh, it was a long time now, forty-five years," she replied.

Forty-five years, Nick pondered. *If the man were thirty at the time, he would be seventy-five now. Perhaps he had never paid for the crime in any way. Possibly he had died a peaceful death, or maybe he was still living contentedly somewhere, while the object of his savagery lives forever changed, fragile and fearful.* Nick fretted over the question of the man's history in an effort to block out the horrible vision haunting the fringes of his mind. But everywhere his mind pushed the thought of the woman's ravaging it was met by the horror of Julianne's death. *What are the ravagers of his family doing tonight, at this moment? Are they free?* He fought the visions but there followed a series of cartoon-like macabre illusions graphically illustrating their continuing mayhem.

Nick was startled from his fantasy as the woman urgently called out, "This is the market." Nick pulled into the parking lot as near to the door as possible. He wasn't going to allow anything to happen to the woman, no matter what. Getting out of the taxi, he opened her door and let the woman walk into the all-night market.

Nick fished into his pocket for the book of matches containing the roach. He looked around the barren parking lot and, seeing no one, leaned back against the cab, lit up, and took a deep drag. He held the smoke in his lungs and fiercely tried to press all thoughts from his mind, but to no avail. The three men standing over his wife's body loomed forward into his mind as though brought into sharp focus through a wide-angle lens. Instinctively, Nick thrust his right hand into his pocket and found the large folding knife he'd begun carrying. His fingers clasped the contours of the handle and pressed it against his palm. It gave him some comfort to feel it and, for a moment, he fantasized flicking the sharp blade open and slashing the phantom killers. He had never used the knife for anything other than cutting cheese, fruit, and rope, but its potential was much greater.

Nick had seen the weapon in an antique store in France on the Normandy coast when he had been working his first job overseas photographing WWII Veterans as they visited the grave sites of their friends. He was enough of a craftsman to look at the knife and understand its rarity. The jovial proprietor of the store had been uncertain of the complete history other than a local man had taken the knife from the body of a dead German soldier. Then the proprietor added, "Although, knowing the man, he could just as well have taken it off the body of an American or English soldier." The proprietor leaned in and studied the knife. "I reluctantly conclude the craftsmanship is German, but it is now in the hands of an American." The man looked up at Nick and smiled. Nick had been interested in the knife regardless of the story. It was obviously one of a kind. He noticed the rough dark staghorn and brass fit together with great precision. "You can open the blade by just flipping your wrist and then *voila*, it locks into place. Uncanny," the man said.

Nick lightly held the heavy knife between his fingers and flipped his wrist. The finely honed steel blade catapulted from the handle and locked into place. He admired the locking device, the unique power of the knife, and the almost hypnotic shape of the blade. He wanted it, no matter the price. It was then that his eyes focused on the fine etching on the blade. Lifting the blade close to his face, his eyes followed the swirling lines and saw them intricately form the letter *N*.

The automatic door to the market sprang open. Nick took a last hit off the roach and flicked away the sparking remnant of weed and Zig-Zag Wheat Straw paper, then walked forward to meet the woman. He could see the long trip had taken its toll on her. As they made their way across Los Angeles, he had noticed her visibly wearing down. Nick theorized that people unconsciously timed their energies for the ending of the flight but seldom considered the wear from airport to home. To most, the flight was the trip. As he held the door open, the woman stiffly reentered the cab. He looked down and observed the contents of her bag: a quart of milk, a loaf of bread, a half-dozen eggs, and a pint of whiskey.

She gave Nick directions and they drove the rest of the way up the steep Hollywood hills in silence. When they arrived at a small stucco house with iron bars over the windows, she said tiredly, "Would you mind very much putting the luggage inside my house near the bedroom?"

"I don't mind at all." Nick would have done anything for the woman. With a pleased sense of discovery, he realized he could still care about another human being, no matter how little he knew them.

Inside, the house appeared very dark and tiny. He placed the bags near the bedroom and glanced around at the melancholy pictures on the walls and sparse furnishings. Nick realized the anti-burglary devices that had been installed were not so much to protect possessions but to protect the woman's person and psyche.

As he returned from the bedroom hallway, the woman paid Nick and tipped him two dollars. "Would you mind shutting the door as you go out? I have to get these groceries into the refrigerator."

Nick assured her he wouldn't mind and, for a moment, he watched her walk with increasing weariness toward the kitchen and few drinks that would put an end to her long trip. Closing the door quietly but firmly, he heard the heavy latch spring shut. *Safe,* he thought. Then a paralyzing question leapt to his mind. *What if there was a prowler in the dark house when they pulled up and now Nick locked him inside with the woman?* A moment of stoned paranoia struck him and he reflexively rang the woman's doorbell several times. After a moment the woman came to the door and asked who it was. "It's the cab driver, ma'am. I just wanted to make sure you're all right."

"I'm fine. Thank you, young man."

"If you like, I'll look around your house for you, just to make sure."

There was a lengthy silence. "That's quite all right, it's not necessary. Now please leave."

Nick realized he must be frightening the woman and he backed off the step. Yet, he still wasn't sure. He had a feeling someone could be inside. He waited at the door for a full five minutes listening and then slowly walked to his cab, opened the door, then turned to the house and listened again. There was not a sound to be heard from any house and finally he admitted to himself she was going to be safe until morning.

Nick leaned forward in the beat-up taxi, started the engine, and expertly played with the broken automatic gearshift until it engaged in reverse, backed slowly out of the driveway, and pointed the cab down the steep hill. Taking a last glance at the house, he pulled the gearshift from reverse to second. The newly selected gear engaged with a loud thunk, and a moment later, he and the taxi rapidly rattled down the twisting hill to the middle of Hollywood. It was a quick transition from small stucco houses half hidden by yucca and bougainvillea to neon-laced streets openly displaying garish hustle.

JIM PEARSON YANKED THE door to his house closed hard. He'd had a few on the way home. Jim thought some of the guys at the Station House would have taken him out for a drink to celebrate his arrest of the serial rapist, but they didn't. So he celebrated a bit on his own. The rapist with the faded orange sneakers was much sought after. The press had been ringing alarm bells about the man and were critical of the police for their lack of progress on the brazen cases. When a reporter for the *Santa Monica Chronicle* questioned him about the arrest he made, Pearson had been generous in his praise of the department and all the vigorous detective work the officers had done. Now that the rapist was caught, the press was going to give the police some breathing room and credit. But many of the detectives were jealous. They had been searching for the man for months and Jim had practically fallen over him. Grabbing a bottle, Pearson poured himself a whiskey and grinned as he remembered the dumb expression on the man's face when he showed him the badge. He strolled over to the fireplace to glance at the pictures on the mantle. Looking at a picture of his daughter, he wondered what it would be like to get raped by a creepy-looking guy who hadn't showered or changed clothes in months. Tossing down the whiskey, he pushed the question away and moved unsteadily toward the bedroom.

NICK WASN'T TOO FAMILIAR with the Hollywood area. Most of his fares kept him around Venice, Santa Monica, Culver City, and Westchester with drops at the downtown hotels. Hollywood was a rare destination. At that hour, he knew he should pay attention. Holding onto the wheel with one hand, he reached around and pushed all four door buttons down to lock them. He learned to keep them locked ever since his first Friday night when three mean drunks yanked open the front and rear doors, piled into the cab, and created a very unpleasant ride.

Merging onto Hollywood Boulevard, he turned west, called the dispatcher, and told him where he was. It was nearly one in the morning and the street looked deserted. He drove steadily, his eyes scanning the sidewalks on both sides of the dark pavement. The boulevard amazed him and betrayed preconceived notions. He never got over the way it looked compared to the way he thought it should look. Like many people, Nick had been seduced by media to think of the street as a gleaming magical place. But he discovered Hollywood Boulevard at night was a furtive, uncomfortable stretch of blacktop that held as much potential for crime as any street in the country. Approaching Vine, he began to see people shuffling along the sidewalk or standing in doorways. By the time he reached Cherokee, the population increased and he noticed a few hookers grimly keeping a careful lookout for johns and cops. Within a block of Highland Avenue, the street population included tribes of young people, tourists, late-night movie patrons, and prowlers. Nick intently peered at them all. Not only was he looking for a fare, Hollywood was good hunting. He made it all the way past Grauman's Chinese Theater and the Roosevelt Hotel to La Brea and no one flagged him down. The CB crackled his cab number. "Pick up at Tiny Naylor's," the dispatcher said.

"Two-four-five, check."

Making a left on La Brea, he rapidly drove the few blocks to Tiny Naylor's on Sunset Boulevard. Standing on the corner was a young man carrying a paper bag and a box of expensive champagne. Nick looked at the guy carefully as he approached, then lifted the button to the back seat and let him into his cab. "Oh, man, I can't hardly believe it. Am I glad to see you. I've been waiting here forever."

"Did you call us for a cab?"

"Oh yeah, man."

A car pulled up behind Nick. "Where are you off to?" he asked as the car behind them impatiently sounded its horn.

The young man gave him an address in Culver City and Nick knew it would be at least a seven-dollar fare. "We're just gonna stop there for a second to pick up this chick. Wait till you see her, man. She's a singer, un-fucking-believable. Then we're going to the airport. We're going to tour Australia and the Far East, man."

Nick took Sunset to La Cienega as the young man continued to talk on without prompting. He was not dressed like a rock-and-roll musician, but rather his wardrobe suggested a business-world dropout. He looked down at the heels but Nick knew better than to judge people that way in Los Angeles and the music business in particular.

"Want to smoke a joint?" the young man asked.

Normally, Nick would have done it, but he had just smoked a roach less than half an hour before and there was something about the young man's karma that didn't quite hold together. Nick declined but told the young man he could if he wanted to.

"Nah, I'll wait for the chick to get in and then on the way to the airport, we'll blow this one. It's Thai stick all the way, man. I'll bring down some glasses and we'll do this bottle of champagne and the weed on the way to the airport. Not every night a guy gets to take off for the Far-fucking-East, man. I've got some goodies in the bag, too, 'cause this chick gets the munchies bad." The man leaned forward a little and grinned, "It's too bad we couldn't kill some time up in her apartment before we go to the plane because this chick, when she gets going and a little high, she'll fuck the planet. I mean the entire planet. I got a hot one in her, man."

He continued talking about the girl and obscure rock groups all the way to Culver City. By the time they arrived at the apartment building, Nick found he was more than a little curious about the girl and what she would be like. The idea of smoking the Thai stick and having a little glass of champagne began to appeal to him. Nick pulled to a stop.

"Okay, man, I'm going to leave the goodies and the bottle of champagne here. I'll go up and wake her, then come down and maybe you'll come up and help us with the luggage. You're not gonna leave the meter run are you? I mean I'd rather lay the dough on you at the end. Know what I mean? It's up to you man, I'll be right down."

Nick didn't like the setup. The guy started to get out of the cab and Nick stopped him with, "It says seven dollars and forty cents on the meter and I need that before you leave."

The young man had one foot out the door and turned to Nick indignantly, "Listen, man, I got my fucking road money upstairs. I blew my change partying tonight and on the champagne and goodies. I'll be right down. Stay cool, man." The young man quickly slipped out the door, leaving it open.

The man's indignant tone was convincing and there was a forty-dollar bottle of champagne on the back seat, so Nick watched him walk the pathway that led to two large apartment buildings. Despite the assurances, Nick began to feel uneasy and just before the man drifted quickly from sight, Nick reached over to the back seat and lifted up the box of Moet Chandon. It felt deceptively light, so he opened the box and saw to his chagrin it contained an empty nonreturnable bottle of Pepsi Cola.

Springing from the cab, he started off at a dead run but the path between the apartments led past multiple entrances and finally to an alley that, in turn, led to other pathways and streets. The man was nowhere in sight. Defeated, Nick returned to the cab. Reaching inside the rear door, he extracted the bag supposedly containing the "goodies," and glanced at its contents. As suspected, it contained nothing but an assortment of garbage.

Putting the bag back on the seat, he thrust his hands into his pockets and paced up and down in front of the apartments thinking of what he should do. It was the first time in months of driving he had been successfully hustled, but he had been hustled beautifully. He had betrayed his own instincts and he felt the implications of the betrayal keenly. Considering what he was trying to accomplish, he needed his instincts to remain as sharp as possible and, more importantly, he needed to listen to them.

Picking up the garbage and the champagne box, he carried them over to the side of the apartment and left them there. He was against littering, but this time he mumbled to himself, "Fuck it, I'm not carrying that guy's shit around." Then he added, "This is a neighborhood problem." He spontaneously grinned because he realized no matter how he looked at it, the joke was on him.

Back in the cab, he decided not to call the dispatcher. He didn't want to announce he had been hustled and have a conversation about it over the air. No, he would just pay what it said on the meter himself and forget it. It was definitely a time for a change of scenery. At that hour, he knew the airport was only twelve minutes away and several flights were due just before 2:00 a.m.

IN THE LATE NIGHT, Mose and Big TC cruised the Oakwood part of Venice. They were slicing up the town block by block. Currently, they were traversing the narrow streets between Electric Avenue and Lincoln Boulevard. Big TC had spent his life in Los Angeles but had only been to the Venice beachfront once in his life. His father had taken him there when he was five. Big TC remembered the outing with some nostalgia. It was the last time his father ever took him anywhere. A week later, after a very successful robbery, his father managed to get himself shot. The robbery had gone well, but one hour later the other two thieves shot him and took all the swag. That was an important lesson for the five-year-old. Big TC nodded at the memory. He was getting tired from the long night but they still needed to find something. He and Mose had already spent the evening looking at the characters on Ocean Front Walk and the happenings from Marina Del Rey to the Santa Monica Pier.

Big TC liked what he saw. Now, in the late night, as he looked out at the small wooden houses and sad little apartment buildings and added up the evening's information, he realized it came to a big plus. Then they saw what they most wanted to find. On a corner, a lone black man rubbed his nose and peered intently into their car as they slowly drove by. "Pull over here and talk to that raggedy-assed motherfucker," Big TC said.

Mose parked down the block and walked back to the eager dealer. After a few minutes, Mose sauntered back to the Cadillac and got behind the wheel. He turned to Big TC and grinned as he said, "They be short on supply and long on need."

Big TC nodded his head and flashed the diamond and gold on his teeth. "We slide into this place, let the Stabile-man watch our ass, and we'll do so very fine."

ENTERING THE AIRPORT, NICK decided to make the loop. There were three cabs on TWA, one on American with very little happening, but when he got to Western he saw a cab heavily laden with passengers drive off, leaving one person on the cabstand. Nick realized with a sinking feeling that the person left was the one who was not going someplace desirable, otherwise the cabby would have taken the one standing and left someone else. As he drove up, he saw it was a black woman of around eighteen. She had a small bag with her and Nick noticed no other luggage, so he reached over and pushed the rear door open. The girl leaned into the car and asked in an irritated way, "Ain't you gonna help me with my bags?"

"Where are your bags?" Nick asked.

"They're inside on the roller thing."

"Well, I'm not allowed to go in there to pick up luggage. The Sky Caps get their noses out of joint if cabbies carry luggage out of their territory."

Clearly, the young women thought Nick was jiving her. Nick was speaking the truth but he was also stalling for time because he was hoping someone else would come out and he could double load. No other taxi had driven up and everything was his to deal with. He got out of the cab and walked around to her. "Where are you going?" Nick asked, keeping an eye toward the luggage area to see if anyone else was coming out.

"I need a taxi, are you a taxi?"

"Sure, I'm a taxi," Nick said, taking some pleasure in the metaphor. "And I'm going to take you wherever you want to go, but I can't go in there and take out your bags. Bring them to the doorway and I'll carry them outside to the car."

The girl strode angrily into the luggage area. From his view, Nick noticed there were few people left. Glancing back toward his taxi, he saw two other cabs whip into line behind him. The first driver, a very overweight black man with a NY baseball cap sprang out of his cab and walked rapidly toward Nick. "What's happening man, you got a fare?"

"Yeah," Nick admitted, "I've got one."

He turned and noticed the young woman struggling with two medium-sized bags. She was neatly but inexpensively dressed in subdued colors. She was not attractive, in large part because her face was constricted into an attitude of anger. The anger, Nick felt, was not directed against him personally but was something that had total possession of the woman. She dropped the bags in front of Nick who bent down to pick them up. She allowed her gaze to fall on Nick's eyes for an instant and then she dropped her head down and pouted. "That other trunk is heavy."

Nick nodded his head in the direction of the two porters who were leaning on their handcarts. "Why don't you ask one of those guys to help you?" Nick offered nicely. He was feeling more kindly disposed toward the girl. "Just tip him half a dollar, a quarter even."

The girl regarded the two porters chatting together. They glanced in her direction but she turned and walked off to the other trunk.

"Hey, man, where's she going?" the other driver asked.

"I don't know."

"You don't know? Shit, man, what do you mean you don't know?"

"I mean, I don't know," Nick answered stonily and turned and walked over to the taxi and placed the two bags by the car.

Returning to the entrance of the luggage area, Nick saw the young woman dragging a large suitcase along the ground. Her coat had fallen open and Nick noticed she was around five months pregnant. Instinctively, he stepped forward inside the doorway and relieved her of the weight. He heard the other driver ask, "Hey, sister, where you going?"

"I'm going to Forty-First near San Pedro Street."

The black cabby turned to Nick and said, "Shit, man, you don't want to go there, I'll take her if you don't want her."

"I'm taking her," Nick said and briskly carried the heavy bag away.

As he walked away, followed by the angry girl, he heard the other cabby call after him. "You're lucky, that's almost an eleven-dollar fare."

Nick got irritated because the man had tried to talk him out of the fare and because he purposely quoted the lowest possible price to go to that area. He thought he could frighten Nick out of going into the black ghetto and then quoted the lowest fare so he wouldn't rip the girl off by driving the long way around. It had been so deliberate and intentional that Nick felt obliged to respond. He turned around as well as the heavy trunk would let him and, with his free hand, he gave the cabby the finger. To Nick's surprise, the man laughed heartily and pointed his finger back at Nick good-naturedly. Nick grinned despite himself.

The girl stood watching until Nick finished loading the trunk. "Aren't you going to open the door for me?" she asked before Nick was really near it.

"Sure," Nick said. He regarded her with interest. Why was she so angry and out of sync? Nick began to open the back door when she cut in.

"I don't sit in back, I want to sit up front."

Nick didn't like people sitting up front unless there were more than two or three people already in back. His Thomas Guide, maps, thermos, and bag had a way of spreading across the seat. Normally, had it been anyone other than a seven-foot person or that particular angry girl, he would have insisted they sit in back. However, Nick obediently opened the front door, bent inside, and pushed his possessions over to the middle of the seat. He noticed the girl was surprised to see so many things there, but she said nothing and sat her small, thin body down onto the edge of the seat and pulled her coat around her swollen belly. Nick observed she wore no rings.

Getting into the cab, he started it, found drive, and floored it. This was the time of night he had grown to love. It was past two in the morning and the city would be nearly vacant of cars for almost two and a half hours. He could have the girl home in less than fifteen minutes. He followed his plan to take the girl the shortest way possible, and the old car bounced and swayed across La Cienega to Stocker, over to Crenshaw, to Santa Barbara, and onward into the heart of the old city.

They rode in silence, whipping through the night. Nick glanced at the young woman from time to time sitting rigidly on the edge of the front seat. "Where you coming in from?" Nick finally asked.

"Charlotte, North Carolina," the woman said bitterly.

Gradually, Nick noticed her face begin to change. Her eyes widened and she fell back against the seat, her breath coming in gasps. She quite suddenly began to choke back a series of sobs. The anger from her face drained and she let out a high moaning sound as she shook her head back and forth and cried out, "Oh, niggers can lie, they can lie and lie." She plaintively sang out the word "lie," and then broke down sobbing.

Nick listened as she wailed and incoherently sang the song of herself and he knew she was returning home, pregnant, jilted, unmarried, and with no job. He felt sorry for her and wondered what she was going home to. After a while, the girl began to regain control and Nick couldn't help but notice as the sobs and crying diminished, the anger slowly returned. By the time Nick pulled the taxi to the curb in front of her apartment building, she had dried her tears and the mask of anger once again dominated her face.

"You're gonna have to help me up with the bags."

"Sure," Nick said kindly. "That'll be ten dollars and forty cents."

"I got no money. My brother was supposed to pick me up at the airport but he wasn't there."

"So how am I going to get paid?" he asked, not anxious to get stiffed twice in one night.

"My mother is upstairs and she gonna pay you."

Nick got out of the cab and took the two middleweight suitcases and carried them upstairs. He wanted to find his way with a moderate load and ensure he'd have the most valuable luggage in the trunk should he not get paid. As long as he had the luggage, getting the money was in his favor.

It was a long journey to the top-floor rear apartment and Nick paid attention in the dimly lit corridor. They arrived at the door and the girl knocked several times, but no one answered. She knocked again, loudly, and in frustration she finally called out that she knew someone was inside and to open up. There was a long silence but then a smiling elderly woman slowly opened the door. Over the woman's shoulder, Nick saw a young man sit up on the couch and hold a blanket over his nude body. The angry young woman pushed her way into the apartment and immediately berated the young man on the couch for not picking her up. He tried to explain the car was broken, but she didn't listen; rather, she turned around on Nick and asked, "Aren't you going to get the rest of my things?"

"Sure," Nick said, "as soon as I get paid the fare."

"Oh," the kind-faced mother apologized. "How much is it?"

Nick told her and after a long trip to the kitchen, she came back and paid him eleven dollars. "Keep the change, young man."

Nick thanked her and returned to the taxi for the large suitcase. Lugging the heavy load upstairs, he puzzled over the fact that lately, something was happening to him. It was as if he was beginning to see the various encounters between himself and passengers who rode in his cab as though he were watching a play where he was both audience and actor.

Nick placed the bags inside the door. The soon-to-be grandmother thanked him nicely but the girl sat in the one stuffed chair with her coat still wrapped around herself, gazing at her luggage. The young man, for want of anything better to do, pulled the blanket over his head and went back to sleep. As Nick walked down the hallway, he wondered where the young woman's father was. Then, he realized, her father was probably gone, just like the father of the child in her belly. Nick shook his head in amazement at the kindly nature of the older woman. How had the women become so strong and many of the men so weak?

Outside, the air was moist and still. He leaned against the cab and surveyed the neighborhood. Was the young black man who helped murder his wife in an apartment nearby? Los Angeles was largely a segregated city, boasting one of the largest ghettos in the country. Few people would admit it, yet it was there. A ghetto that sprawled and shifted from Adams Boulevard just south of the Santa Monica Freeway for many miles down through Inglewood, Watts, Compton, Bellflower, Carson, and into Wilmington. As it spread east, the city became more Hispanic. It was a massive area holding millions. It made the odds of finding any of the men remote. Yet they were out there.

Nick got back in behind the wheel. He held the ignition key in his hand but made no move to put it in the lock and start the engine. He stared through the windshield as the image of the young black man took over his mind.

◆◆◆

AT THE MOMENT, RAINEY, the young black man Nick had been obsessing about, was standing seven miles away on the corner of Western and Santa Monica. He was hoping to land a trick that would get him money for a fine fix. When he was needy, which was often, Rainey sometimes thought about the robbery in Venice, months earlier. "Those two guys were mean motherfuckers," Rainey mumbled to himself.

Rainey and the men had met casually at a gay drug dealer's apartment in Oakwood. Running into the burly Mexican and the hard-looking white guy weeks later, Rainey made the mistake of approaching the two men about a possible and profitable robbery. He had seen a guy with a lot of expensive photography equipment. He knew where the photographer lived and the place was low security. Suddenly, he had two partners and that's when things went really wrong for Rainey. He had wanted some protection and size for the job, but all he got was fear. Those guys were not only straight and mean, they didn't have a problem with killing anyone. Rainey shivered in the cold. He didn't like to remember that evening but it kept repeating in his mind. Watching those guys rape that poor woman with the baby there and everything, and then the way they killed her. He had cried right then and there. He tried to shut the memory from his mind and sought deliverance by turning and staring hopefully at the late-night passing cars.

NICK'S OBSESSION WITH THE image of the young black man gave way to the reality of his location. That part of Los Angeles was certainly not cab country, not for him, not for anybody. There were seldom any orders, it was a dangerous place to cruise and pick up, especially late at night. *Dangerous?* Nick mused. *I'm supposed to be tracking killers.* However, he knew it wasn't out of fear he decided to leave South Central. It was because he instinctively declared the killers weren't there—possibly the thin black man, but not the others. It was a long drive to anywhere in the city he felt he could make some money at that hour.

He didn't feel like checking in with the dispatcher. He decided to return to the airport. If he could pick off a fare as soon as he drifted in, he would have had a good night. More and more, economics began to drive the cab and less and less hunting.

Inside the airport, the three American Airline flights that usually came in a little after 3:00 a.m. had arrived early and Nick lucked out with a double load. He dropped off a couple in the southeast flats of Beverly Hills and then continued on toward Los Feliz with an elderly businessman going to visit his son. Nick took Olympic Boulevard from Beverly Hills past Koreatown to Western, turned left, and headed toward Los Feliz. He just missed the light at Western and Santa Monica Boulevard and immediately took the opportunity to peer at his Thomas Guide for the fare's specific destination. His good eye found it in the dim light.

Standing at the corner, Morgan Rainey looked hungrily at Nick's cab, for sometimes tourists liked to take cabs around the city to find tricks. As the businessman glanced out the window, Rainey struck a provocative pose. The man quickly turned away from the hungry stare. Rainey's hopes were dashed. The light turned green as Nick flipped closed the Guide and laid it on the seat beside him. Nick glanced at the light and drove off. It was only in his peripheral vision with his bad left eye he caught a blurred glimpse of the desperate young man on the corner.

Financially, it was a profitable trip as he left his meter on and charged the first passengers full fare, and the gaunt old businessman paid full fare as well but didn't tip because of the detour. The thirteen dollars the young couple paid to get to Beverly Hills went into Nick's tips. As was his learned custom, Nick wrote up the double load as a single fare to Los Feliz. It was how all the drivers who had driven for more than a few days played the game, and the owners knew it. As long as the drivers made book, the company made money. Regardless, the meters always recorded the fare, so they let the drivers play their side games.

Leaving Los Feliz, Nick took a cruise along Santa Monica Boulevard toward the Westside.

Thirteen blocks ahead, Rainey bitterly decided to call it a night, and he turned east walking toward Vermont and the little room his friend Rene had. He hoped Rene would be home. He didn't have the energy or money to make it to his apartment in South Central. Maybe Rene had scored and would share. Buoyed by the slim possibility, Rainey pushed rapidly on. A four-door rental car slowly and invitingly passed by and pulled around the corner onto a dark side street waiting for Rainey. Rainey walked rapidly to the car and peered inside. The driver, a middle-aged English tourist, had a moment of sudden panic and shook his head at Rainey and pulled away. Rainey stood up, disappointed. *Another fucking shopper.* He turned in time to see Nick's cab cruising down the boulevard only forty feet away. Rainey walked from the darkness of the side street toward the boulevard and thought, *It'd be bitchen' to hop a cab home.* But, he didn't have the fare

⬗⬗⬗

NICK MADE IT ALL the way to Beverly Hills without anyone waving him down, when he heard the dispatcher ask, "Anybody clear for Westwood?"

He answered the call and punished the car up Wilshire Boulevard. Years earlier, Westwood had been Nick's favorite town in Los Angeles. He remembered it as a quiet university town with nice houses, low-profile apartment buildings, stunning UCLA campus, a few movie theaters, nice shops, and broad streets and sidewalks that made the town pleasant to spend time in. Less than ten years later, it had become a large business community with high-rise office buildings, a huge influx of tourists, and fast food.

It replaced Hollywood as the new film capital of Los Angeles, and on any evening twenty movies could be showing within a half mile.

Westwood was brightly lit, no matter the time, and it was all the more apparent when no one was on the streets at 3:55 a.m. Nick turned off Wilshire, looped around the National Theater and saw a young woman wave to him from the doorway of the Criterion Restaurant.

She was wearing a pale blue cape, a short pink disco dress, and red wedges. She was tall and ladylike in the way she slid onto the rear seat. Leaning back and crossing her legs, she told Nick she wanted to go to Manhattan Beach. Nick started the meter and headed toward the San Diego Freeway. She asked him how much the fare would be and he told her it would run about thirteen dollars. "Well, I've got that stashed in the apartment," she said, letting her head drop back against the seat. "What a night, unbelievable."

"Good, I hope."

The young woman let out a moan. "I came to Westwood with my girlfriend in her car. We met a couple of guys at Dillon's and my friend took off with one and the character I wound up with was supposed to take me back to his place in Topanga but he turned out to be a little weird."

"Weird?"

"Yeah, he started asking me if I liked to talk dirty and stuff like that. It was the way he asked it, you know? Anyway, I get a little scared and so I tell the guy I'm hypoglycemic and got to have food right away, that I'm getting faint. Well, in the bright light, I get a look at this guy over a cheeseburger and he definitely has a look in his eye I don't like and the conversation gets more and more bizarre. So I tell the guy I have to level with him, that I didn't dig him in the right way to go to bed with him and would he mind just backing off and driving me home. Well, he calls me a bunch of really horrible names and walks out leaving me with the check. It was a small price to pay to avoid...whatever. So I called a cab and it doesn't show, so I call your cab company. Really brings me down, so many creeps out there." She sat up a little and asked, "You wouldn't have some grass, would you?"

"Yes, but you'll have to roll it."

"Sure, hand it over."

Reaching into his pack, Nick fished out a thirty-five-millimeter aluminum film can and a sheaf of wheat straw papers and handed them to the girl. He caught a quick glimpse of her face as she bent forward to take the makings from his hand. She was around twenty-one, striking, with a long thin nose, large hazel eyes, and a wide, nicely shaped mouth. She also seemed to have a kind of brash honesty about her. He knew the kind and didn't mind.

In the dim light of the back seat, she expertly rolled a joint, put it between her lips, and lit up. She took a deep, experienced drag, stared out the window holding her breath, and then silently blew a cloud of smoke around the cab. Casually taking a deeper hit and holding it down, she silently passed the joint to Nick. He took it from her, and as she released her hold and pulled away, her fingers lightly brushed over his hand. Nick was immediately aware of the gesture but not certain it was intentional. He could sense her looking at him. Taking a hit himself, he heard the girl give a loud smoke-filled exhalation and exclaim in a half purring voice, "Oh, this is a definite improvement."

She leaned forward, and when Nick once more proffered the joint, she lightly held his wrist with her left hand as though to steady Nick's arm, while with her right hand she retrieved the joint. As she released her hold, he felt her long fingers slide lightly across the smooth underside of his wrist. It was a provocative movement and he suddenly felt numb and aroused. It was the first time something like that happened to him in the four and a half months since his wife had been killed. Women had flirted with him but he ignored them with a distant politeness the women found baffling. After his wife's death, he'd made a vow to not seek out women until the killers were caught. He had deeply suppressed his normal high-level sexuality, but with the mere brushing of his hand

and wrist, the girl in the back seat had caused him to involuntarily swell beneath his dark corduroy pants. The girl leaned forward and rested her arms on the back of the seat. She took another hit off the joint and then reached forward and still holding it, pressed her fingers and the joint to Nick's lips. He took a long noisy inhalation and went almost dizzy from the sensation of the girl's fingers lightly resting against his lips. Glancing in the rearview mirror, he saw her sit back, take the last hit off the now tiny roach, and lay the burning remains on her wet tongue. There was a light hissing sound as her saliva extinguished the embers. She closed her mouth and effortlessly swallowed the bits of soggy paper, ashes, and marijuana. Leaning forward again, she casually peeked over at the picture on Nick's cab license and read his name aloud.

Nick cut off the freeway at Rosecrans Avenue and began heading west toward the ocean. The girl turned back from studying the picture and leaned closer to him. Nick could smell her heavy perfume mixed with the smell of grass and he was nearly overcome with desire.

"I'll bet you're a New York guy, right?"

"Yes," Nick answered quietly, his voice hoarse.

"I can tell, I'm good at that. My name's Nancy." She paused, waiting for Nick to say something, and when he didn't reply, she continued. "That was some nice weed. I can feel myself getting ripped." Nick swung the cab south on Manhattan Avenue. "You've got to make a right on Twenty-First Street. I'm down by the Strand. Then you'll have to come up with me while I get the money."

"Okay," Nick said. Little electrical sparks seemed to be zapping his fingers and cheeks and he realized he was breathing heavily.

"I didn't bring much money because I was riding with my girlfriend and besides, they always rip your purse in discos when you go to dance. Creeps."

Down near the ocean, she told him where to park. They got out of the cab and Nick followed her up the stairs of the apartment building. Nick could hear large swells pounding the sand rhythmically against the shore. Removing her cape, she draped it over one shoulder. She was even better-looking than he had thought and he couldn't help but notice her long, nicely shaped legs and tight little bottom waving at him up the last few steps.

Unlocking the apartment door, she stepped inside and with a toss of her head invited Nick to follow. Throwing the cape over a wooden chair, she went across the cluttered living room and listened at the bedroom door. Nick noticed a pair of men's shoes by the sofa. The girl was satisfied all was well in the bedroom and, smiling at Nick, she went to the kitchenette. Opening a bag resting on the counter, she extracted some money. Nick hung out near the door trying not to stare around too much, but the effort was beginning to make him feel ill at ease and claustrophobic. The girl walked toward him, her large hazel eyes staring seductively, and he noticed how nicely her small breasts nestled beneath the thin pale pink fabric of her blouse. She came close to him and he detected she now too was a little nervous. She reached out with both hands and took his hand in hers as she placed the money into his palm. "We could roll another joint and smoke it if you wanted. My girlfriend is using the bedroom with this guy but we could sit over here," she said, indicating the couch.

She held onto his hand allowing Nick to think over the offer. It was late, it would be innocent enough. He waited for the barrier of Julianne's image to intercede but it didn't. He felt only the closeness of the pretty young woman, the aching in his groin, and the dazing effects of the marijuana. When he finally spoke, his voice sounded distant, even to himself. "I'm sorry, I'd like to but I can't."

The girl gave a little shrug. "Well, if you can't, you can't," she answered, trying to sound unaffected. But she still looked at Nick invitingly, her mouth slack, not moving, as though expecting him to change his mind and take her in his arms.

"Good night," Nick said. Pulling his hand gently from hers, he shoved the money in his pocket and started to walk from the room.

"Thanks for the joint and ride home," the girl said a little loudly as Nick left the apartment and quietly closed the door behind.

The cool ocean breeze came as a shock to the numbing heat that had taken hold of him. Climbing into the oil-reeking cab, he drove slowly southward in a stoned daze. Finally, on instinct, he parked his cab by the entrance to the Manhattan Beach Pier. He got out and walked slowly onto the long concrete promenade. A fresh set of waves from the winter swell rolled in and underneath he could feel the huge structure trembling in rhythmic vibrations as heavy waves crashed from piling to piling.

In the middle, a solitary fisherman occupied the long walkway. He glanced suspiciously at Nick. He paid the man no attention but walked the distance to the long pier's end. Glancing around, he saw he was alone. The breeze was stronger at the end of the pier but the smell of old bait and countless gutted fish still scented the atmosphere.

Nick walked to the south corner and faced out toward the incoming Pacific swells. He took deep breaths as he gazed over the night-black water but he could not calm the burning sensation in his groin. The feeling was not to be denied and slowly he reached down, unzipped his fly, and removed his swollen cock from the confines of his pants. He caressed it, squeezed it, and gently rubbed it up and down. It was the first sexual thing he had done since Julianne's death.

He continued for a time. Gradually and with more and more clarity, the image of Julianne sitting astride him moved into his mind. He remembered their lovemaking and, phantom-like, he saw his wife aroused, moving with abandon, repeatedly moaning his name as she began to come. The image floated in front of his mind as the onshore wind blew and soothed his face. Then, with a muffled cry, he sent his sperm flying out into the sea below. Spent, he leaned forward, rested heavily against the railing, and stared down at the freshly gathering black swells.

Driving back along the ocean, he welcomed the relaxation from sensual preoccupation, but the longing for Julianne intensified. He thought of her and of Melissa and the emptiness crashed upon him. He turned east on Imperial Highway and passed the airport without as much as a thought of entering and seeking a fare. His longing and despair gave way to a rising anger. Looping around the airport, he made the light onto Lincoln Boulevard and headed around the north side of the airport where the boulevard paralleled the runways. He thought of the men who had taken Julianne from him, and as the rage took possession, he floored the accelerator and the old cab slowly began to gather speed. He knew the road well by now and often drove it rapidly, but never so flat out. By the time the straightaway ended, the car was doing its maximum of ninety as Nick took the turn where the road pulls away from the airport. The loose old body creaked and protested in a low moaning sound and the tires added their shrill shrieking to the noise. With his eyes flicking constantly at the rearview mirror, he kept the accelerator on the floor and, squealing out of the turn, he saw the light by the Airport Marina Hotel turn green in his favor. The cab roared through the intersection and miraculously made the other short light into town before dropping down the winding hill over the Hughes Aircraft acreage and rattling toward Marina Del Rey.

He didn't notice the headlights up Jefferson Boulevard as his old cab propelled by the steep descent crossed the intersection at ninety-eight. The cab quickly began to lose its momentum from the hill and slow to its normal maximum speed.

In the police car, two officers saw the glowing light on top of Nick's cab streak across the intersection. The cops looked at one another, nodded in mutual assent, and roared after the speeding taxi.

Nick missed the light at Mindanao Way and braked hard to stop. As he sat at the light, the engine idled at a slower speed than normal, exhausted from the five-mile plunge from the airport.

The rapid drive had temporarily kept his mind off what was generating his anger. He was wandering from his quest. As each night had gone by, he had gotten more and more involved with the business of driving. To do it well and make maximum money, it was an all-consuming thing. Then to be confronted with myriad personalities night after night had the ambivalent effect of drawing him more and more out of himself and yet making him feel more and more apart from the real world. The people who got in and out, they were real. The things he observed were real, buildings, roads, trucks were real, but he was not. Rather, he was like some extraterrestrial creature, a visitor from another dimension, driving along in a shiny beetle-like capsule running through the corridors of the darkened city.

The light changed to green and Nick made a left turn into the marina on his way toward Venice when the interior of his cab lit up with a reddish hue. He knew it was cops and the back of his neck began to burn from the rush of blood to his brain as the red glow filled the cab, followed by a garish white light from the police car's spotlight. He glanced at the rearview mirror and saw the cruiser unbelievably close.

He completed his turn and started to pull off to the side by Admiralty Way, but he delayed briefly while he traced down where his marijuana was. He remembered he had put it in his pocket after Nancy had passed it back to him. He quickly reached in and pulled out the papers and can of weed and stuffed them well down between the front passenger seat and the back rest. A loudspeaker harshly blasted directions. "Pull over to the side. Now!"

Irritated, Nick complied and immediately got out of the cab. He hated remaining in a car when cops came up on him or, in less friendly countries, soldiers and militias. It made him feel vulnerable to be seated.

In turn, the cops were surprised by Nick's quick exit. They got out of their cruiser, gun hands at the ready, and from behind their bright lights, they peered narrowly at the wild-eyed driver who advanced slowly but boldly toward them. The cop on the passenger side stepped onto the sidewalk and moved even farther off to the side with his hand remaining near his gun. The driver stayed behind the glare of the cruiser's headlights. "Stop where you are!" the policeman shouted firmly. Nick froze. "Step up onto the curb," the officer harshly demanded.

Nick did and the officer asked for his license and registration. The second policeman moved purposefully to Nick's taxi, pulled out his flashlight, and pointed the beam inside the idling cab. Nick observed the second officer's inspection and felt relieved when he turned off the flashlight, stepped back, and resumed his gunfighter posture. Nick turned around and studied the first officer as he handed over the license and registration to him. "Why am I being stopped?"

"What's the matter, you don't have a clue?"

That response was a little better. "I like to know what's going on."

"You drove through the light at Jefferson and Lincoln between seventy-five and eighty-five miles an hour."

The officer turned and walked back to his car to radio in. The second officer just stared at Nick, with his right hand remaining inches from his gun and left hand clutching the long flashlight.

The first officer returned and pulled out his book. He was going to write Nick a ticket. "How did you clock me, was it on radar?"

The cop looked up, pissed. "No, we didn't have you on radar. We estimated, we're allowed to estimate. Especially if you were going as fast as you were."

Suddenly, a code came across the police radio. Nick had long since lost concentration on the radio, which was constantly squawking, but the cop with his hand on the gun ran to the CB and got back to headquarters. The cop writing the ticket handed Nick's license back to him and hustled to the cruiser. "Don't let me catch you speeding again, you hear me? Never!" he yelled over his shoulder.

"Don't worry," Nick said.

The police cruiser backed down to Lincoln Boulevard and pulled away with a powerful surge, heading south, no siren, but with lights flashing.

A once-in-a-lifetime break, Nick thought.

Back in the cab, he drove to Admiralty Way and swung into a restaurant parking lot. He left the cab and walked around the restaurant and down to waiting sailboats. He walked past the various docks tethering million-dollar yachts and moss-encrusted dinghies. The water, with its reflections of light, supporting the floating, bobbing crafts, calmed his speeding feelings and he came back to himself. He had been driving like a jerk with nowhere to go. He had lost his plan.

He walked all the way to the end of the marina. While listening to the musical clinking of rigging on masts, he mulled the problem of how to find the three men. After driving for months, he realized they could be anywhere—El Monte, Pacoima, Whittier, San Pedro, South Pasadena, Pennsylvania, you name it. He considered it might be better to go onto day shift and search when more people were out. But he was comfortable driving at night and reasoned they were the kind of men who would be out at night. At night, he could go from the airport to Hollywood in twenty minutes, and during the day, with just normal traffic, it could take an hour. The ability to cover a lot of ground appealed to Nick and any important information he learned at night, he could personally and more easily investigate during the day. He determined to take a copy of the collages he had constructed along with him, show them around, and ask questions when appropriate. He'd dice up the city into those little squares in his map book, checking it out, piece by piece.

By the time he got back to the cab, he had settled himself, felt more confident, and began the makings of a workable plan. But first, he had to see Pearson.

CHAPTER SIX

COMING INTO HIS APARTMENT, Nick downed a mouthful of tequila, cracked open a beer, and called the Venice Police Station. He left word he'd be dropping by at three in the afternoon to see Pearson. Then he placed a call to Melissa. Nick had initiated his Sunday calls to Melissa and Lillian. For the first three weeks she let the service pick up and listened to Nick's message. It never got returned. On the fourth week she picked up and, after lecturing him for what seemed a tedious length of time, she put Melissa on. It was brief and awkward. Hanging up, Nick thought about how he might get better at it.

This time, it was Thursday but also Melissa's birthday. When Lillian answered, she sounded excited and pleased with herself. "You should be here, Nick, I'm giving Melissa her birthday party and there are six children coming to celebrate. I've got balloons and cake and pralines and lemonade and oh, just so many sweets those little darlings are going to be turned to sugar."

Nick smiled. He was pleased Lillian was sharing information and speaking to him kindly. He also knew she was doing it to make him feel guilty. He could tell by her tone. When she finally put Melissa on, he was near tears and found it difficult to speak. "Hello, sweetheart." There was a silence on the other end of the phone. "Did you get the present I sent you?"

"Yes."

"Did you open it?"

"No. Grandma says it's for my birthday."

"Today is your birthday, Melissa. Happy Birthday, honey."

"I'm going to have a cake. Bye," and she hung up.

Nick stared at the telephone, then Melissa's picture on his nightstand. Taking a slug of beer, he fell back across the bed. "Oh, fuck," he said. Still clutching the beer bottle, he gave way to lonely exhaustion and slowly passed out.

◆◆◆

PEARSON'S PARTNER FRANK WAS out on medical leave and Jim missed him. The guy had eaten about three thousand cheeseburgers too many and had a massive heart attack. The doctors had bragged about what a great job they had done with the triple bypass. Pearson sobered them up with, "We'll see."

Despite offers of help, Pearson didn't want anyone new. He would wait for Frank to return. When Frank wasn't out having a heart attack, he was solid. The idea of a new or temporary partner left him cold.

It had been a hell of a rough day. Early in the morning, some Crips and Hispanics fired enough shots at each other to leave three dead, his ex-wife had called to yell at him just for old time's sake, and Nick Cullen was waiting to see him. Pearson glanced at his watch, got up, and walked around his desk for a stretch. He circled the desk five times, reaching back and pulling on his stiff neck. By the time he sat back down, he was slightly looser and a little dizzy, a definite improvement. He stared at the tall pile of papers on his desk. The Venice Division averaged a homicide case every ten days. He got thrown many, but he was only batting .324 in convictions. In baseball that was good, but in homicide it meant there were a lot of killers getting across the plate without being tagged.

It was hard enough to keep track of all the local murders, let alone solve them. In Japan, they had only twenty-seven murders with firearms for the year. The tiny city of Venice beat that running away. During that long war, more citizens had been killed by guns in the US than soldiers in Vietnam. *It was just that in Vietnam we were shooting locals instead of one another*, thought Pearson. *You didn't have to solve the killings. It was all sanctioned.* In his personal daily reminder, Pearson had the total of people killed by guns in many other "civilized" countries. It made him more comfortable knowing tens of thousands of American citizens were getting killed by guns annually. As he thought about the number of bodies in his casebook compared to the national statistic, it gave him a sense of proportion. Pearson took out his gun and had a look. It was a Smith & Wesson .38 revolver with a three-inch barrel. Some of the men tossed comments at him as they strapped on their .44 automatics, but Pearson liked his old gun. He was used to it and knew it would never jam. Miraculously, quite a few murders did get solved at the Venice division, but Pearson knew better when it came to the Julianne Thombridge-Cullen case. That one was tough. There was a Mexican-looking guy, a black guy, and a white guy. The Shoreline Crips and Mexican gangs were banging each other all over Venice. So it was unlikely those three killers were all working together. Hell, he was investigating seven murders within the Crips alone. As to the white guy, well, Venice had more than enough white creeps and transients. Pearson reassessed where he was with the Cullen case. They had a few partial prints that could be associated with the killers. There was the possibility of finding the expensive camera equipment. Even though Cullen had let his insurance lapse because he was broke, they at least had the serial numbers. A camera might show up somewhere; they might get a lead but it was unlikely. Pearson remembered Nick's last visit and knew he'd better prepare himself with facts and a stern attitude. Most crime victims he dealt with were easy to read, but Nick Cullen presented a different profile. The guy had been around. He'd seen a lot of shit, done a lot of things. It was easy to see. The man wore it but he did so like it was a casual part of himself. The guy was also a little off, you were never quite sure what to expect. He'd obviously strayed from the mark because a man like that, in his midthirties, shouldn't be driving a cab. Pearson took a last look at the blue steel of his gun, put it in his holster, slipped on his jacket, and decided on the old "better get on with your life" speech. He rehearsed what he was going to say by muttering it to himself, "We're making every effort but much as I hate to say it, we've got a potentially unsolved case, and until we catch a break it's going to remain that way." Yeah, that's it, give him the honesty approach and get-on-with-your-life pep talk. He reached for the intercom.

As Nick entered, Pearson busily shuffled paperwork on his cluttered desk, glanced up, and welcomed Nick by giving his hand a solid shake and gesturing for Nick to take a seat. Pearson looked back to his paperwork and inadvertently did a double take of the man sitting in front of him. Nick did not appear to be the same guy he had met with months earlier. Some things were quickly obvious: Nick looked thinner, more haggard, his eyes had dark circles under them, and were stonily glazed over. But there was something more. Certainly, the guy had been knocked askew by the murder, but now he looked like he had entered another dimension. *Fuck*, Pearson thought to himself. *What's been going on with this guy?*

A few seconds after entering the room, Nick realized he had seen enough. He sensed there was nothing new to the case. He had seen the manufactured activity Pearson was initiating with papers on his desk dozens of times in editor and managers' offices and he knew what it meant. So Nick went right to the point. "Tell me you've got some news."

Pearson looked at Nick, started to say something, and then thought better of it. He instinctively knew he couldn't bullshit the guy. "We're working on it."

Nick didn't say anything, just waited. Pearson leaned forward, stared at Nick, and said, "You know, you look like a guy who should go to Florida and lie in the sun for a while."

"Let's not change the subject."

"Don't you have a kid in Florida or Georgia, someplace with your wife's mother?"

That burned into Nick and he burned it back to Pearson. "Tell me what you've got and quit steering me and using my family to do it."

"It's my way of telling you to stay out of this. Let us do our job."

"I don't see a job being done."

"We're doing our best and you're not helping by running yourself and some cab into the ground."

Nick felt his anger kick off in another direction and inexplicably, he found himself telling Pearson a story. "Let me tell you something about myself. A guy spit on me once. His name was Angelo. He was a tough guy, and for a living he hurt people. He spat on me and I bashed him in the nuts. So he waits and then he and two other guys beat the shit out of me. Put me in the hospital with tubes going in and out. I learned my lesson. I learned how to wait."

"That's what I'm asking for."

Nick ignored Pearson's remark and pressed on. "The guy got into trouble, shot somebody. Victim lives to testify, so Angelo gets nailed but is going to get out in five years with good behavior."

"So you're off the hook."

"I keep track of his stay at Attica and finally learn Angelo is getting out. So, I fly back to New York. I know what he's going to do. He's going to go to his mother's, get cleaned up, and then head out to Jilly's. There, he'll meet some of his friends and the boys he's going back to work for. They'll throw him a party, probably get him laid, too. I wait until he comes out of his mother's apartment all dressed up to go to his big homecoming. I make sure he's far enough away from the apartment so I don't cause his mom any auditory emotional distress."

Pearson leaned in closer trying to get a bead on Nick and thought, *This guy's got a sense of humor and he's using it to pin me to the wall.*

"Angelo steps around the corner and, *wham*, I smack him between the eyes. Then I hit him with twenty or thirty good ones. Then I give my feet and legs some exercise." Nick leaned in a little and stared at Pearson. "They had the party for him, three months later."

Pearson nodded and figured Nick wasn't kidding.

"Now those fucking guys out there killed my wife, whom I loved. You think I'm just gonna go home and forget about it?"

Pearson spun a paper clip with his finger on the desk and thought, *There goes my "get on with your life" line.*

"Here's what I'm going to do." Nick pressed. "From now on, I'm going to bug the shit out of you and the department until you nail 'em or you all fucking retire."

Pearson leaned back in his chair. The backrest pushed his gun into his kidney and he reached around to slide the worn holster forward on his belt a couple of inches. That reminded him, he patted the gun once and asked, "You don't have one of these now, do you?"

"No," Nick said. "But I should. If I see the killers, I can't even shoot a picture of them. I don't have a camera." There was no humor in the way Nick said it.

"Well, you should get one, a camera that is, and get back to photography." Pearson couldn't resist giving advice after all, but when Nick said nothing Pearson knew he'd have to give the guy something. He reached over and opened the file. "Here's what we've got. There were two break-ins in these last months and people described two guys, one white, one Hispanic. They were dressed very similar to what you've described. In those instances, there was no violence, but people did see them near the building and we have a couple statements. We're trying to track the stuff that was stolen through our Pawn Shop Detail. But that's all we've got, so if you think you can just call them up, forget it. We've just got to wait until they get nailed on this or something else."

"Is that it?"

Pearson nodded. Nick stood up to go. Pearson noticed the guy hadn't gotten a haircut since the last time he saw him. "There is one other thing," Pearson heard himself say. "I think it's time you got back to your life, as it was before your wife's death. She would have wanted that."

That stopped Nick. He leaned across the desk and stared Pearson in the eyes. "I hated my life before I met my wife. I was totally turned off, strung out, wasted, and had blown my career until it was almost dead. But she believed in me, even loved me. She was a beautiful woman and despite all the shit I had gone through, she had just about put me back together when those fucking pigs murdered her. She stuck by, she helped, she was my savior. I can't move on from something like that."

Pearson peered down at the open file on his desk like there might be something more. But there wasn't. "We'll let you know when we've got something."

"I'll keep in touch." Nick said.

When Nick got to the parking lot and slid into his, '68 Camaro, he was both surprised and angry with himself for telling the story of Angelo because it wasn't true. Sure, Nick had whacked Angelo in the nuts and gotten severely worked over in return, but Angelo never got out of Attica. He murdered someone in there as well. Angelo wouldn't be getting out for another twenty-five years, if ever. As for Nick, he had been left with only a fantasy of revenge. Whether or not he would have ever acted on the Angelo fantasy was always a dark and haunting question. Before he learned of Angelo's added sentence, he had played the revenge plan so many times to himself, there were moments when Nick actually thought he had accomplished the violent act and he had taken satisfaction in the notion. He would quickly realize his mind had been playing tricks. It frightened him that he could lose touch so completely. This was a kind of madness. Now he had a new and more compelling revenge fantasy, but he didn't want to let this one drift into counterfeit. He wanted it real.

✦ ✦ ✦

JIM PEARSON WORKED IN his office until six. His encounter with Nick Cullen had left him curiously depressed. He decided to pack it in for the day and stop off for a couple drinks before heading home. As he left the building and walked toward his car, he saw Detective Arnold Frederickson talking to some guy he had recently noticed around the station house. Pearson didn't like the looks of the new kid on the block. The guy had a middle-aged weight lifter's body and a comparatively small head that gave the guy a cartoon-like quality, but what Pearson didn't like was the way the guy looked behind the eyes. "Hey, Jim, I'd like you to meet my new partner," Arnold said.

Reluctantly, Pearson stopped and turned toward the men.

"Jim, this is Lou Stabile, came over from Central. He's working narcotics with us."

Jim and Lou Stabile shook hands. "I've heard you're a big-time fisherman," Stabile said.

"Hardly big-time. Do you fish?"

"No, just for players in the drug trade."

Pearson hated guys who did that, brought up a subject they had no connection to. Regardless, he decided to be friendly and cut the guy some slack. "You do something other than busting drug dealers?"

"I do some trap shooting, work out at the gym, play a little racquetball."

There's nothing in common there, Pearson thought. "Well, good luck, I'll see you around." Pearson turned to go, but Stabile put a hand on his arm and squeezed it. Pearson didn't like that.

"Listen, it's none of my business, but I hear you've got a son in Chino."

Pearson stared at Stabile. Then, he slowly turned to Arnold. "You giving out my life's story, Arnold?"

Arnold's jaw dropped like he was going to say something, but Stabile covered for him and easily beat him to the answer. "I heard it from one of the guys. I didn't mean any disrespect. I just thought maybe I could help."

"My son is in there for vehicular manslaughter. How you gonna help that?"

"Well, truth is, I know a lot of guys in that prison. Most of them I put there," Stabile smirked.

"Oh, that's gonna make my son real popular."

"No, you don't understand. I know the assistant warden and a bunch of those cons I actually helped out. Some were just steerers and pitchers but with an aggressive prosecutor, they might have been doing fifteen to twenty after the bust. I talked to the DA and worked some of them down to just a couple years." Stabile grinned.

Pearson thought Stabile's grin looked as though someone had put fishhooks into either side of his cheeks and pulled them back. Lou showed a lot of teeth but there was no warmth; it was more like the smile hurt. He turned directly to Stabile and spoke quietly, "You worked it down after they informed on their friends and associates. If you don't mind. I just want my son to do his time and skip the hanging out with players and informants."

"Hey, you got me wrong but forget it, no offense," Stabile said.

Again, Pearson decided to cut the guy some slack. "Listen, you're new here and I know you want to help out but as far as my son is concerned, he'll do his time and he'll be fine."

"Hey, I stuck my nose in where it doesn't belong and I'm sorry." Stabile flashed his dead smile, reached out, grabbed Pearson's hand, and shook it like a good salesman.

Pearson had enough. He nodded, got into his car, and drove away. "What a fucking asshole," he said as he swung out onto Venice Boulevard.

CHAPTER SEVEN

THE RAIN POUNDED ON the windshield, creating hypnotic patterns as it slid down the glass. Nick watched and inwardly concentrated on the image of the three men. Was there something he hadn't noticed, anything he hadn't put in the collage he gave to Pearson? He knew there must be something else.

When he would weary of the concentration, his eyes would drift down the mental picture of the murderers and focus on Julianne. It was inevitable, and as he did, his spirit would crash. On this night, with the sound of the pounding rain enveloping him in the cab, the thoughts were more painful than ever. Earlier, he had gone hunting through the Oakwood section of Venice and into Culver City. It was a cold trail as always. He had nothing on his trip sheet, so he'd moved to the airport but now found himself stuck waiting for weather-delayed planes. As he waited, the images would not go away and the gloom of the dark, rain-drenched night assisted in conjuring the horrific memory.

Gradually, Nick came to fixate on a small aspect of the scene. He was dwelling on Julianne's hair. It was long and full, with an overall deep brown hue, but there were individually different tones of red, amber, and colors Nick could only describe as dark honey and nutmeg. He made her promise she would never cut it short. He obsessed on the remembrance after she had been murdered, how hair cascaded from her head out onto the floor like a commercial stylist had placed it there. Nick reasoned she must have been held by one man with a hand over her mouth, while another stabbed her chest those many times. When the assailants released her, she had fallen to the floor. Then, with her last strength, she tried to turn back toward Melissa's playpen in an effort to see her baby, her hair fanning out behind her as she moved her face across the floor toward her child. As Nick stared at the shifting patterns of rain on the windshield, the scene played over and over before him until he was mercifully snapped back to the present by a knock at the passenger window. Looking out through the cut-off view, Nick saw three gold buttons he immediately knew were army. Squinting more closely, he tried to see if any rank or history showed on the sleeves. It was a habit he had inadvertently learned from his time taking pictures of soldiers around the world and in Vietnam. The sleeves at the window were bare.

Nick opened his door, got out, and stared at the soldier. He didn't like what he saw. He sensed a negative emanation immediately. Popping the trunk, he dropped in the soldier's duffel bag. The soldier gripped a small athletic bag tightly in his right hand. "You want to put that bag in the trunk?"

"Fuck no," the soldier said and giggled nervously.

Nick studied him as he entered the back of the cab. The young man's eyes were bloodshot with dark circles under them. He wore a tight grin that seemed to have been placed there. His hair was too long for him to have come from basic training, so Nick reasoned, with no stripes or markings on his sleeves, he'd probably gotten busted all the way down. Nick calculated that whatever the young soldier had done had been a serious offense but not serious enough to get him a lot of time in the stockade. He had a sudden and unsettling thought. *Maybe he was no soldier at all.* Nick got in the cab and turned around and stared at the young man. "Where you going?"

"The bus station downtown, but I'm really going to San Bernardino. How much would it take to get to San B, man?"

"That'd be around one hundred fifty bucks," Nick answered. He pulled the cab away from the curb and cut around the back of a bus that was spewing black diesel plumes like a ground-cover smoke bomb.

"I can't make that; I've got forty-two dollars. How about doing it for that?"

"No can do, it'll cost you almost twenty to get downtown, but you can pick up a bus to San Bernardino for about ten or less, so you're okay." Nick decided to take the soldier the cheapest way over the hill. He turned partially around and glanced at the soldier who had seated himself directly behind Nick. The guy had a cynically shrewd attitude beyond his years, but there was something else as well. "Where you coming in from?"

"Came in from Germany, man. Was there almost nineteen months."

As he worked the cab through the light traffic on Century Boulevard, Nick studied the face again in the rearview mirror. Despite the grin, there didn't seem to be any humor in the face and again Nick was hard-pressed to put a finger on the intensity of the young man. "Move over to the other side of the seat. I don't like single fares sitting directly behind me." The soldier's grin grew a little but he obeyed. "If you were in Germany all those months and you don't have any stripes, there must be a story."

"Yeah, I got a UD," the kid replied in a matter-of-fact manner.

"What'd they find so undesirable about you?"

"Speed, man. I was doing speed."

"They actually catch you doing it?"

"Shit, man, my sarge knew I was doing it. He knew about it for a long time."

"Why did he finally turn you in?"

"I fucked up a couple of things; I think he got tired of that. Shit, he knew I had a bunch on me to bring home and he didn't say anything. He just wanted to get rid of me."

"Looks like he did. An undesirable discharge and a bag full of speed, doesn't sound like much of a future."

"Oh, man, you won't believe this speed. This shit I got is unbelievable. This is pure crystal, crystal pure."

"Where were you getting it from?"

"Holland, man, I'd go to Holland and get it."

"Yeah, I heard you could just go and buy stuff there."

"It wasn't that easy, man. But I could get it."

The young man paused, and then his voice took on another tone, somewhere between repressed glee and religious fervor. "I'd like to do some right now."

Nick had a momentary chill at the inflection in the kid's voice. "When was the last time you did it?"

"A few hours ago, on the plane."

"And you want some more?"

"Yeah, I do it five, six times a day. I'd like to do some right now. You mind if I do some? I got my works right in the bag. I could do you, too, man. Why don't I do you and you take me to San B?"

"I don't think so," Nick said.

"I'll give you a couple grams and you can snort it, man, you don't have to shoot it. I do it that way 'cause that's the way I like it but you could snort it. Man, on a couple of grams, you could drive for weeks with no sleep."

For a moment Nick seriously considered the notion. He was no stranger to speed. He had shied away from it during his career because for him and photography, it didn't go at all well. Still, it could be a handy thing to have around some nights. As quickly as the temptation entered his mind, he shrugged it off. *No,* Nick thought. *I'm leaving that bitch alone. I've got work to do.*

"You look like one of them Vietnam vets. Were you ever in Vietnam?"

"Yeah," Nick answered warily.

"All right!" the kid said eagerly. "Were you some big hero, did you bang a lot of 'em?"

"I was a civilian photojournalist. I just took pictures."

"That sounds hot, man. How long were you there?"

"Forty-nine days."

"Only forty-nine? What happened?"

"I had spent Christmas with my dad, then went to Vietnam on assignment. It was one of my first real jobs. I hustled a small paper into giving me the gig. I got there just in time for the Tet Offensive."

"The what?"

"It was a big battle they had, went on for a long time. Killed over eighty thousand people."

"Holy fuck," the young man said and wiggled excitedly in his seat. "So, what happened?"

"After they kicked our ass and we kicked back, things quieted down for a bit. One day, an eighteen-year-old GI asked if I'd take his picture. I always did when they asked me. I carried a little Olympus for the shots, so I could keep them separate from my work stuff. The guy sees a water buffalo about fifty yards away and takes off at a jog, yelling back at me to come and take his picture by the buffalo." Nick recollected the heat and rich pungent smell of the rice paddy near the dirt road. He remembered the boy's bright face turning and grinning back at him over his shoulder as he trotted down the road. Nick quit talking, as he got stuck on the image of the boy's face.

"So, what happened?"

"I ran along after him, almost caught up when the kid steps on an antipersonnel mine, blows his legs off and fills me full of shrapnel. That was the end of my tour. Sent me home for a couple months in the hospital."

"Why didn't you go back?"

"When I got better, they sent me to Biafra."

"Where's that?"

"Africa."

"Africa! Holy fuck."

"There was a civil war going on and they needed some pictures of starving people."

"Did you get the pictures?"

"Sure."

"That must have been a weird trip, man. What was that like?"

"Imagine what it's like to see thousands of starving people, little kids, and you don't even have a candy bar to give them, let alone a freight full of wheat."

"I'll bet you could get things cheap there, especially pussy."

Nick was repulsed by the guy and lost interest in talking. He didn't like relating stories of his past to jerks and fools. But the ex-soldier had a way of coming back with an eager attitude, like an insidious captivating salesman.

"Did you do much drugs there, man? I mean in Vietnam."

"I smoked some OJs."

"What are those?"

"Opium joints. I'm sure you've heard of them. You dip a marijuana joint into liquid opium and smoke it."

"Was it a great high?"

Nick thought about it. "Yes, it was."

"Man, if I was over there, I would have done a lot of drugs, I would have done a lot of that OJ shit."

"Some GIs smoked it because they hated what they were doing or because they were getting shot at all the time. Nobody was shooting at you in Germany, so how come you're doing yourself so much?"

The kid reached over and clutched the back of Nick's seat and stared at him earnestly. "Don't you understand, man? This shit's *good*."

"Yeah." Nick admitted. "I understand."

"Once I stayed awake for twenty-two days. My sarge couldn't believe it."

"Well, you must have crashed for a long time."

"No, I just slept for two, three days, but my sarge got pissed off anyway 'cause I slept through some duty assignments. But, shit, I had stayed awake for twenty-two days. That should have counted. Another time I went over two weeks. Come on, let me do you and then we'll go to San B. I got some friends there. We'll party."

Nick immediately rejected the offer but wondered if having the drug available could help him with his quest. The men who murdered his wife and robbed him were most definitely into hard drugs. That notion was Nick's firm belief. It was also Pearson's speculation. Digging around through the drug world was probably a good way to try and find them. *Crystals*, Nick thought. The image was one of sparkle and clarity.

The voice from the back seat confided again, "Pure crystals, man. I do you and you won't believe how high you feel. You can do anything."

Nick prepared for the descent down the steep wet hill toward the freeway by glancing in the rearview mirror to see if there were cops around and, finding none, he easily ran the speed of the cab up for the long downgrade. The rain was diminishing, and as the wind whistled into the leaky old cab. Nick reasoned he should run the kid out to San B and get the crank off him. He speculated by offering some to the right riders, he could further his investigations and see where it took him. Whether from the cab speeding down the dark lonely hill or from Nick's silent thoughts, the young man in the back seat grew paranoid as he sensed something.

"You're not going to rip me off, are you, man?"

Nick had to grin at the kid's powers in responding to Nick's fantasy. He'd better quit those mind games. He could slip further back himself and quickly. He had to go on. "No," Nick answered. "I'm just taking you to the bus station and dropping you off. But you've got to watch your ass in that place. It's a bad section of town and they eat young GIs for midnight snacks, especially whacked-out ones with duffel bags."

"Take me out to San B, man, and I'll give you crystal."

"Now that you're stateside, why don't you quit? That shit's not going to get you anywhere."

"I can't do that, man, I love my crystal. I don't care if I die. I stay up, man. I live more in a day than people live in a week, in a year."

"That's what you think," Nick offered.

The Santa Monica Freeway was looming in the distance and Nick slowed the cab and ran over the railroad tracks near

Jefferson Boulevard. All Nick had to do was to swing up onto the freeway and stay on Route 10 all the way and he could have the kid home in seventy minutes. The idea of getting the crank ate its way back into his brain, but there was something about the kid that just didn't make it. "Is San Bernardino your home?" Nick asked.

"No, man, I've got some friends there. We're going to party."

Nick let Route 10 easily swing by overhead. He decided then and there not to take the kid to San Bernardino and not to take the freeway into downtown lest he be tempted further. Save the kid another buck or two, Nick reasoned, and forget about getting the crystal. If the kid had been going home to Mom and Dad, Nick was just about ready to take him, but to drive to San Bernardino so the kid could shoot up with buddies he may or may not find was a waste.

In the misting midnight rain, the bus station looked even more sinister than usual. Drifters and derelicts huddled under the marquee and inside the doors waiting for deliverance. They watched with barely concealed interest and hope as Nick pulled the young soldier's bag from the trunk. The kid tipped Nick a dollar and hoisted the bag onto his shoulder. For a moment, there appeared a look of apprehension on the kid's face as he contemplated the doorway nearly barricaded with men. Once again, Nick warned him, "Listen, just go buy your ticket and then sit by the entrance where your bus departs and don't wander around or go to sleep."

"Man, you're talking to the wrong guy about going to sleep. I'll just go into the john, shut the door and do myself. I'll be so fucking awake the sun will be in my head." The kid reacted to Nick's deadpan stare. "I can take care of myself."

The soldier headed into the station and the men reluctantly parted for him. A short, squat Mexican man came up to Nick and asked in halting English, "How much money to go to First Street and Ramone?

"About three dollars."

The man slipped into the cab and within five minutes, Nick drove him to the address. After the man left the car, Nick thought about his next move. The bus station was as close as any other place to grab a fare. As a rule, his cab company didn't service east of the Harbor Freeway. Since he had to deadhead back to the Westside, he reasoned the station was on the way but his primary motivation was to see how the soldier was making out after his shoot-up in the john.

Many of the same crowd were still outside the station, hoarding the comparatively dry area under the metal canopy. Nick carefully locked the cab and went inside the large terminal. The cavernous building was nearly deserted except for a security guard, a clerk, and a few passengers lingering at numbered doorways. There was no sign of the soldier, so Nick went to the desk.

"When's the next bus to San Bernardino?"

"One will be leaving in forty-five minutes," the bored clerk told him.

"Did a bus just leave?"

"No, the last bus was over two hours ago."

Armed with the information, Nick went to search the men's room.

Inside, there was an ancient black man mumbling incoherently and rhythmically washing his hands in what seemed to be an endless ritual. No one else was in sight. With method, Nick opened the doors to the stalls and peered inside as though he might find the young soldier sitting there putting a needle into his arm. In the next to last stall, Nick found the soldier's overseas cap on the floor. He felt a sense of panic, left the men's room, and searched the station again, but to no avail. Outside, he got into his cab and combed the surrounding neighborhood, but the soldier had vanished into the wet night.

◆ ◆ ◆

FOR SOME REASON, THE pain in his stomach began its nightly visit stronger than usual, possibly because of concern over the soldier. He chastised himself for the thought. Why was he concerned for a man he didn't know and didn't like? It wasn't that Nick was interested in the crank; he had just toyed with the idea. Nick came to acknowledge that he felt responsible for his fares. They were in his care for a brief period and implicit in that was a certain responsibility. A year from now, Nick estimated, the soldier with the undesirable would be doing stickups to get dough for a fix. He stopped at a drab little liquor store on Fifth near Hope. More and more frequently, the insidious pain crept into his belly and concentrated two inches above his navel. Nick had found a ready cure. He bought a nip bottle of Cuervo Gold and a bottle of Dos Equis. In the cab, he uncapped both bottles, and, holding the tiny nip bottle in his fist to hide it from sight, he drained the tequila in one shot. It went greedily to the painful spot and clobbered it. He rolled down the window and tossed the bottle into an open wire trash basket. A security guard at the nearby Mexican cantina watched without any apparent opinion. Macho music blared from within and Nick permitted himself a few seconds of break as he slowly wrapped the brown paper bag tightly around the neck of the bottle and took a long pull of the dark amber liquid. Wedging the bottle between his legs for easy access, he dropped the cab in gear and began a deadhead run to the airport. The men he was looking for wouldn't be hanging out in the downtown rain.

Entering LAX, he realized he had made a mistake. There were a lot of cabs at every stand. It would be a long time before he got a fare. With resignation, he parked at American Airlines in anticipation of their post-1:00 a.m. arrivals. Slipping the now empty Dos Equis bottle into his pocket, he walked into the terminal, went into the bathroom, ditched the bottle, washed his hands, and grabbed his usual dozen paper towels. Out in the lobby, he checked the arrival board. It would be at least a half hour before the first plane landed, so he returned to his cab and settled in for the wait. Gradually, as he stared out into the night, the mist on the windshield mercifully induced a memory of one of his favorite moments with Julianne. After Julianne would emerge from her shower, she had a way of putting lotion on her legs that Nick found both calming and sensual. She approached the ritual slowly, with effortless concentration, as she casually worked her long fingers up the muscles of her beautifully formed legs. He would watch her from the bed with the morning light slanting upon her enchanting nakedness. She was framed by the doorway, which billowed forth residual steam from the bathroom. It reminded him of a painting by Maxwell Parish. Alone in the cab, the memory softened him and made him ache. *I should have taken a picture of it,* he thought but then consoled himself with knowledge the most memorable moments don't need to be photographed. They were for the mind's soul and not to be shared.

Abruptly, there was a brief rapping of knuckles on the front passenger door. The door was pulled open and a young man's face appeared. Nick had seen the guy around. He was a night driver for the same company, but the only thing Nick knew about him was that he drove fast. He'd seen him blowing away from stands like he had a supercharger under the hood. "Want some company?" the young man asked. Nick never wanted company but he didn't want to be overtly rude, so he just shrugged. With a disarmingly open grin, the young man got into the cab and held out his hand. "Billy Houston," he said.

"Nick," he said, shaking the young man's hand.

"Yeah, I've seen you around. You got some style," Billy said, and fished in his breast pocket and pulled out a well-rolled joint. "Colombian, good shit."

The match flared, illuminating Billy's face. He had a well-groomed narrow mustache and a full head of wavy light brown hair. It gave him the look of a French Musketeer. He passed the joint to Nick who took a couple of hits. It was rich and heavy and Nick knew he was going to get very stoned almost immediately. "Nice weed," Nick said.

"Yeah, it's good. If you ever want any, just ask."

"You dealing?"

"Not really. I just sell to some of the drivers and a couple of friends. But if you want any, you'll be able to find me pretty quick. I'm going to start dispatching nights," Billy said, grinning at Nick.

Nick turned and passed the joint back. "Is that something you want to do?" he asked.

"Well, I like driving, but as soon as I go to court on this last ticket I'm gonna lose my license for a while. So if I can't drive a cab or tow truck, I might as well dispatch. Besides, I always felt I could dispatch better than the guys doing it, especially that asshole Tony."

Nick nodded agreement.

"You know," Billy said. "I've been looking over the trip tickets and you are one hell of a high booker, especially since the dispatchers don't throw you any long fares."

Nick was surprised by Billy's remark, both that his records were so available and that Billy would take the trouble.

"You book way up there in the top two or three percent of the company. They should give you a good cab instead of always sending you out in pieces of shit."

"That'd be nice," Nick said.

Billy took another hit off the Colombian and passed it back. "There's a day driver, Clyde Nestle, real mellow guy. He's picking out a cab over at the shop in the Valley and will be looking for a night driver who's cool and clean to share it. Clyde only drives from eight to four thirty. The rest of the time, you could have it, long as you want. I'll speak to him about it. You guys would like each other."

"Great," Nick said without too much enthusiasm. Nick couldn't understand why Billy was being so considerate. All the reclusion Nick had been hiding behind was jumping up in his mind, trying to block any openings. Could this guy be a friend? It had been so long since anyone seemed genuinely kind, he was suspicious. He took another whack off the smoldering roach and said, "Well, I know where I'm gonna go for my weed from now on."

"I only sell weed, no coke or anything. Strictly weed."

"That's all I need."

Billy confided, "Stop by anytime during the night when I start dispatching. We'll do a number. I'm going to need some friends and guys I can count on out there." Billy looked down at the hack license in the holder and studied the laminated picture of Nick. "What'd you do before you started driving?"

Nick took another drag and the roach burned into his thumb and forefinger. "I was kind of a renegade photojournalist."

Billy grinned and nodded his head. "Sounds really hot, man."

Nick impulsively liked this guy. He had a straightforward, no-nonsense, positive vibe that spoke to Nick. Maybe he could confide in Billy. The guy knew the territory. Nick had kept to himself even though he knew networking among the cabbies might have brought him something. What could Nick say? *Hey, keep an eye out for some guys that look like this because if I find them I'm going to kill them.*

"So why would you give up something like that?" Billy asked regarding Nick's lost career.

Whether it was the big Columbian weed, the lulling rain, or Billy's receptive manner, Nick decided to slowly bring the story to him. "Being a freelance photojournalist is a business you've got to hustle in. In recent years, there were fewer and fewer assignments and more and more photographers, they also want video now. If you're good and you get around, you see a lot of terrible shit. If you let it, it gets to you. I started drinking a lot and fucking around with drugs, didn't scurry for work, and here I am. Except I gave up the hard drugs, but I'm back into weed and booze."

"I don't drink," Billy said. "You can't do it all and I love my weed." Billy waited, then prompted, "Sounds like you could make a comeback."

"Some months ago, my apartment was ripped off and I lost a lot of equipment, TV, every camera and lens I had. I always thought I got robbed by guys who were into drugs. You know quick score, sell the stuff, buy drugs, trade around. I've been trying to get a handle on where guys like that would hang out, sell the stuff."

"Could be anywhere in the city from East LA to Venice, Pacoima to Compton. Where were you living when it happened?"

"Venice."

Billy fished out a roach-holder from his breast pocket, clamped the half-inch resin-stained remains, and took a long slow inhalation, shrinking it back to the steel clamp. "Well that still leaves a lot of territory and shit, you don't even know what they look like."

"Yes, I do," Nick said.

Billy slyly glanced at Nick. "You sound pretty serious about this."

"I am."

"I can understand you could love your gear that much. I'm still pissed off about a crescent wrench somebody lifted." Billy removed the roach and pocketed the holder. "Well, like I said, there's a lot of territory out there. We'll talk about it and I'll give it some thought. There are a couple of other drivers I could run something by."

"I'd appreciate that, as long as it was kept quiet and they didn't know it was me asking."

"No problem." Billy paused for a moment as he rolled down the window and flicked the impossibly tiny roach from the holder onto the wet pavement, then turned back to Nick and asked, "If you find them, what plans you got for the person or persons who did it?"

"Depends on the who, what, where, or when."

Billy nodded approvingly, and then said, "I'd better get back, they'll be coming out soon. Tomorrow, talk to me about that cab for you and Clyde."

"I will, and thanks for the smoke."

"Anytime," Billy said.

Peering in the rearview mirror, Nick watched Billy go back to his cab. He walked with a short bouncing gait in keeping with his personality. Nick admitted to himself he liked the guy.

He had to wait for the second plane in, but he got off with a pretty good fare. A guy was going to the Sheraton Universal. He explained he was checking in there, going to find an apartment, and then become an actor. Nick glanced at the fare in the back seat. He must have been in his midthirties, kind of dumpy-looking and, as far as Nick was concerned, didn't have much spark. "You must have worked in the theater in New York for a while, huh?"

"No, I haven't acted yet. It's just something I've always wondered about and wanted to do."

"So were you at a good time in your life to try something like this?"

"Well, I had a great apartment on Fifth Avenue, a good job, and I just up and left it all. It's something I've got to try, you know?"

"Yeah," Nick said.

Nick couldn't resist a last look in the mirror, then shook his head, and thought,

There's a dream a minute coming into LA. He knew. But his had become a nightmare.

CHAPTER EIGHT

I

T TOOK A FEW days, but Billy made the introduction between Nick and Clyde. Clyde lived with his mother, drove a cab from 8:30 a.m. to 4:30 p.m. Monday through Friday, and that was that. He had a childlike face that had seen some thirty-five years. How Clyde had spent most of those years remained a mystery. Nick thought there was a feeling about the guy, like he had been a member of a religious cult or something. But all in all, he seemed pretty together and curiously nice. Nick liked him well enough, but had seen in an instant they'd never become close friends. That suited Nick just fine.

Some drivers were watching them carefully, so the three walked off to a distant part of the yard where they wouldn't be overheard or interrupted. Cabbies could smell a business conversation and had an innately curious nature.

Clyde turned to them and hesitated as though it were going to be painful to speak. "I had hoped they'd have the cabs painted by now, but it's taking them some time."

"How long you think?" Billy asked.

"I don't really know."

"They're just wasting their own money having cabs waiting to be painted and not out making dough," Nick volunteered.

"Yeah, well, the painting is one thing but the licensing is something else. And though they're not saying, I think they're having a problem with the city on that score," Billy said.

Nick turned to Clyde. "I'm happy I'm someone you'd like to share a good cab with. So whenever it's ready, that'll be fine. "

"I went over and had a look at them. There are a few nice cars, but there's one I've got my eye on," Clyde said in his shy manner.

"When I start dispatching, I'll see what I can do to get the bosses to hustle things along," Billy said.

Business done, the three of them walked back toward the dispatcher's window. Clyde turned in his paperwork and headed for home and Mom.

Billy was pleased with himself that the introduction had gone well. Billy turned to Nick. "You know, the best thing about working with Clyde is he comes in at the same time every day, so you get your cab and go out right away. None of this waiting around, and if you're late the car will be here waiting for you."

"It's a good deal all around for me. I want to thank you. I should lay some dough on you or something. This is going to translate into money for me."

Billy shook his head and grinned. "I don't want any dough. This is part of being a dispatcher. I want some teamwork. It will work out on all sides down the line."

"Well, no matter, I owe you."

A silent minute passed as Billy stood beside Nick and kicked at the ground with the sole of his boot as though trying to uncover something in the asphalt. "I've been thinking about your robbery and everything. You don't have to tell me, but I can't fucking believe you're going to all this trouble just because some guys ripped off your cameras and shit. There's gotta be something else."

Here it was, Nick thought. He had opened up just a crack, confided in him, and now Billy smelled the big story and wanted more. It was his own fault, he reasoned. He had created an implausible story out of a tragically real one. He reached back and reflexively pulled up his collar against the growing evening chill. "You're right. I left out part."

"The big part?" Billy asked.

"Yeah."

"Well, if you ever want to talk about it, we'll grab a cup of coffee or something." A cab swung into the yard and Billy waved at the driver. "I'm driving three-seven-one tonight, pretty good cab. See you later." He started off but then turned back toward Nick. "If you really want some help, it would be better if I knew what went down."

Nick watched Billy go over and greet the day driver of 371. Together, they began to service the cab. It looked like Billy had quite a few friends. Nick thought, *Maybe I should tell him everything. What good does it do keeping it all in and just doing crisis sharing with Detective Pearson?* Nick nodded his head and the nodding slowly turned to a shaking motion. It was the same old problem. If he told Billy and he somehow helped find the guys and Nick killed them, then Billy, and maybe others, would know he'd done it. That was the danger. But on the other hand, the real dilemma was in not finding the killers. Nick studied Billy from across the way and realized Billy reminded him of some of the guys from the old neighborhood. He suspected Billy had a code and that code included not telling a sensitive story about a friend to anyone.

During the next few days, Nick worked out a new routine he thought would optimize possibilities for success in finding the killers. Nick reasoned they could be anywhere. He would start at the airport. The 5:00 p.m. airport traffic was always intense. He could usually get out right away and 75 percent of the time he would find himself driving from LAX to somewhere on the Westside of LA. Those were areas he wanted to concentrate on regardless. The capricious nature of getting fares and their different destinations often defeated his plans, causing him to have to go with the flow. Sometimes, he'd wind up in other cities like Anaheim or Long Beach, and while he wanted to concentrate on the area within which he thought the killers operated, he'd have to leave himself open to all possibilities. *Look through the trees, not at the trees.* That was the problem. There were millions of men burrowing into bars, movie theaters, clubs, bowling alleys, all impossible to keep track of. Nick remembered the feeling when he'd be on a photographic assignment and would check into a motel in the middle of Texas or sleep in the back of a truck in some remote part of Egypt. No one would know where he was. He was a man stopping at a place where no one knew him and no friend, relative, or editor had any real notion of exactly where he was. Often, for safety's sake, he didn't even use his correct name. That increased anonymity, lessened the chances for interference and reprisals. For brief moments of time, he was unknown and alone on the planet, disconnected from every acquaintance. It never ceased to affect him. He always found the experience extremely liberating and, to a degree, Nick concluded, that's why he was in the cab. Then he remembered, the killers were living much the same way.

That might be what the killers are trying to do, Nick thought. *Get to a spot where no one knows them.* If that were true, then Nick was wasting his time. How far could they have gotten with what they stole? Nick had run some calculations in his mind that with his wife's jewelry, most of which had come from her family, and his camera equipment, they stole the equivalent of $45,000, if not more. Then there was the ruby ring. They had not appraised it, but it could have been worth as much as $50,000. If the thieves hocked it for 10 percent of value, they'd have enough money to get anywhere they wanted. They could buy a supply of drugs, get out of town, and still have some whip-out money. But what if they didn't leave town?

That's what Nick was banking on.

CHAPTER NINE

"RAINEY DAZE," AS SOME of his acquaintances called him, had been back for over two months and, as usual, had spent much of his time looking for his next trick on Santa Monica Boulevard. After the killing, he had fled to San Francisco. He crashed at a friend's house and did the scene until he ran out of money.

For his share in the robbery, he had gotten some of the jewelry. Cal and Jesse gave him the least expensive swag, keeping the best jewelry, all the cameras, and ruby ring for themselves. Furious, but knowing he couldn't safely complain, Rainey took his meager share to San Francisco. He sold the jewelry, piece by piece, to acquaintances of his friend who came in and out of the apartment. The money kept him on some not-very-good drugs and food for weeks and weeks.

NICK HAD GOTTEN SEVERAL calls from the custom lab where he had left the exposed film he had taken of Julianne and Melissa. The proof sheets had been ready for months. He avoided getting the pictures because he feared looking at photographs of Julianne on the last day of her life would be more than he could take. Finally, out of fear the lab might misplace or throw them out, he retrieved them. Taking the proof sheets out into the sunlight, he spent an hour leaning over the hood of his Camaro, studying them. Some shots were very fine and Julianne looked happy. Emotions swirled within him and he requently had to quit studying the proofs as tears moistened his eyes. Finally, he selected a few, took the proof sheets back into the lab, and asked to have them enlarged to five by seven inches. After a discussion of exposure, paper selection, and cropping, he left.

A few days later, he studied the prints. The two-inch negative from the Hasselblad gave a deep richness to the prints and Nick was pleased with the results. Consulting with the lab technician, he learned of a good framer and took the pictures there. He spent a lot of time with the custom framer and finally decided on the beautiful matte cherrywood frames. He had an individual shot of Julianne framed for Lillian. He would send it to her for her birthday. But it was Melissa he was vitally concerned with. He took two beautiful and identical pictures of Julianne seated on a bench holding Melissa in her lap. Two weeks later, he picked up the artfully framed pictures. Back in his apartment, he wrote, *Dear Melissa, I hope you will put this picture of Mommy and yourself in a special place by your bed. I have one as well and have put it by my bed. As you can see from the picture, your mommy loved you so much. I miss you honey and love you, too. Daddy.*

The next day, he taped the note to the back of the picture, carefully wrapped it, and sent it.

JESSE AND CAL WERE not easily panicked by the events of the robbery and had casually tried to fence the stuff the day after. They were trying to work their way back into some money so they could buy a decent quantity of drugs cheaply and start dealing again. That was where the real money was, and they knew it. It was a plan Jesse had been working on. Six months earlier, they had actually begun to prosper in the drug trade. Then, they made a mistake trying to sell to a powerful East LA Chicano gang and had summarily gotten ripped off. Next time, they'd know better.

They hadn't left Los Angeles right away. Rather, they hung out and over the next weeks committed two more robberies in the Venice area. They partied over Christmas with the halfwit girl they picked up in Pacoima, then dropped her off nearly comatose alongside the highway twenty miles outside of Las Vegas.

With a sense of dread, Cal let Jesse talk him into stopping in Las Vegas. It was not part of the plan. The plan was to bomb down to Texas and get in touch with a dealer Jesse knew who moved large quantities of drugs. He'd cut them a great deal. Then it was supposed to be back to LA to begin selling and making "the big easy trade-up." Instead, they got a swank hotel room and, still flying high, Jesse took their money to the tables and left it there within three hours.

Angry, Cal almost headed off by himself. Instead, he found himself driving the car with Jesse lying down in the back seat. Cal scrunched down behind the wheel and back to Los Angeles, broke. Jesse's last words before he fell asleep from weeks of partying rang in Cal's ears: "Hell, we got the dough together before, quick as a mustang out a gate. So, pardner, we'll just do her again."

They were now driving a Chevy Nova down Interstate 15. Cal had dropped in a powerful LT1-350 engine he got from a chop shop in Wilmington for a solid gold cigarette lighter and a ladies' silver bracelet. That had pleased Jesse. The car was half restored with patches of primer on the body. While Jesse would have preferred a big new pickup or Lincoln, he liked the way the powerful engine sounded when he was sleeping in the back seat. "Like it's carrying me to a mountain of maidens," he said.

As Cal drove along, he thought for a moment of the woman with the ruby ring. She had been beautiful, and Cal remembered when Jesse had taken his knife from him and stabbed the beautiful woman all those times, then casually handed the blade back with a grin. In reaction to the memory, he glanced in the rearview mirror at Jesse crashed on the back seat. Jesse didn't seem to have much problem with the fact that he had stabbed her to death. But Cal had Catholic remorse. He also wondered about the chances they'd get caught.

For his part, Jesse always knew he was going to get caught; he theorized he'd just keep living his wild life until they got him. As he often repeated in his flat Kansas accent, "Something's gonna get me, either the law or the grim reaper. It's just a question of which one gets to me first."

Cal didn't speculate much on death. It was too frightening, and he had a lot to answer for. Some of the crimes he had already done time for, but his time in prison didn't frighten him as much as the idea of getting caught again. It was the surge of guilt he felt when he got caught that he feared most. He often considered leaving "the team," as Jesse called them, but he didn't know what else to do. He was attached to Jesse like a lamprey to a shark.

CHAPTER TEN

J UST AFTER MIDNIGHT, NICK got a call to pick up Irene. Unaccountably, he felt a little excitement as he drove to the hotel. She was outside waiting for him, and he watched her gracefully open the door and slide into the back seat. "I've asked for you several times but a different driver always shows up."

"Well, either I was not in the area, or the dispatcher didn't give me the order. Supposedly, they have a rule about personal fares, but a new dispatcher is starting soon and I'll speak to him about it."

"I would prefer you driving me," she said in her prim but slightly abstract manner. Through the rearview mirror, Nick studied her from time to time as they drove toward her motel. Uncharacteristically, Irene suddenly stretched an arm up to the top of the back seat and relaxed. Nick noticed the fabric of her small print dress pull against her round, surprisingly full breasts. "I had a really good night," she said, then looked out the window and quietly repeated, "A really good night."

Nick wondered about her definition of "a really good night" but didn't ask.

◈ ◈ ◈

DROPPING IRENE OFF, HE rapidly deadheaded to LAX and pulled up to American Airlines to get the flights from New York and Chicago. A fog had gently drifted in and the planes were going to be delayed. Across the concrete divide, the loudspeakers monotonously droned out to no one in particular, "The white zone is for immediate loading and unloading only. No parking." Nick settled in for the unanticipated wait when the door to his cab was suddenly pulled open and Billy slid into the passenger seat. He sparked a new sample and handed it over to Nick. No one else was around, so Nick lowered the windows to let out the smoke.

Silently, they passed the joint back and forth until Billy turned to Nick and said, "We've got some time, why don't you tell me the big part?"

It took him a full minute, while he stared at the smoldering weed between his fingers until gradually he began to talk, "I had a wife. Her name was Julianne. She was beautiful and I loved her." As the story continued, Billy reclined his head onto the backrest and stared out into the night, listening. This time, Nick didn't leave anything out, and when he finished speaking, Billy didn't waste much time on sympathy. After one quick heartfelt shake of his head, he turned to Nick and said, "You gotta get those guys." He sucked down the last of the roach, reached out the window, and flipped the tiny remaining ember over the back of the cab. "Definitely, definitely, you gotta get those guys," he repeated. "But you probably won't."

A couple of porters and passengers were making their way toward the waiting taxis. Billy got out of the cab and leaned back in through the window. "I'll help any way I can."

"Thanks," Nick said, getting out of the cab himself. He watched Billy walk away and then turned and faced the oncoming hoard. The first person who made it to him was an elderly black lady. Nick guessed correctly that she was just going to Inglewood. He knew it would be a five-dollar fare at best, but he accepted it graciously and took good care of the kindly old woman. Short fares, long fares, they were all part of the game and, in the long run, they averaged out. After he dropped her off, he thought of heading back into the port and getting the balance of the American flight rush but he heard a call for anyone outside the airport. He decided to go for it and answered the call.

The fare was to be waiting at the Full Wing Arms, a small two-story green stucco hotel on Century Boulevard, two miles east of LAX. It was a depressing joint and Nick felt right at home. Walking into the lobby to locate the fare, he saw two young women look at him expectantly. Pale and worn, they came forward slowly. "Are you the cab driver?"

Nick nodded in response.

"We called because there's a guy in the bathroom over there and he needs a ride. He was real nice to us and we want to make sure he gets out all right." The girl who spoke looked as though she might have been a telephone operator from Oklahoma. Two short starch-fed white girls, Nick observed. They didn't look much like hookers, but they surely were.

An Asian American in workingman's clothing stumbled out of the bathroom. His face was shining with a thin patina of greasy sweat. He reeled and looked around, not really seeing. He was nearly blind drunk. Nick turned to the two hookers. "Has he got any money left?" The girls didn't object to the question but they also didn't exactly know how to answer. "I don't want to drive a guy that can't pay or is too drunk to figure out how to find his address."

"He'll be all right. He's a really nice guy," the other woman said earnestly.

Nick looked at the man and then back at the girls. He wondered what kind of a scene they'd had. It looked to Nick like he'd balled them for a while but then must have spent most of his time drinking because the guy was beyond functioning. With some reluctance, he walked over to the man and said, "I'm your ride."

The man nodded once and searched with his eyes for the lobby door. After the hooker's concern, Nick figured the man would give them a big smooch goodbye. To his surprise, the man left the hotel without even an acknowledgment. Nick watched him get into the cab and saw he could still manage some semblance of coordination. The guy wanted to go to a section of downtown LA off Alameda. Nick knew it to be a place truck drivers parked their tractors to await load assignments. "I'm a trucker," the guy volunteered, confirming Nick's hunch.

Nick didn't feel like talking. He was recalling his confession to Billy about Julianne's murder and discovered he felt better for having told. The fare in back leaned forward and held one hand on the front seat for support. "I drive an eighteen-fucking-wheeler all around this fucking country."

"That's great," Nick offered.

"I'm Korean. I'm from Korea. I fought in the Korean War and the motherfucking Vietnam War."

This time the guy waited a while for Nick's response. Nick didn't have much to say about that except the idea of a Korean fighting in the Vietnam War and now being a truck driver in America struck him as a little odd.

"I don't go back to Korea no more. I'm American. I drive my truck all over the motherfucking country. It's me and my truck, pardner." The man fell back into the seat. "It's my truck and nobody messes around with it. I've got a nickel-plated forty-four and anybody mess with my rig, I'll fucking shoot their ass."

"Yeah, I'll bet you would," Nick ventured.

"I'm a registered Korean black belt, sixth degree and carry a forty-four magnum, anybody mess with me I'll fuck 'em in the ass. Nobody killed me in Vietnam, nobody gonna kill me here."

The guy was talking all-American country slang but he still had a taste of a Korean accent left. Nick suppressed a grin. It was a funny combination, but that's where the humor about the guy ended.

"That gun is a fucking beauty. You want to see it?"

"Only if you want to sell it."

"I wouldn't sell my motherfucking gun, not for a thousand dollars. That gun is mine. We travel together, pardner."

"Where did you get it?" Nick found himself asking.

"I fucking bought it in Amarillo, Texas. Where do you think I got it? Walked in there, saw gun, and fucking bought it."

"Where do you keep it?" Nick quickly realized it was the wrong question, and right away the guy got paranoid.

"What do you want to know that for? You gonna rip me off? Come see where my rig is and then come back and steal my gun?"

"No, I mean when you're driving across the country, where do you keep it in case you want to use it?"

"I keep that motherfucking gun right next to me, in my bag on the seat. What use have motherfucking gun if can't get to it fast?"

Nick thought, *This man understands a big hunk of America, the swearing and shooting.* The guy was trying real hard to be an American man and he got parts of it perfectly, the anger and the lonely pain. The Korean in the back seat came back out of his momentary dizzy drunk spin.

"The girls at the truck stops, man, they don't give a flying fuck what you look like. But man, those were some fine women tonight. Weren't those fine gals?"

"Yeah, they were really sweet."

"What?"

"Sweet, they were sweet. They told me to look out for you. They said you were nice to them." Nick glanced in the mirror and saw a look of confusion come over the man's face.

They drove on in silence for a while. As he neared Ninth Street, he heard the man say, "Pull over here."

"Here? There's nothing around here. Let me take you to your rig."

"No way," he insisted. "I'll get out here. I show you my rig, you'll come back and steal my gun. I'm getting out."

Nick stopped the cab. He wasn't going to argue. The man leaned forward and paid, tipping Nick a couple dollars.

Getting out of the cab, the guy staggered up onto the curb. A telephone pole rose up into the night and the new American put out his hand and leaned against it for support. He swayed where he stood and stared with glassy eyes off into the distance, a weird grin on his face. *God knows what he's grinning about*, Nick thought. He dropped the cab into gear and drove through the bleak industrial streets toward downtown to see what he could pick up. The man who had just gotten out of the cab was right about one thing. Having a gun was very much on Nick's mind.

AFTER THEIR TEXAS TRIP got thrown away at the crap tables, Jesse, Cal, and their Chevy Nova drove into LA and holed up. Jesse had come down from his manic drug-assisted high and they had stashed themselves at a motel just off the Pacific Coast Highway near the Wilmington-San Pedro city line. Being from landlocked Kansas, Jesse was fascinated by the harbor and big ships. Cal felt comfortable in Wilmington. He could hang out with a couple homeboys he knew from his time in jail and could visit with his cousin who lived in a trailer and was waiting for a job as second mate on a long-haul tuna boat. When his cousin got a boat, he would be gone for months, and Jesse and Cal could stay in his trailer.

Cautiously, they sought out some drug buyers as part of Jesse's plan for "the big easy trade-up." Jesse decided his first choice was a tall, dark brown-skinned man they'd been introduced to in Oakwood. He called himself "Cranberry" and both Jesse and Cal thought he was sharp. Cranberry didn't give out any information about prices or minimum buys, but did say he'd be ready for them when they showed up with the goods and check with him first no matter what they had. As much as safety would allow, Jesse asked around about Cranberry. The few people he spoke with confirmed Cranberry was "the man" and could handle any size transaction. The rumor was Cranberry worked for a major dealer out of South Central Los Angeles called Big TC. Cranberry was opening the Venice territory for the major player.

Most of their days, they headed north to scout possible scores, and in good time had them lined up. Jesse referred to their coming thefts as "storming the walls."

Jesse's hunting abilities and uncharacteristic patience yielded eleven houses and condominiums from the Pacific Palisades to Marina Del Rey that looked promising. The idea was to take all the places down in a very short amount of time, get out of LA, and head to Dallas for the drug buy. Jesse estimated they could average a minimum of $15,000 in jewelry and goods from each house. They could fence it for 10 to 20 percent of value and wind up with at least $20,000. Secretly, both Jesse and Cal told themselves, next time, they could walk away from their fence, Koss, with more than that.

They had a couple two-foot square magnetized signs made proclaiming: *Meade's Plumbing*. Meade was Jesse's father's middle name and Jesse thought it a good joke to use his name on the sign. They stole a large white van, stole some license plates, switched them onto the van, and stuck on the signs. The next day, they drove north to Pacific Palisades to begin "storming."

CHAPTER ELEVEN

DETECTIVE PEARSON LOVED POLICE statistics. He rolled his new favorites around in his head. In the last year, Los Angeles had 3,285 people murdered by guns. The entire country of England had sixty-three. He was checking on how many were in his neighborhood. The number seemed to be going up quickly. Two nights ago he had a case where four guys shot up a bingo parlor in an attempted robbery, killing three. They had one of the assailants in jail and Pearson figured they would have them all locked up in due time. But there was a new case he learned of. It wasn't in his direct territory and it was less sensational than the bingo mayhem, but more interesting. He reviewed it and tried to learn more details.

It seems two guys—one Hispanic, heavyset, with shoulder-length black hair and one Anglo, tall, dirty blond hair, of medium build—had terrorized, robbed, and attempted the rape of a woman in a condo in Marina Del Rey. The tall Anglo had begun to strangle her when her boyfriend unexpectedly walked into the apartment. The tall Anglo picked up a gun and quickly shot him twice, once in the throat and once in the cheek. The girl took the opportunity to run. The Hispanic guy was about to stop her so she took a shortcut around him and, still naked, crashed through the third-story window. The sounds of the glass shattering and screams brought out some neighbors and the two men fled the building. Once the poor girl was stitched up and her arm and leg set, she gave the investigating officers a very good description of the two. One of the most interesting things Pearson read was that the tall guy wore a sleeveless sheepskin vest and had a tattoo of a black leopard on his left arm. She described their behavior. The deduction was they were some kind of speed addicts. The guy had her on the bed but never got an erection, which seemed to piss him off. He told his heavyset accomplice to leave the room, which the guy did by going into the bathroom. When the boyfriend came in, the tall guy stood up to get his gun, put his cock back in his pants, and shot the poor guy practically all at the same time. That's how the girl managed to escape. Pearson pulled the file on the Julianne Thombridge-Cullen murder, studied it and the collage Nick had made of the killers. It was probably the same guys in both cases. It made a kind of special sense to Pearson because the Anglo-looking guy shot the boyfriend in the head, the same as he had Nick. It was a risky, but potentially very effective way of stopping someone, forever. It was the killer's signature, as much as if he always left an ace of spades. Maybe this time they'd have some luck with prints, but the pair would probably need to fall on the hood of a patrol car in order to get caught, as their physical descriptions could match two hundred others walking down the boardwalk.

Pearson tossed the file onto his desk, leaned back in his chair, and put his feet up. He thought to himself about how the poor desperate woman whose boyfriend got killed didn't warrant an article in any paper. However, the shoot-out at the bingo parlor made it into all the papers, and that's where he was expected to spend his time. One of the suspects was coming out of surgery from a gunshot wound he received from a security guard, before the guard himself was blasted dead by the robbers. He had to go down to the hospital and question him. It had been a long day. Questioning the guy, calling in the results to headquarters, and talking with the press would be enough until Monday.

He picked up the file and started to walk back to the cabinet. It was then he thought again of Nick Cullen and wondered what he'd been up to. He made a mental note to call him next week, but not mention the similar murder case. This was something he wanted to follow by himself. He'd like to present Nick with three killers, sitting behind bars. After a moment's hesitation, Pearson pulled Nick's collage of the killers from the folder and stuck it under his arm. Maybe he'd take an hour over the weekend, stop by the hospital, and show it to the woman who had taken the swan dive through her window.

CHAPTER TWELVE

THE DARKNESS OF MANY nights surrendered to daylight, but no new cab appeared. Nick didn't want to bring it up and embarrass Billy or Clyde, so he went about his business.

Implementing his new plan, nightly he scoured the bars from south Santa Monica through Venice, from the bottom-rung joints to the workingman and drinker's saloons.

One night, between some meager fares, he spent over three hours checking all the places on his growing list and found no one filled the killer's descriptions. It was disappointing as always but way past time to make some money. A quick drive to LAX was in order. Entering the airport, he saw some cabs on the first two stands, so he continued around until he came to American. There were no cabs, but there was a woman standing with one small piece of luggage and a shoulder bag as Nick pulled in. He got out of the cab and moved around to her. She had a full mouth painted with deep red lipstick, but that was where the fullness ended. He was startled at how thin she was. The pink coat with matching fabric buttons was cut narrowly in the shoulders and waist but it still hung on her like an oversize garment. He thought right away she might be anorexic. "Hi, where you off to?" Nick asked.

"Just going down to Continental, I'm flying down to Texas in a couple of hours." She had a slight accent to go with her destination.

Nick looked past her and noticed two men with carry-on luggage heading for his cab. They each started to lengthen their stride to see who could make it to the stand first, but there were forty yards between them and the taxi and a lot could happen in that distance. Behind them, a mass of people was moving in to wait for their luggage to begin the secret trip from the airplane down to the spinning carousel. Nick turned back to the woman. "I'm sorry, but I can't take any rides inside the airport," he fibbed. "There's a free shuttle that comes by every few minutes and it'll drop you at Continental."

"Well, I've got a couple of hours to kill. I thought I might see some of LA," she casually answered.

"LA is pretty tough to find, it doesn't sit on one main section and there's nothing much right around the airport. If you've only got two hours, I suggest you hang out here." Nick prepared to meet the arriving passengers.

"How about if I just ride around with you?"

Nick looked at the woman and she stared back at him. There was something very frank and open about her, as though she had cut through all pretenses and was living very much in the moment. Despite her frail appearance, she seemed to be taking charge. She held Nick's eyes and he found himself saying, "Let me see where these guys are going and if it makes sense, you can come along." Nick quickly wondered to himself why he said that. It meant he'd have to return to the airport regardless of circumstances. She was into touring but he didn't think she was into paying. He began to explain. "These guys are probably going downtown. Normally, I'd just stay there after dropping them off because it doesn't pay to deadhead back. So..."

She seemed to anticipate Nick's objection. "I'll pay the fare from where you drop these guys off back to here."

With twenty yards to go, the two men that had been scurrying toward the stand had by some unspoken mutual consent stopped the race and begun walking toward the cab lest they blow a gut from the drinks they'd had on the plane As they closed in, one guy who was wearing a green silk tie and cashmere topcoat hopped quickly up onto the curb to plant his foot on the taxi stand concrete first. "Where you off to?" Nick asked.

"Going to the Bonaventure Hotel."

"Are you with him?" Nick asked the smaller, bald-headed man.

"No," the guy said, irritated as hell for being beaten to the stand.

"Where you going?"

"Hancock Park." Nick glanced toward the terminal. The carousel was playing its clunking tune with the luggage and people were picking up their belongings and going through baggage check. "I'll take both of you. Drop you at Hancock Park and then head down to the Bonaventure. The gentleman going to Hancock Park pays full fare and you, sir, get three dollars off the meter."

"Fine," the Hancock Park man said.

"Why do I have to ride with him and go out of my way?"

"It'll only take an additional few minutes."

The man in the green tie wasn't happy, but he was in a hurry. Nick regarded them evenly. "You gents can refuse this ride if you want and wait for another cab."

The man took a look at the throng coming out onto the sidewalk from baggage claim, then walked toward the trunk, handing Nick his carry-on bag.

"Where's she going?"

"She's taking a tour." Nick didn't care what he said because there were more rides walking his way and he was already upset with himself for letting her come along. Thin and bony as she was, she was taking up space and there was more money coming at him and very possibly better rides. He straightened the luggage in the trunk and slammed the lid.

"Where should I sit?" the woman asked.

Nick instinctively answered, "Sit in the back with the gentlemen."

"Oh, great, pack us in now," the man with the green tie said.

Nick ignored the remark and if the woman had any feelings about the matter, she didn't say. "Where should I sit back here?" she asked.

"Sit in the middle."

"But I can't see," she said.

"You can see on the way back," Nick said. They all got in the cab and Nick quickly drove away.

"If we're both going to different places, why don't we share the meter?" Green Tie asked.

"Because if you were going to the Bonaventure by yourself then it would have cost you sixteen, but I'm giving it to you for thirteen."

"But this man is paying full fare."

"Yes, he is."

The bald-headed man's frustration with the guy wearing the green tie began to audibly surface. "It's so nice to have these financial matters worked out for me. I only happen to be chief accountant and partner at a large firm."

Nick grinned and half turned to green tie. "Listen, it's thirteen for you and the meter for him. If you don't like it, I'll take you back to the airport and you can get another cab. No charge."

"Ha, ha, very funny," the man in the green tie said. Then he paused in thought, glanced at the woman and asked, "How much is she paying?"

"She?" Nick asked.

"Yes, this woman sitting one inch away from me."

"She's not paying for the ride down; she's paying for the ride back."

"Oh, that's just too beautiful," the guy said with genuine distress.

"Hey, relax, will you? Enjoy the ride. I'm driving my cab and I'm supposed to get paid for it. You're riding in it and getting to your destination and so you have to pay."

"Yeah, great, I get to give somebody a tour, too. I got to ride with this accountant guy, give the lady a tour, and pay full fare."

The bald man spoke up again. "Must I really listen to you go on and on about this? I've had a very tough and unsuccessful week and you are just about driving me nuts."

"It's easy for you, you're going home first," Green Tie retorted.

Nick directed his words to Green Tie. "Listen, you're behaving like a jerk. You're here, you might as well have a conversation, enjoy the company, and the enjoy the ride."

Nick watched as the guy got red in the face but realized his only options were to accept the situation or get out. He gradually responded to Nick's suggestion and turned to the woman. Glancing back to the mirror, Nick inwardly nodded at the progress. "Where you flying to?" the man asked.

"Off to San Antonio."

"Texas is one of those places they should have left to the Mexicans."

That ended the conversation for a few minutes until the woman stared into the rearview mirror and complained, "I can't see anything from back here."

"We'll work it out later, it's the same sights both ways," Nick said. He disliked people riding up front.

She turned to the bald man and asked, "Why'd you have such a bad week?"

"My firm was arguing a case. A subcontractor put the wrong material and fire retardant in a whole line of children's sleepwear. We took the delivery, paid them, and now we have to dump the entire inventory."

"Do you want to have some flammable polysynthetic material melting all over some little baby's body?" she asked.

"Oh Christ, I know, I know," the man weakly protested. "I've heard it a thousand times. But it still hurts. We took a big hit for a little mistake that wasn't ours. We've got a huge inventory of the stuff."

Green Tie jumped in with advice. "Why don't you send them to South America or someplace, like manufactures do with banned pesticides and things?"

"We can't do that."

"Sure you can. Why not?" The man with the green tie queried.

"Fucking regulations. Oh, excuse me," he said, looking at the woman.

She said nothing and turned away from him, not because of the swear word but because of his lack of strong character.

"Well, you did the right thing," Nick said.

"Yeah," the bald man replied, but Nick didn't think the guy sounded convinced.

They rode on in silence and Nick dropped the bald guy in Hancock Park and took Wilshire downtown. The woman slid across the seat as far away from Green Tie as her bony frame could. He thought the ride down Wilshire might give the woman a view of some of LA, despite her back seat sight line. As they continued in silence, Nick had a thought. *If Downtown LA was basically where Wilshire Boulevard ended, amid the hotels and office buildings, then where was uptown?* LA was a city with no uptown.

At the entrance of the Bonaventure, Nick noticed several cabs waiting and was thankful for the woman's tour and the paid ride back to the airport. The woman got out of the cab when the man did and looked up at the towering, modern hotel and the tubular exterior elevators rapidly hauling guests upward. The doorman grabbed the luggage, and, with some exaggerated deliberation, Green Tie gave Nick exactly thirteen dollars and headed into the hotel.

The woman moved to the front passenger side of the cab. "May I sit up front?"

"Yeah, I guess so." Nick didn't want to hear her complain again about the lack of view. She glanced down at Nick's bag and moved it to the center of the seat and got in. A moment later, Nick started the car and drove off. Cruising back down Wilshire Boulevard, the woman studied Nick's hack license in the drop-in frame, then sat back in the seat quietly peering out into the night, apparently deep in thought. Nick was glad he wasn't expected to do a running narrative about sights of the city.

He glanced over and briefly studied her. Now that he was used to her remarkably thin appearance, he noticed her clothes were clean and neat but inexpensively tailored. Her light blonde hair was evenly cut at the neck and topped with a small Jacqueline Kennedy pillbox-style hat. Considering her look and direct manner of speaking, Nick thought she must make her living at some sort of sales, but he couldn't be sure. By the time they got to La Brea

Avenue, he had tired of the stop-and-start driving with the traffic lights and he swung south. "I should start heading back to the airport if you're going to catch your plane."

"Yeah, I guess so. We're running out of time," she said in a meaningful way, though Nick couldn't surmise what she was implying. "Do you mind if I put this bag on the floor?" she asked, nodding at Nick's canvas bag.

"No, I guess not. Just keep it upright when you lower it." It was a curious request because she had plenty of room on the seat. The bag didn't take up much space and she was no wider than a sheet of paper. She handled the transfer of the bag smoothly and moved to the middle of the seat. She turned toward Nick and in so doing she lifted one leg half up onto the seat. Her coat parted and Nick glanced down and saw an impossibly thin thigh. Noticing his reaction, she smiled at him in a sly manner. Momentarily thrown, Nick started to make small talk. "Where'd you come in from? Oh, by the way, I'm Nick."

"No names," she said.

"Well, I noticed you were looking at mine."

"I looked at it, yes," she admitted. She reached in her bag, pulled out a cigarette, and lit up. "I came in from Hong Kong. Now I'm on my way to Texas. I travel a lot. I travel a *lot*," she said again for emphasis.

"What were you doing in Hong Kong?"

"I've got cancer," she said matter-of-factly. "There are things you can get over there that you can't get here."

"I see," he said, as much about her seemed to fall into place.

"I travel a lot. I'm never in one place more than a few days."

"That's got to be hard on the system."

"Yeah, but part of it is I'm searching."

"We're all searching for something. But it's tough on the road after a while when you don't have any friends."

"Oh, I make friends: bus drivers, airport people. You have to take things where you find them." She waited a moment for her comments to register, then gently took Nick's right hand off the steering wheel and placed it on her thigh. The gesture startled him but not as much as the feel of her thin leg. His hand involuntarily began to withdraw but she held onto it. "You're not going to deny a dying woman's last request, are you? Are you that ungallant?" Confused, he involuntarily let her pull his hand slowly down and she rested it on the inside of her thigh. When he lightly closed his hand, he nearly encircled her. The cab crossed the railroad tracks and began the ascent toward Baldwin Hills. "Are you married?" she asked.

"Yeah."

"So this is a big something, huh?"

"Yeah," he said hoarsely.

"Well, believe it or not, this is a big something for me, too. It's life or death." She reached over and put her fingers lightly onto Nick's groin. Her hands gently caressed him for a few moments and she stared intently down at him, watching him grow beneath the fabric of his pants. Nick glanced down and carefully noticed her hands for the first time. They were beautifully shaped but extremely thin and white. She had painted her manicured nails the same deep red as her Lips. Her fingers progressed with their teasing and exploration. It didn't take her long with the belt and zipper and, suddenly, to his own surprise, she had him and he was out. Her thin fingers began to work him and he felt himself continue to grow. She stared at Nick's face and for a lingering moment, his eyes left the road and he glanced at her. She was studying him. His face and eyes had gone soft with the hazy dizziness from being touched for the first time in a long while. His mouth went slack. The woman smiled, showing an even row of white teeth, and then she glanced down at his swollen hard penis.

"I guess I'll see the greater part of LA down here."

He almost laughed at her comment but her insistent fingers made rational thought less and less possible, and he was overwhelmed with a desire he had almost forgotten. He drove slowly and carefully so he could more easily concentrate on what was happening. As her fingers rubbed and lightly pinched his cock, she stared at his face, enjoying the feeling she was creating in him. Then she looked down and he heard her whisper, "Come to Mama." Her fingers continued to play with knowing grace and Nick watched with helpless fascination as the tiny woman dreamily bent down the rest of the way and took him between her lips and into her mouth.

Nick's head began to spin and he knew he had to stop the cab before he passed out or lost control. He had a flash of concern that if the cab was seen parked on that lonely stretch of road, it could only be assumed by passing drivers and police that something was wrong. Nick had to get off the road because it wasn't going to take much longer. At the top of the hill, he made a right onto Stocker, and, as he began his descent through the working oil rigs, he gratefully caught sight of a utility entrance by one of the fields. He turned into the opening. Dropping the car into park, he turned off the lights and the engine. The harsh security lights around the field were made softer by the evening's dampness and vapor from the oil wells. The birdlike pumps clanked their heavy metal beak-shaped counter weights up and down. Nick reached down and with both hands rubbed the woman's frail back and caressed her delicate blonde hair. She moaned approvingly and increased her attention on him. Nick looked around the surreal surroundings of the oil fields and had a momentary stroke of panic. He felt a sense of betrayal to Julianne's memory and his emotions were cleft in half, part of him feeling the eager attentions of the woman on his lap and part of him searching for Julianne and her forgiveness. Suddenly, the moment was upon him and his head sank back and he silently whispered Julianne's name as he shuddered and came. The woman comfortably stayed with him until he went completely soft. Then, she slowly sat up and looked at Nick, whose head was still resting back against the seat as he stared at the ceiling of the cab.

"Well, that was quite a big ride. Thanks," she said and put her arm up on the seat. After a moment, she gently and playfully pulled on Nick's ear. Though Nick was leaning back, he completely relaxed, sank into the seat, and for the first time in months completely let out his breath. "That was a heavy sigh," she said.

"Yeah, by way of thank you."

He reflexively reached down and zipped his pants and fastened his belt. The woman smiled and looked at Nick. Her lipstick was smeared across one of her cheeks and her pillbox hat lay alongside Nick's bag on the floor. She seemed pleased with herself and continued smiling. Nick felt he should say something, but felt awkward. He reached down and turned the key in the ignition and started the cab. Suddenly, her smile began to fade and a momentary look of fear came into her eyes. "Hold me for a moment, would you, honey?" she asked.

Nick felt a pain in his chest for the woman and he reached over and slowly pulled her close to him. He was startled again by the touch of her, like a small bird, and he gently held her. When she finally pulled away and looked at him, there were tears in her eyes. "I could miss a plane for some more of this, but I've got business to do on the other end." Nick hadn't planned to but he bent down and kissed her. It was a kiss he needed as much as she. As she hungrily returned his kiss, he could taste himself in her mouth and, in that moment of need and kindness, two lonely people shared their pain and fear.

When they arrived at the airport ten minutes later, she had cleaned her cheek and reapplied the deep red lipstick, and the hat sat primly on her head. As Nick got her bag from the trunk, she asked, "How much do I owe you?"

"Ride's on me."

"No, I said I was going to pay and I will." She formally gave him twenty dollars, just the way a lady should, picked up her small bag, and walked away. Nick folded his arms, leaned back against the cab, and watched her. He found himself mentally snapping a picture of her delicate frame walking through the wide doors and into the garish light of the terminal before quickly disappearing into the swirl of passengers.

His body was so altered from the experience with the woman that he searched to regain contact with his surroundings. Much of his anger and desperation was temporarily gone and he was left with a feeling of hollow loneliness. He rested against his cab until his next fare arrived. It was a middle-aged salesman going to the Sheraton Universal. Nick drifted into a sort of mental autopilot and drove slowly and quietly. At the hotel, he said the obligatory pleasantries to the salesman and returned to his cab. He drove the loop in front of the hotel and mentally traced the route to Hollywood Boulevard. He didn't want to sit in front of the hotel, even though at that hour with no other cab around, it could have been the cool play. He felt he had to continue hunting.

The thin little woman had changed him. He realized how badly he needed the touch of a woman, the comfort, even from a desperate little creature like the one he had just encountered. He was injured and alone with no woman to ease the pain of his life with her curves and softness. Loneliness was a feeling he was used to in his life, but when he'd married Julianne there had been a realization of how much he needed constant and loving companionship. The frail woman had matched his need with hers, and it all had seemed so logical and natural. Now he was left again with a void, and with Julianne gone he understood how desperately he missed Melissa. He missed her spirit, her inquisitiveness, her hugs, the smell and smoothness of her tiny body. It had been another female's smell in the apartment and he had gotten to love it. By the time he drove past the Hollywood Bowl onto Highland Avenue, he found himself weeping. He turned and cruised Hollywood Boulevard until he recovered. No one flagged him down and no killers showed themselves. As he left the tourist section behind, the boulevard before him darkened into a long black corridor randomly sprinkled with harsh white lights. Nick gripped the wheel and plunged in.

CHAPTER THIRTEEN

NICK WALKED INTO THE yard at ten to five in the afternoon. He noticed drivers were crowded around some cabs he hadn't seen before. They were not factory new, but late-model cars that had been repainted and renovated. They looked sharp and were quickly coveted by eager drivers. Nick wondered which, if any, was his. Walking to the dispatcher's window to put in his name, he was surprised to see Billy happily smiling up at him. "Your cab is on its way in. Clyde picked it up today but you can't drive it until tomorrow night. They've got to install and calibrate the meter and stuff." Vern, the regular dispatcher, came in the back door and Billy took off the headset and handed it to Vern, who silently sat down with practiced resignation. Billy came out of the shack. "I start dispatching regularly tomorrow night, same night you get your new cab." Billy grinned.

They walked together toward the long hurricane fence. Nick nodded to the new cabs. "Some new ones over there."

"Yeah, but yours is a hell of a lot better. Wait till you see it."

They continued walking across the oily blacktop past condemned cabs waiting for the mechanics to strip needed parts. Billy fished into his pocket and grabbed a half-smoked joint. He lit up and shared it with Nick. "Listen, I've been thinking about your problem. Something bothers me. One guy's white, one brown, and one black, that's an odd combination in a deal like that."

"How do you mean?" Nick asked.

"Well, I don't think these guys were any rock-and-roll band. The kind of mixed groups that hang together don't usually rob and rape people. They're together because of other things. They're on the same football team, they're actors, advertising executives, highway workers, or they might all be gay."

"They raped and murdered my wife."

Billy glanced at Nick and then down at his beatup dark brown hiking shoes. "Once somebody tells me something like that, I don't forget it."

Nick felt a flush of embarrassment from Billy's retort, then thought about what he had implied with the homosexual angle, and offered, "But gay guys don't usually rape women."

"Sometimes guys are bisexual, especially if they've been in prison for a long time. No big deal, just how it is," Billy offered.

Nick felt like a jerk. He wasn't thinking clearly and wasn't listening. He was letting his emotions color what he was seeing, hearing, and saying. "They raped her and murdered her. That's what went down," Nick said, reassembling the big facts in his head.

"Do the police have any idea which guys raped her?"

Nick was getting uncomfortable with the conversation, but he went along with it. "No."

"Well, I've got a way loose rounded-out theory. Want to hear it?" Billy asked.

"Sure."

"What brought these three guys together was drugs, or the cameras, or both. They needed to score some money so they could buy. Maybe the white guy and Mexican guy hung out together, maybe not, but they probably did."

Nick took a toke and blew the smoke from his inhalation into the air and watched it expand outward, disappearing against the darkening sky.

"So the black guy says he knows where some money or camera equipment is. I think it's the black guy because otherwise the white and brown don't need him. If there were two black guys and one white guy, it would be the black guys that needed the white guy. "

Nick didn't argue. It was starting to fit.

"The black guy shows them where the place is. They see you leave and they bust in, but the wife and kid are there. The black guy didn't know about them or anybody being home." Billy looked down at the blacktop, shrugged his slight shoulders, and said quietly, "And the rest you know about."

"I don't know everything about it. L ke who raped her, who they are, nothing."

"Well, you said that the black guy reacted in a very female way when he saw you."

"Yeah, he threw his hand to his mouth like this," he put his hand to his mouth in feign shock, "and kind of shrunk back. More like Greta Garbc than some tough dude I saw plenty of that in New York."

"So, that's a break because if the guy was hustling scores or tricks, you know, a street fag, it tightens where he might hang out, the boardwalk or Hollywood."

Arnie had totally broken Nick of the habit of calling gay men fags, but he understood the implications of what Billy was telling him.

Suddenly, Billy's name was called on the speaker. Billy waved across the yard to Vern, flicked the roach out through the chain-link fence, and turned back to Nick. "We'l keep talking about this. See ya out there."

Nick watched Billy walk off slip into his cab, and power out. Leaning back against the fence, Nick closed his eyes for a moment as the grass began to do its thing. As the cold months wore away, the sun set later. He felt the setting sun brushing him with the last warm rays of the day and became acutely aware of the mechanical sounds of cabs being serviced and driving in and out of the yard. Suddenly, Nick sensed a change; a silence came over the men and the mechanical sounds halted. He opened his eyes to see what was going on and immediately spotted an impeccably clean cab pull up to the mechanic's shack.

As Clyde opened the door and got out, drivers immediately converged around the cab. It was a machine so far superior to anything new or old that had ever come into the yard everyone was instantly in awe. Nick didn't want to join the rush, and resisted the impulse to walk over. Instead, he walked to the shack and waited for Clyde to turn the cab over to the mechanics and go to the dispatcher. Clyde was doggedly pursued by night drivers wanting to know how he got the cab and who was going to be driving it at night. He shyly muttered something about how the cab was spoken for at night, but the drivers were not to be put off. "Let me drive that cab, man, I'll give you ten bucks a night," Nick heard one man say.

"I'll take good care of that cab for you, brother," another said.

Clyde came up to the window where Nick was waiting. "We'll talk about this some other time, instead of in front of all these guys, okay?" Clyde asked quietly.

Nick nodded and strolled away. Clyde handed in his paperwork and walked out of the yard. One particularly aggressive driver followed Clyde out of the lot, and Nick ambled over to the gate to make sure Clyde was going to be all right. He watched Clyde walk down the block, turn to the man, shake his head, and get into his car. The man came back to the yard, hands thrust deep into his pockets with a mean look on his face. Clyde drove by Nick and gave a light nod of acknowledgment. The aggressive drivers chasing after Clyde reminded Nick of reporters and photographers swarming around a man who had firsthand information on a story with blood in it.

Walking back into the yard, Nick saw Manuel, the chief mechanic, get into the cool cab and drive it into the garage port. Nick allowed himself to walk close by the cab and its admirers on his way back to the fence. The cab's body was perfectly straight, without a dent or undulation. It had been painted the yellow and blue colors of the company and numbered 405. Nick studied it more carefully and noticed it sat evenly on four new tires. Glancing at the interior, he saw it was immaculate. Letting his eyes drift down to the trunk, he confirmed his suspicion that the cab was a Ford LTD. He didn't have to look—he knew instinctively the car had the big V-8 engine and all the interior luxury items that model chose to offer. About the time he got to his familiar position at the fence, he heard his name called. At the dispatcher's window, Vern looked at him and asked, "How you like your new ride, Nick?"

Nick was happy with the question because it meant it was officially recognized he'd be driving it. "It's the best-looking thing I've seen outside a show room."

Vern nodded. "If I was still driving, I'd have loved to have that cab."

"How come you don't drive anymore, Vern?"

"It's too crazy out there. I got a wife and kids."

"Well, I'm glad you're not driving because if you were, you'd probably get the cab."

"That's the truth," Vern said. "You're lucky to get it."

"Yeah, I know,"

"But your luck hasn't started yet. Tonight you're driving one-four-four," Vern said as he handed Nick the trip sheet.

When Nick heard the low number, he automatically knew he was in trouble. He thought momentarily Vern was messing with him because he was getting the beautiful new cab. He liked Vern, but this time he gave him a hard look.

"I thought I'd have a decent cab for you tonight, but all the regulars are already out driving them. So if you want to get out right away, you got one-four-four."

Nick looked over at the cab and shook his head ruefully. He knew the cab; he had seen it at the airport a few times. It was a smoker, totally trashed, but Nick had the itch to go. "I'll take it."

"Maybe you can switch it out later."

"We'll, see. One more night won't kill me," Nick said, heading toward the crumbling cab. Somehow, Nick still had the feeling Vern was playing games by dealing him the near wreck, but he didn't mind too much because the step from 144 to 405 would be all the more sweet. He glanced over at his new cab. "Four-o-five, you're going to make a big difference in my life." Turning to 144, he knew his tips would drop that night. The million-mile cab sat at a slightly off-kilter angle on the oily blacktop. "You belong in a compactor, old Mr. One-Four-Four."

There had been a lot of pressure on the company from the Transit Authority to get the old cabs off the street. After the washout of Yellow Cab, they had been lenient because there were not enough to service the city. Enough time had gone by now, many spectacular accidents with the old clunkers had occurred, and they were leaning on the cab companies again to upgrade and upgrade fast. But business was very good, and though they were bringing in newer cabs, they kept the old ones on and simply added more drivers. As the fleets grew, Nick couldn't help but notice business was starting to get increasingly tight on the streets. Competition was on the rise.

Nick walked once around the cab to make sure it had four tires and no recent damage they could blame him for when he came in later. Although there were a lot of dents, they were all weeks, months, or years old. Looking inside the cab, he saw two McDonald's coffee cups on the seat. Instinct told him what was next. He looked under the front seat and confirmed his hunch by removing a McDonald's bag crammed full of crushed containers, soiled napkins, and bleeding micro ketchup packets. With 405, he'd never follow a slovenly driver or have a cab like this again. Nick speculated the day driver was merely reflecting his low opinion of the car, then realized the slob probably could have had a Rolls-Royce and still left it a mess. The ashtray was full and the windshield looked as if it had been brushed with used fry oil. He jumped to the important stuff, lest he clean up a car that wouldn't move. The cab's fluids were all at the proper levels and it was gassed up. The preceding driver had at least done the mechanical check. Putting the key into the ignition, he snapped it over and the engine merely groaned. Nick tried pumping the gas pedal and after uttering a few coughs like a sick patient, the engine reluctantly rattled to life. Nick ran it up to a high rev and held it there. The engine seemed to settle in and hold the rev fairly steady, so Nick knew it would probably run the night. He finished cleaning the cab, got in, and dropped it into gear. It took a moment, but he was rewarded with a loud clunking sound as the transmission managed to engage. He drove out of the yard into the gathering darkness and began his hunt.

The night seemed to have an odd spin to it as the rattling cab and fares led him away from the yard. Five hours later, Nick found himself in Downtown LA and he got a quick fare off the bus station. An old woman had just come back from San Diego and probably Mexico before that. She was only going to Sixth Street near Bonnie Brae, but Nick was thankful to be working his way back toward the Westside. He didn't trust the cab too far from the garage. The woman sat silently in the back seat with her bag held carefully in the center of her lap. She had a kindly face and Nick could sense the grace in her presence.

Arriving at the woman's destination, Nick got out of the cab, walked around, and opened the door. She gathered up her belongings and with surprising agility, spun her legs around on the seat toward the open door, stepped out of the cab and up onto the curb. "*Muchas, gracias,*" the old lady said.

"*De nada,*" Nick said and watched her walk off and step into a three-story apartment building.

Sweet old thing, he thought to himself as he walked around the front of his cab and got in. Through the windshield, he stared down the street to the intersection of Sixth and Alvarado. There was a cabstand on the west side of Alvarado next to MacArthur Park. Nick made out the landmark sign of Langer's Delicatessen and nodded his head in recognition. Staring at their beckoning neon sign, he realized he was hungry. The long nights and resulting exhaustion were taking their toll on his regime. He'd missed going shopping for days and hadn't packed his customary lunch. He'd heard a few things about Langer's and it was supposed to be New York "authentic." It had been a while since he'd had anything like that, and the thought of pastrami on rye with hot French mustard began to stir him. Deciding, he drove to the cabstand, walked over to Langer's, and treated himself to a beer and anticipated sandwich. For a moment, it did feel like New York.

Arriving back at the cab, he slipped in behind the wheel, sat for a moment, and became aware of the pastrami grease emanating from his stomach and throughout his body, like an oil spill in a river.

During his odd reverie, a young black man knocked at his window and, after glancing at him, Nick pulled up the lock on the back door. Suddenly, two other figures appeared and three teenage guys immediately slipped into the back seat and slammed the doors closed. The lingering smell of pastrami was quickly replaced with the real smell of trouble. "Drive," ordered a voice from the back seat.

Nick turned around and faced them. "No."

The young men were seated rigidly in the back seat. They were slender and did not appear very tall. Dressed in the black ghetto version of sharp, they were definitely trying to be serious and cool, but Nick had thrown them by refusing to drive and turning around to stare. They groped at the unexpected turn in their plan. As he studied them, Nick figured them to be around sixteen or seventeen years old.

"What you lookin' at, man?" demanded the one nearest the passenger door side. He wore a deep purple colored beret.

"I'm looking at you guys."

"Well, quit looking and drive."

"No."

"What do you mean, 'no'?" demanded the one in the middle, as he shifted a little in his seat and pulled at the scarf around his neck.

"By 'no,' I mean, no. I don't drive anywhere unless I have a destination. I don't just drive around with three guys in the back seat not knowing where I'm going."

"We're going to Eighteenth Street and Central," said the kid with the purple beret.

Nick called the dispatcher. "One-four-four, going to Eighteenth and Central.

"Sounds like fun," the dispatcher said and clicked off.

Nick had a flash of fear and uncertainty. The whole setup didn't seem right. As he pulled away from the curb, the kid with the scarf confirmed his fears by asking, "You cab drivers do all right, don't you? You make some heavy bread."

Nick responded to the lack of subtlety, "Are you kidding me? You don't make hardly shit in this job. Figure, man, otherwise everybody be doing it."

"Yeah, but you got to get some bread coming through here. I mean, that's the nature of the thing."

"Well, look at it this way. I came out at ten o'clock tonight 'cause I'm a night driver. I've been cruising around for an hour, looking for a fare. I finally pick up a cleaning lady and get five dollars. My cut is forty percent, so I've been working two hours for a little over two dollars. No, man, this business sucks. Take my advice, stay in school and learn something."

That was enough for the kid in the purple beret. "Pull over, man. We'll get out here."

Nick was suddenly happy. He had actually talked the guys out of ripping him off or worse. He pulled over to the curb as the meter clicked up to $1.50. Shutting the meter, Nick got out of the cab and walked to the sidewalk. There were still people on that part of Alvarado and Nick wasn't taking any chances sitting behind the wheel with his back to the kids. He felt safer out of the cab. The kid with the beret got out, paid Nick exactly $1.50, and the punks turned and walked up the street in the direction they came from. Nick heard the kid with the scarf complaining, "Goddamn, what kind of shit was that…?"

Nick could see they were upset. They had made a dollar-and-a-half investment instead of getting some money. Nick allowed himself to be a little smug. He drove back to the cabstand on Alvarado, parked, and went back across the street to Langer's to use the bathroom.

When he got back to his cab, he noticed a newspaper on the floor in the back seat. He unlocked the doors reached in and picked up the paper. The dispatcher's voice cracked in, calling for a cab downtown. It took Nick a moment to get to the front seat to answer. By the time he did, he lost the order to another cab. Frustrated, he pulled out a roach from inside a matchbook, rolled the window down halfway, lit up, and concentrated on his next move.

The punks had walked the five blocks back to MacArthur Park. They had been arguing whether they should have ripped Nick off and how much money the driver was actually holding. They had almost no money left, were hungry, and wanted to score. Once in the park, they stopped not too far from the cabstand to determine what they should do next. Seeing Nick's cab, they began to reconsider. They collectively agreed the driver had to have more than the old lady's five dollars and their buck and a half. They were feeling conned. They wanted to set things straight. Staying back in the shadows they had watched Nick come back across the street from Langer's and get into his cab. They waited a few minutes to make sure everything looked right, then made a wide arc behind the cab and approached from the rear, staying clear of the mirrors.

Inside, Nick took a last hit off the roach and put the small burning remains on his moist tongue and swallowed. He rolled his window down all the way and let the smoke drift outside. As he did so, he came to a decision. He decided to drive west on Wilshire and see what he could pick off the hotels along the way. If nothing turned up, he'd cut up La Brea to Sunset and cruise the Strip, hunting along there. As he reached for the ignition, he heard his rear doors pulled open and the punks quickly slid inside.

"We decided we're goin' home, man. Take us up to Forty-Seventh and Hoover."

"No can do," Nick said. "I just got a call for a pickup at the Hilton. I'll call you guys another cab."

With amazing quickness, the kid with the scarf pulled a .38 revolver with a four-inch barrel out from under his jacket and pressed it to the back of Nick's neck. "Start the car, motherfucker, start the car."

The guy under the beret suddenly sniffed the air inside the cab and announced, "This motherfuckers smoking some weed, man."

"We gonna help us to that shit, too," said the silent one.

"Smells like some righteous boo. How much of that weed you got, man?" asked the guy with the gun.

"I carry enough for two or three joints. I'll roll you a couple and you can go off and smoke it but I ain't driving you anywhere."

"You ain't driving?" asked beret kid incredulously.

The kid with the gun abruptly jabbed Nick in the back of the head with the tip of the barrel so hard Nick had a second of blackness and could feel blood start to trickle out of a half-moon-shaped cut in his scalp. "You drive this car, motherfucker!" the kid screamed.

The blood slowly flowed down the back of Nicks neck. He shook his head in an effort to throw off the dizziness and stall for time to think. If he got out of the cab, they'd probably shoot him. If he didn't pump the accelerator, the old cab probably wouldn't start and the tired battery would run down fast, so Nick turned on the lights to increase the drain on the battery and avoided stepping on the gas. Turning the ignition key, the old engine groaned for a few moments and then caught and sputtered to life despite Nick's idle foot. Nick winced at the old machine's betrayal. "Drive, motherfucker, or I'll waste you right here," said the gunman.

"And don't go usin' that radio thing," said the kid in the beret.

Nick cursed silently to himself and, stalling for time, he slowly reached over to start the meter. "Hold it man, what you doin'?" the guy with the gun asked.

"Got to start the meter, otherwise the light stays on the top of the cab. People see you in the cab with the light on, they'll think I'm either high-flagging or there's a problem."

"Oh yeah, why you doin' that?" Purple Beret asked.

"Hey, when I drive somebody someplace, I start the meter. You guys are gonna pay for the fare, aren't you?"

The guy with the beret reached over and pulled the gunman's hand down—to keep the gun from view. The one with the gun said, "Okay, man, go ahead. Start the meter."

Nick reached over and flipped the flag.

The one with the beret turned to the gunman and asked, "You gonna pay this, man?"

The gunman turned to him and grinned. "Yeah, I'm gonna pay him. I'll give him a big tip, too." The young men looked at the pistol and laughed.

"Yeah, man, give him some big tips," said the quiet one, and more laughter came from the back seat. They suddenly realized Nick hadn't driven anywhere. The gunman leaned forward and, holding his scarf with one hand and pressing the gun into the back of the driver's seat with the other, hissed, "You drive this car motherfucker, now. I can pop you six times through this seat and no one will hear shit. Get this cab moving."

Nick dropped the car into second and started slowly forward. He pulled up to the light at Sixth and Alvarado. It was red. Nick tried to examine the situation and not panic. The least the kids would do was rob him, but it would probably go beyond that because Nick could clearly identify them all and they seemed up for anything. He sensed the tension in the back seat and was aware of the kid with the scarf leaning forward and aiming the gun at his back. He thought of the knife in his pocket but knew that wouldn't help, and down the line it might even be a liability when and if they discovered it. He came to a bitter conclusion. *These little fuckers are going to waste me.*

Nick looked around. There was still a little activity on the sidewalks. That was positive. Before him, the street made a slight rise through an area bordered by low-grade shops and restaurants but Nick knew, as Alvarado descended on an angle toward the distant freeway, the area would become increasingly dark, and there would be fewer cars and no one on the streets. He would be at their mercy. While there were still pedestrians around, he had to do something immediate. Across the four-lane street, he stared at the nearest parked car. It was an old station wagon illegally parked in a red zone at the corner. He saw no one in it and no one directly behind his car. The light changed to green. Nick dropped the transmission into low, eased the taxi forward a few feet and then stomped the gas pedal to the floor. Surprised, the cab lurched ahead like an old nag stung by a bee. The guy leaning forward with the gun was involuntarily thrown back against the rear seat with his friends. About the time he recovered enough to try and sit up and possibly shoot, he watched incredulously as Nick popped the gearshift into neutral, opened his door, and rolled out the cab.

Nick nearly made it out clean, but when his foot slipped off the gas and he rolled out the door, his shoe got hooked under the worn steel break pedal. His shoe tore loose and Nick's leg was violently twisted and his foot gouged from the steel.

The gunman instinctively tried to shoot Nick as he fell onto the street, but his friends' distress distracted. They were screaming frantically as the driverless cab headed toward a crash with the parked car. The gunman realized too late what was happening and put his hands up in defense. The cab crashed violently into the rear of the battered old station wagon and hurled the three young men forward. There was a moment's confusion as they clawed and scrambled over one another to get out of the cab.

Cars momentarily stopped in disarray. Nick got up and, favoring his wrenched leg, skipped away from the cab toward the opposite lanes. Along with a gathering crowd, Nick watched as the three punks tumbled out both sides of the cab. Bewildered, they stared at the growing number of people advancing toward the wreck. A moment later, they turned and ran through the last opening in the tightening circle and quickly disappeared from view.

Nick limped awkwardly as he returned to inspect the damage. The walk across the grime- and chewing-gum-spotted street attacked his sock as blood greedily entered the soft wool, making it soggy and loose.

He could see the old wagon had taken the hit pretty well. However, turning toward the front of the cab, he confirmed he wouldn't be going anywhere in Taxi 144 that night. The station wagon had risen up over 144's bumper and brutally crashed backward into the cab's grill. As the grill caved inward, fractured pieces of it stabbed their way into the radiator. Nick watched as yellow-green toxic coolant drained from the impaled radiator, ran to the corner sewer, and began its long slow journey to Santa Monica Bay.

The driver's door was impossibly sprung from being open at impact and refused Nick's efforts to close it. Nick hobbled around the back end of the taxi as the front and side was littered with shards of glass. The engine had died with the collision but, regardless, Nick leaned inside the cab and switched off the ignition. Suddenly, he was aware of a red glow infusing the cab's interior. He thought possibly he might be passing out, but the sound of a police loud speaker crackled. Nick looked up as the speaker bellowed. "Step out and away from the cab, keep your hands up and move over to the hood of the car."

Nick wanted to bend down and get his shoe but he knew that could be a fatal mistake. He didn't want nervous officers shooting him full of holes, so he did as instructed. Getting out, he hopped along on his good foot through shards of glass to the front of the cab. He immediately felt himself being patted down for weapons, drugs, whatever. "Remove your belongings from your pockets and put them on the hood."

Nick complied but decided to speak before the cops cuffed him and hauled him away. "You should be catching the guys who just tried to rip me off instead of wasting your time with me."

The cop said nothing. Nick glanced up and saw his partner, a powerfully built African-American cop talking to some people on the sidewalk. After a moment, the cop left the sidewalk and came over and nodded for the other officer to join him. "Stay as you are, hands on the hood of the car," the first officer said and left Nick to confer with his partner.

Still a little numb, Nick tried to carefully develop his reasoning for the anticipated search and interrogation. He thought about the can of weed in his bag as well as the bottle of Dos Equis. Well, he thought, there wasn't enough smoke to get him into serious trouble. The beer was unopened and the weed was less than a fifteenth of a lid. If the cops asked, he'll claim it was his stash for when he got off work, or better yet, he had found it in the cab earlier. The knife might be another story, but it was closed and not on his person. Still, the weed, beer, and knife together didn't present a positive image. *This is gonna be trouble,* Nick thought.

The cops sauntered over to him. The one who had patted him down asked, "You say you were getting robbed?"

"That's right. Three teenage kids, black. One with a purple beret and one wearing a long scarf. They ran off into the park. Why don't you get in your car and go look for them instead of jacking me around?"

"You sure you're not dreaming this up?" asked the black cop.

"Yeah, that's right," said Nick. "Every time someone gets into my taxi, I always roll out the door and crash my cab into a parked car."

"Don't be a wiseass," the first cop said.

The cops walked away again. He was getting to dislike the LAPD. He longed for the cops of New York. He knew those guys from experience. Despite a certain authority trip, the New York guys with their ill-fitting uniforms had some humanity going and a bunch of them even came from his old neighborhood. But these

LA guys, where the hell did they come from? He couldn't get a grip on it. The two cops walked back over to him. "We'll need a statement. Tell us what happened."

"I want to call my dispatcher and tell him what's up, so they can get a tow truck here and get this heap off the street. This cab is finished."

The cops nodded and Nick reached in and turned on the ignition and picked up the hand mike. As he did so, the first cop shined his flashlight inside the cab for a cursory inspection. "One-four-four," Nick said.

The dispatcher shot back. "One-four-four?"

"I've had an attempted robbery and an accident. I'm on the corner of Sixth and Alvarado. We need a tow, for sure."

"Are you or anyone else injured?"

"Nothing serious I know of," Nick said, despite his throbbing leg, foot, and aching head.

"We'll have a tow there in twenty minutes. Meantime, you'll have to make a statement to the police. Do you want us to call them?"

"Won't be necessary. They're right here on my ass. Over."

"Check, one-four-four," the dispatcher said and the radio went dead.

Nick switched off the ignition and turned to the cops. "I guess I've got some paperwork to do."

"Just step up onto the curb and we'll bring it to you," the black cop said.

"How did you get that cut on the back of your head?" the other cop asked.

Nick smiled ruefully. "One of the guys head-jabbed me with the barrel of a gun."

"That's assault with a deadly weapon."

"I can tell," said Nick.

"That's more paperwork," said the cop.

The black cop returned with the accident and robbery forms. Nick reached into the cab and brought out his shoe and slipped it onto his bloody foot without lacing it. The flow of blood was beginning to diminish and coagulate with the blood on his sock.

"You want us to call a paramedic?" the cop asked.

"This can wait, but here's what I would like: I want you to note that the station wagon was illegally parked and there was no one in it or injured. I'll leave a note on the guy's windshield, but I don't want the company to have to buy him a new Cadillac."

The policeman grunted with what Nick took to be a grudgingly affirmative response. He shook his head at the fact that the two cops never made a move to catch the punks. Maybe they called it in and another patrol car was making the search, but Nick didn't have much faith in the notion.

By the time he finished the paperwork, the tow truck from the yard showed up. He was surprised to see Manuel, the chief mechanic, driving it. *Manuel must work sixteen-hour days,* Nick thought. Manuel walked over to him, glanced at the cab, then back to Nick. "Night mechanic sick and *mucho* cabs to service."

I hope 405 is one of them, Nick thought to himself.

As they towed 144's corpse back to the yard, Nick examined the cut on his foot. There was a nasty irregular slice along the side that was still oozing blood. He didn't like the idea of taking the time, but he'd have to get stitches. As Manuel drove, Nick filled out the backside of the trip sheet regarding the accident. He didn't want to hang out at the yard longer than necessary.

The dispatcher wanted to hear all the details. Nick begged off telling the long version, saying he had to get to the hospital to get stitched. He walked back to 144 where it had been ignominiously dropped near two other wrecks. Some things had bounced out of his bag at impact and he wanted to make sure he retrieved everything. Another look confirmed no one would see 144 on the road again, ever. Taking the small flashlight from his bag, he shined it around the floor and looked under the front seat where the McDonald's garbage had been. He noticed an odd, dark shape near the back of the driver's seat. Hopping around and opening the back door, he knelt down and shined the light under the seat. Neatly wedged against the seat's runners was the punk's gun. Nick pulled it out, slipped it inside his jacket, and limped from the yard.

Hoping it wouldn't be as busy as other hospitals, Nick went to the emergency room at Marina Mercy. It was a good decision. Almost immediately, a doctor by the name of Lombard came into the small room where Nick waited. He was an odd-looking little man with very pale skin and black hair slicked straight back. Dr. Lombard questioned him about how he got the cuts and Nick didn't mind telling him. Lombard got to work and seemed to take real pleasure in doing a good job of putting twenty-three stitches in Nick's foot and eight in his scalp and giving a tetanus shot.

When he left the hospital, his leg was throbbing and he wanted a drink. He had drunk the bottle of Dos Equis in his Camaro on the way to the emergency room, but it hadn't done much good. He needed a real drink. He stopped at Friday's in the Marina, which was the nearest bar he could find. The bartender apologized; they had already given last call. Nick looked at his watch and saw it was thirteen minutes before two. "Customers are allowed to drink until two," Nick said.

"Yes, but we stop serving at one thirty so people can finish their drinks and go home."

"You pour me a double tequila and I'll finish it in five seconds," Nick said.

"I'm sorry," the bartender replied. He noticed the back of Nick's blood-soaked shirt and added, "House rules."

Nick was getting to despise the rigid rules of California. If they chose, New York bars could stay open until 4:00 a.m. and if it was later than that, Nick knew a couple candy stores in lower Manhattan that served drinks at the soda counter from four until six when bars reopened. There had to be something like that in LA and he made a mental note to find it. Still feeling jangled, he drove home.

In the apartment, he closed the door, stepped into the kitchen, and dropped the keys on the table along with his tip money and the gun. He stared down at the pistol. It was a .38 Charter Arms Comanche with a four-inch barrel; it was an inexpensive gun and probably had an interesting history. He'd have to fire it sometime to make sure it was working and check its accuracy. Regardless, the bullets were real and so was the gun. At close range, it could kill you as well as a Howitzer.

Picking up a tequila bottle, he tempted fate by flipping it in the air several times before he quickly knocked down a couple stiff ones. He opened a beer, drank some from the bottle, went into the bedroom, and slowly got undressed. Favoring his bandaged foot and sore leg, he carefully got into bed. Lying there, he found he couldn't sleep. He glanced at the clock and saw it was twenty minutes before three. *Five hours before my usual bedtime.*

He closed his eyes again and, as he often did, considered he could be wasting his time driving. He could go around and look for the killers just as efficiently without a cab, even more so. But how could he make a living? He had to admit to himself, he welcomed the all-encompassing swirl of what he was doing. He feared what might happen if he let it go and stepped out into the void. The cab had become a destination in itself and he needed both its confinement and its mobility.

His thoughts returned to the evening's attempted robbery. What would the punks have done if he had told them the truth? At the time, he had $69.40. Would that have made it worthwhile to kill a man and risk prison? In his travels around the world he'd known of people killed for far less than a three-way split of $69.40. The kids had a gun and attitude like nothing could happen to them, and that was a dangerous thing. Nick was certain they would have shot him. Plenty of drivers had been killed in similar situations. Nick had read the statistics. The odds were one in two thousand you'd get killed while driving a cab. As a night driver, the odds were much greater.

Now Nick had their gun. The thought gave him no pleasure or comfort; it seemed like another complication. He had wanted one but never made an effort to buy one. Suddenly, a gun presented itself. Now that he had it, he felt things would never be the same. He didn't feel it would make him safer during the night. It was something to be held in reserve for the moment of discovery, when and if it ever came.

He remembered what Vern had said before he'd gone out earlier that night. "It's too crazy out there. I got a wife and kids."

Well, he didn't have a wife anymore, but he did have Melissa. He suddenly realized if he did get killed, Melissa would have nothing other than what Lillian was able to provide. He turned and looked at the picture of Melissa seated on Julianne's lap. He felt an unquenchable longing in his chest to see and hold her. Though he wanted to, it was too early to call Lillian's home. Gradually, fatigue and tequila spun him down into a fitful sleep.

CHAPTER FOURTEEN

WAKING UP, NICK'S EYES adjusted to the light and he found himself looking at Melissa's photograph from the same position when he'd passed out. A feeling of guilt and self-loathing overcame him. He felt selfish that he had thought of little but his obsession of catching the killers, while the most important and precious thing was right there in photo and life.

Before he went to work the next afternoon, Nick got out the telephone book and studied lists of insurance agents. Three hours later, he had initiated a $400,000 life insurance policy for Melissa. One half was to go to Lillian for Melissa's support and the other half to be held in trust for Melissa's education and future. It was the first insurance, other than car and theft, he'd ever had. He remembered with some bitterness, because of finances, he had let his New York theft insurance policy lapse when he'd come to California. The loss from the theft had been total. Whether driving a cab at night in a massive city or being a photojournalist in combat zones, the occupations were high risk. With Julianne gone, taking care of Melissa was the most important thing.

The business with the insurance company got Nick to the yard late. Clyde was waiting for him with the new cab. "I didn't want to leave the cab without you being here. Some of these guys are just waiting to swoop on it."

"I appreciate it. After what happened last night, I had some personal business to take care of."

"Yeah, everyone's been talking about your little adventure. You're not gonna go leaping out of four-o-five and shoot it into a truck, are you?

Nick grinned. "Not even if they put a gun to my head."

"Well, don't go getting yourself shot over it. It's just a car."

"No, it's more than that," Nick said. He looked at 405, then back at Clyde. "It's a whole new way of riding and looking at things. Thanks again for picking me."

Embarrassed by the thanks, Clyde turned his attention to the car. "I didn't get out with it because they didn't calibrate the meter until three. But I have driven it. It runs really good. The engine is strong. Everything works and the radio is exceptional."

"You mean the CB?" Nick asked.

"No, I mean the car radio. Got a really good stereo system." Nick nodded in appreciation. "Well, good luck with it and be careful out there."

Nick reached out and shook Clyde's hand. "Thanks, Clyde. I owe you."

Clyde looked at Nick's bandaged foot and loose open shoe. "You all right, after last night?"

"Yeah, I'll be fine," Nick said.

Nick watched as Clyde walked out of the yard, then turned and headed back toward the dispatcher's shack. His foot was beginning to throb. He walked carefully, trying not to limp and show how badly he was hurt. Individually, three different men came over to ask him if they could drive the cab when Nick wasn't driving. They all led with a comment about Nick's late-night adventure and asked for the story, but before Nick could relate anything, they asked him who had 405 when he wasn't driving it. The night driver called "Stepper" got right into Nick's face. "I need a cab like that man because I get out there and go, man, I just go. I'm a high booker and I been here way longer than you. I deserve that cab, man. If I can't have it, I should at least get it the two nights you don't drive."

Now, that's a different approach, Nick thought. He studied Stepper up close for the first time. His right index and middle fingers were stained with tobacco and his hands were gray with experience and lack of washing. He looked at Stepper's face and stared squarely at him for a long moment. It didn't put the guy off right away, but after a while Stepper looked down at Nick's knees. "I need a cab like that, man."

As though airbrushed against his pale white skin, there was a faint trace of yellow nicotine emanating from his lip up toward his right nostril illustrating where the cigarette was held when it wasn't between his fingers. His eyes were sunken and dark circles traced under them. His worn, black leather jacket was two sizes too small and his wrists stuck out from the cuffs, emphasizing his lanky form. The jacket rode an inch above his waist, showing the large belt buckle with the outline of a Harley Hog. Nick knew he had to set the guy straight right away. "Listen carefully, so you and anybody you talk to gets this. I drive six and seven nights a week just like you and when the car is not being driven by me or Clyde, it's one of the bosses in there decides who will. I can't and don't want to pick the driver. I wish you luck with finding a good cab, brother."

It took a little time but, finally, Stepper nodded his head and seemed to accept the situation. Nick stuck out his hand. "I've seen you around. My name's Nick."

"Mine's Elkins, but you can call me Stepper. Everybody does."

The two men lapsed into silence, then Stepper looked at Nick shrewdly. "Why you driving, man? You don't look like you should be here."

"If you are here, you should be."

Nick wanted to end it, but as he turned, Stepper reached out and grabbed him by the shoulder, leaned in, and whispered in Nick's ear, "We got to stand together against the niggers in this yard."

Nick glanced down at Stepper's hand and Stepper immediately removed it. Nick turned to face him and quietly asked, "What are you talking about?"

The guy looked momentarily nonplussed. "The niggers get in control of all the best fares because they've got the black guys dispatching." Stepper nodded toward Vern.

Nick glanced at Vern, then directly at Stepper. "Vern goes home at nine and then it's a white guy dispatching and a new white guy starts tonight. You're a night driver, so what's your beef?"

Stepper had a moment's confusion from having his theory blown, but then recovered. "You just see how many good fares that nigger Vern sends your way."

"Stepper, don't get me into that shit. As far as I can see, this is one of the few jobs where you can do your own thing. There's no point messing with it."

Stepper was getting to him, and Nick felt the familiar shell forming around himself. Then something odd happened, something that hadn't occurred in a long while. Nick wanted to shoot a picture. In particular, he wanted to shoot a picture of Stepper. The guy was a definite "leaper," as Nick used to call them. A face that leapt through the lens at you as though demanding a photo be taken. Usually, Nick found leapers to be either great personalities with expressive faces or conversely typically stereotypical persons but in a heightened way, as though the individual in question could define an entire class or group. But then, some leapers defied the pattern and went so far out they wound up in another dimension. Stepper was one of those. Reflexively, Nick wanted to take a picture as Stepper put his nicotine-stained finger up to the darkened shadow under his right eye and rubbed it in reaction to the rebuttal. Nick's impulse was fleeting, a snapshot taken at high-shutter speed.

Nick turned and crossed to the dispatcher's window realizing he had taken a mental picture of Stepper, and the negative burned into his memory. He wondered what Stepper did with his money. Driving thirteen hours a night, six nights a week, he must be making top-driver money. He certainly didn't spend it on his wardrobe. Maybe it went up his nostrils like the nicotine stain on his lip. Vern was on the radio and heavily into the business of rapidly tossing cabs around the city like cards from a casino dealer. Nick waited patiently. Finally. Vern reached over, picked up a trip ticket, wrote *405* in the cab identification box, and wordlessly passed it sideways. Nick took it and walked over to his new cab. He could feel the other drivers' eyes on him and he wanted to get out of there. Opening the door and slipping inside, he noticed with pleasure the wide, firm, and comfortable seat. He put the key in the ignition and turned it. Almost noiselessly, the engine jumped to life with muffled strength. Dropping it into gear, he drove out of the yard under review of the other drivers gaping with envy.

He drove to a quiet residential street in Venice, pulled to the curb, shut off the engine. Getting out slowly and painfully, he hobbled across the street. Small but creatively individualistic houses graced the street. Sharing the space were lawns sporting homemade sculptures, children's playhouses, and old-growth trees and palms. It was the area Julianne and he had decided they'd like to move to as soon as Nick's career was resurrected. At the time, it had been a modest enough dream; now it was abandoned. At the far corner, a tall slender young woman with waist-length black hair held a baby in her arms as she watered her early spring garden. Nick turned back to the car. He shielded his eyes as the sun set over the houses and squinted into the glow to admire the car's perfect outline. For the first time in a long while, he felt a little lucky. He crossed the street and circled the car once, stopping at the trunk. He popped it open. *Copious*, Nick thought. A word, Arnie, his first boss and mentor, had used excessively, but it rang home with Nick as he stared into the deep, wide trunk. He searched the metal in the slanting light and saw it all ran straight and true. The engine revealed itself to be a clean, huge, sturdy V-8. He inspected the wiring, radiator, hoses, and connections, rubbing his hands around the panels that ran over the curves and angles. No new panels or parts declared themselves. Nick stepped back and wondered at the unknown history of the car. Not hit and less than thirteen thousand miles on the odometer.

As the company owners fenced with the city over the license, the cab had sat idly outside the paint shop for weeks. Despite being recently washed, a light gray film covered all the windows, the result of smog baked on by hot Santa Ana winds. It was resistant to the window spray and towels but starting outside, slowly and painstakingly, he began its removal. The ammonia from the spray ate into his nose and lungs. Getting into the driver's seat, he stared at the windshield. "I've got a new lens," he said with genuine satisfaction, and set about spraying the windshield and the rearview mirror and cleaned them with the last of his "liberated" paper towels. Readjusting the now-clean mirror, his reflection leapt out at him. In the fading light, he noticed with some amusement the dark circles under his eyes and the intense, haggard look. "You keep at this too long and you'll wind up looking like Stepper," he warned his reflection.

He sat back and stared vacantly down the street, which glowed orange in the last minutes of the sunset. Nick allowed himself a moment of quiet, then reached for the microphone and called in. Resulting fares pulled him around until a rabbi gave him a short trip to Fairfax and Beverly. He decided to drop down and cruise Santa Monica Boulevard and check out his adaptation of Billy's theory. Nick was obsessing on particular sections of the city and a big candidate was the strip that ran from La Brea to Robertson Boulevard. At night, that mile and a half turned itself over to a hunk of the gay community—not the best of it, probably not the worst. It was a string of blocks starting just west of La Brea stretching past the darkened walls of Goldwyn Studio, restaurants, gay bars, and idiosyncratic businesses to Robertson Boulevard. On the east end, it was prime territory for male prostitutes. Sometimes they stood furtively in the shadows, at times languidly walking. Some paraded curbside in sequined drag or bare-chested bravado, waving their shirts, openly soliciting. The display was determined by their personalities and the LAPD. The gay prostitutes had held that turf for years like a gypsy caravan owns a country road. For Nick, it was now hunting territory for finding the young black man he'd seen in his apartment. He had driven through the area many times but apart from noticing the activity, he had refrained from looking too pointedly. He didn't want to send the wrong signal. This night was different. He had a plan.

It was Friday and the boys were out in large numbers hoping some nice guys would want to pluck them off the curbs and loosen their pants and payday wallets.

Heading west, Nick dropped the cab into second, maintaining a slow, steady pace. He noticed most of the young men were subdued, hanging back, while a few were more active in their self-assigned spaces. One, despite the chilly temperature, had taken off his shirt, displaying a well-built body. Others were half-dressed as females, wearing mesh stockings, shorts, and high-cut waist jackets. Nick's task was comparatively easy; the guy he sought was black. That eliminated two thirds of the gathering. But then as he searched, he wondered if one or both of the other killers were gay or bisexual?

According to the report Pearson had shown him, there had been no semen detected in Julianne's autopsy. Nick subsequently learned that was quite common with forcible rape. The act of rape is the important thing. If the thrill for some attackers is to penetrate and violate but not necessarily ejaculate, that makes the act of rape a whole other thing. It would be a direct assault and the sex, if one could call it that, would be more of a by-product. But then possibly Pearson's report was incomplete or Pearson was holding something back. He'd never know. By introducing the bisexuality equation, Nick found himself disoriented at the notion of having to check everybody. Nick stumbled at the myriad possibilities.

Many of the men on the street were around the ages of his wife's killers. Staring out at them, they stared back, for every passing car was a potential trick. He watched and speculated on what they were thinking. Was someone hiding in the back seat, was Nick simply going to pick up some boys and then take them to where the Johns were, was Nick looking himself? Young men licked their lips in a sensual way. Some moved their asses in an almost floating motion, while others flexed their powerful biceps. Nick suddenly remembered he'd seen an antithetical display during the early mornings when he was returning to the yard. Immigrant Latin American day laborers, who congregated at various corners around LA, had that same hungry look. They peered into the trucks and cars trying to make eye contact so the drivers would choose them out of the large gathering to do manual labor. But the boys of the night were different. They were into a service of a much more personal kind, more expensive, exciting, and dangerous.

Nick completed the run down the boulevard and no one flagged. Impulsively, Nick made a U-turn, drove back up to La Brea, hooked a right, and parked at the first open meter. It was near enough to the corner that Nick thought the cab would be safe. "Four-o-five."

"Four-o-five?" Billy called back.

"Going dark for about fifteen."

"Check."

Nick reached down into the bag and slipped out the pistol, wedging it down the back of his pants, pulling his sweater over it. Leaving the cab proved difficult. His back, leg, and especially his foot ached miserably from the previous evening's stunt.

When he started down the boulevard, he tried his best to walk slowly, casually. It wasn't hard. Without overstating it, his injured foot helped him legitimately walk leisurely, enabling him to look around. The atmosphere was palpable among the young men. At turns, they glanced at Nick suspiciously, flirtatiously, and with dismay brought about by the thought of possible competition. A few of them recognized him as a new face and asked casually, "What you looking for, honey?"

Others concluded he was an undercover cop. Most recognized he wasn't one of them and sensed he wasn't looking. But they were wrong. Nick was looking, but it wasn't for sex.

For his troubles, he saw no one bore the slightest resemblance to the men he sought. By the time he neared Fairfax, his foot and ankle were throbbing unbearably. He waited patiently until there were few passing cars, then crossed the street. As he did so, he forced his mind to refocus on the young black man. It was then that Nick remembered how Pearson had questioned him from every angle on details regarding the robbery and murder. It was on one of those angular mental forays that Pearson had led Nick to fleetingly recall seeing the slender black man the afternoon before the killing.

At the time, Nick was going to sell his Hasselblad and one of his Nikons. An old client had given Nick a job in Alaska. However, there was no immediate money for Julianne and Melissa with which to live while he was gone. He still had a full complement of equipment he could use. The other two cameras were a luxury with which he could part. He took Julianne and Melissa outside and the three of them walked the Venice Ocean Front Boardwalk while he photographed them with the last of the film in the Hasselblad. Arriving back at the apartment, Julianne took Melissa inside. Nick walked across the street exchanging the Hasselblad for the Olympus and shot off the last two exposures on the roll, capturing the building in which they lived.

It was during that time Rainey saw Nick. He watched as Nick rewound the film. Sensitive to people around his equipment, Nick glanced up the block and noticed him. Rainey crossed the street at an angle away from Nick and Nick finished putting his cameras into the bag then headed back into the old apartment building. Once Nick was inside, Rainey turned around and moved rapidly back up the street. He entered the open lobby door and listened as Nick walked the second floor toward his apartment. Rainey heard the key go into the door and he lightly trotted up the stairs and glimpsed Nick's door closing at the end of the hallway. Rainey quickly turned and split. Nick had forgotten about Rainey, but Rainey didn't forget about Nick and his cameras.

Rainey had gone to jail at eighteen and learned in prison his true attribute and talent lay in prostitution. He had given up breaking and entering because he lacked the courage and requisite mechanical skills, but he did make occasional money as a spotter. If he saw an opportunity, he would share it with one or two of the thieves he knew. They'd cut him in for a piece of the action. He had run into Cal and Jesse at a dealer's apartment in Oakwood and was introduced. He thought Cal and Jesse were there selling, rather than buying as he was doing. He overheard they had recently ripped off a couple of houses in Long Beach and scored pretty well. Rainey turned his full attention to the men and listened. Rainey didn't like to work with white guys, but sometimes one couldn't be choosy. At first glance, Cal and Jesse appeared cool and seemed like the type who wouldn't get caught. Rainey liked that. He told Jesse and Cal if he ever found anything good, he'd cut them in.

On the day Rainey discovered the potential camera score, he reached out to Cal and Jesse and met up with them on the Boardwalk. Rainey told them of Nick's place.

Rainey was intent on just selling the information, but the guys insisted he come along. They weren't going to allow themselves to get set up. Jesse stared hard at the hesitant black man. "Listen, Rainey, I'll ask you right out here in the street where you're safe. Are you setting us up? If you are, we're just walkin' away and nothing's goin' to happen."

"No, man, I wouldn't do that. Why would I do that?"

"Then how come if it's such a good score, you don't just go and do it yourself?" Jesse asked.

"I told you, I don't do that shit."

"You sure about this?" Jesse asked.

"Man, this dude's got cameras that are quality. It's quality shit and that's just what I know about. There's gotta be more."

Jesse reached out and lightly poked his finger into Rainey's chest. "So, I ask again, why don't you just go get them yourself?"

"Man, I don't carry no piece and the man what lives there is a tough-lookin' motherfucker. He comes back in while I'm there, he's gonna mess me up for sure."

Jesse laughed at Rainey's admission. He reached out, grabbed Rainey by the shirt and slowly pulled Rainey toward him. Just as suddenly, Jesse let Rainey loose and put his muscular arm around his shoulders. "Well, you just come along, Rainey. We'll look out for you. But if you're setting us up, you're gonna learn what gettin' messed up really means."

Snickering, Cal reached over and pinched Rainey on his ass, hard. "Puto."

Jesse put his hand in the center of Rainey's back and pushed him forward. "Show us where it is." After a moment's hesitation, Rainey started walking, turning the corner toward Nick's apartment. Jesse and Cal followed.

◄◖◗►

THE PAINFUL WALK THROUGH the scattered groups of young men had brought him no reward, and Nick sought relief by returning to 405. Lifting the pistol from behind his back, he rubbed the spot where it had pressed into his spine. Then he reached into the bag and exchanged the .38 for a bottle of Dos Equis. He opened it, took a large mouthful, and was rewarded as the warm amber liquid exploded with foam in his mouth. He pulled out a newly rolled joint and lit up. He switched the ignition to accessory, put down his window, and blew the rich smoke out into the night air.

Watching in the rearview mirror, he could observe the small groups of men on the corner. He started the car, bumped the heater to high, and lifted his throbbing leg onto the seat. He wondered why he had such a deep chill. For a moment he thought it was because of his foot. He realized walking among the young men made him feel as though he were on the right track. The possibility of actually confronting one or all of them was, for the first time, incredibly real.

Sliding his leg off the seat, he dropped the shift into gear, looped around, and cruised the rest of the boulevard with its bars, bookstores, and boutiques all catering to the local clientele. Just then, a young man ran out of a bar and flagged him down.

Nick watched as the young man got into the cab. He was not much older than eighteen, startlingly good-looking, with light blond hair that hung to the nape of his neck. He was upset and on the verge of tears. Nick stared at him and the boy turned immediately hostile. "Look, I don't want to talk. I just want to go home." Then, as an afterthought, he added derisively. "Home, ha." Nick continued to regard him, waiting, and the boy squirmed in frustration. "Well?" the boy demanded.

"You going to tell me where home is, or do I get the address telepathically?"

"Oh, my God," the young man called out. "Sorry. I'm going to student housing at UCLA. Do you know where it is?"

"Sure," Nick said.

He started the meter and drove off. The young man was silent for a while, but as Nick began to cut up to Sunset Boulevard, he started crying. For the most part, he stared out the window as the tears slowly trickled down his beautiful face. Sometimes he gathered himself to stop crying with a dab or two of a handkerchief until he groaned and started in again, hitting a constant level of quiet heartache. Nick didn't say anything but remembered from his apprenticeship experience with Arnie how gay men could be unbelievably supportive and could also be incredibly cruel. *This boy got the bad end*, Nick thought, then mentally slapped himself for the inadvertent pun. Nick had never gotten completely into the destructive life rhythm and acerbic banter Arnie had indulged in.

It wasn't until he hit the light at Beverly Glen and Sunset that he remembered to turn his CB radio back on. A moment later, he heard his cab called. "Four-o-five?" Billy questioned as though for the tenth time.

"Four-o-five."

"Haven't heard from you since you said you were going dark for fifteen. You go dark and we don't hear from you, we get nervous."

"Sorry, got preoccupied. Have a fare and going to the Westwood area."

"Call me when you drop."

"Check," Nick said.

It may or may not be a good thing to have a friend dispatching. He knew Billy wanted to show off and keep him hopping all night, but Nick liked operating anonymously. He dropped the kid off at one of the student dorms that sat high on the hill overlooking campus. *Nice spot*, Nick thought, but his opinion was tempered by the miserable appearance of the good-looking young man. The kid tipped him 10 percent and Nick watched the young man wipe his eyes and ready himself for the entrance into the dorm. It was still only nine o'clock and Nick could see movement in the dorm lobby. As he watched the kid walk away, he wondered what kind of a life he was going into.

"Four-o-five."

"Four-o-five," came the reply.

"I've dropped and I'm on the UCLA campus."

"Go to UCLA Medical Center Emergency and pick up a party there."

"Roger that." *That's handy*, Nick thought and drove across campus to the hospital emergency entrance, shut down his cab, and walked inside. A lone man was seated in a chair. Nick studied him and didn't like what he saw. The man was extremely overweight, in his late fifties, and dressed in a slovenly way. He seemed to have little awareness of what was going on around him. Hoping he was not the fare, Nick walked to registration. The woman behind the counter asked Nick if he was there for the pickup, and when Nick acknowledged he was, she nodded in the man's direction. Disappointed, Nick crossed to the man who slowly got to his feet and shuffled toward the exit. Nick walked a little ahead and opened the door, wondering all the while why he was being discharged when he looked in such bad shape. With effort, the man lowered himself into the taxi and Nick got in behind the wheel. "I'm going to Palms, near the corner of Motor and National." Nick dropped the new cab in gear and cut through the campus, hoping to make this fare as quick as possible. "I had a heart attack this morning," the man offered.

"You just had a heart attack and they let you out tonight?"

"They gave me some medicine," the man explained simply.

"It still seems a little extreme," Nick ventured.

"I'll be all right," the man said.

Nick glanced at him in the rearview mirror and didn't believe him. Although Nick was driving slowly, the curving ride along Motor Avenue began to take its toll. "I'm going to be sick," the man said.

"Wait!" Nick exclaimed. "I'll pull over." Nick hit the break and pulled toward the curb, but the man moved forward slightly and noisily threw up all over the floor, himself, and the seat. Nick's heart sank at the desecration of the new cab and he flushed with anger, but he found himself asking, "Are you all right, do you want to go back to the hospital?"

"No, I'll be fine. Just get me home."

Nick did just that. Despite the fact that the man had thrown up in his cab and tipped him only half a dollar, he watched with concern as the man walked into the small apartment building. *That guy isn't going to see the morning*, Nick thought. *I'll probably get a call to take him back to the hospital around five.* Then Nick corrected himself. *Dead men don't take cabs to the hospital; they go to the morgue.*

He drove to Lincoln Boulevard near Venice where there was a twenty-four-hour do-it-yourself car wash. Nick put quarters into the cash box, took the washing wand, and fired it directly onto the floor and back seat. It took three different deposits of quarters, but he finally felt he had blasted all the vomit from the car. He vacuumed the excess water, started the car, switched the air system to "Floor," and turned the heat on high.

As he drove toward the airport, he put down all the windows. Despite the hard washing, the dense odor of vomit hung so heavily Nick could taste and feel it in his body. "What a way to christen you," Nick said to the car. He hoped it wasn't an omen.

It was just before eleven when he stopped second up at United Airlines. He knew there wouldn't be a flight for twenty minutes, but he needed a break. His whole body was beginning to stiffen up. In places where there hadn't been any bruises in the morning, new ones were declaring themselves. He half hobbled to the men's room where he washed his hands and collected his nightly ration of paper towels.

His foot protested from the constant sitting position, so once back in the cab, he raised his leg onto the dash. The movement brought some relief. Sitting there, he felt the evening's close reconnaissance in West Hollywood had been promising. He realized with his new plan, he must continue to cruise the hangouts of the male prostitutes, including the bars. He wasn't excited about the idea of constantly combing the area and he especially didn't like the thought of going into gay bars. It wasn't that he cared about their existence one way or another, but he knew if he went in there searching, it would be misinterpreted and he'd get hit on. That would quickly get tiresome, but it was what the hunt required. Then a nagging thought entered his head. Was he way off base with the notion of the young black man being a gay hustler? Just because the young man was gay, if indeed he was, why would that have him pulling tricks on Santa Monica Boulevard? The thoughts fueled his frustration but he had to follow through. It was a plan, the only one that made any immediate sense, and instinct told him he was on the right track. He'd stick to it.

The theory had another advantage. The hustlers on the boulevard represented a small but very visible section of the community. Nick had no problem with hustlers of either sex. His predominant thought about prostitutes was they were some of the bravest people in life, or the most uncaring. There they were, getting into a car, an alley, or hotel room with anyone who said they had the money. Considering the potential danger made Nick shake his head in wonder. Then a funny notion hit him. He had strangers jumping into his cab sitting close behind and staring at the back of his neck all through the night. The thought made him briefly laugh out loud for the first time in a long while. The grin felt funny on his face.

CHAPTER FIFTEEN

C AL WAS DEPRESSED. THEY had made a bad estimate of what they'd get "storming the walls." Most of the houses had no high-grade jewelry. In two they found wall safes and had neither the skill, tools, nor time to crack them. Jesse insisted on taking some paintings and artwork but had bad taste and stole reproductions while passing by some small but valuable originals. It hadn't been going well, but then things got really bad. The last place on their list was an upscale condominium in Marina Del Rey. Hitting it, they discovered a beautiful young woman, alone. Jesse ordered Cal to collect the valuables while he took the woman into the bedroom. Jesse always took the women first, and even though Jesse was now having trouble getting hard, he still wouldn't let Cal step in. Jesse's selfishness burned at Cal, but he bit down on his anger and went into the bathroom. Taking off his gloves, he dropped his pants and sat on the toilet. Sitting there, Cal reasoned he should go first with the women because he could always get a stiff one going. Suddenly, he sensed another presence entering the condo and a moment later he heard a man's voice call out, "Honey?" A few seconds later, there were loud gunshots. Hastily exiting the bathroom, Cal put his hands all over the toilet, sink, walls, and door. Emerging, he saw a man lying on the floor. Blood was pumping out of his throat and his head had half exploded from the bullets of Jesse's gun. A moment later, he heard smashing glass and a shrill scream. He turned in time to see the young woman hurtle naked through the air and drop three stories to the lawn below. Jesse came hopping across the living room, pulling up his pants and yelling, "Let's go, let's go!"

As they roared away in their stolen van, Cal turned to Jesse in a fury. "See what shit you got us in now, killing that guy. That bitch can identify us, we left prints and we didn't get nothin', nothin'." For once, Jesse didn't say anything. He knew they had to get out of town. Victor Koss, their fence in El Monte, knew it as well. They walked out of his place with $5,500, less than a quarter of what they had estimated. Jesse further infuriated Cal by buying an ounce of cocaine at retail price: $1,900. Cal tried to do the math as to how much they had left when Jesse slapped Cal on the back. "Cal, don't get so worked up. When we get to my old buddy Steve's house, he's gonna take care of us and we'll be like bulls in fields of clover."

With Cal driving the Chevy Nova, they hit the road for Texas. Cal hoped the remaining money would last them for a while, but he didn't have much faith.

DETECTIVE STABILE DROVE HIS personal car into the garage of a tall building in Westwood Village. On the top floor of the building was Monty's, a restaurant with a great view of Beverly Hills and the surrounding Westside. It was a nice place to go after work, have a drink or two, maybe chat up a woman you wanted to get to know. Stabile, however, had no such plans. He waited in the underground garage until he saw the Cadillac belonging to Thomas Cleveland Williams slowly drive by. He got out of his car and walked around the corner, up the dimly lit ramp to where the Cadillac had parked, opened the rear door, and slid into the back seat. Big TC nodded to Mose who took the hint, got out of the car, and walked across the garage to wait. Stabile studied Big TC. The little man had gotten a couple more gold chains and they glowed against his dark brown skin. "You know, with all that gold hanging on you, you look like some kind of drug dealer," Stabile said.

"Drop the jokes, man. S'up?"

"There's a lot of heat coming down from the press, the city council, and the captain at my new division to produce serious arrests and convictions. With all the murders, gang activity, and drugs, things are out of control in the precinct. If it was in my old precinct it would be expected, but Venice is transitioning. Citizens are moving in and they want the place clean."

Big TC nodded toward the envelope on the seat between them. "That's what I pay you for, so I won't have to listen to this shit."

Stabile didn't make a move toward the envelope. "I'm going to repeat myself. There's a lot of dealing and a lot of killing going on there and the place is getting invaded by the middle class. They like the air by the beach, but they're fucking nervous and making noise. You know this can only go so far before people are going to have to go to jail. Sure, you pay me, so you won't have to go, but you've got to give me somebody, somebody good."

Big TC studied Stabile in that deadpan way that normally would bring most people knee-knocking fear, but Stabile knew the game. "All the money I pay you and you still dress like shit," Big TC said.

"I've got to be careful how I spend my dough. I can't go around dressing like some pimp. The guys in the station look at me like I'm a leper and I've got to bust some guys to look clean. You hear what I'm saying?"

Big TC heard it and he was beginning to get an idea or two. That's why he was the main man, and he explained, "I'm in a building phase in Venice right now, Lewis. So I can't go taking down any of my brothers. I can't take no losses. But there is one or two who are beginning to slide out of line. You wait six months or a year and I'll give you one."

"I can't wait a fucking year. In a year, we'll have the DEA swarming us like hornets and I'll be long gone. They'll put me on foot patrol in Watts with a baton up my ass."

"Isn't that how you started, my man?" Big TC laughed and showed his big array of white teeth, one of which had a small diamond embedded in it.

"Fuck," Stabile uttered, realizing he couldn't push Big TC too far. "I'll tell them I'm onto something good, but I've got to come up with some serious collars within a few months or I'll be history and they'll put some Elliott Ness on your ass."

Big TC turned and stared at Stabile, his black eyes expressionless and dead. This time, Stabile grabbed the envelope full of cash and got out of the car.

IT HAD BEEN A long haul to Steve's house. Cal had never met Steve, but Jesse went on and on about him until admitting he hadn't actually called Steve because he couldn't remember Steve's last name, but he sure as hell knew where he lived.

"We drove all this way and you never told him we were coming?"

Jesse protested loudly, "I didn't call him because I lost his number and Stevie changed his last name every time he met a cop, woman, or husband. I couldn't keep track. Don't worry, we'll find him."

Cal was tired and couldn't get angry. He needed a break from the constant driving, and found himself increasingly eager to see Jesse's old drug contact and have some beers. As they bounced down a muddy road forty miles from Dallas, Jesse peered out the car window trying to remember the exact location. Suddenly, he let out a loud yell as he glimpsed a run-down little ranch house. A few moments later, they pulled into the driveway and Steve's wife Sherry came out onto the raised porch. Not too long ago, she was very pretty, but over the last two years worries, pregnancy, and a bad diet had conspired to add some wear. To Cal and Jesse, her big blue eyes and red hair were still worth looking at. She wore a pair of tight denim cutoffs with frayed ends and her large, round, drooping breasts pushed against a white sleeveless T-shirt. In her arms was her one-year-old son, Stevie Jr. Jesse immediately began chatting her up.

"Old Steve didn't tell me he had a beautiful wife and baby boy."

"You're friends of Steve's?"

"Didn't Steve ever tell you about Jesse Carmody and our times in Oklahoma?"

"I reckon he mentioned a few things."

"Well, I sure as heck think he would. Where is that old dog?"

Sherry looked across the weed-strewn yard and her eyes came to rest on the "For Sale" sign on the corner of the property. "Jail," she said. She caught her breath and a few tears sprang to her eyes.

"Son of a bitch," Jesse said, and kicked the front step, startling Stevie Jr. "When's he getting out?"

Sherry distractedly reached under her red hair and pulled on her ear. "It doesn't look like Steve will be around for fifteen years or so." Sherry's face flushed and two lonely tears worked their way down her cheeks.

Jesse stared at her white thighs and the dangling threads of denim. "Hell, this here's a bad situation. I'll bet those narcotics boys confiscated about everything, didn't they?"

Sherry nodded and choked back a sob the tears flowed freely now. Seeing his momma crying, Stevie Jr. followed suit. Jesse put a boot up onto the second step and said, "Well, my compadre Cal and me, we're gonna do what we can. Won't we, Cal?"

Cal nodded his head but couldn't take his eyes off Sherry's large breasts. Jesse climbed onto the porch and put his arm on Sherry's shoulder. "Do you have anything to drink?"

"No, it's pretty much all drunk up."

"What would tickle your fancy?"

"Southern Comfort and Coke."

"Hell yes, you could use a little Southern Comfort." Jesse turned to his partner. "Cal, go on down the road and get us a bottle of Southern Comfort, some beer, chips, and stuff like that, and a little milk for the baby." Jesse glanced at Sherry's breasts and laughed. "Though I reckon he won't be needing any."

Sherry sniffed and gave a little sad laugh.

Six hours later, Cal was drinking his fifth can of beer and watching cartoons on TV with Stevie Jr. He watched as the Road Runner beeped and zoomed around the TV screen and listened as the bed creaked and thumped against a wall in the bedroom. Cal was disappointed because he knew he could have pleased Sherry more, even if Jesse got his hard back.

IT WAS A QUIET night along Santa Monica Boulevard, and as Nick hunted, he noticed there were less than a dozen boys cruising the sidewalk. At the corner of Curson, Nick thought he saw someone who resembled the young man from his apartment. He looped the block, pulled up to the curb, and slipped his hand in the bag and felt for the gun. With his other hand, he pressed the control button and lowered the passenger window. As though drawn to a magnet, the hustler came over to the cab. "You lookin' to take me somewhere?"

Nick immediately realized it wasn't his man. "I was looking for someone who looked like you."

"Ain't nobody looks like me, Sugar."

"Well, this guy has a resemblance."

"Darling, if you're looking for a certain type, why then it looks like you found it. But if you're looking for someone specific, I can't be no help. But, honey, I love that reddish-looking hair you got."

The man reached inside and tried to touch Nick's hair. Nick pulled back. "Forget about it. But if I get any passengers looking for what you're offering, I'll bring them right to you."

Nick pulled away and continued cruising. When he hit Robertson, he had a choice. It was an unusually slow night for the hustlers and for him. He swung left and headed for the airport as a light rain began to fall.

✦✦✦

THE GENTLE MIST CONTINUED as Nick's cab cruised into the airport. Studying the taxi stands, he made his way around the long U-shaped facility. TWA, the International Terminal, and American seemed slow, so Nick pulled up to Continental where he was second up. He could see people moving toward the luggage carousel to get their belongings. He knew it would be just a matter of minutes before he'd get off. He left the motor running, sat back, banked the heater up a little, and lifted his right leg onto the passenger seat. His ankle continually bothered him and he found he was getting increasingly stiff from sitting behind the wheel more than eighty hours a week. The lack of exercise didn't help.

The heater took away his chill and, gradually, the soft patterns of the rain and airport lights on the windshield lulled him. His thoughts drifted to his father in New York. He could visualize him sitting atop an old cushion on the radiator cover, staring out the tenement window to the street below, lonely and stoic. His mind drifted to the image of Melissa toddling around Lillian's backyard, and he rubbed his head to force the longing from his mind. What surfaced in turn was the unsettling thought that if he left Melissa in Macon too long, it might prove difficult to get her away from Lillian both emotionally and legally. That possibility was not something Nick was prepared to live with. Instead, he called in and told Billy he was headed out of the airport. Billy stopped him with, "Four-o-five, pick up Irene."

✦✦✦

SLIPPING INTO THE BACK seat, Irene said, "I'm glad you were around. There was another driver that came to pick me up, but I wouldn't go with him."

"Why not?"

"I didn't like the way he looked at me. Sometimes cab drivers see a working girl and think they can do what they want. Lately, I've been getting worried."

"What's worrying you?"

"I'm just afraid something is going to happen. I don't know what."

"Things can happen anywhere. My wife was killed right in our apartment." Nick surprised himself by making the confession. They rode on in silence before Irene asked.

"Did you love her?"

"Yes, very much."

Irene pulled her dress down over her knees and folded her arms over her chest. "You didn't kill her, did you?"

Nick was momentarily nonplussed by her question, finally he answered but it sounded strange, even to him. "No, of course not. There were three men in the apartment and one of them shot me as I came in."

"Sometimes, men say they love you and then they kill you."

Nick was shocked by her comment but let it pass. The conversation was unsettling and Nick was content to simply drive, but then Irene asked, "How did you meet her?"

"I was hanging out in London, doing work for different magazines. Well, at the time I was actually doing more partying and drugs than work. Then, I met Julianne at a play. She was in London visiting a friend from college."

"But how did you come to be with her?"

"I invited her to dinner. I dragged her behind me through clubs and bars for a few dates and then invited her to my apartment. She looked at some of my photographs I had stashed in a pile in the corner of the bedroom. Then she turned to me and said, 'You're too talented to be behaving the way you are. You should put more energy into your work.' It was as simple as that. I laughed at her because at the time, deep down, I was trying to forget about my work and the images I had witnessed through my lens. I was trying to party my way out of it. I made dinner, broiled salmon, new potatoes with garlic and leeks, and a beautiful bottle of Sancerre. And for dessert, I snorted some heroin. That was that."

"She did the drug with you?"

"No, to the contrary. She said she liked me and admired my work, but wouldn't see me again unless I was going to get straightened out."

"You must have because she married you."

"I thought about her much more than drugs, so she made it comparatively easy. After a while, I convinced her to move in with me and I stayed straight. By the time we were living together and married, I was not drinking or doing any drugs at all. She had that effect on me. She was the only woman I've ever truly loved. She was..." Nick glanced in the mirror and noticed Irene was crying. She removed a tissue from her purse and wiped her eyes and blew her nose with it. Nick didn't know how to react, but suddenly he felt tears spring to life in his eyes as well. They rode on in silence, quietly crying in their respective spaces and for their own reasons, until they arrived at her motel. Irene reached over and put the money in Nick's hand and with her other hand grasped his wrist. "I'm so sorry about your wife, Nick." She quickly let go of him and slipped out the door.

Suddenly, Nick felt terribly depressed. He wished he could follow Irene up to her room and lie down with her for a month or two. Instead, he sat and watched as she maneuvered her tall, shapely body up the stairs. *It's got to be a lonely life she's living,* he thought.

✦ ✦ ✦

THINGS WERE NOT GOING well in Texas. Jesse and Cal were nowhere near getting the cash they needed. Sherry's father and mother had come to the house and taken her and Stevie Jr. back to Oklahoma. The house was foreclosed on by the bank and padlocked by the sheriff's department. Jesse and Cal had to find another place to stay.

Too much money was getting spent on partying. Too much was going up their noses. Jesse especially loved his coke, and Cal would grind watching the money disappear, snort by snort. The LA coke was going so fast, Jesse continually cut it, and the drug had less and less effect. They sold some, but the fantasy of hitting their target of twenty to fifty thousand to buy big remained just that. They were near broke.

They got a good deal on some newly cooked methamphetamine from a couple Chicanos for personal use and switched from coke to crystal. Jesse continued to sell an occasional gram of cocaine for a hundred dollars. They seldom knew who they were selling to and the profits were very small. Cal complained, but Jesse insisted they were just doing it until they found the right score and got their money for the easy trade-up.

The meth spurred them to party on for two solid days and nights before impulsively they drove toward Houston. They reasoned they could easily pull off a quick robbery or two in that sprawling city. On the third night, in a roadhouse on the city's outskirts, Jesse walked two truckers into the men's room and sold them a tiny brown bottle of his worthless coke, while Cal kept a careful watch from the bar. The truckers planned to share it between themselves and their dates. One of the truckers was a large fat man who made the tiny urine-reeking bathroom much smaller and more odorous than usual. The other trucker was a short muscular guy in a black T-shirt, sporting a full mustache. The truckers looked with greedy anticipation as Jesse pulled out a small bottle of his radically cut cocaine. Inside the bathroom, the truckers each parted with fifty dollars of their hard-earned cash and Jesse dropped the bottle, half the size of a cigarette, into the fat man's palm. "Hang onto your boots, boys, because this shit could blow them off."

Jesse left them greedily snorting behind the locked door and returned to the bar. Cal was nervous. He knew Jesse had been cutting the coke so much those big boys and their fat dates could snort a truckload and not get high. Once at the bar, Jesse grinned at Cal who turned and watched the men come out of the bathroom, go to the booth where their girlfriends eagerly waited, and slip one of them the bottle. Smiling in anticipation, the ladies got up and headed for the ladies' room. Cal chugged down most of his beer in a few gulps and turned to Jesse. "We got to get out of here, before they catch on."

"Hey, that's good coke," Jesse protested.

"You know how much you stepped on that? You stepped on that more than a bull steps in shit and those boys look like they'd know good blow from bad."

"Shit, those boys are drunk, and when their women come out of the bathroom smiling and grabbing their cocks, they're gonna be just fine."

"I don't like it," Cal said, but as usual he went along. Three minutes later, the women came out of the bathroom giggling. They flashed their spandex-covered asses to the room as they climbed over their men and settled back into the booth. Jesse began to chat up a pretty twenty-year-old that stumbled up to the bar; she was working on draining her seventh Harvey Wallbanger. In the reflection of the large mirror behind the bar, Cal nervously observed the two couples in the booth. Upending the last of his beer, Cal swallowed, blew the foam from his mustache, and watched as they put their elbows on the table and began to discuss how high they were. They gave it almost a minute, but Cal could see it coming as they went from discussing how high they were, to if they were high, to the sad realization they were not high at all. Cal felt a rush of adrenaline as the two couples looked across the crowded dance floor to Jesse. Cal nudged Jesse, who pulled his attention away from the girl next to him and glared at Cal. "Hey, can't you see, I'm making some very serious progress here." Jesse turned back to the girl and bought her Harvey Wallbanger number eight. She smiled at him glassy-eyed, and Jesse knew he was in.

He stared at her pert little breasts pushing against the snap buttons and red piping of her western shirt, and for the first time in a week he felt himself begin to get hard.

Cal returned to his observations in the mirror and watched the two men slide out of the booth and walk purposefully toward the bar. Cal knew they weren't coming to buy drinks. He turned and kicked Jesse's foot hard. "Here they come, asshole. Just like I told you."

Jesse glanced in the mirror, saw the men almost upon him, then, with his left hand, he impulsively grabbed his Lone Star beer bottle by the neck, cracked it in half on the bar, spun around and quickly stabbed the big trucker twice in the face and eye. The trucker's short friend moved in quickly and belted Jesse a solid blow to the left side of his forehead, spinning him around and down to one knee. Cal swung a tremendous punch from the middle of the bar, but missed the short man's jaw and hit him just under the neck by the collarbones. The man went down. All was a blur after that, but the fat man screamed and writhed on the floor, while his friend, not seriously hurt, leapt up and, snarling under his large mustache, plunged into Cal. By now, Jesse had ditched the broken bottle, shook off some of the effect of the punch, reached the snub-nosed .32 in his stash sock, and pulled it out. The short bull-like man had some good professional boxing talent and he belted Cal four or five times before Jesse stood, put the gun behind the man's ear, and fired. It took a second, but the man dropped like a stone to the wooden floor. Blood spurted rapidly from the man's head and floated sawdust and cigarette butts on a tiny red river toward the bar. The Harvey Wallbanger girl screamed like a siren and Jesse and Cal reflexively plunged toward the back door. Seven seconds later, they discovered the back door was locked. Cursing, they quickly veered away and moved through the scattering crowd toward the front. Gun in hand, Jesse led Cal in their dash to the front door.

Alerted by the sound of the gunshot and screams, the bouncer, a recruit from the local weight-lifting establishment, saw them coming and mistakenly thought all his weight training would help him in the situation. He authoritatively flexed his deltoids and pecs, stretched to his full six-foot-two-and-a-half-inch height, and held up his massive arms to block their exit. In response, Jesse shot him three quick times at close range through the heart. Jesse and Cal pushed through and plunged out the door. Behind them, the owner toppled backward and landed with a reverberating thud.

A fine-looking young woman with great eyes and memory got the license number of the Nova as it made a squealing, swerving exit from the parking lot. The cops were impressed with the young woman's memory, description of the events, and round ass that showed so well in form-fitting jeans. They put out the information, but it was 1:14 a.m. and by that time Cal and Jesse were pulling into a Best Western parking lot twenty-eight miles from the roadhouse. As Jesse quickly went through the car and pulled out their belongings and guns, Cal went through the parking lot and selected a four-door Pontiac he knew was a rental. He quickly broke in, hot-wired it, and pulled to where Jesse stood waiting. Cal popped open the trunk and Jesse rapidly threw in the guns and covered them with their clothes and overnight bags. They were out of there in less than six minutes. Cal drove the car onto Highway 84 West and put it in cruise control at sixty-one miles an hour. "Can't you get this car going any faster? Goddamn!" Jesse said.

"You want us to get stopped for speeding?"

Jesse didn't answer, but opened the glove box and was happy to see the registration and rental receipt. He peered at it in the dim light. "We're now the good friends and employees of Wesley T. Hagen, in case anyone should ask. I believe we should be in the construction business, shopping malls and all."

Cal stared down the highway. "We've got to get out of Texas. This car is rented by a guy who is gonna walk out into the parking lot at six or seven in the morning, realize the car's stolen, and, half a minute after that, the news will be out. That only gives us about five hours. Shit, things ain't going to go so fast. We can swap some plates."

"We got to get out of Texas, for sure, but we got to get to El Paso."

"El Paso is in Texas, fuckhead."

"Don't go calling me fuckhead, you fucking greaseball. You're getting way too cute, you know that?" Jesse stared at Cal with wild menace.

Despite the potential danger, Cal allowed himself more anger and ranted, "I can't take this shit no more. You going around popping people whenever you feel like it, doing such stupid shit. You call yourself the brains of this outfit; well you act like a fucking lunatic. I'll steal you a car down the road and you can take off and do your own thing, I've fucking had it."

Jesse began to reach for his gun, then stopped himself and forced a little laugh at Cal blowing off steam. Jesse knew he needed Cal, and he wasn't going to let him go. Cal was fluent in Spanish, and for what Jesse had in mind that was a necessary thing. He reached over and patted Cal on the shoulder and grinned at him. The shooting had somehow calmed Jesse. He was happy to be on the road and the run again, so he started to mollify Cal who was in a dangerous state. "Listen, we just carefully drive to El Paso and then..."

"I told you, El Paso is in Texas, you Gringo asshole..."

"I know where El Paso is, and it's right across from Juarez. See, I know my Mexican geography, too."

Cal seethed, "It'll take us eight to ten hours to get to El Paso, this state is so fucking big. I hate this fucking state."

"Yeah, but that's where we can score and make the buy."

"Where we gonna get the money?"

"Here's how we do it, pardner. I got cousin lives in Roswell, New Mexico. He works at the Air Force Base there. We can hang with him. Take a few side trips down to Juarez and line everything up. Then we do a few jobs up in Flagstaff, get some dough together, make a hot buy in Juarez, and begin the big easy trade-up."

It was a plan, which was something Cal never had, so he quit complaining and bumped the cruise control up to sixty-six.

Jesse opened a small bottle of coke, loaded some on the spoon, and stuck it under Cal's nostril. Cal tried to snort but his nose was swollen shut from the trucker's punches. Jesse didn't have any such problem, so he tooted up and let his head flop back onto the seat. "Man, this coke sucks," Jesse hooted.

Cal didn't laugh at the joke, and Jesse impulsively reached down and rubbed his crotch. "Man, if that fat fucker hadn't come over, I would have been balling that little honey in the back seat right this second."

With the back of his hand, Cal dabbed at the blood coagulating on his split lip. It bothered him how the little guy had slipped inside and caught him with those hard punches. It was probably that, as much as anything, that made Cal back off from arguing with Jesse. In a way, Jesse had saved him from a bad beating. The little tank of a guy had been a skilled boxer and might have gone through the two of them. They could have been caught in that place, holding coke, selling coke, and wanted. As usual, he started to forget it was Jesse that got them into the mess in the first place.

CHAPTER SIXTEEN

A T 9:15 P.M., NICK picked up a nice fare at the Hollywood Roosevelt Hotel. Two German businessmen and a businesswoman were checking out and going to the Beverly Hills Hotel, a definite upgrade. The neighborhood around the Hollywood Roosevelt left them offended. Nick didn't blame them. The Germans had taken the long journey to Hollywood only to discover its tarnished identity. It was an area made famous by a gilded past and fanciful history. Though the glitter and gold had abruptly left the city a long time ago, studio executives and famous actors still made the journey from their homes in the hills or surrounding studios to Musso & Frank Grill or The Brown Derby and there were still premiers at Grauman's Chinese Theater. But most tourists didn't know of Musso & Frank, and if they did, they couldn't afford it.

The only stars to be found were the ones embedded in the sidewalk on the Walk of Fame. Many of those too had faded from memory. Sleazy tourist shops and the flotsam of lost hopes bordered the constellations of forgotten stars up and down Hollywood and Vine.

The German passengers were looking forward to leaving and settling at the Beverly Hills Hotel, which had a reputation for catering to the famous stars who stayed, swam, and dined there. The meetings and power lunches at the Polo Lounge were legendary. Nick fit most of their luggage in the trunk but two small handbags wound up on the front seat. The men got in the back seat, letting the woman squeeze up front by the bags and Nick. She was heavyset, in her midthirties, and just missed being very attractive. She had an air of business efficiency about her. Nick surmised she was strictly working for the men and there was no romance. He listened as the two men spoke in German about the area. Though Nick knew very little of the language, he could tell they were disappointed. As they were talking, Nick decided to take them on a cruise down Santa Monica Boulevard. He should have taken Sunset all the way, but by taking Santa Monica, he could add another pass to his current routine.

By then, Nick must have scoured the street hundreds of times as fares from different parts of the city allowed him to intersect with the critical blocks. Apart from Venice, it was the one consistent place he could search and feel like he might actually discover what he was hunting for. It may have been a false lead, but Nick felt good about doing it. It kept him connected with his purpose. He started the meter and turned off Hollywood Boulevard, maneuvering over to La Brea and heading south to Santa Monica Boulevard.

RAINEY WAS LOOKING FORWARD to the night. He walked down Santa Monica toward La Brea. He wanted to work the area between Fairfax and Crescent Heights. He was starting a little late, but with a good night he might be able to pick up some decent money, and Friday night was not a night to be missed in the hustling trade.

NICK DROVE DOWN LA Brea and crossed Sunset. The woman in the front seat who hadn't said anything suddenly piped out with a logical question delivered in perfect English. "Why aren't you taking Sunset? The hotel is on Sunset."

"It's crowded on a Friday this time of night, bumper to bumper. I'll just cruise Santa Monica Boulevard and then run up Holloway Drive to Sunset and it'll be faster and the same distance."

It was the truth, but the woman was going to show off for the Germans. "I'm not sure about that. I used to live here for three years."

"Trust me, this is better," Nick said, flatly.

"Whenever a cab driver or someone in this country is going to steal from you, they say, 'trust me,'" the woman said to the men in the back seat.

Apparently the men had perfect English as well because they laughed in appreciation. Nick didn't bother to defend himself. He had to stop for the light at Fountain and La Brea. As he sat there, he suddenly became aware of the perfume the woman was wearing. It had a pleasant, delicate scent and Nick found himself briefly glancing at the outline of her large breasts and full round thighs. He wondered what she was like if and when she ever dropped the officious attitude. It might be exciting to see.

RAINEY CROSSED LA BREA and looked around. A lot of boys were already on the boulevard. He had expected it, but the number worried him. He needed a good night. At the corner of Detroit and Santa Monica, he saw two acquaintances—Mario, a recent muscular transplant from Christopher Street in Greenwich Village, and a tall, thin, black transvestite who called herself Sharone. Sharone was dressed in three-quarters drag. Mario had the opposite image going, that of the macho blue boy—this was fitting, as Mario had grown up on the tough streets of Queens. He always carried a five-by-one-inch pipe for protection, which became a weapon when held in his fist, or a compact bong when a joint was wedged in the hole he had drilled in the end.

Rainey walked toward them, all the while turning to the traffic on the street. He would love to pull a trick before Mario and Sharone and tease them about it later.

♦♦♦

As THE LIGHT AT Fountain changed to green, Nick pulled away and a few seconds later swung right onto Santa Monica Boulevard and began his search. He studied the hustlers as he slowly cruised along. Inside the cab, the Germans followed Nick's eyes as he studied the men on the sidewalk. As he approached Detroit, Nick noticed three hustlers standing on the corner. One appeared to be a transvestite wearing a blonde wig, white blouse, and tight cutoff jeans. The second one was built like a bodybuilder and was dressed in blue pants with a denim shirt open down to his navel. But the third... He studied the man as he slowly drove past. Encouraged by the interest from within the cab, the three hustlers responded with different degrees of flirtation. Sharone leaned forward, shook her ass, and blew the cab a kiss. Mario, who had his thumbs hooked into his front pants pockets, rubbed his fingers on his abdomen near the steel pipe in his pocket. Rainey gave a little jump and waved with his right hand.

It was Rainey's looks and movement that riveted Nick's attention. The outline of the man's body and the position of his arm was much the same as Nick had seen when he surprised the men at his apartment. Rainey's gesture made Nick focus in, like racking a long zoom lens. He went cold inside.

It took Nick a half block to recover, and by that time he was at the corner of Formosa. Impulsively, he made a right and accelerated up the block. The woman next to him turned in alarm. "Where are you going now?"

Nick had trouble dealing with the question but finally hit on a half truth. "There's a man back on the corner who owes me money and I'm going to get it."

The older German man in the back seat spoke to Nick for the first time. "You may collect your money at a later date. We are already late for friends we are meeting."

"This will only take a moment, and I will deduct the added charges from the meter."

Nick powered the cab onto Lexington Avenue and ran it back to La Brea for another pass. He had to be sure it was him, and if it was, he couldn't let the man get away. There was a moment of uncertainty. How could he be sure, when he had only seen the man for a second from fifteen feet away? "We don't care about your deductions, we have a dinner meeting to go to and we are late," the woman said.

Nick turned right on La Brea, floored the accelerator, and quickly arrived back at Santa Monica Boulevard.

Nick thought of the gun in the bag. If he pulled out the gun, the passengers would completely panic. As he approached the corner of Detroit, Nick stared hard at the man and, obligingly, Rainey stared back in the vain hope the returning cab held promise.

There was something about the way Nick stared at him that quickly unsettled Rainey. It was not the kind of sizing up he was used to, except by police.

For his part, Nick decided he was almost certain it was him, but he had to be positive and make sure the man didn't disappear on him. Nick drove the short block to Formosa and parked at the loading zone in front of Port's Restaurant. "Now we are stopping?" the woman demanded.

"Just for a minute." Nick left the engine running, quickly opened the door, and, taking his bag with him, got out of the cab. Kneeling close to the rear tire, Nick pulled the gun from the bag and stuck it in his belt, pulling his jacket over it. Standing, he walked to the driver's door and tossed the bag onto the front seat. The younger man in the back seat suddenly became extremely animated. He leaned toward the front seat and yelled at Nick, "This is something you should not do! We have business to attend to. We will inform your superiors. There is no..."

Slamming the door, Nick cut off the man's words, turned, and purposefully walked back up the boulevard toward Rainey.

Mario and Sharone had followed the cab with their eyes and watched it stop the short block away. When they saw Nick get out and begin to walk in their direction, they instinctively separated themselves from Rainey. Rainey had a few good instincts and something didn't seem right, but maybe the riders in the cab wanted him for a scene. He hung back from Sharone and Mario, waiting to see what would happen. It didn't take long as he watched Nick walk right by them toward him.

For a half second, Rainey's vanity allowed the thought that Nick was a John coming to score him for the passengers in the cab because he was the one they desired, but that thought almost immediately went from his mind. There was something else about the appearance of the man. Apart from looking eerily familiar, Rainey had seen that look on men in prison when they wanted someone hurt. Instinctively, Rainey knew someone was going to get it and after a moment's wavering, he came to the realization it was him. His hand flew to his mouth and he arched backward in shocked horror.

Nick saw Rainey's outline repeat the gesture he had seen in his mind a thousand times married with the memory of the odd low hairline, broad flat nose, and, just before Rainey's hand covered it, the split lip, and Nick knew it was the man.

Rainey watched as Nick's eyes clicked in on positive identification, confirming he was definitely the target. He looked in vain toward Mario and Sharone at the corner, but they were concentrating on the passing traffic. Nick surged toward Rainey and Rainey noticed the bulge under Nick's jacket, a bulge where there was no reason for one. Panicked, Rainey bolted out onto the street into traffic. His fear intensified as he glanced over his shoulder and saw Nick run through traffic after him. Cars honked and the hustlers watched in interest and amusement as the two ran down the south side of Santa Monica Boulevard. Mario turned to Sharone and asked, "What the hell's up with that?"

"Honey, I don't know," Sharone replied.

Rainey was light on his feet and moved swiftly. Nick was heavier and was barely keeping up. Rainey cut through the parking lot behind the Formosa Cafe. Nick followed and the injury to his ankle sprang back to consciousness. A car swung quickly into the parking lot and almost collided with Rainey. As Rainey momentarily had to stop, Nick made the move to cut him off, but Rainey quickly slipped around the car and ran down the alley behind the lot. Nick ran full out after him, feeling his ankle weakening with every stride. He was going to lose the chase when Rainey made the error of turning around to see where Nick was. In his panic, he kept his eyes on Nick a moment too long and stepped into a pothole. The tip of his shoe caught the crumbling edge of the hole and he tripped, falling clumsily to one knee. He struggled to his feet, but Nick was on him. Nick grabbed Rainey by his jacket, spun him around, and threw him forward into a chain-link fence bordering the alley. Nick started reaching under his jacket to pull his gun when Rainey whipped around and shot his leg out in a karate move and struck Nick in the ribs. The blow was not strong, missed Nick's solar plexus, but he was knocked off balance for a moment. Again, Rainey tried to make a break, but Nick was able to reach out and grab the tail of Rainey's jacket. Rainey spun and swung wildly at Nick, who took a punch to the cheek. Nick quickly stepped in close, hit Rainey with two hard punches to the stomach and a straight hard right that caught the punk flush between the eyes on the bridge of his nose. The force of the punch knocked Rainey backward, landing him on his ass. Rainey held his face and shrieked in pain and fear. Nick pulled the gun and fell down upon Rainey with his knee landing in Rainey's stomach and his left hand driving Rainey's back flat upon the ground.

Rainey's head hit the blacktop with a sharp crack and he nearly lost consciousness.

Nick stuck the tip of the barrel of the gun at the end of Rainey's nose and for a moment all time seemed to stop. Blood and snot bubbled from Rainey's nose as he gasped from the run, punches, and Nick's knee in his stomach.

Recovering a bit, Rainey screamed in frustration, "What you want with me, man? What the fuck you want with me?"

"You killed my wife."

"What you talking 'bout?"

"You know what I'm talking about. You and two other guys, in Venice, six months ago, raped and killed my wife in front of our child."

Suddenly, Rainey's eyes went wide and wild and he sobbed. "I don't know nothing about that..."

Nick cracked Rainey over the eye with the side of the gun. The metal split open a deep gash on Rainey's eyebrow. "Oh, Jesus, don't kill me, man, I didn't hurt that woman. I don't do nothing with women, man. It was those other guys. They was bad motherfuckers."

"You're not telling me shit." Nick lifted him by the neck and cracked his head back onto the ground, too hard.

It took Rainey a half minute to open his eyes and see Nick again. In his state of shock, he lost his panic and, for a moment, spoke quietly to Nick. "I didn't know they was going to hurt nobody, I just showed them the apartment." Gradually coming back to full consciousness and aware again of the gun under his nose, Rainey asked, "You going to kill me?"

The question caused Nick to pause for a moment, and he considered it. "I don't know. I think I will. Give me your wallet and tell me about those men."

"I ain't got no money, man. What you want my wallet for?"

Nick cracked Rainey on the eye again, opening the cut even more, and Rainey howled in pain. Nick pressed the gun against Rainey's nose. "Give me your fucking wallet. Pull it out slowly, and tell me about those guys."

Rainey awkwardly groped into his back pants pocket, handed the wallet to Nick, and began talking. Nick opened it with his left hand and stared down at Rainey's California driver's license. Rainey went on about how he didn't know the men and had gotten hardly any of the stuff that was there. It was some guys named Jesse and Cal. He wasn't even sure those were the right names and he hadn't seen them since. "I never want to see those mean-assed motherfuckers again, ever."

The light was too dim to read the name and address on the license, so Nick pulled it out and put it in his shirt pocket, then fanned through the rest of the wallet. There was nothing except some club cards, a picture of a middle-aged black woman, and a registration card to the Free Clinic.

Pulled by the curiosity of what was going on between Rainey and the man who chased him, Mario and Sharone had tracked them to the end of the dark alley. They observed the man holding Rainey down. From where they were, they couldn't see he held a gun on Rainey. Mario turned to Sharone and gestured for him to follow.

Terrified, Sharone shook her head and slowly backed away. Mario quietly pulled the steel pipe out of his pocket and stealthily walked up the alley over the crumbling black top toward the man atop Rainey.

Rainey's confession was over. Nick had gone through the wallet and now the moment of truth had arrived between the two men. Suddenly, Nick was aware of how exhausted, numb, and lightheaded he felt. He stared down at Rainey. The man looked pathetic, tears in his eyes, face contorted, bleeding from his nose and eyebrow. Nick hated him. He hated everything about him, but he didn't pull the trigger. He just stared at him, his mind blank.

Rainey seized on the moment of indecision. "Let me go, man. You got no problem with me; it's those other dirty-assed motherfuckers, Jesse and Cal," Rainey wailed.

Nick's mind remained blank. The moment could have gone on and on but, he felt another presence and Nick noticed Rainey's eyes dart off to his left as Mario arrived directly behind him.

Looking down, Mario panicked at the sight of Nick's gun and swung his pipe-clenched fist at him with his entire strength. The blow caught Nick on the side of his jaw, knocking him down onto his shoulder. Rainey shrieked and pushed the gun away. Mario quickly threw another heavy punch and hit Nick above the temple. Nick went limp, the gun loosed from his hand. Rainey pulled himself out from under Nick as Mario wildly punched Nick again, hitting him on the forehead. This time, however, the blow shattered Mario's first knuckle and as he felt it go, he cursed. Nick was distantly aware of what was happening but could not move. Mario reached down and took the gun from Nick's limp hand. "I'll keep this for you, sweetheart."

Rainey looked down at Nick and kicked him in the stomach. "Motherfucker!"

Rainey was going to kick Nick in the face, but Mario pushed him away. He bent down and picked up Rainey's wallet, handing it back to him. Rainey took it as blood continued to stream from his split eyebrow, blinding his left eye. Breaking into tears again, he turned and hurried down the alley.

After a glance at Nick to make sure he wouldn't be following, Mario slid Nick's gun inside his shirt and buttoned it up. He put the piece of pipe back in his right pocket and turned and followed Rainey. At the end of the alley, Rainey emotionally fell against Sharone, who recoiled from him. "Fool, don't be getting your blood and snot all over my blouse."

Nick lay in the alley for several minutes without trying to get up. For some reason, and for the first time in a long while, he felt oddly at peace. Rainey had gotten away. It didn't seem to matter. Nick was relieved he hadn't killed him. What Rainey had told him made sense. He slowly turned his head toward his right hand and confirmed the gun was gone. He was reconciled to that as well.

Gradually, he staggered to his feet. His ear was ringing loudly and head throbbing, but otherwise he felt unaccountably relaxed. Fighting off dizziness, he began to walk back down the alley. When he reached Formosa, he turned toward Santa Monica Boulevard. A moment later, he could see his cab. There was a Celebrity taxi double-parked just in front of it and the Germans and the driver were loading luggage into the trunk. *They must have flagged him down,* Nick figured. Not wanting to deal with them, he turned the corner and walked into the Formosa Bar and Cafe.

The restaurant and bar were crowded. It was dimly lit and had booths of dark wood with deep red vinyl. One end, where tables lined the walls, it looked like an old railroad car had been attached to the building. The place was ringed with pictures of stars from earlier years, complete with a bizarre little shrine to Elvis Presley. The bar was long and crowded with serious drinkers, most of whom were engaged in animated conversations. Nick immediately liked the looks of the place and moved to the far end of the crowded bar.

It took a while for the overworked bartender to make his way to him. Nick ordered a double Cuervo Gold in a rocks glass, neat. The bartender swiftly sprang into action, and when he finished the pour, he looked at Nick carefully for the first time, and pulled Nick's drink back and held it in his hand. "You all right?"

"Sure," Nick said.

"That'll be four fifty," the bartender said, still possessively holding Nick's drink.

Nick was insulted. The bartender acted as though he didn't think Nick was good for the money. Nick tossed a twenty onto the bar.

After another cautious look, the bartender placed the double tequila in front of Nick, picked up the twenty, and went to make change.

Nick opened his mouth, tossed half the tequila down, and noticed his jaw felt very stiff. He turned and found the entrance to the men's room close by.

Stepping into the small, poorly lit room, he locked the door and turned toward an old, scratched mirror. He peered into it and was surprised by what he saw. The left side of his jaw was swelling grotesquely. There was a large red welt declaring itself on his forehead and Nick was able to make out the markings of Mario's knuckles and ring. A little blood trickled from his ear. His face glistened with an oily-looking patina of sweat. Pulling off some paper towels, Nick wiped the blood and gingerly opened and closed his jaw. He didn't think it was broken but he couldn't be sure.

He stared at his image in the dull mirror and asked, "All right, Nick, tell me, how did all that help?"

The doorknob turned as someone tried to enter. Nick unlocked the door and walked past a young man who looked at him curiously. Back at the bar, Nick tossed down the rest of his tequila, dropped a dollar on the bar, and decided he'd better check on his cab. He hoped they didn't take his keys.

The cab was still there with the keys in ignition. He had left the engine running as a gesture to keep the Germans from panicking when he left to investigate Rainey. But now, the engine had been turned off. The other driver must have taken the keys out of the ignition, opened the trunk to take the luggage, and then returned the keys. *The Celebrity driver must have enjoyed stealing the ride,* Nick thought. Suddenly, Nick heard the meter click over. The meter had been running all the time. Nick stopped it, knowing he'd have to make up the money. The extenuating circumstances were not something he'd care to relate. The fare was a small price to pay for solving part of the crime, if indeed that's what he had done. Remembering, Nick fished inside his shirt pocket and found Rainey's license. He switched on the overhead light and studied it. The picture of Rainey showed him smiling. He looked innocent enough. The identification read: Morgan Clarence Rainey. He was five foot nine, weighed 139 pounds, and was born May 19, 1957. That would make him twenty years old, Nick reasoned. Despite the young age and smile, Rainey looked like he had seen a lot. Nick should show the license to Pearson, but he'd have to wait until morning, though waiting might not be a good plan if Rainey was going to move. Nick's head was throbbing. He was having trouble thinking clearly. What could he say to the police on night watch? It was a long story, and then there was the missing gun. If Rainey knew his license was missing, he surely would not go home that evening, or any other night, for some time. Nick decided to wait and visit Pearson first thing in the morning.

Carefully putting the license into his wallet, Nick was surprised by a knock at his window. He looked outside and saw a thin street hustler leaning down, looking in at him. Nick switched on the ignition and lowered the window a few inches.

"Hi," the hustler said. "I need a ride just down to Robertson."

Nick nodded and the young man slid into the back seat. Nick pulled out into traffic. "It's crazy out there tonight," the young man said. "People chasing one another like cowboys and Indians. Earlier, a John drove up in his car, rolled down his window to start the banter, and had a heart attack. Do you hear what I'm saying? The guy looks out his window and says, 'I'm looking for some hips,' and then drops dead."

"Amazing."

"Amazing is hardly the word. It was like some weird scene from Hieronymus Bosch out there. I mean, how's a boy to make a living with all this shit going down?"

Nick didn't answer because at that moment, he didn't care, but he was impressed with the knowledge of art the boy in the back seat provided. *Art major*, Nick thought. He dabbed at the blood dripping from his ear, switched on his two-way radio, and listened as Billy began getting into his shift and riff.

GRIPPING THE STEERING WHEEL of his badly rusted Dodge, Mario knew his knuckle was broken, or worse. He had felt something go when he'd hit the man with his last punch, otherwise he might have kept going. He was upset with himself for getting involved. He hardly knew Rainey and didn't even like him much. Now he'd have to go to the hospital and get his hand looked at. Rainey needed stitches for his eye, and his normally broad nose looked pancaked. The whole thing was lousy. Then he remembered the gun in his belt. That was a positive. A gun might come in handy in LA; plus, he had been itching to get one since he'd moved to town. He should have gone through the guy's pockets to see what else he could have picked off.

Sharone didn't want to go to the hospital with them and Mario was glad when she asked to be dropped off at Western to see what she could pick up. Mario barely tolerated drag queens. They weren't his thing. After she left, he and Rainey headed to the emergency room at Brotman Memorial, in Culver City. Mario figured they'd avoid the pits of County General and knew they should stay away from the hospitals near West Hollywood in case there was some fallout over the beating.

NICK DROPPED THE KID off at Robertson and headed home to clean up. He could also call Pearson and leave him the news. Then, he could go out again, or turn in the cab for the night. No matter what, he didn't want to show up looking like he did. He'd make himself as presentable as possible. Suddenly, Billy's voice found him. "Four-o-five?"

"Four-o-five," Nick answered.

"Four-o-five, call me on the phone, or come on by."

"Four-o-five, roger that."

Nick wondered what Billy could want, and he quickly drove home.

Walking into his apartment, Nick went straight to the bathroom, turned on the light, and studied himself in the mirror. His face did not look good. It was continuing to swell, but he concluded nothing was broken. There was blood on his neck and shirt collar from where it had trickled down from his ear. *The ear could be a problem*, Nick thought, as he listened to the ringing inside his head. He popped three aspirin, put some ice in a towel, and, holding it to his jaw, called Billy.

"Four-o-five, what the hell did you do out there tonight?"

"Why?"

"Some lady called in, said you just left them alone in the cab with the meter running, the engine running, and you ran out. She said you never came back."

Billy's tone was not friendly and the fact he had called him "four-o-five" instead of his name showed he was distancing himself. Nick reacted defensively and lied. "Well, I found a guy who had run out on me some time back and I went after him." Even though it had been Billy's idea to scout the neighborhood from the beginning, he didn't want him knowing the truth just yet.

"Four-o-five, they want to lodge a formal complaint and asked me how to go about it. I told them to give me all the information and I would put the paperwork through, personally."

"Are you going to?"

"Hell no, but this lady was trying to raise a shitstorm. She's got your name, license number, cab number, everything but the oil level. So I want to know what's going on." There was a pause as Billy waited, and then backed off. "Let me ask you this. Did you get the money from the guy who had jumped on you?"

"It wasn't without some pain, on both sides." Nick hoped this would cover how he looked when Billy saw him.

"Well, I'll dump this complaint, but you better watch that shit. I gotta do the phones now. Check with me when you're back on the road."

Nick hung up. He felt bad about lying to Billy but wasn't ready to give the whole story. He had to think the whole thing through: what to say and what to do with Rainey's license. He wanted it all to go the best way possible, but for now he felt good; he had made some progress. Maybe when they picked Rainey up, they'd get more.

RAINEY AND MARIO WALKED into the emergency room and were told to take a seat and complete the inpatient forms. The waiting area already displayed various Friday night complaints: stab wounds, car injuries, and overdoses. Rainey and Mario fit right in. Mario's hand was still swelling and throbbing painfully, but he could still write. Rainey remained high-strung and nearly hysterical. The long cut over his eye was continuously leaking blood and he was having trouble seeing. Despite the pain in his hand, Mario said he'd fill out Rainey's form. Gingerly dabbing at his cut with his shirttail, Rainey recited the needed information until Mario asked for his license number. "Shit, I can never remember that," Rainey said. He pulled out his wallet and abruptly shrieked, startling everyone in the room. Suddenly remembering, he wailed, "He's got my license, my license. That man has my license."

"What'd he want with your license?" Mario asked in irritation.

"You don't understand, there was some bad shit went down."

The admitting nurse feigned disinterest, but leaned her head in closer with a ballpoint in her hand. Mario pulled Rainey a few feet away from the curious woman and hissed a question at Rainey, "You mean he's going to the cops?"

"Either the cops, or he be coming back to get my ass his self."

Mario didn't like that at all. His own record wasn't exactly spotless and now he was involved in something that could come at him. He'd have to distance himself from Rainey. "You're going to have to find some other place to stay than your apartment, so they can't find you."

"Can I stay at your place?" Rainey asked plaintively.

"Fuck no."

Rainey thought for a few moments. "I can stay with my aunt Louise in Inglewood. Get my friend to bring my shit from my apartment. Then, if I can squeeze money from Aunt Louise, I'm moving my sorry ass to San Francisco."

"Good idea," Mario said and thought at least he'd be rid of the hysterical fool.

Rainey turned to Mario, hopefully. "Maybe they'll give me some Percocet or something good for my cuts."

"Man, they're not going to give you anything good. They're just gonna give you stitches, painful stitches." Rainey put his hand to his heart and stared around the waiting room, terrified.

✤✤✤

IT WAS ALMOST TWO in the morning and Nick decided to turn in the cab while the yard was quiet, talk to Billy, go home, and get rested to see Pearson first thing in the morning. He drove 405 into the yard and began to service the cab. He was pleased to see almost no one around. A night driver was gassing his cab and Nick avoided him. It appeared as though Billy was alone in the dispatcher's room and the night mechanic was eating a burrito in the back of the shed. Nick finished preparing the cab for Clyde and parked in a safe spot in the yard. Instead of counting up inside the driver's shack, Nick turned on the overhead light in the cab and did his paperwork. Regretfully, he had to add some of his own money in the cash envelope to make up for the running meter and the angry Germans. With some reluctance, Nick took his paperwork and money over to the dispatcher's window. To his dismay, he saw there was a guy in the shack with Billy, answering phones. Nick angled back from the window out of the sight line of the man in the booth. Billy finished giving out an order over the dispatch; Nick handed his paperwork and cash envelope to Billy. "Holy fuck." Nick shrank back from the window and Billy's exclamation. Billy took off his headset, got up, came outside the shack door, and stared at Nick. "So how's the other guy doing?"

"He ain't looking so good."

"Damn, I hope it was worth it. How much was the fare you collected?"

"There wasn't a fare at all. Actually, it was one of the guys I was hunting. The one you suggested I hunt Santa Monica Boulevard for."

Billy studied Nick's face, then stuck his head inside the shack window and told the new guy he'd be back in a few minutes. Fishing inside his pocket, Billy pulled out a freshly rolled joint and he and Nick walked into the middle of the yard where they could not be overheard. As they passed the number back and forth, Nick related what had gone down. It hadn't been his intention to do so, but after a second's hesitation, Nick couldn't think why he shouldn't share the night's events. It was Billy who had put him there. "Too bad you didn't have a gun with you. You could have just wasted his ass."

"Yeah, maybe," Nick said.

Billy reached out and lightly poked Nick in the chest. "But if you do something like that, you have to watch out where you do it. A cab is like a beacon, you might as well be parking a fire truck or an airplane. In LA, people remember cabs, especially when they happen to be sitting in them, like those Germans." Billy laughed.

"Yeah, I wasn't thinking too rationally." Nick pulled out Rainey's license.

"You got his license?" Billy said excitedly. "Let me see it."

Nick handed over the license and as Billy took it he dropped the roach into a little metal tube and slipped it in his shirt pocket. "He sure doesn't look like much, but he lives in a hell of a neighborhood. My guess is the other two guys wouldn't go within five miles of that place. So he was probably telling the truth. You call the cops?" Billy asked, handing back Rainey's license.

"I'll go see the detective first thing this morning."

"Good idea to call him now, if you've got his number."

"Yeah." Nick was beginning to realize how hard he had been hit in the head. He had been thinking slowly, as if in a dream. "Why wait, I guess?" Nick questioned himself.

"This is definitely a situation where you want to work all the possibilities fast, especially if you want to catch the main guys. From what you told me, my guess is this Rainey guy was telling the truth. He set up the score but the other two did the nasty shit."

"That's how it looks." Nick looked down at Rainey's license. "I just wish it was them I found instead of this fucker," Nick said, sliding the license back into his wallet.

"Well, now you know. But, if you ever do find them, you'd better have it together because those guys don't play."

WHEN PEARSON CHECKED THE messages on his machine, he learned Nick had called his house at 2:23 a.m. Fortunately for Jim, he was in bed with an affable middle-aged tourist from Cleveland. He met her at a bar in Brentwood and they went to her hotel. She was plump, funny, and wanting. She was his first success in four months.

After Nick's last visit, Pearson decided to share no more information with him. He didn't need some half-crazed amateur investigating. Some leads were coming in better than expected. In particular, there was the woman who had jumped through the window and could positively identify the men. Based on the similarity of the crime and assault, Pearson surmised they were the men who killed Cullen's wife. From fingerprint information, he had their names—Jesse Carmody and Cal Santiso—and all their multiple priors, a most impressive list. All he had to do was wait for them to slip up again or get caught in the net. Criminals who behaved in such a brazen manner were always caught. Their time would come, and, based on their multiple crimes, they would never get out of prison. End of story.

As he often did when he was unsettled, Pearson spun around in his chair and looked at the picture taken of him holding a huge tarpon. He remembered that first tug on the line better than he remembered his first time having sex. His friend had told him how lucky he'd been to catch such an elusive, strong fish. Pearson liked to credit himself with some fishing talent, but deep down, Pearson understood how luck played a big part. Along with instinct and patience, luck was an ingredient a good fisherman or detective needed. But instinct, patience, and experience also played a big part in how one's luck would go. At the moment, Person's instinct was telling him the case was unfolding nicely, but Nick was going to be trouble and likely bad luck.

✦ ✦ ✦

As Nick walked down the crowded hallway, he felt he was making a mistake. He knew not sharing information limited the possibility of success, but something nagged at him. His personal pain and resulting obsession were not something he wanted to spread around too freely. He had grown possessive.

It was too late to back out of the meeting. With a sense of resignation, Nick walked into the office.

Pearson was shocked when Cullen came in. He thought he'd seen the major transformation in Nick the last time he saw him, but now the man standing before him was even more sunken-looking and he had obviously been worked over very well by someone. His face was a swollen mess. Pearson got up, shook his hand lightly, and closed the door "I'm sorry I wasn't around when you called last night. I got lucky for the first time since puberty, so I wasn't by my phone."

Nick nodded at Pearson's attempt at humor.

"I know you wouldn't have called at that hour just to see how I was feeling, so what's up?" Pearson asked.

"I wanted you to have this information, personally. I didn't think it was anything for the night desk." Nick tossed Rainey's license on Pearson's desk. Pearson picked it up and studied it. "That's one of the guys who robbed my place and killed my wife."

"Judging by the way you look, this guy didn't just come up to you, hand over his license, and tell you all about it."

"No, and I don't have him waiting outside your office either. He got away from me and this is all I have. I figure you can find him with that."

"Why don't you tell me how this all went down."

As Nick told Pearson the story, Jim listened intently. He bent his head down, stared at the top of his desk, and poked a paper clip around a few times, occasionally glancing up at Nick's battered face. When Nick hit his stride, Pearson put his finger on the paper clip and slowly pushed it into the desk. He could feel the metal press into the flesh of his finger, creating a U-shaped pattern. When Nick finished, Pearson lifted his finger, studied the creases in his flesh, and thought there were a few things missing in Nick's explanation. He was correct because once more, Nick left out the part about the gun. Nick had learned as a kid how to shave the truth for whatever reason made sense and Pearson made a living out of finding the whole story. "It sounds to me like you really panicked this guy. Did you threaten him with something, a knife, a gun, a club?"

"Not exactly. I was sitting on his chest, whacking him from time to time. That might have helped."

Pearson studied Nick's bruised knuckles and figured that part was probably true, and he decided to leave that question and circle back. He studied the license carefully and began to question from a slightly different angle. "Tell me again what makes you think this guy Rainey had anything to do with it."

Nick grew frustrated and angry. He had just gone through it all. He blurted it out again, loudly. "I've been looking for this guy. I had something better than a mug shot. I had a full-figure view of him imprinted in my head. I know I only saw him for a few seconds, but I know this guy."

Pearson nodded as though to say, *All right, I understand.*

Nick went on. "I've been hunting him and even mentioned to you I thought he might be hanging out in the West Hollywood area. It wasn't like a miracle happened. I've been looking for him for months, the way you were supposed to be doing, and I found him hustling along Santa Monica Boulevard. He saw me coming and ran, like he recognized me. I caught him, smacked him around a little, and he confessed. Then someone jumped me and he got away."

"I'd confess too if some crazy guy started chasing me out of the blue and then stomped me. During the Inquisition, the most innocent people confessed to the most horrible crimes because they were beaten or tortured."

Nick thought he had explained everything so logically; he objected to Pearson's deflection of the story. His Irish temper flared along with the fatigue, pot, booze, and stress. He tore into Pearson. "This guy Rainey did it. He knew things only someone who was there could have known. He gave me their first names, for Christ's sake, Jesse and Cal!"

At the mention of the names, Pearson betrayed nothing. He continued to listen carefully as Nick went on again, telling Pearson everything Rainey had said about his accomplices. Pearson sat like a psychiatrist in an asylum with a chain-link fence between him and the crazed. In the end, he still suspected he wasn't getting the whole story, but that was okay. He wasn't sharing either. Surprisingly, Nick had uncovered part of the puzzle, but Cullen didn't have to know all about Cal Santiso and Jesse Carmody, especially with the way he locked and was behaving. It was with some relief he observed Nick calming down from his outburst. It was time to get him out of there. "This is helpful, Nick, and we're going to pursue this with a lot of vigor."

"When are you going to check this guy out?" Nick asked.

"As soon as you leave."

"I don't have to leave. I could go along, identify him, or maybe he kept something that was stolen..."

"We've got the list you gave us of the stolen items. We're just going to pick the punk up and bring him in for questioning. When we do that, we'll give you a call and let you know."

Pearson's comment, "Let you know..." unexpectedly drove Nick over the top and he stepped forward and violently scraped half the stuff on Pearson's desk to the floor. "This is bullshit, I know this fucking guy, I had him by the throat and you tell me I'm just supposed to go home? 'You'll let me know?' Get real, Pearson."

Pearson rose from behind his desk like a giant walrus. "Don't rip on me, fuckhead. All you had to do last night was call the cops and send them to where you saw this Rainey guy and that would have been that."

Nick wildly threw his hands in the air. "They couldn't have done jack shit. A patrol car pulls up to twenty hookers soliciting on a corner; cops jump out and try to find some guy I described over a microphone? He would have disappeared faster than a snake in weeds."

"We would have caught him."

"That's bullshit," Nick raged and swiped the remaining papers off Pearson's desk. "What are you jiving me for? Let me in."

Pearson looked with dismay at the pile on the floor. It was the only organized stack of papers in his office. He reached for the cuffs on his belt and pulled them. "We are the police and this is the work we do. That's the way it's supposed to be, Cullen. That's the way I told you to play it: cool." Pearson held up the cuffs in front of Nick's eyes and threatened, "If you take the law into your own hands again, I'm going to bust you for it and bust you as hard as I can. There's no excuse for that."

"There's every excuse in the world!" Nick shouted.

Jim closed the handcuffs in his fist and the sound of the locking teeth on the cuffs ground loudly and effectively. Nick found himself staring at the jagged locking teeth in Pearson's hand. Jim went on, "Just so we understand one another, you start beating up potential suspects again, I'll have you locked up for a long fucking time. I can't condone that. I promise you, I won't even blink to get your ass off the street. I've given breaks to people like you in the past and it turned to shit. I'm not going there again."

He observed Nick with his wild sunken eyes, looking first to the cuffs and then at the havoc he had wreaked in the office. Another four seconds went by; Nick turned and walked out the door.

Attracted by the yelling, Lou Stabile came down the hall and stared at Nick walking away. He then turned and peered through the doorway to Pearson and his littered office. "You invite people in here to yell and trash your office? Invite me in here sometime. I could use that kind of release," Stabile said.

"Hey, Stabile, go out and bust some kid smoking a joint and leave me the fuck alone."

Stabile grinned. "Just trying to be of help," he said and walked back down the hall.

"Asshole," Pearson muttered. In the crowded confines of the precinct halls, he had bumped into Stabile a few times since his transfer and didn't like him at all. Stabile was too much of an in-your-face-then-off-to-the-shadows kind of guy. Something wasn't right with him and Jim was happy they didn't have to work together. Pearson sat down behind his desk and said to himself, "Hey, Jim, you let a potential killer go again."

A half hour later, Pearson had picked up all the papers from the floor, consumed three ounces of whiskey from the bottle he kept in his drawer, and cursed Nick a thousand times. He should have busted Cullen, or at least made him clean up the mess. "If I had made him pick everything up, he probably would have made my filing system even worse," Pearson muttered. After one more nip of Irish to achieve a perfect calm, he got up and did as promised. He drove over to Morgan Rainey's and, using two patrol officers from South Central as back up, he approached the large, run-down Victorian house that had been divided into small apartments. Upstairs at the end of a hall, the door to Rainey's studio apartment was wide open. Inside the little greasy brown furnished room, the dresser drawers had been pulled to the floor and were gaping empty, save for one lone sock with a hole in the toe draped over an edge. Rainey's wardrobe and personal effects were gone. So was he.

✦✦✦

NICK WENT BACK TO his apartment, chugged some tequila from the bottle, opened a beer, popped a few aspirin for his numb jaw and ringing ear, and lay down on his bed. He turned and looked at the pictures of Julianne and Melissa with the toy taxicab parked in front. "Well, what did you think of all that?" He paused for a moment as though expecting an answer.

The images stared back. Nick took a slug of beer, rolled over, and stared at the ceiling. He forced his mind away from Melissa and Julianne. He felt drained. He had found Rainey, but he knew if they ever picked him up, Rainey wouldn't be able to give any more information than Nick had gotten from him. There was also a very good chance Rainey would be gone. In a real way, it was his fault. With Rainey, Nick had a nightly destination and, consequently, an anchor. That anchor was lost. The real killers were still out there.

CHAPTER SEVENTEEN

PEARSON SHIFTED HIS WEIGHT on the stool inside Chez Jay's, a small joint on Ocean Avenue in Santa Monica. It had a funky nautical motif, peanut shells on the floor, and an atmosphere conducive to drinking. On the wooden bar, Pearson turned his Manhattan on the rocks, dragged it toward himself, and watched with interest the condensation sliding along the glass. He liked Manhattans on a rainy night. They had a warming and stomach-settling effect that made him feel cozy in a place that had gotten cold from disappointments. He liked Manhattans so much he was on his third. His daughter, who was home from college for a few days, had passed on going to the Lakers game with him. She had been a big Lakers fan when she was in junior high school. At the time, she was a pretty fair basketball player herself and could out shoot her older brother on a regular basis. Pearson was surprised when she declined. Maybe it was because he could only afford nosebleed seats. Or maybe it was because she really wanted to go up to Sunset Strip, get high with her friends, and listen to music. Probably the latter. He gave the tickets to Hastings, a man in the squad room who made Pearson feel even worse by saying, "Hey, I'm gonna see my boy tonight. These tickets will knock him out."

Pearson was feeling sorry for himself, but his third drink lifted him out of self-pity and released his obsessive mind to dwell on his murder cases. His thoughts drifted to the Tombridge/Cullen case. Things had been grinding slowly. But now he could see them unfolding like a developing hand in gin rummy. More and more stats were coming in about the perpetrators who had left prints at the crime scene. They were wanted in Texas for murder, as well as Denver. As Pearson checked around, it definitely sounded like the same guys who killed Nick Cullen's wife. Definitely the same MO, at least, a modus operandi of total whacked-out stupidity and meanness. He admitted if it hadn't been for Cullen getting information from the Rainey guy, it might never have been so clear.

That fucking Cullen, the guy had actually helped, even if he did let the perp get away. Still, having Cullen for a partner was a little like having a crazed, untrained pit bull in your bathroom. You were never sure when it might bite you on the ass. The way Nick had trashed his office, he should have put him in the tank for a few hours to calm down. He didn't want another Reginald Post. If Cullen ever pulled anything like that again, he was going to have to take the consequences. Pearson shoved Cullen from his mind and thought of his caseload. He had made good progress on a few murders and collared one guy who killed a bartender on Lincoln Boulevard. Yes, it had been a pretty good week in all, so why did he feel so fucking down and lonely? He looked around the bar. There were a couple of good-looking middle-aged women warming their barstools and sipping white wine. Maybe if he got lucky, one would fall on top of him on her way to the ladies' room.

NICK ANSWERED A RADIO call for a pickup in Playa Del Rey. As he drove to the fare, his outburst in Pearson's office came sweeping back into his mind. Why had he done such a thing? That was not like him to trash an office like a spoiled three-year-old. What was it about Pearson that made him behave like an asshole? He reached for the answer and dwelled over whether he actually wanted the police to find the murderers. He could lose his personal vendetta, if that's what it was. Vendetta? No, it was more like a personal obligation. It was his. The obligation did not include Pearson, the LAPD, or anyone but himself.

He pulled alongside a pale-green stucco apartment building, fronted with thick clusters of bird-of-paradise, illuminated by gaudy red-and-blue spotlights. It was an unfortunate, garish sight singular to urban Southern California. He turned off the engine, and as he waited for the fare to arrive, he concluded Pearson wanted nothing more to do with him and in turn he had nothing left to share with Pearson. So he would just let it all play out and see who found them first. After all, it seemed to Nick that he was out in front of the cops on the case.

A moment later, a woman about thirty years old came out of the breezeway and arrived at the passenger door. She was modestly attractive, a little heavyset, with dark brown hair, wearing what Nick assumed to be a business dress. She got in the cab and gave Nick the address of a place in Sherman Oaks. It was going to be a nice fare if the freeway wasn't too crowded.

The woman settled herself in and asked if she could smoke. Nick said he didn't care as long as she cracked the window. She lit up and put the window down a half inch. It took over seven miles and two cigarettes but she began talking. Lighting her third smoke, she said, "I'm going to see this guy. I must have broken up with him at least three times." Nick's lack of response didn't slow her down. "He's the only one who can push my buttons, you know what I mean?" Nick acknowledged he knew, so the woman continued. "There are guys, I date them, well, I date a lot, but nothing seems to pop, it's just been this one man, my button pusher." She paused for effect. "Want to know something weird?" Nick wasn't sure he did and kept silent. "I don't even think I like him." She glanced at Nick through the rearview mirror to see how he was taking their conversation. Nick looked passive, and she took a deep drag on her cigarette and slowly blew the smoke out the cracked window. "I don't know, sometimes I think I should just forget about men. Just get a vibrator and jam it against my clit until I have one galactic, explosive orgasm, one of those total body-racking kinds. What do you think?"

"That might be a temporary solution to a deeper problem," Nick said absently. The woman seemed to consider Nick's comment until they finally cruised up to a large new apartment complex. The woman silently rummaged inside her bag and Nick groaned to himself and thought the woman was like an elevator panel with a thousand unmarked buttons. Nick felt sorry for the guys she'd been dating, trying in vain to hit the right button. He was glad the ride had ended. When she placed the three-dollar tip in his hand, he heard himself say, "I hope he hits every button." Despite her preceding immodest dialogue, Nick sensed the woman didn't like his familiarity. She gave him a dirty look, snapped her purse shut, got out of the cab, and walked toward the apartment building. He mulled the possibility she was miffed because he didn't volunteer to press a button himself.

THINGS HADN'T GONE WELL in Juarez. They had parked the stolen rental car on the American side and spent three days searching for a suitable supplier. Their search resulted in them having a brief sit-down with a dealer named Raul. The dealer was a thin, dangerous-looking man in his early thirties, with piercing black eyes. The man quickly dismissed them by saying, "This is a cash-and-carry business. Come back when you have cash."

They promised Raul substantial future business. Going by foot over the Cordova Bridge from Juarez back to El Paso, they blended in with tourists and the thousands of Mexicans who made the daily pilgrimage. Cal turned angrily to Jesse. "Any fool could tell you, go see a man like that, you've got to have a briefcase full of green."

"Hey, compadre, we accomplished a lot. Next time, we know where to go and won't be wandering all around Juarez with a ton of cash looking to make a buy."

Cal slipped behind the wheel of the punished rental car. "Right now, I'd take five hundred bucks and a bottle of tequila," he said and pointed the needy Pontiac toward Roswell.

CHESTER MORLEY HAD BEEN living well and lost much of his muscular profile to Budweiser. He had been a cook for four years in the Air Force, stationed on Guam during the Vietnam War from 1966 to '67. When he was discharged, he used his GI Bill to put together two years toward an AA degree in Restaurant Management from a St. Louis junior college. He now worked as food coordinator at the Air Force Base. He was doing well for himself. He had a small house on the outskirts of Roswell, complete with three cars and a truck. The truck he used for work and the occasional delivery. He had purchased a 1970 El Camino from an Airman on the base. The kid had bought it new, run it into the ground for two years, and then shipped out to Germany. Chester had it in his garage where he had been rebuilding it into what he knew would be one of the greatest pickups of all time. He put in a huge LS6-454 engine, a Muncie 21 transmission, and a superbly balanced and strengthened suspension. He expertly applied seven coats of maroon paint and added detail heaped upon detail. The El Camino stayed covered in the garage. It was going to be his exit car. He also had a Ford Fairlane, which he drove when not using the truck. His next automotive project was an 1970 Pontiac GTO he planned to bring back to cherry condition. The good life was largely afforded by the fact he did some part-time dealing of weed, speed, quaaludes, and cocaine to the kitchen staff. In turn, they got the goods to any Airmen who wanted to buy, and many did. Chester kept the side business small, lucrative, and steady. He deposited much of his money at a bank in Kansas where he had opened his first account when he was nine years old. He planned to return to his hometown when he hit his target of $250,000, then open a small restaurant. The plan was working because he didn't get greedy and didn't flaunt it. For security, he had three handguns: a .44 Ruger Super Blackhawk, a .32 snub-nose Colt, and an 8mm Nambu Japanese Officer's pistol. He got the Nambu in Guam but never fired it for fear it might blow up in his hand. He had heard stories of Japanese booby traps during the Second World War. Added to the small arsenal was a beautiful 12-gauge Remington pump action shotgun he kept hidden in a closet by the front door.

When Jesse arrived towing along some sullen-looking Mexican dude, Chester Morley wasn't happy. He knew Jesse from childhood and it didn't look like he had improved much.

"Howdy, cousin. You're a sight. You put on more weight than a heifer in springtime," Jesse said and gave Chester the old glad hand.

Chester reluctantly admitted them into his home and said they could stay a day or two until they got themselves rested, but that was it. "I got to be firm about this, Jesse. I've got business to tend to."

"Hell, Chester, looks like you got plenty of room, but whatever you say, pardner. Me and Cal here can use any kindness a close relative can give."

The brief visit got extended, day by day, week after week. Chester pouted and complained bitterly from time to time, but the boys were impossible to dislodge. Jesse and Cal took short hunting trips around Roswell looking for places to rob, but it proved more difficult than Los Angeles. Roswell only had thirty-eight thousand people, was too open and exposed, and they concluded it was going to take some time to find proper scores. Meanwhile, they were only too happy to live off Chester's largesse and stay holed up with him until things calmed down from their crazed run through Texas. Sadly, Chester found he occasionally enjoyed their company. He realized he had been lonely. Some talk recollecting the folks back home in Kansas was nice and the boys were fun to party with. Chester thought Cal turned out to be a pretty decent guy, was a good mechanic, and at the worst of moments seemed to be a calming influence on Jesse. But it wasn't enough to make up for the wholesale intrusion into his closely guarded private life.

To his dismay, his life was revealed, layer by layer. Jesse discovered the El Camino under the car cover, the many pairs of expensive cowboy boots, the porno collection, his Remington shotgun, the Nambu and Ruger pistols, and his weekly relationship with Natalie who was a rare and expensive hooker in Roswell. Jesse also figured out and confirmed Chester was modestly but successfully dealing. One thing in particular fed Chester's increasing discomfort: he feared it was only a matter of time before Jesse discovered his secret stash.

◆◆◆

NICK HAD BEEN DRIVING constantly for thirteen straight long nights. When he came into his apartment at 7:20 a.m., he went to the kitchen, poured himself four ounces of tequila, tossed it down like medicine, popped open a bottle of beer, and cooled his burning throat with the welcome liquid. Reaching into his pocket, he slowly pulled out his tip money and dropped it on the kitchen table where it lay atop a growing pile of cash from the previous twelve nights. There were hundreds of dollars in small bills as well as a couple of checks from the cab company. He needed to take a day off, go to the bank, send Lillian some money, get a present for Melissa, and pick up groceries and booze.

He blankly stared around the kitchen. It had been many weeks since he'd lost Rainey in the alley. Since then, he'd been driving and hunting, driving and hunting, night after night. Walking into the living room, he glanced down at a place on the gray rug. The morning light slanted in through the windows and illuminated the vague outline of the area where Julianne's blood had run out. When the police investigation concluded, Nick had cleaned the carpet, but there remained the trace discoloration. Nick slowly got down onto his knees and stared at it. He bent over and ran his hand back and forth along the stain. Against his diminishing will, he weakly descended onto the carpet and passed out. Released from his grip, the bottle fell over and the beer spilled out, foaming and settling into the old stain.

CHESTER MADE UP HIS mind to get Jesse and Cal out of his house. He was rehearsing what he was going to say when, to Chester's extreme dismay, the boys turned over the last layer of Chester's life. Beers in hand, the three of them had walked into the garage to do some work on the GTO. Crowned with boxes of auto parts, motor oil, and coolant, Chester's four-foot metal locker was hidden in the corner of the garage under some old canvas. It was probably the only place Jesse hadn't searched and Chester had scrupulously avoided any mention of it. Earlier, Chester had gone to put some cash in the locker, but before he'd completely covered it back up, the telephone had rang. It was still slightly exposed when the three men walked into the garage. Chester's heart sank at the sight of the partially revealed locker. As they began their tinkering with the GTO's engine, Jesse kept eyeing the locker and finally asked what was in it. "Some old tools and shit," Chester answered, trying to remain casual. Jesse knew better. Chester was organized and meticulous with his tools. With a welded steel strap and forged padlock, the locker resembled a Brinks armored truck.

A little later, Chester went into the house to go to the bathroom. On the way back, he stopped to get three more beers from the refrigerator and vainly search for the pretzels Cal had greedily devoured earlier. During that short time, Jesse took Chester's large ring of keys out of the GTO's ignition and quickly tried several in the large padlock until he found the right one. He removed the steel strap and popped the locker open, revealing several kilos of marijuana, over six ounces of coke, a fair supply of speed, and over $9,000 in cash. When Chester came in and saw Jesse and Cal looking into the locker like kids into a Christmas window, he quietly went over and closed the doors, put the steel strap back on, secured the lock, took back his keys, and went over to the GTO as though nothing had happened. 'No good tools in there," he said.

Chester went on trying to act like they hadn't seen anything. It was like dropping a mouse into the terrarium of a captive rattlesnake and then writing the snake a note saying, "You do not see a mouse!" The snake wouldn't pay any attention to the denial. It would take the prize when it felt like it. So would Jesse.

"That's a nice little stash you got in there, cousin. Glad to see you're doing so well," Jesse calmly commented.

THAT NIGHT, CHESTER COULDN'T sleep and his mind whirled with questions and concerns. Increasingly panicked, when he left work the next day, Chester went to his steady hooker. He confided his fear he was going to get ripped off by his cousin. Natalie gave him some reasonably good advice: "Take the stash to a locker at the bus station, or out to the desert and bury it all under a rock. Then tell them you sold the stash and all the cash went to get rid of some old gambling debts. Tell them you did it so you wouldn't wind up hurt or killed."

In his desperate state, Chester grabbed at the idea. He gave Natalie $200 for the good advice and secretly vowed to bury his stash behind the abandoned gas station on Highway 285. He'd get up early while Jesse and Cal were still sleeping. Yes, he'd hide his treasure and then get rid of his crazy cousin and his lumbering sidekick.

When he went back to check on his stash and his guests, he found only Cal kneeling in front of the living room coffee table. Cal was moaning loudly, accompanied by sounds of Mariachi music blaring from the radio. Cal was flipping through some of Chester's porno magazines, wildly exclaiming in Spanish over the different women he'd discovered. He was masturbating violently and near orgasm. Chester watched as Cal visually locked onto what was obviously his favorite picture, and as he started moaning the centerfold's name he came all over the washcloth in front of him, the magazines, and the centerfold. Chester sensed he'd better go and get one of his guns and keep it on him.

He went to the bedroom, reached under the mattress, and pulled out the chrome-plated .32-caliber snub-nosed Colt Cobra. Going to his closet, he reached inside a gym bag, removed an ankle holster, strapped it on, and jammed the pistol in. "What the fuck," he mumbled in frustration. One way or another, he was going to get those guys out. He went back to the living room and saw Cal lying on his side, spent and content. Suddenly, he heard the sound of the GTO pulling up outside. Chester hated Jesse driving it, but the boys had said they had to get rid of their rental car, as they couldn't afford it anymore. Chester could understand that; they'd been drinking his booze, smoking his weed, and eating his food for weeks and weeks.

In actuality, that same morning, as Jesse followed in the GTO, Cal drove the stolen rental car two hundred miles to El Paso. They left the GTO on the El Paso side, then drove the rental across the Cordova Bridge into Juarez. While they were there, they had a conversation with Raul. Jesse talked of doing a big buy in the next week. Raul assured them whatever they required would be waiting, but to not waste his time again by showing up with no Yankee dollars. Almost as an afterthought, Jesse asked Raul if he had a small amount of quaaludes he could buy. "I got some of that, but what you want that shit for? You look like a stimulant guy," Raul said with a sneer.

Jesse explained it was a gift for a friend. Raul wouldn't sell any for less than a hundred dollars, so Jesse took the twenty pills and paid the hard-looking young man, leaving him and Cal with eighty-two dollars between them. Cal didn't understand why Jesse would buy quaaludes, but he didn't ask. He knew when to leave Jesse alone and it was obvious Jesse was planning something. In Juarez, they left the rental car on a dirty side street with the windows down, keys in the ignition, and walked back over the bridge spanning the Rio Grande to El Paso. It took forty-one minutes before a burned-out itinerant worker discovered the dusty sedan with the keys in the ignition. He thanked Jesus and Our Lady of Guadalupe, started up the pounded rental, and headed for his home in Jalisco.

Cal and Jesse drove the GTO back to Roswell. They had conducted their meeting with Raul and made the 420-mile round trip in less than ten hours. Jesse dropped Cal off at the house, telling him he had shopping to do. For Jesse, it was all coming together, and though Cal knew something was in the works, he didn't try too hard to figure it all out.

BOTH FASCINATED AND REPULSED, Chester watched as Cal slowly cleaned himself up from his sexual encounter with the porno collection. Jesse walked into the house as Cal completed cleaning himself up from his porn indulgence and grinned at Chester. "Well, cousin, we're out of here first thing tomorrow."

Chester repressed an urge to give a loud rebel yell. Cal got up from the floor; Jesse's declaration was news to him.

"Yes, sir, made some calls to LA and a buddy has some work lined up for both me and my Tex-Mex compadre here." Jesse threw the GTO keys to Chester. "We won't be needing this fartin' GTO of yours anymore. You just drive us down to the bus station in the morning and we'll be out of your hair, cousin, 'cause we've got business in L-fucking-A."

Chester felt lightness inside and couldn't suppress a grin. "Well, I'm happy for you boys, getting something going and all."

"Shit, we've got it all goin', cousin. Let's party, I want to party, then we'll hit the road first thing."

Chester wished he had made the decision to sequester his stash earlier. The guys were leaving in the morning and they still might be tempted to dip into it. But he had the key to the heavy lock and a gun at the ready. He watched with some misgiving as Jesse reached into the bag he was carrying and spun the top off a pint bottle of Jack Daniels and handed it to him; then he reached back into the bag and pulled out a quart of tequila and two six-packs of beer. "You're the Mr. Jack Daniels man, cousin, and me and compadre here will do the tequila." He threw the bottle of tequila to Cal, then popped open three beers and passed them around. "To a brilliant fucking future, whatever we may be doing."

Chester brought the bottle of Jack Daniels to his mouth and something inside him warned against taking a drink, but he pushed the feeling aside and took a healthy belt. He followed this with a good slug of beer, Cal and Jesse doing the same. Jesse lit up a joint, took a couple of hits, and passed it along to Cal, who passed it on to Chester. As Chester took his scond hit off the joint, Jesse held the tequila bottle aloft and grinned. "Here's to you and your cars, cousin. The cars are great, but you're the best."

Chester took another big slug of Jack and noticed it had a slightly acidic taste that seemed beyond the normal sour mash flavor. He stared at the label on the bottle and then washed the offending taste from his mouth with beer. Feeling unusually mellow, he held his bottle of Jack up and proposed a toast. "Here's to the future of the unholy and wild trip of Jesse and Cal. Let the wind be behind you and women on knees in front of you."

Jesse and Cal laughed as they all drank. Inspired, Cal proposed a toast to their mothers. That cracked Jesse up and he fell down, rolling around on the floor. Giggling, Chester, took another deep drink. He stared glassy-eyed into the now half-empty pint and noticed some sedimentation on the bottom. He tried to sit erect and study it more closely in the light, but he had trouble lifting his body more than an inch.

Jesse had crushed and dissolved eighteen quaaludes into the Jack Daniels and so far, Chester had drunk at least eight of them. He stared across the room at his guests and realized things were not right. Jesse was staring at him like a leopard, a slight smile playing across his lips. "Hey, Ches, what's the matter with you, bro?"

Chester tried to articulate something but the cocktail had done its work. He mumbled and managed to shove his feet straight out in front of himself in a lame effort to stand up, but it was no use. Jesse rose up and glanced down at Chester's extended feet, noticing the .32 Colt stuffed into the ankle holster. "Hey, cousin, what you got there, some little pop gun? You're making it too easy for me, Chester." Jesse went over and pulled the gun from the holster, then reached down and straining mightily, hauled Chester's bulk into a more upright position on the chair. "You got to sit up, bro, or you'll slide onto the floor." Cal and Chester watched fascinated as Jesse flipped open the cylinder, spun it a couple of times, examined the bullets packed in, expertly snapped the cylinder back in place, and pushed off the safety. Pulling out the tail of his cowboy shirt, he meticulously wiped the gun all over. "You got to keep a chrome-plated gun like this clean, cousin, nice and shiny." Jesse reached down and put the gun into Chester's right hand. "Here, I'll give it back to you nice and clean." Chester tried to push him away, but it was a feeble effort and holding his hand over Chester's, Jesse put the muzzle of the gun against Chester's temple and pulled back his finger. The gun fired and across the room, Cal jumped up as though he had been shot himself. "*Madre de Dios*, what did you do? That's your cousin, man."

Chester flopped over to his left side. Blood spurted from within the blackened hole in his temple onto his shoulder, stuffed chair, and Jesse's jeans. Jesse jumped back. "Goddamn, this is my best pair of jeans."

Cal stared at Jesse, and tears sprang to his eyes and trickled down his cheeks. He liked Chester. "How could you do that, man? Your own family?"

Jesse turned to Cal and looked at him like he was the stupidest man on the planet. "Don't you see? We take the keys, raid his locker, take the Camino nobody knows he's got, and drive out of here. We've got the most bitchin' wheels, a stash, and cash. We're on the road to 'the big easy trade-up.'"

Cal understood once and for all—if Jesse would murder his own cousin who had shown them respect, given them shelter and money, then Jesse would kill him faster than he could down a shot of tequila.

They cleaned up the place, wiping fingerprints from everything they could remember touching. On their way out the door, they stopped and looked at Chester slumped over the edge of the chair. A fly was walking around the wound in his temple, checking it out. "Suicide, that's what they'll say," Jesse said. "He was such a sorry ass he should have shot himself anyway. Hell, that porky fucker didn't even belong in my family."

Fearfully, Cal went along with everything. They went into the garage, emptied the locker, stashed the cash under the rear seat, removed the spare tire from the rim, shoved the weed and drugs inside, and remounted it.

Four hours later, they reached El Paso. Parking the El Camino in a safe place, they took nearly $10,000 over the bridge into Juarez. They checked into a hotel and partied with some Mexican hookers for two days. With the rise in their fortunes, Jesse seemed to have reclaimed his sexual vigor and always took the best-looking women. Cal didn't say a thing. He'd have to be patient. Now was not the time to get into an argument with Jesse over anything. *Maybe there would never be a time,* Cal thought.

When Jesse had enough partying, they went to Raul and purchased $7,500 of Mexican brown heroin. They placed it inside condoms and, at Raul's suggestion, hired two young men to act as "mules" and carry the drugs across the bridge jammed up their rectums. They added it to Chester's collection inside the spare tire. Getting behind the wheel, Jesse cheerfully punched Cal on the shoulder and exclaimed, "Compadre, we're on our way. I told you, stick with me, buddy, we're gonna be rich" He grinned and turned the El Camino toward LA.

CHAPTER EIGHTEEN

VERN DROPPED AN ORDER on Nick as he drove out of the yard. The late summer sun was still well up as Nick made his way through the angling shadows to a narrow street in the Palms area. Stopping outside a dull, gray two-story apartment building, Nick briefly sounded his horn. A few moments later, a couple emerged from a ground-floor apartment. Despite being in her early thirties, she appeared a worn woman. The man was in his midtwenties with a long, thin brown beard and straight hair to his shoulders. He had a vacant stare, as though he were present somewhere other than earth. The woman opened the door for him and he quietly accepted the courtesy. She walked around the cab and slid onto the seat and looked at the disturbed man. "Are you all right, Doug?" she asked with meaning. Doug said nothing but might have moved his head. It was hard for Nick to tell. "We're going to the VA Hospital up on Ohio."

Nick nodded, started the meter, and pulled away. Glancing in the mirror, he felt a familiar concern and asked, "Is this a Vietnam thing?"

"Yeah. He's gotten much worse over the last week. I'm afraid I'm going to have to leave him in the hospital again for a while. I can't take care of him full-time. I've got a job."

"What happened?"

"What happened? They took my brother, sent him over there and ruined him. He used to be a great guy, a bright, great guy, and they ruined him," she declared, her voice full of anger and bitterness. "They just fucking ruined him."

Nick glanced in the mirror to see how Doug would react to her statement, but he just stared vacantly out the window. They rode on in silence and Nick remembered when he had arrived in Vietnam seeing soldiers waiting to return stateside. They were deeply changed people. Nick felt his bitterness about the senseless war swiftly resurface. As a photographer, he was supposed to have been dispassionate, but it seldom worked. "Those sons of bitches," he said aloud to himself.

"What?" the woman asked.

"Those dirty sons of bitches."

"Yes," she said.

When Nick dropped off the woman and her lost brother, he remained for a few minutes watching them make their way into the hospital. A blizzard of photographic images he had taken overseas flooded his mind. He tried to shake off the montage, but all he could do was push it down; it wasn't going anywhere, it was part of him. "Fuck that noise," he abruptly said to himself. "I got shit to do." He angrily drove away to the closest liquor store for his usual half pint of tequila and three twelve-ounce bottles of Dos Equis Amber.

With the booze carefully sequestered in the trunk, he caught a good fare out of Westwood going downtown to the Clark Hotel. Five minutes later, Nick picked off a well-dressed man at City Hall. He was headed to Baldwin Hills and as the man relaxed into the seat, Nick watched as he slowly stretched out his long dark brown fingers and began to crack them one by one, relieving the tension. "What a day, what a day, what a day," the man said.

They began to talk and Nick learned the good-looking man was a prosecutor for the District Attorney's Office. Without too much subtlety, Nick steered the conversation to a question he had long wanted to understand. Presenting the situation fictionally, he went on to explain what had happened to Julianne and about the robbery. "If they caught those guys, what do you think the chances are they would get convicted and what would they get?"

The prosecutor made a living ferreting out half truths and immediately saw through Nick's attempt at deception. "Well, from what you told me, I'd say the chances are not very good. The only witness is you and you're prejudiced." The man paused for a moment. "You are prejudiced, aren't you?" The man smiled at his own joke, showing a beautiful set of white teeth. When Nick didn't answer, the prosecutor got serious. "We put a lot of people in jail. The system loves to put people in jail, especially men who do what you say those guys did. But it doesn't sound like there's an airtight case. Chances are they would have no stolen property left and there were no witnesses, unless you could find and get that one hustler to talk again. No, I'd say they would walk out the door on this one. But let me say this, people like that will get caught eventually and they'll go to jail. It may not be for your case, but they'll wind up in jail one day."

"How much time would they get?"

"I don't know. It depends on what they get caught for, what else they're wanted for. But even if they are convicted and sentenced to death, there is no guarantee. Look at Gary Gilmore. He killed someone, said, 'I did it,' they gave him the death penalty. He said, 'Good! Go ahead. Please kill me. I want to die,' and they still haven't killed his ass. It's been years."

Nick dropped the man in front of an old craftsman house with red rosebushes lining the path to his door. The man leaned forward and handed Nick the fare and tip. "I'm sorry, but you shouldn't grind on this too much. Someday, those boys are going to get theirs," the man said, getting out of the cab.

"Someday" was too long for Nick to wait, and he sped into the gathering darkness.

◈ ◈ ◈

AT 10:40 P.M., HE got a call to pick up at the Airport Marina Hotel.
He thought it too early for Irene but as he arrived, he saw she was
standing outside and a short, thin, nervous-looking man in a cheap
gray suit was earnestly speaking to her. As Nick pulled alongside,
a man about thirty-five years old who looked like a former football
lineman pushed the front door to the hotel open so hard it bounced
loudly off the stop. He was barefoot and the tail of his white button-
down shirt was hanging outside his rumpled black pants. The man
drunkenly lurched toward Irene and grabbed her by the arm. "You
got to come back upstairs." As he pulled on Irene's arm, she began
to lose her balance.

Nick quickly got out of the car. "Hold on, pal, the woman's
getting in the cab."

The man turned to Nick. "Fuck you. She's coming upstairs with
us. She's a prostitute," the man said, as though it were the same as
a rental car.

"The woman called for a cab, so she's going to get in it. Please,
let go of her."

"I don't take orders from cab drivers."

"Listen, you and your friend can either let her go, or I'll pick up
the mike, get the cops, and have you arrested."

"You're going to call the cops?" the man asked derisively.
"The woman's a prostitute," he said again, loudly, still holding onto
Irene's arm. Irene stood like a store window mannequin, waiting.

Nick glanced at the smaller man who had backed off a little and
Nick estimated he didn't want any trouble. The big fella, however,
was another problem. Nick knew the type. The man would be
just as happy getting into a fight as getting laid, probably happier.
Nick spoke quietly to the man. "You ought to think this through.
She doesn't want to go with you."

"She doesn't have a choice. She did my friends and she's gonna
do me."

"What are you going to do, rape her? That's what it's called
and that's trouble, even for you, pal." As Nick said this, he observed

the tendons in the guy's neck begin to stand out as he gritted his teeth in mounting fury. Nick refrained from stepping up onto the curb to make the situation less confrontational, but he felt vulnerable standing between the huge man and the taxi. His only advantage was by standing below the curb; he was a smaller target by almost eight inches. Nick tried the quiet approach again. "You don't want to get into a mess over this, especially, when you're wrong."

"Wrong?" the big guy snorted the question and began to move toward Nick, dragging Irene along.

Nick felt the familiar buzz of fear-provoked adrenaline rushing through his body.

"Wrong?" The guy repeated, letting go of Irene and turning completely to face Nick.

Nick tried his last quiet voice. "Yeah, you're..."

"Wrong!" the big guy shouted and swung a huge roundhouse right for Nick's head.

Nick had a lot of warning and anticipated the punch. He ducked, sidestepped, and quickly moved behind the guy as the man lurched forward and stumbled off the curb from the force of his tremendous drunken swing. Quickly grabbing the back of his hair and thick neck, Nick rapidly slammed the man's head onto the edge of the car's roof a few times. Furious, the man bellowed, recovered his footing, and pushed back violently from the cab with all his strength. Nick knew the move and helped by pulling him backward. The big guy's ankles caught the curb; he fell heavily onto his back and cracked his head hard on the pavement. The man almost went out, but after a few second's delay, he started to get up and Nick quickly stomped him twice, high on the stomach and solar plexus to encourage him to stay. Turning to the other man, Nick asked, "You coming into this?"

The nervous man backed off a few more feet and declined by shaking his head. The man on the ground suddenly roared again in anger and tried to get up. Nick stomped on his stomach again, even harder, and the man groaned and rolled to his side. Turning away, Nick quickly opened the back door of the cab for Irene.

"Thanks," she said casually, as if he had lit her cigarette.

With his body whirring, he quickly jumped in behind the wheel and tore out of the driveway.

Irene turned around and looked out the rear window at the big man stumbling to his feet.

"Christ! What was that all about?" Nick asked.

"He was drunk."

"No kidding, but what was going on?"

"I had just finished a party with three of their friends. There's some group here for a motivational seminar on how to sell more soda cans or something. But then those two got motivated to come into the room. The big one came in naked and very drunk, as you could see. I didn't like that. I left, but then they followed me downstairs. I don't know what would have happened if you hadn't come. The night manager doesn't like to call the police."

"I was lucky the guy didn't connect with that punch. He would have knocked me all the way to the Bronx."

Irene paused; she seemed concerned about something. "Do you think I can go back to the hotel tomorrow night?"

The woman is persistent, Nick thought. "I'd wait until you're sure they've left. You could call the hotel and ask when their seminar is over."

"That's a good idea. I don't want to miss any work."

He drove on in silence, catching his breath. He felt completely exhausted and his fingers were hurting from yanking the huge guy around. He was surprised and worried at how vulnerable he felt.

"I've been thinking for a long time what you said about your wife and how you met her. It sounded nice. Tell me again of your life with her."

Nick couldn't believe Irene could leave the recent fight so quickly behind. *It must be what she does with her tricks as well,* he thought.

"Could you tell me?" she asked again with an eagerness he found almost alarming.

"What do you want to know?"

"I want to know how you were when you wanted to get married. I want to know about the beginning."

"I was a mess when I met Julianne. I had no idea."

"That's what I want to know. Why were you a mess?"

He hadn't seen Irene so animated before. As he caught his breath and came off the adrenaline buzz, he began to tell her. "I didn't think about getting married. I had been traveling for years and had no idea how burned out I was, seeing children dying of malnutrition, people's lives wrecked by disasters, families blown up in wars." Nick thought about what he had been saying and corrected himself. "Burned out may not be the right words, I just didn't know how not to care. If you care, that stuff can get to you. During that time, I drank quite a bit, smoked a lot of weed, and did the occasional psychedelic, but when I started hanging out in London, I really started partying. It was as though I just wanted to let it all go. I was getting into some hard drugs, forgetting about work—well, worse than that, just blowing it off. I'd only just begun to realize it, but I didn't have a clue who I was, what I was doing, or where I was going. I guess you could say I was having a huge identity crisis." Nick gave a short laugh at his last line.

"And then you met her?"

"Yes."

"Well, what happened?"

"She was like an old soul, beautiful with that softness some southern women have. I just went for her, totally, but she was holding way back. Then she saw some of the work I had done, my photography, and she looked at me and said, 'This is important. You do important work.'

"I never forgot that. It was a great compliment but it was also like a slap in the face, a rebuke," Nick said, as he drove along, stuck on the memory.

"Then?"

"I got sober and tried to get going with my work again, but I had burned a lot of bridges. It wasn't easy starting again."

"But you did."

"I'm driving a cab. That should tell the story."

"But something must have happened from what you were doing, getting sober, trying again."

"Well, yes. I finally did get a great assignment to shoot the building of the Alaskan pipeline, but the week it was to start, my wife got killed, so I didn't show up. If you have to give an excuse for not showing up, I guess that's a winner, but they moved on to someone else."

"I think you're going to get going again."

"We'll see."

"No, I do. It's going to happen for you, if you want it to."

Nick swung the cab into the motel parking lot and turned back to face her. "How about you? What do you want, Irene?"

Irene placed the money for the fare in his hand. "I want to get going again, too. I want my own little house, in a very private place."

"Do you have a place in mind?"

"Yes."

"Okay," he said, not caring to pursue it.

"Waldron Island, off the coast of Washington," she said shyly, and slipped out the door.

Several short fares later, Nick slowed 405 to a stand in Culver City. He called in his position. "You planning on retiring, or is that the best you can think of?" Billy asked.

Nick left the question unanswered. It was a dead stand, but he had physically ground to a halt. Getting out of the cab, he opened the trunk and took a grateful nip of tequila, snagged a beer, and returned to his position behind the wheel. He suddenly remembered the half-smoked joint in his bag the young man with Trudy Girl had foisted upon him. Nick stared at Bruno the Apocathary Man's creation and slowly took the last four hits the stubby joint provided. He could not identify the scent of the mysterious ingredients. Turning on the car stereo, he heard the familiar opening bars of Gabriel Fauré's "Pelleas et Melisande." Riding on the beautiful melody, Nick stared out the window down Culver Boulevard, and as the music brought him along, his mind followed a logical trail back through the night's fares and moments of opportune tracking of Cal and Jesse. He went past Irene, the fight with the huge jerk, then skipped over some uneventful fares, the handsome prosecutor with his unhappy conclusions, and came to rest upon Doug, the Vietnam veteran of late afternoon.

That fare stood out as the most vivid. He had been in Vietnam for less than fifty days in all, but it had been enough. He had seen Doug's lost, spaced-out expression on many of the young men returning to the States. It was the leaping glazed expressions on some of the men he photographed that haunted Nick. He remembered the kid jogging over to the edge of the rice paddy to have his picture taken near the water buffalo and then he'd watched his subject's lower legs fly off, followed in turn by the startled and sickening expression on the boy's face as he crumbled to the ground like the Scarecrow in the *Wizard of Oz*. It was then he felt the stiletto-like stabs in his stomach.

The Vietnam War had left a hole in Nick. He hadn't realized it, but it had. It was not the perforations in his stomach from the shrapnel, but a spiritual hole he hadn't completely acknowledged: the recognition of our collective responsibility of what a toll it had taken, on him, on everyone. He had seen horrors all over, but Vietnam was personal insofar as it was his country and countrymen perpetrating the mayhem. As with the murder of Julianne, it was something you couldn't turn your back on and say, "Forget about it." It was always there and always would be.

He had carried the anger back stateside and suddenly nothing seemed to make sense. After he'd recovered from his physical wounds, he was sent on other assignments to Africa and Turkey, but the Vietnam War banged on and on. With a feeling of resignation, he told himself he didn't give a shit about the war that was morally and financially bankrupting the country. He didn't care about anything except getting high, which he did with more and more frequency and higher dosage. But deep inside, he did care and he agonized over it. Instead, he shot pictures of both sides. It was all so stupid, so pointless. His pals and former classmates were getting wasted one way or another. So was he. He harbored a fierce hatred and desire for retribution that was constantly suppressed beneath his objective photojournalist exterior. It was an emotion not to be denied, it had to get out, but there was nowhere for it to go except down deeper inside.

It was then that he remembered the discouraging words of the prosecutor from early evening. Nick had subconsciously been avoiding the implication of what the man had told him, but realized if there was a good chance the killers would go free, then it was all on his shoulders. He remained immobile, feeling the weight for a long time. Gradually, he came back to himself and felt the phantom presence of the joint he'd just smoked.

The night was entering the late, quiet pulse of diminishing activity. The tequila, beer, and the joint had done their work far better than usual. Nick acknowledged he was very stoned. He'd have to watch that; if he wasn't careful, it could get away from him. *If it hasn't already done so,* was a thought fleetingly touched upon. For now, he welcomed the feeling of being totally spaced and tripping out in his glass and metal container. Glancing down, he stared at the speedometer and odometer, as though seeing them for the first time. Behind the plastic frame, they looked like an art object. The odometer read 46,243.7 miles and he realized the car had been driven over 33,000 miles since he'd first driven it out of the yard those months ago. Considering Clyde drove only about a third of what he did, he calculated he had driven well over twenty thousand miles. That would be seven trips across the US. Six thousand more miles and he could have circumnavigated the earth at the equator. From his seat, he glanced back at the MGM gate and, as though illuminated by an arc light, he visualized young Judy Garland in her ruby slippers skipping toward his cab. Toto was cradled in her left arm nestled against her gingham dress. Arriving at the cab, she bent over and peeked through the window at Nick. He delighted in her sweet soft face and braids. She gave him a lovely delicate smile and said, "We'd like to go to Kansas, please."

"I'm sorry, but I'm not allowed to drive out of state."

"Oh," she said. "That's disappointing, it would have been such a nice ride." She clicked the heels of her ruby slippers and disappeared. Nick sadly remained behind. He became aware of the entire area the cab occupied between Culver and Washington Boulevard, the lights, telephone poles, white lines on the street, and occasional cars passing. Then, as though from a thousand feet above, he observed his cab parked under the lights of the quiet streets. He might have remained up there enjoying the view but Billy's voice called, "Four-o-five?"

Regretting the interruption, Nick reached for the mike. "Four-o-five."

"Pick up at the Red Lion."

Nick understood Billy threw the order his way just to pull him off the dead stand. Red Lion was a small, modestly priced chain of hotel restaurants. As Nick drove up to the entrance, he saw a petite woman wearing a prim but inexpensive dress waiting for him. She was around thirty-five, had a demure third-world manner, and as she got into the cab Nick sensed a certain formality. "I'm going to Arbor Vitae not far from Sepulveda," she said, with a very light Hispanic accent.

It wasn't much of a fare. But he didn't care. Nick glanced at his watch: 1:27 a.m. The bar at the Red Lion must have been getting very quiet by that hour. "Have a nice time, tonight?" Nick found himself asking.

"Very nice, I did a lot of dancing. They had some salsa music and some American kinds." There was a long pause from the back seat and Nick didn't feel inclined to disturb it. Then she followed with,

"I danced with one man most of the night and we had champagne, but at the end he said he had to go. He was with some business associates." The pause extended and even though she had mentioned the rebuff so lightly, Nick could sense the sadness, the loneliness.

"Many times, business keeps people from doing what they would really like to do," Nick offered.

"I suppose so." She rested back in her seat and added with a light laugh, "He said what he really wanted was to take me home and kiss me all over."

Surprised by the comment, Nick's eyes glanced into the rearview mirror. The woman was still seated demurely, hands folded in her lap, lost in the thought of the poignant end to her evening. "I don't blame him," he said. Nick returned his eyes to the road, but her image stayed in his mind as though he had taken a picture.

They drove in silence until they got near her apartment building and she gave final directions leading them to a beige one-story apartment complex. He shut off the meter as the woman checked in her purse. "I don't have quite enough money. I'll have to get some more. You may come and wait while I get it, if you wish."

Nick got out of the cab, opened her door, and they followed the narrow walkway to her apartment. She used two different keys for the locks. Without looking at him, she said, "You may come in." Once inside, she turned on a table lamp and went to the bathroom and shut the door.

Nick glanced around the neat little apartment. There was a kitchenette with a breakfast nook and a tiny and sparsely furnished living room with a stuffed chair upholstered with tropical print fabric. He was acutely aware of sounds as the small refrigerator in the kitchen kicked on and he heard the woman move from the bathroom to the bedroom. He remained in the living room, not moving. The details of the room stood out like an etching and Nick acknowledged that the weed he had smoked maintained its strong, psychedelic edge. He had learned that when a drug kicks in with unexpected power, you don't give in to fear or remorse over taking the drug because by then it's too late. You acknowledge where you are, what you've done, and ride it out. There's nothing else to be done, so go with the flow and it will gradually end. He noticed beneath the lamp on the corner table was a simply framed black-and-white photograph. Nick lifted and studied it closely under the light. It was of a middle-aged couple standing in the doorway of a small house graced with flanking avocado trees. Nick heard the bedroom door open and heard the rustle of the woman counting the fare in singles. "My mother and father," she explained as Nick replaced the picture.

"I like the photograph very much. They look like nice people."

"They sent me here from El Salvador." In the reflected light from the lamp, Nick studied her, noticing her surprisingly pale skin, thin lips, and aquiline nose. "So I would be safe," she added with meaning and pressed the dollars in his hand.

"It's in our Bill of Rights, 'freedom from fear.' There's too much fear, don't you think?"

The woman gave a sad sigh of acknowledgement and looked at the picture of her parents. Nick looked down at her, feeling for the first time in a great while an emotional kinship, an aching and a longing. He was surprised to hear himself say, "You are such a gentle and beautiful woman, you should have what the man promised." Her gaze slowly returned from the photograph to him. Her large brown eyes opened wide and penetrated directly into him so completely he felt the room spin and his breath became short. There was a palpable tension, sadness, and vulnerability in her look that affected Nick completely. He bent down near her ear and quietly whispered, "If you wish, say, 'Please leave,' and I will." He stood erect looking down at her beautiful sad face. The woman said nothing, but her eyes moistened as she continued to look at him waiting for love and kindness, comfort and protection, however fleeting. Seconds passed and gradually Nick's right hand found her lower back and rested there as he said, "Let's be close." The woman's face relaxed and her lips parted as she took a deep, quiet inhalation. Nick leaned in and softly kissed and touched his tongue to her neck. It tasted lightly of salt from her night's dancing and Nick followed a trail with his lips down under her dark brown hair onto the nape of her neck. He could sense her breathing get increasingly heavy and her breasts rhythmically and lightly touching his chest with each inhalation. With the hand on her lower back, he slowly pulled her toward him. Letting her head tilt backward, she looked up at him and from the close angle her brown eyes were enormous.

Nick was completely taken by her eyes. Feeling suddenly weak and vulnerable, he lowered his head gently upon her shoulder and rested it there. She neither embraced him nor moved away. A few seconds later, his heart pounding and head swimming from the weed, the booze, the need, he turned and kissed her lightly below the ear and quietly said, "I would like to..." Nick paused to slow the spinning of his head. "I need to kiss you all over." At his comment, the woman's inhalation caught in her throat, yet she said nothing and did nothing. Nick returned his hand to his side, pulled his head back, and, avoiding her eyes, he found himself starring down at her well-formed breasts. He returned his gaze to her eyes and spoke quietly. "I will kiss you gently. When and if you like, you may stop me with a word, but I want to kiss you. I want to kiss you all over." Without putting his hands on her, Nick leaned in and kissed her again up and down her neck. He moved his hands back to her waist and as in a dance movement she gracefully glided into him, into his hands, body, and lips all at once. Nick knew then he couldn't stop what was happening, only she could and she didn't. Her arms encircled his neck and her mysterious brown eyes and deep breathing told him, "Yes."

He wanted to ravage her with his need and pent-up emotion, but he forced himself to take time to kiss and lick the underside of her arms, her wrists, hands, and fingers. In an excruciatingly slow manner, he returned to her neck and face and with his head spinning in near delirium, he unzipped the back of her dress.

She impatiently pulled it down to her waist, revealing round, well-formed breasts straining against a lime-colored bra. She quickly unhooked it and absently shrugged the straps from her shoulders, letting the bra fall to the floor. Nick bent down and caressed and kissed the pale firm breasts and sucked her erect dark nipples. He could have continued the pleasure for a long time, but the woman groaned, leaned back, lost her balance, and, staggering backward, fell onto the armchair behind. Looking up at Nick, she impulsively grabbed her gathered dress and quickly pushed it down along with her lime-colored bikinis. Nick knelt before her and plucked the garments from where they had snagged on her high heels. He slowly removed her shoes and rubbed the soles of her feet and kissed their arches. Looking up, he was astounded to abruptly see Julianne reclining alongside the woman on the chair. She was as naked as the woman and sensually reached her hand down and slowly began touching herself. She smiled at Nick and put her hand on his neck as though to pull Nick down between the woman's legs. The woman seemed unaware of Julianne's presence and she reached her hands to where Julianne rested hers and pulled Nick forward. Nick looked at Julianne in elation and astonishment. Julianne continued touching herself, smiling at him peacefully with kindness and love. Wishing to stay with her presence, Nick resisted the pull against his neck until he watched as Julianne, continuing to touch herself, bent over and kissed the woman's breasts. For a charged moment, Nick and the woman looked at one another. "Come to me," she said.

Nick allowed himself to be pulled forward and he kissed the smooth inside of the woman's thighs. She moaned with pleasure as he put his arms under her legs and continued upward. He thought he could feel Julianne's hand rub his head and then move it down onto his back and gently caress him. The woman moved her hands to the back of Nick's head and again tried to pull him to her. He resisted in uncertain desire and confusion but continued taking his time kissing the inside of her legs, ever higher, enjoying her incredible smoothness and deepening scert. She pushed herself toward him and pulled on his head and, before he had intended, he was there. He licked her and after a momentary bitter taste, he felt a welcome wash of sweetness flood onto his tongue and into his mouth. He began to suck and explore her with his mouth and tongue. For a merciful time, Nick was completely lost in the wetness between her legs, the softness and rhythmic undulations as she held and rocked his head back, forth, and around. Thinking Julianne's phantom presence would no longer be there, he opered his eyes and saw the faint spirit of Julianne nearing orgasm in that gentle, almost girlish way she had. He lost himself in the moment as he felt the woman swell in his mouth and her groans lower in timbre and vibration. The time seemed all too short, because suddenly, the woman began to moan loudly, and as she did, she raised and dropped her legs over his back, held onto his head, and, as she began to come, sang out and swung his head around between her thighs. Nick closed his eyes, and with his hands under her hips, he pulled her closer and gratefully felt carried along with her rhythm and flow. He opened his eyes again and Julianne was there as well, participating, and as she began to orgasm her body shifted in color and density, chameleon-like, from a faint presence to opaque. The woman's legs continued to seize and rock him, and Nick's intoxication, exhaustion, and emotional need flung him into a draining blackness and for a long time he was lost he knew not where.

When it was over, Nick opened his eyes. Julianne was gone. The woman lay back against the chair cradling his head as he rested between her thighs. She rubbed the back of his neck and when he finally looked directly at her, she said, "You may stay if you wish."

"It's better if I don't." He wasn't sure why he declined.

"Come to me again," she said, reaching out and taking hold of his hand as the light tinkling Latin accent of her words fell upon him. He rose up on his knees, held her small nude body next to his, and gently kissed her mouth. She eagerly pulled him toward her and he knew for certain, he couldn't stay. If he remained, he would forget everything.

A few minutes later, he found himself walking through the damp night air toward his cab. A wave of astonishment came over him at the tangibility of his hallucination of Julianne. Her participation and personal immodesty and abandon were uncharacteristic, unthinkable. Julianne had been passionate but private. Her visitation was confusing and a reminder of both his loss and his failed quest. Guilt descended upon on him. Was he being unfaithful to Julianne's memory? It had only been nine months. Was he being diverted from his search? Driving along, the conflict raged in his brain and, out of frustration, he slowed 405 just outside the airport entrance, pulled off the road, and got out. He watched through the hurricane fence as occasional planes roared low overhead and landed not far from where he stood. His mind spun with uncertainty and questions. Should he give up driving, retrieve Melissa, and find another relationship? Sooner or later, he would have to allow himself to freely have sex, but when? He thought back to the beautiful Salvadoran woman. What had been the harm in two lonely people finding one another regardless of how briefly? Only one thing was keeping him from living life as he should: avenging Julianne's murder. He needed that peace. He could not just walk away. He knew with certainty that if Julianne could speak to him, she would tell him to please relinquish the violent quest and get on with his life, take care of Melissa, and find someone new. That was what her visiting spirit must have been telling him. That was a kind gesture, but not a thought he could live with. He had to go on.

Back in the cab, he drove into the airport and circled the terminals. Things seemed slow. It was then he unexpectedly saw a sight that completely unnerved him. As he passed by the United terminal, he noticed two lanes were blocked by a crew painting new white lines for pedestrians over ones that had been worn away by incessant traffic. Nick realized it was the second time he had seen them painting those exact lines in precisely the same spot since he'd started driving. He had an image of himself gradually disappearing, as were the lines. Unsettled by the thought, his breath hung in his throat and he inexplicably began to cough. He fled the airport to cruise the cheap hotels, strip bars, and fast-food joints down Century Boulevard. Just maybe the men he was looking for were hanging around. He had to find them before he too was completely worn away.

THE SUN WAS WELL up when Nick pulled to the front of his apartment. Letting himself inside, he walked around staring vacantly at everything there: his wife's' clothes he couldn't allow himself to get rid of, the baby crib and playpen, the boxes of negatives stacked in the closet. Everything was as it had been, except creeping in and around all the articles was chaos from months of inattention. The sights and memories suddenly became overwhelming and he half staggered toward the bed. He stared down at his wife's picture and the little taxi parked in front. "I don't know how much longer I can do this, baby. I don't know if I'm doing anything but disappointing you. I hope not, because I've done enough of that already."

Nick picked up Julianne's picture and held the cool frame to his chest as the sweet, rich scent of the woman from El Salvador swept through his nostrils. A moment later, he passed out.

CHAPTER NINETEEN

RAINEY HAD TAKEN A bus from LA to San Francisco. He would have preferred to fly, but he didn't have a license for airport security. The license! That crazy fucker who had broken his nose and cut his eye had his license, or worse, the cops had it. He didn't know what to do, but the fright of getting arrested for robbery and accessory to murder was subsiding from absolute total panic to gnawing fear. One thing that helped was good smack. That always took care of things for a time, and now he had some money to make things right. Rainey had a good week culminating in a great night, pulling in four tricks in six hours just by cruising the Castro district.

A white boy from a farm community in Ohio by the name of Jeffrey Oltin had mercifully come into Rainey's life. They met while hanging out waiting for tricks. Rainey moved in with Jeffrey who began to appreciate Rainey's love of heroin. Jeffrey had heard of a new source of supply. "In Oakland they're selling something called China White. It's supposed to be unbelievable and a little bit goes all the way," Jeffrey exclaimed.

"Jeffrey, you don't know nothin' 'bout smack. All you know is potatoes, cows, and shit," Rainey teased.

"Maybe, but I heard it from Stiles and he knows what he's talkin' about. He told me what the man looks like, his first name, and gave me the address of the liquor store the man hangs out by," Jeffrey insisted.

Rainey thought for a moment. "China White? Sounds like some sexy bitch to me. Let's get some."

The next day, they got into Jeffrey's old Ford and headed across the Bay Bridge to Oakland. They searched from noon until dark to find their man. Just as they were about to give up and leave to hustle for the night, the man appeared. The dealer was cautious. He had them park a block away while he went to get the China White. When he finally walked back to their car, Rainey slipped him $200. The dealer leaned inside, bent over, and kissed Rainey on the mouth. Even though Rainey was expecting it, he was surprised when he felt the man's tongue shove the small drug-filled rubber balloon into his mouth.

Driving back across the bridge, Rainey and Jeffrey ran the experience over and over in their conversation as they anticipated the high. The night's hustle could wait.

Once inside the small apartment, Jeffrey walked into the kitchen and got himself a Diet Coke. When he came back to the bedroom, Rainey was emptying out the balloon into a glassine envelope and then in turn dividing out a couple shots. "You know I'm not shooting, I'm just snorting," Jeffrey said timidly.

Rainey didn't respond. Jeffrey was relatively new to the drug and that was fine with him. He could hold back on what he gave Jeffrey and there would be more for him. Rainey was certain what he was going to do with his fix. "There's so much. This was such a motherfucking great score. We'll be good for a week," Rainey exclaimed and handed Jeffrey a small piece of folded paper containing his snort. Rainey began to cook down his shot and then added a pinch more for good measure. He wanted to be sure this high was extra special. Jeffrey snorted his, got up, staggered around the room, and began chanting in his Midwestern twang, "Oh, Lordy, Lordy, oh my, oh my..." He stumbled into the living room and fell back onto the stained sofa they had found curbside. He stared at the ceiling trying to hold on, but he was being taken inward by a beautiful, frightening rush.

From Jeffrey's reaction, Rainey saw they'd really scored. He finished cooking his and loaded the syringe. Tying his arm, he smacked it a few times until the abused and reluctant vein finally bulged up. Rainey gave himself the jab. He didn't quite manage to get the needle out before the overdose slammed into his brain. From the other room, Jeffrey heard his friend groaning and gasping. He sensed something was very wrong but he was too wasted to get up from the sagging sofa. The rush was still pulling him along and he didn't want it interrupted. Fourteen minutes later, he reluctantly made his way to the kitchen. Rainey was lying on the linoleum floor, a pool of vomit under his head. As far as Jeffrey could tell, he wasn't breathing. Dazed, he walked to the telephone and dialed 911. Before the cops and ambulance came, he managed to get to the planter box outside the kitchen window. He hid the small glassine envelope containing the China White amongst sprigs of long-neglected, withered Lobelia.

At the hospital, a young intern diligently continued the paramedics' efforts with Rainey He managed to jump-start his heart, but that was all that would ever start again. A resident doctor came in and examined the young intern's work. "Nice job, I guess. Obviously the one strong thing left in this guy is his heart. But he's brain-dead, a taxpayer's burden for the rest of his life." The doctor picked up Rainey's chart and began writing the technical description of what happened while he mumbled the true prognosis, "Life as a vegetable."

AT 11:13 A.M., NICK's telephone started ringing. At the ninth ring, Nick managed to reach near consciousness. No one ever called him, so he thought it might be Pearson with some news. He picked up the receiver. "Hello."

"I'm trying to get in touch with Nick Cullen," a voice replied.

"This is Nick."

There was a pause. "I'm looking for a Nick Cullen, from New York. A photographer..."

"Dad, is that you?"

"Yeah. Christ, it doesn't even sound like you, Nick. You okay?"

"Sure, I've just been working all night and haven't woken up yet."

"Sounds like you've been asleep for a month."

"I'm okay, Dad. What's up?"

"That's what I want to know. I haven't heard from you in over six months." There was another pause as Nick tried to think of some excuse but couldn't. "It ain't as though I had thirteen kids like Jimmy O'Shea down the block. I got one kid and I'd like to hear how he's doing from time to time. I wouldn't even mind if he asked how I was doing."

"How you doing, Dad?"

"No complaints, except I don't hear nothing from you. How's my little baby Melissa?"

"Fine."

"Fine? That's it?"

"I'm sorry, Dad, I've been working nights, a lot of hours and..."

"Yeah, well, I don't know what the fuck you're doing that for. In case you hadn't noticed, you had a pretty interesting career going. If you need some money to get some new equipment, I could dig around and advance you some."

"I'm okay with what I'm doing right now."

"It doesn't sound it." There was a pause while he waited for Nick to say something, but Nick was fighting the urge to fall back to sleep. "I've been thinking about coming out to LA. Get away from this muggy fucking tenement. It's so hot in New York right now; I break a sweat walking from the window to the kitchen."

"That would be nice, Dad, but this isn't a very good time for me."

"Oh, really?" There was another long pause. "Well, when it's a good time, give me a call."

The line went dead. Nick fumbled in his effort to hang up the telephone. The awkward conversation made him feel like crap.

He continued to lie in bed staring at the ceiling, and after a few moments he inexorably sank back to sleep. When the alarm went off at 4:00 p.m., he staggered toward the shower. Nick couldn't remember if the call from his father had been real or dreamt. Regardless, he should get his father out to California, but not until after he had found Jesse and Cal. As Nick stepped into the shower, he remembered what his father had said to him those many years ago: "Killing is a bad business, all around."

"It sure is, Dad," Nick muttered. "And it's not over."

BEING CAREFUL NOT TO tip his hand, Stabile drove an unmarked car a block or two behind Cranberry's Corvette. He had been tailing Cranberry the short distance from an apartment in Culver City, but it was risky as Cranberry could spot him on the quiet streets. However, Stabile wanted to see where the man would go and who he'd meet. Cranberry wended his way into Oakwood, parked his car, and entered a two-story stucco building. Stabile pulled into a space by a fireplug and waited. Eighteen minutes later, a grime-crusted maroon El Camino that looked as though it could fly cruised the block looking for a place to land. Stabile watched as it found a spot a block away and observed two men exit the car and come back in his direction. A tall, lanky, cowboy-looking guy with a sheepskin vest led the way. He was followed by a shorter, powerfully built Hispanic character carrying a gym bag. Stabile watched the two men enter the same sad-looking stucco building. Thirty-two minutes later, the cowboy and the Mex left the building without the gym bag. Eight minutes later, Cranberry came out with the bag. He put it into the trunk of his Corvette and drove off. Stabile decided against following Cranberry to Big TC's place.

WHEN NICK WALKED INTO the yard, he could sense something had gone wrong. The night drivers were huddled together in a few tight-knit groups. They all glanced at Nick as he walked in but kept conversing among themselves. Nick walked over to the first group, made up of four black guys. One of them he knew reasonably well, a cool older guy called Kingpin. "What's goin' on?"

"You don't know?"

"Know what?"

"Shit, I thought you'd be one of the first to know," Kingpin said.

Nick waited. Another driver volunteered an opinion. "They probably didn't tell him, 'cause they 'fraid he'd quit."

"There some sort of job action going down?" Nick asked, looking around at the groups.

"Job action? What the fuck's a job action?" Kingpin asked.

"Just reminds me of what I used to see on the docks in New York," Nick offered.

"Man, this was murder. Stepper got robbed and shot last night," Kingpin said.

"Shot right in the back of the head as he sat behind the wheel," added another.

Kingpin looked down at the ground and confessed, "I didn't like that bony-ass motherfucker, but I didn't want to see him get shot. That's a soberin' thing."

"Where did it happen?" Nick asked.

"Downtown, southwest corner, Second and Hewitt," Kingpin said, being specific.

"Man, he should have rolled his ass out of the cab the way you did, Nick," volunteered one of the drivers. Nick glanced over at the cab Stepper had been driving. "Took all day to get the blood and shit out," the man continued.

There was a momentary silence as the four men regarded Nick and waited for him to say something. He felt awkward and finally said, "Stepper was a wild man and nobody's friend, but that was a bad deal." He turned away from the men and walked over to the shack to see Vern and get his trip sheet.

Vern was busy dealing orders. He grabbed a trip sheet and handed it to Nick and without looking said, "It's crazy out there. Watch your ass, Nick."

As he left the yard, he thought of the mental photograph he had taken of Stepper all those months ago. He tried to imagine the scene where Stepper got it, who might have shot him, but his mind kept lunging toward its obsession with Julianne's killers.

DRIVING INTO HOLLYWOOD FOR a night on the town, Cal and Jesse parked the El Camino in a lot with a security guard next to the Huntington Hartford Theater on Vine Street. "Not gonna leave my ride on the street in this neighborhood," Jesse said. Cal didn't like it when Jesse called the El Camino 'his ride." Sure, it had belonged to Jesse's cousin, but how much legal proprietorship do you get if you kill the owner? It had been over three months, Chester was long dead, and they still had the car. The El Camino had served them well driving the three round trips to see Raul in Juarez, but Jesse was abusive to it, never changing the oil or letting it get washed. "Cops love shiny red things," he said.

Cal coveted the El Camino. He hoped to buy it from Jesse with his share of the money when they did their "final divvy-up," as Jesse called it. Cal reasoned the El Camino should belong to both of them, but he kept his mouth shut. He wouldn't win the argument. Still, the plan was finally working out the way Jesse had promised, and the few trips back and forth to Juarez had multiplied their assets eightfold. Their profits would have been more, but Jesse loved to spend money.

Walking out of the parking lot, Jesse turned to Cal and slapped him hard on the back. "Follow me, compadre, we're gonna celebrate, get us some steaks and shrimp and shit, then we're gonna find us some pussy." Cal walked along with Jesse who led them off in the wrong direction, away from Hollywood Boulevard. A block farther away, realizing his mistake but not admitting it, Jesse led Cal over to Ivar Street and back up toward Hollywood Boulevard in search of steaks, women, and action. Jesse knew how to find all those.

◆◆◆

THERE WERE SOME SLEEPY, deadbeat drivers on stands in front of the hotels, so Nick headed to the bus station. He was first up and caught a ride to his favorite old neighborhood, Alvarado and Sixth Street. He dropped his fare, then took a long look at the taxi stand across the street where the three punks had jumped him in his cab. The whole incident seemed like it had happened on Mars, light-years ago.

◆◆◆

JESSE AND CAL DISCOVERED a nice, dimly lit bar on Hudson Street. Seated at the bar next to them were two women in their midthirties. Currently, they were telephone solicitors by trade, though one of them had done some soliciting of the more traditional kind in Reno. The ladies had left off calling Los Angeles residents during their late dinner hour to offer them a "great opportunity" for a cruise to Baja, Mexico. After work, the women had separated from the dozens of other callers and headed down from the crowded lair in the gray office building on Hollywood and Vine to the bar for a couple rum and cokes before heading home. They were friends. Together, they had done some swinging around town and liked action when they could find it. Jesse was giving them the eye and that was okay with them, as he had a lot of money lying on the bar.

But it was the Hispanic-looking guy who seemed like hot stuff. The ladies whispered between themselves and agreed to be picked up.

❖❖❖

NICK DIDN'T THINK LONG before deciding not to hang out at the stand on Alvarado. Heading west along Sixth Street, he turned on impulse toward Wilshire Boulevard and pulled in front of the Sheraton. A woman in her late twenties stood there as though waiting for him. A moment later, a man wearing an expensive black leather jacket came out of the lobby and followed the woman into the back seat. "We've been waiting for you, I just called again," the man said.

Right away, Nick knew he had inadvertently stolen the ride from another cab company. It was too late to do anything about it without dislodging the passengers, plus whatever driver had gotten the call was obviously late for the pickup. Nick looked in his rearview mirror to see if another cab was coming in. "My company put me in this hotel. It's not near anything. Deadsville. We're going up to Gazzari's, you know where it is?" the man asked. Nick grunted he did and, with no taxi headlights behind him, pulled out. "You're not a cop, are you?" the man asked.

"No."

The woman turned to the man questioningly. "Sometimes cops drive around in cabs, you know, undercover," the man explained. "But you're not a cop, are you?"

"I'm no cop."

"Good. You mind if we do some blow?" Nick shrugged his shoulders and drove the couple to the Sunset Strip as they tooted up in the back seat. The man didn't offer to share and as Nick listened to the sound of them snorting, he wished they would. He remembered the drug very well and just the sound of them violently snorting brought the alkaline taste back to his mouth.

The Strip was awash with rock and rollers and as he dropped the couple by the line of people waiting to get into a nightclub, he remembered how long it had been since he had done something as simple as listening to music and having fun.

Making his way west, he kept his eyes open for a new rider. He didn't get far when a young woman flagged him down and gracefully slid into the back of the cab. "Man, this is the worst, needing to have a car out here or take a cab everywhere." The traffic behind Nick closed in impatiently.

"Where you going?"

"The Montecito Hotel. Christ, what a zoo this Strip is."

Nick glanced at her in the mirror. She was attractive in an almost hard way. Straight black hair fell down to her breasts, which were nicely shaped and rested easily under the soft fabric of her gray blouse. He could tell she wasn't wearing a bra. The woman smiled at Nick's observations. "What's the matter? Never seen a gal from New Yawwk before?" she joked.

"I've seen maybe a couple hundred thousand. That's where I'm from."

"Christ, you like it out here?"

"It hasn't been very good to me, so I guess not."

"I'm staying at the Montecito. I've seen more actors I know at that place then I ever saw in New York. It's like they emptied out Broadway and put them all up at the Montecito."

"I've heard that about the place."

"There was this one creepy guy in my acting class who kept hitting on me. I come out here thinking, well, at least I'll get away from that fucker and he's right down the hall from me. He's right down the fucking hall! I'm talking to the manager in the morning to switch floors, or moving out." The young woman looked out the window and made running comments about the architecture, the signs, the cars, all the familiar comments Nick had heard other New Yorkers make about Los Angeles, including himself. As they neared the hotel, she uncrossed her shapely legs and leaned forward. "You're not an actor too, are you?"

"No."

"You look like you could be, you've got intensity." The woman paused for dramatic effect and studied Nick openly. "Most times, I don't like to date actors or people in my business, you know what I mean? It's all so close." Nick didn't say anything. He was beginning to feel uncomfortable from her gaze and the slight smirk pulling at the corners of her thin mouth. "You look like an interesting guy. How could a girl get in touch?"

Nick was surprised by the question. "Call the cab company and ask for Nick in four-o-five." It never entered his mind to give out his home number.

"Well, like I said, I don't like to spend too much time with the same people and my fellow actors gossip more than old Brooklyn ladies over a game of canasta. I like to meet different types, so, maybe I'll give you a call. Name's Carla." Nick stopped in front of the residence hotel and accepted the money she proffered. "Wish me luck, Nick. Got a callback audition tomorrow out at Warner Brothers. They flew me out for it."

"Luck, Carla. Good luck all the way."

Carla gave him a wink and thumbs-up and slid out of the cab. He watched her enter the hotel and as the door was closing, Carla turned and gave him a flirtatious wave. The thought of having sex with her penetrated his mind and wedged there as he watched her disappear into the lobby. The notion occurred to him to hurry into the lobby and ask her to have a drink. Instead, he started back out along Franklin Avenue and after a moment's hesitation decided to drop down and cruise Hollywood Boulevard, which lay just two blocks south. Making a right on Las Palmas, he quickly covered the distance and hit a red light at Hollywood Boulevard. He was frustrated with himself. Carla had clearly given him the signal and, as always, he'd let it slide. His mind rolled back and forth considering the possibilities and whether or not he had done the right thing. Two men and two women were crossing the street in front of him, heading east. Nick's eyes were drawn to them as they walked close by.

Jesse Carmody turned and, with speed-fed eyes, glanced through the slightly tinted windshield into the cab. He and Nick briefly flashed on one another before Jesse turned back to the woman beside him.

Something clicked deep within Nick, but the spark was immediately flooded by his ongoing preoccupation with Carla's come-on. He waited as the couples stepped up onto the curb and prepared to cross the boulevard with the light. The light turned green and as Nick pulled out, he had to pause for them to pass before he could complete his left turn.

Cal Santiso instinctively turned and glanced in Nick's direction just to make sure the cab was going to stop. Once assured, Cal looked back at the woman he was with. He dropped his hand down and slid it across her ass and then reached up and pulled her thick waist toward him.

Leaving the two couples behind, Nick headed down the boulevard looking for a rider. He got all the way to Vine without any possibilities and decided to double back to the Strip and see if he could pick off a fare on his way to the Westside. At Sunset, it hit him. Those two guys…looked like what he has been looking for…the look in their eyes, their attitude, their clothes… It was them. It had to be. He had been thinking about Carla's dancing breasts and the sexual possibilities and not much else and had allowed them to get by him. The thinner man was wearing a Western-style shirt, Levi pants, and a vest, while the Hispanic-looking man appeared almost exactly the same as Nick's recollections. He floored the accelerator and drove down to Cahuenga, made a screaming right, then a hurtling right on Selma, quickly came to Las Palmas, and turned back up toward Hollywood Boulevard. Pounding the steering wheel in frustration, he drove as fast as he could without running over some of the Hollywood multitude. He made a right onto the boulevard, pulled his knife from his bag, and began hunting the south side, past Frederick's of Hollywood, past the tourist shops and army-navy stores. He peered at the dark figures walking across rose-colored stars with inlays of televisions, movie cameras, and microphones paying homage to the names beneath.

Jesse, Cal, and the women peered down at the names and didn't have a clue who most of them were. Jesse steered the women off the Hollywood Walk of Fame and down Ivar Avenue in the direction they had mistakenly taken earlier. Being from Kansas, Jesse was uncertain about his Hollywood/LA directions, but he knew his backtracking would get them to the El Camino. Nick neared where they had just turned and would have spotted them, but pedestrians and a vacant tour bus rounding the corner conspired to block his view. A few minutes later, Jesse got behind the wheel of the El Camino, his date next to him. Cal got in and put his date on top of his lap. They laughed at the tight confines and Cal felt himself quickly getting hard with the woman's ample behind pressing down on him. Jesse started the motor and revved it a few times to hear its sound. Cal's date cooed and wiggled her ass. "Oh, what a big engine you have."

Cal smiled and Jesse chimed in, "Oh, yeah? Wait till you see what's coming." Amid the half-drunken laughter, Jesse drove quickly out of the lot and off toward the ladies' apartment.

Nick cruised Hollywood the rest of the night, leaving people flagging him for a ride stranded behind on curbs and corners. He drove until well after the sun came up and he had to return the cab.

Exhausted and cruelly frustrated, he returned to the lot. After servicing the cab and turning it over to Clyde, he informed the management that for the foreseeable future, he wanted to drive seven nights' a week. The two beefy guys in the back room counting receipts just shrugged. They were happy to have him driving as much as he wanted. He was their high-booking star.

✦✦✦

WHEN NICK GOT TO his apartment, he called Pearson's home.

"Hello?" Pearson sounded awake, which was more than what was going on with Nick.

"It's Nick Cullen, Detective."

"What's up, Nick?"

"I saw them last night. I saw them in Hollywood."

"So, why didn't you call me?"

"By the time I realized it was them and went back to spot them again, they were gone."

"You should have notified us. That's why we have different police headquarters around town and they have a lot of police cars with officers who ride around in them. They even have some helicopters, in case you haven't heard."

"I'm sorry, I just thought I could find them. I guess I wasn't thinking straight."

"Doesn't sound like it." Pearson thought about it for a moment and then took a less-sarcastic tone, "I know you don't have a lot of faith in us, but you've got to share when something happens, otherwise we can't help."

"Do you share everything with me, Lieutenant?"

There was a perceptible pause. "You sure it was them?"

"How often do you see two guys look as different as those guys together? And the man the taller guy had on the same sheepskin vest."

"I'm going to put out an APB, and you should come into the station and we'll go over this. Just stay away from the paperwork on my desk."

Nick ignored Pearson's wisecrack. "I'm telling you I saw them in Hollywood, right on the Boulevard by Cherokee. I'm certain it was them. So, why should I come in?"

"Maybe it's not necessary, but if you think of anything else, let me know. Were they in a car when you saw them?"

Nick went on to explain precisely what had happened. He was thorough enough, but exhaustion was pulling at him and he was grateful when Pearson let him off the line. One thing he realized before he passed out: he didn't actually want Pearson or anyone else finding those men. He wanted to. This was his.

CHAPTER TWENTY

A S THE WEEKS BLEW by, Big TC grew more and more concerned about Stabile's remarks. He knew he couldn't just keep on growing without having to give a little soldier to the police from time to time. Some of his men were branching out, trying to set up their own shops, getting greedy, and that could make things dangerous for him. In particular, Cranberry seemed to be losing the good-soldier mentality and was beginning to think more like Al Capone. One of Big TC's girls came in the door carrying a cup of coffee, the way he liked it, black with half a shot of Courvoisier. As she left, he watched her firm butt straining against her red leather pants. He'd get some of that later but for now, he sat back, sniffed the aroma of the fresh coffee, and took a sip. It tasted very fine, and as the steam from the coffee wafted in front of him, it suddenly became clear how to solve all his problems with Cranberry, Stabile, and the angry citizens of Los Angeles. It would take a little time and some maneuvering, but who better to maneuver things than he?

As weeks passed in an exasperating rush, Nick hunted with a frenzied intensity. Every time a fare brought him near the Hollywood area, he drove more quickly to get to the boulevard to continue the hunt. The reflex action of his foot pressing down harder on the accelerator resulted in two speeding tickets within ten days. As he cruised the Hollywood area, the thought of the two tickets ate into him; he needed to be careful not to get another one or he could lose his license. A call from Billy startled him.

"Four-o-five?"

"Four-o-five."

"Pick up at Beverly and La Jolla."

The company didn't get telephone orders midtown very often. They were primarily a far-Westside outfit. Nick surmised whoever had called the cab company didn't know that. It should be a good fare, otherwise Billy wouldn't have sent it his way. Careful not to speed, he made his way to the pickup. When he arrived, he saw a man sitting on the curb ranting with a young woman bending over trying to console him. Not far away, a tow truck was lifting a tricked-out Chevrolet Impala that had the front end smashed in. Nick surveyed the scene and was thinking of leaving the fare. The man was verging on tears of rage and looked like bad news. A large, heavyset man came over and said, "We called the cab. He needs a ride to Artesia."

The man who sat on the curb was small and thin, with strong, wiry muscles and a hard, lean face. To Nick, he seemed high, speeding. *Why didn't cops arrest the guy?* Nick wondered.

"He's all right," the man said, reading Nick's thoughts.

It was a good fare, but Nick still didn't like the setup. "Are you coming with him?" Nick asked the sensible-looking man.

"No, I live around here. It'll be okay."

"It'll cost around twenty-five on the meter and there's a five-dollar surcharge to go there. I want thirty dollars up front, or it's no go." The man with the gentle disposition nodded and went over to the guy sitting on the curb. The tough little guy roared at the suggestion, but the girlfriend and heavyset man talked him into parting with the money. Once Nick had the money in hand, he let the couple into the cab. Unfortunately, the woman got in on the passenger side and the man sat directly behind him. Nick didn't think it worth the hassle to make them switch, but he would have preferred the man on the far side of the cab. Nick had a good view of the young woman. She was wearing a blue-gray dress over her thin body. Her light brown hair was evenly cut just to the bottom of her neck and her pale face was careworn beyond her twenty-three years.

The ride went smoothly enough until they got about three-quarters of the way to Artesia. The young man sat up and leaned forward. "What the fuck you take my money up front for? I never heard of giving money up front."

"It's just how it is on a long fare."

"You know what you are?" Nick didn't care to hear the guy's opinion, so he kept his mouth shut. "You're a whore," the man volunteered anyway. Nick held onto the wheel and tried to keep his cool. "You're a whore!" the man hollered even louder.

This is great, Nick thought. *The guy smacked up his car and feels like a sorry jerk, so now he wants to beat on someone, or have someone beat on him as punishment for being a fool.* Nick couldn't think which choice the guy would prefer, but concluded it could go either way and the man wouldn't care. Nick made a decision and pulled off the 605 Freeway and cruised in front of a convenience store in the city of Downey.

"You can get out here. There's a telephone over there. Call yourself another cab."

"You've got my money!" the man bellowed.

The meter showed twenty dollars and forty cents. "You can have back the difference between the meter and the thirty."

"Please," the thin young woman said, leaning forward and clutching her hands together. "He'll be quiet. Please, just take us home."

Nick knew instinctively the woman had absolutely no control over the guy, so he turned around and put his arm up on the back of the seat and looked at the amped-up speed freak. "How about it, man, you gonna be quiet?"

The man reached forward in the seat and grabbed onto Nick's arm with his small hard hands. "Yeah," he said with a malevolent grin.

Nick had to strain to pull his arm away from the firm grip. The man continued to grin at him. Mistakenly, Nick decided to go forward. It was only another five miles or so to the destination. If he remained, he knew he would probably have to fight the guy to get him out of the cab. It would be best to get him home rather than have an altercation, but there was no guarantee either way. Nick reached into his bag, pulled out his large knife, and wedged it between his legs.

About two miles down the road, the man couldn't stand the silence and started calling Nick a whore again. Nick tried to ignore the insult by asking the woman for directions. "You're a whore and we've got to give directions, too?"

"You call me a whore again and you're getting out of this cab right here."

"Please," the woman implored. "I'll tell you how to get there."

Nick relented and let her give directions to their small house. Glancing in the mirror, Nick noticed fear in the woman's pale blue eyes. *Why would she stay with such a violent jerk?* Nick guessed she was too frightened of him to leave. Mercifully, the man kept quiet, but Nick could sense the guy's chaotic wheels spinning. He wished once again he had insisted the man sit on the back right so he could keep an eye on him. Arriving at their little house, Nick noticed the street was completely quiet. He reached over and shut off the meter, which clicked to twenty-six dollars. "You owe me four dollars," the man said and started to get out of the car. Nick put his hand over the knife and got out of the cab as well. The man stepped in and confronted Nick up close. "You owe me four dollars. You took my money."

"There's a five-dollar surcharge to come down here. You owe me a dollar. Please pay up," Nick quietly retorted. He glanced over at the young woman who stood forlornly by, the look of fear building in her eyes.

"You gonna give me back my four dollars?"

"I told you, you owe me a dollar," Nick said evenly.

"You're taking my money from me. I'm going to get it." The little man advanced on Nick, crowding in close, swaying his shoulders, hands at the ready like a good boxer. Nick backed up involuntarily, instinctively knowing the little guy knew how to fight. "This is gonna be fun," the man said with a sly grin and kept coming.

"Give me my four dollars." Nick was sorry he had the knife in his hand. He could have taken the guy down with his bare hands but the knife made things awkward. If he started anything, he would have to use it. Almost like a dance, with the man swaying and bobbing in close, he slowly backed Nick out onto the middle of the street, where a lone light shone down upon them. Nick worried about the knife but thought if he did something with it, he could plead self-defense. He could simply flick the blade open and eviscerate the man if need be, or he could hit him with an uppercut and would probably connect. The knife in his hand would make it like getting hit with a rock. The possibilities mounted in Nick's mind, but he heard himself say, "All right, I'll give you the four dollars."

"Oh, yeah!" the man exclaimed. "Gimme."

"Over by the car," Nick said.

The man spun around like a fighter going back to his corner at the end of a round and walked the distance back to the cab. Nick used the opportunity to slide the knife back in his pocket and peel off four dollars from his roll. As he handed it to the man, he glanced over and saw a look of disappointment on the young woman's face. From her reaction, it appeared she wished Nick had stomped or killed him. "You're a whore," the man said, grinning.

Nick almost hit him then, but instead got into the cab and left. Before he got back onto the freeway, he went into the trunk and finished off half the bottle of tequila he had stashed. He was rattled and oddly disappointed in himself. It was the smart thing to do, giving the crazed man the money. It wasn't worth four dollars to get into a serious fight, but Nick was thrown by it. The guy was right, he was a whore. He was out for hire. But there was something else bothering him. He felt weak. All the months in the cab had left him out of shape. As Nick felt the tequila work its way outward from his stomach, he realized another thing. There was no anger. Normally, he would have been enraged with the man and his Irish temper would have taken over. There would have been a fight. It was as though he didn't have enough strength for the anger that should have been there. Instead, he was left shaky and dispirited. As he stashed the near-empty bottle, a troubling question entered his mind. If he backed down and couldn't make things right with the crazed little man he had just dropped off, what would he do when he actually confronted his wife's murderers?

◆◆◆

NICK HADN'T BEEN TO the airport for several days. He'd been intent on the Hollywood area. As a result, he was making less money and racking up debt in speeding tickets. He opted to do some airport runs, work the system with Billy, and put more on the books. After a few minutes at United, he snagged a good fare. A merchant seaman wanted to go to Long Beach, then back to the airport. He had to pick up his seaman's papers that had recently been validated and were aboard a ship for him in the Port of Long Beach. He wanted to get them, then get back to the airport in time to catch the last flight to San Francisco. He explained he had exactly ninety-eight minutes to make the round trip before the last flight left. "Do you think we can make it?"

"If your papers are waiting for you, I believe we can."

The ship is leaving at six a.m.," he said and jumped into the cab.

Nick drove as rapidly as the fear of getting another speeding ticket would allow. They quickly made it to Long Beach and after a few frantic moments searching for the correct pier, they found the ship. The young seaman went bounding up the gangplank and disappeared from view.

Staring at the outline of the black ship and reflections on the gray water, fatigue overcame him. Involuntarily, he began to doze behind the wheel. As he did so, the haunting tableau crept back into his mind but this time, Nick discovered new and unwelcome elements in the already horrific scene. The women he had seen Cal and Jesse with in Hollywood were now included in the vision;

one was seated in a chair smoking a cigarette, the other was examining some silverware on the sideboard. They seemed to have made themselves very much at home, despite the gruesome scene that surrounded them. Half dreaming, Nick ran the scene over in his head. Had he forgotten the women were there that day? Why was he confusing an image he had tried so hard to keep clear? The young seaman suddenly appeared and pulled open the door, startling Nick. "Got it," he said. "Thanks."

Nick fought his way back to some semblance of consciousness and reflexively drove toward the Long Beach Freeway. His mind gradually drifted back to the dream and, inexplicably, the women were still there. Rainey, Cal, and Jesse were all dancing around his apartment, holding high his possessions. Occasionally, Jesse would stop and with one of Nick's cameras, he'd take pictures of Julianne lying on the floor and of Melissa's face contorted with terror.

As though from a great distance, Nick heard a voice. "It seems to be taking a lot longer this time," the seaman said, with concern.

Nick snapped back to reality. As he looked around, he had no idea where they were. The land had turned curiously flat and empty. A moment later, he saw an exit for the City of Downey and realized he had gone miles past the turnoff to the 405 Freeway. He reeled in confusion. How had he done such a thing? He admitted his mistake and the seaman collapsed back into his seat with bitter disappointment. Nick stopped the meter and, retracing the miles, drove rapidly back toward the airport. Risking getting another speeding ticket, he arrived at United Airlines with only eight minutes to spare. "I'm sorry," Nick said sincerely. "Go to the counter downstairs and tell them you're on your way to the gate and maybe they'll hold the plane until you get there. Jump in front of the line," Nick said. The young man paid Nick and left without a word but ran as fast as he could to try and catch the plane Nick was near certain he would miss.

He looped the airport and stopped at TWA, which had some flights coming in from Europe. Parking the cab, he went to the trunk, removed the half-pint bottle of tequila, slipped it into his jacket, and went to the men's room. No one was there, so he took a nip from the bottle and washed his hands. He stared at himself in the mirror, and while he knew the reflection was his, he was looking at a stranger. He grabbed some towels and went back to his cab, stashing the scant remains of the tequila in his bag. A few minutes later, he got a long fare going to Glendale.

Two middle-aged women complained bitterly that their sons had refused to pick them up. As he drove along trying not to listen to the ladies complaints, he felt oddly spaced out, even considering his normal consumption of alcohol and weed. He found he had to concentrate hard not to get lost on the comparatively simple run. On the return trip, he dipped into Hollywood to continue his search, but immediately got a fare going to Van Nuys. Two pretty teenage girls had gone to Hollywood to check things out and had a bad night ducking creeps. After dropping the girls, Nick smoked a small resin-stained roach he had stashed in the bottom of his little film can. To counteract the dryness in his mouth, he opened a bottle of Dos Equis. Wedging the bottle between his legs, he drove away from the girls' neighborhood and became momentarily lost while trying to find his way back to the main cross street.

Finally, he stumbled onto the wide expanse of Van Nuys Boulevard. After a moment's indecision, he made his way to the 405 Freeway and began the drive over the hill toward Westwood. He decided to check in and learn what Billy might have for him.

Cresting the hill on the 405, he reached for the hand mike and inadvertently felt it slip from his grasp. He bent over to pick it up and the car swerved as he groped around the floor. He finally found it by tracing the cord to the mike. Pulling the mike to his mouth, he pressed the button. "Four-o-five."

"Four-o-five?"

"Heading to pickup at Gatsby's, in the Brentwood area, if nothing's around, I'll go to the port."

"Roger that." Nick went to put the mike back into the clip and accidentally dropped it onto the floor again. He let it lie and started down the steep, three-mile slope toward Sunset Boulevard. From there, he'd take the shortcut to San Vicente and Gatsby's. His foot powered down on the accelerator and the big Ford engine eagerly followed the command. Reaching between his legs, he brought the bottle to his mouth and drained it. He bent over and shoved the bottle under the seat, and when he tried to sit back upright, his head involuntarily bounced off the driver's door window. Time seemed to slow. As Nick came down the freeway toward Sunset, he no longer felt connected to the car and felt as though he were floating. The cab seemed to hurtle forward with no effort on his part. He glanced ahead at the Holiday Inn, a round seventeen-story building standing like a stack of quarters alongside the freeway. Lights beckoned from random windows. They glowed for him through the night moisture like landing lights in the sky. The cockpit of the car was snug and as the concrete, painted lines, and lights flashed by, he felt as though he were entering some alien planetary vortex that would carry him into the next dimension. Alongside, the lane reflectors shot by like tracers. He smiled in a delirious sort of ecstasy as the white lines of the off-ramp seemed to float near eye level, undulating in his peripheral vision.

It wasn't until he was ninety feet from the curving guardrail that he snapped back to reality. At seventy-two miles an hour, he immediately knew he was going to hit. He instinctively slammed on the brakes, threw the wheel, and two seconds later hit the railing broadside, creating a cacophony of squeals and crashes of metal upon metal. The cab bounced off the curved railing, spun half around, and slid sideways forty feet, coming to rest near the traffic light at the end of the off ramp. During the crash, Nick's head banged the window and swung halfway across the front seat, but he managed to hold onto the wheel and ride out the spin. He didn't seem hurt, but 405 was a mess. He could see the driver's side of the car was completely caved in. He tried the door and knew immediately it was crushed shut, so he slid across the front seat and observed the contents of his bag littered on the floor, his stash, rolling papers, tequila, and an empty Dos Equis bottle that had shot back out from under the seat. Pushing open the passenger door, he crawled outside.

He checked himself out by moving his head and arms. He seemed all right and with adrenaline rushing high, he began gathering the weed and alcohol from the floor. Occasional cars came by, all stopping much longer for the light than normal to stare. From above, Nick was aware of people awakened by the crash standing on their balconies talking about him. He shoved the drugs and booze under his sweater and made his way around the cab and walked some yards away. As surreptitiously as possible, he tossed the possessions into the weeds on the far side of the guardrail. He found it difficult to part with his film can containing the marijuana, so he bent over and placed it behind one of the pilings supporting the guardrail. *Later,* he promised himself. He walked back to the cab and, as he studied it, he was sickened by the sight of the extensive damage. Yes, maybe they could fix it, but 405 would never be the same. The thought of Clyde made him feel even worse. He had betrayed a trust. He had crashed the car, and it was no one's fault but his own. What could he tell people, what could he say to Billy when he called in? Which he would have to do right away, especially before the police showed. The thought of police jumped Nick into action and he slid across from the passenger side and tried to start the car. Miraculously, it sprang to life. Putting it in gear, he drove the car, with the metal screeching and grinding, painfully around the corner. The left tires made low moaning sounds as they rubbed heavily against the crushed fenders. He parked it off the turnout. As he did so, as though totally exhausted, the front tire sank and went flat.

Nick sat for a moment and quickly concocted a story. He didn't like it, but it was all he could come up with apart from a straight, honest admission, which would not go over well with the owners or police. "Four-o-five."

"Four-o-five?"

"Got a problem out here. Cab is crashed up,"

"Are you okay, four-o-five?"

"Yeah, I'm fine, but the cab is ugly."

"Was anyone hurt in the accident?"

"No."

"Was another vehicle involved?"

"The one that forced me off the road, but he split." There was a long pause. Billy wasn't buying it but Nick didn't care. He needed something and he'd have to stick with that.

"Do you need a tow?"

"Yes."

"What is your exact location?"

Nick told him and was impressed at Billy's businesslike manner. But then, why would anyone screw around in such a situation? *Billy handled it,* Nick thought, *but, what about you, Nick?* He hadn't handled anything; he had simply messed up, big time. Nick recognized that every night driver that had his radio on would be able to hear Billy's part of the conversation and put it all together. Billy came back. "Four-o-five, I'll have a tow truck out there in thirty minutes. I'll see you when you get in."

Nick was calm but exhausted. The lightness he felt in his head and the weakness in his body confounded him. The people who had been gaping from balconies of the Holiday Inn had grown bored and returned to their rooms. Apart from the noise of the freeway, the night was quiet. Nick felt suddenly clear and very alone. The moment declared itself with a bright forcefulness that was not to be denied and during that interlude it came to him with certainty: nothing would ever be the same. He had crossed some sort of line and though he wasn't sure what it was, he knew it to be there, just as the white line in the middle of the road was, the white line with his skid marks burned across it.

Nick stayed with his thoughts until Manuel drove up in the tow truck. When Manuel saw the car, he didn't say anything. He just hooked it up and brought both Nick and the car in.

Nick knew Manuel was disappointed in him and he didn't try to change it. There wasn't much to say, it had been all too evident. When Nick got out of the tow truck in the yard, he walked over to the shack where Billy was taking a break. Seeing Nick walk his way, Billy moved away from the shack out toward the yard and Nick knew he was meant to follow. Billy fished into his shirt pocket and removed a half-smoked joint. Sparking it, Billy handed it to him and Nick took a good whack. He had trouble holding it down and when Billy offered him another hit, Nick shook it off. He didn't feel he could handle it. Billy studied him with that curious, elfish expression of his. "That didn't sound so good out there tonight."

Nick took a deep breath and slowly let it out in preparation to tell the obligatory lie, "Yeah, I should have been better about handling the Pontiac Firebird that cut me off, but I've been a little out of sync."

Billy nodded in agreement, "Yeah, you've been acting a little stupid the last few weeks." He paused for effect. "So, what's going on?"

"I don't know, man."

"Well, when people don't know why they're feeling funky, they either go on a vacation or see a doctor."

"I'll be all right," Nick said, defensively.

"Well, let me say this: you're not the same guy I saw drive out of this yard a year ago."

"Ten months, two days."

"Whatever. I liked that guy back then, but I'm not sure who you are now. Driving seven nights a week, fourteen, fifteen hours, it's not improving you. You're looking ugly, kind of like Stepper before he got shot." Billy grinned at Nick, but his face didn't have a lot of merriment.

Nick stared across the yard and watched as Manuel operated the tow truck's winch and lowered 405 next to other crashed cabs. Mortally stricken, it sank to the pavement in final collapse.

Observing the resting wreck, Nick had a flash of silent realization. Deep inside, he understood something was very wrong. "Maybe I'll get myself checked out."

"I wouldn't wait too long. I'd do it right away. Maybe all you need is a little Hawaii, or go to Georgia and see your kid, but it'd be good to know. I'll be getting out of here myself in a few days."

"Where you going?"

"There's a new cab company starting up, called Sea Cabs. I got my license back. I'll be driving for them a couple nights and dispatching others. They let me go here. Friday is my last night. They think I've been dealing drugs out of the shack."

"Well, in a way you have."

"I just sell some weed to some of the drivers who are friends of mine. That's it. I don't call that dealing," Billy said with a trace of irritation.

"Yeah, I guess."

"A few of the drivers from here are goin' over. I've got you figured to come along too."

"I don't know. I'll think about it. I'm going to miss you, though. You were my anchor."

Billy smiled and took a final hit off the joint. Nick turned, looked around the yard, and wondered what the hell he was doing there.

NICK SAT ON THE hospital bed and stared at the nametag of his doctor listening to his heart and lungs with a stethoscope. Dr. Trang, a slender Vietnamese man, put the stethoscope back into his lab coat pocket and stared into Nick's eyes for a moment. "I want some X-rays of your chest." Nick wondered about the man's journey from his country to medical school in California. *They sure could use some more doctors in Vietnam*, Nick thought.

"Do I get them tomorrow, somewhere else, or what?"

"No, you can get them here. I'll give you a prescription. Go upstairs, have them done, then bring them back here."

Nick didn't like it but felt too rotten to object. He went through the paperwork process, which took another half hour. He felt lucky the cab company had major medical. They wouldn't pay for basic things, but if he were very ill, then most of the hospital charges would be taken care of. He had a long wait for the X-rays and a longer wait for Dr. Trang to return. He wasn't sure what the X-ray would say, but he sensed something was wrong. He could feel himself becoming more and more zoned. When Dr. Trang walked in and jabbed the X-rays into the clips on the light box, Nick responded, not so much because they were his X-rays but because they were a film negative and he immediately became interested in objectively studying them. "News is not good. You have very serious pneumonia and must be admitted," Trang asserted.

Nick considered this for a moment. He hadn't figured on that possibility. He thought they'd say he had a little flu and exhaustion and to go home and rest. "Well, I'll go home and straighten out a few things and then come back tomorrow."

Trang grinned at Nick, showing large, irregularly spaced teeth. "No, you must be admitted, now."

"Well, I've got some things to do."

"Don't you have someone who can take care of your home?"

Nick thought for a moment and realized he had no one and there was nothing in his apartment needed taking care of. "Yeah, I guess it'll be all right." He still felt uneasy about having to miss his night hunts then he remembered crashing 405. Had he been feeling even half as well he wouldn't have done that. Gradually, he realized he needed to be taken care of. It was a tough admission.

"I will have a nurse take you upstairs. I'll discuss a treatment procedure with the chief resident, and once that's determined, we will go ahead."

Nick glanced at his watch and saw it was nearly eight in the evening. He couldn't think where all the time had gone. *At least*

I don't have to worry about someone else driving 405, he thought bitterly. He watched as the small, thin doctor left the room. He got off the bed, went to the light box, and studied his X-rays. He wasn't sure where the pneumonia was indicated, but he did notice a slight change in exposure on the lower outer sides of his lungs. A moment of fear came over him, not for himself, but for the haunting image of his little daughter standing alone in the backyard of Lillian Thombridge.

An hour later, he found himself slipping into a gown and climbing into a hospital bed. As the moments passed and he admitted his sickness to himself, Nick felt himself go down fast. He dozed uneasily for an hour and then watched, as though in a dream, Dr. Trang come in with a nurse who stuck him with an IV.

CHAPTER TWENTY-ONE

BIG TC'S BODYGUARD TRACKED Cranberry to a bar in Inglewood. He sat his enormity on a barstool next to Cranberry and, after discussing pleasantries and most particularly a young woman's ass overlapping a corner barstool, Mose got around to business. Through a friend, he learned of a guy coming in from Las Vegas who wanted to buy and buy big, but only cocaine. He wanted a steady supply and would pay top dollar for good stuff. Cranberry had been doing variations on that scheme for some time, but with Mose he was immediately suspicious. "Why you telling me this? Why don't you tell TC? He's your main man. If Big TC wants in, then he'll put you in touch with me. That's the way it goes, fool, you know that."

Mose explained he wasn't happy with Big TC, whom kept him constantly close, 24/7, paid him like a lowly chauffer, and never gave him a bump of coke. He went on to flattering Cranberry as the best at handling buys and sales and he could easily work the deal outside of TC. Then Cranberry might throw something tasty back on Mose, like 10 percent of the sale. Cranberry was interested but cautious. It took another hour and two more wine coolers before he stood up and turned directly to Mose. Holding up his long index finger, Cranberry swung it down toward Mose like a conductor signaling the horn section.

"Deal, brother," enthused Cranberry, and shook the big man's hand.

◈◈◈

WHEN MOSE WALKED IN and informed Big TC, "The man went for it like a dog to a bone," Big TC laughed full out. The diamond in his tooth flashed and his gold chains jiggled. Sitting up, he gestured for Mose to leave. Leaving the couch, he went to the stereo, put on some Marvin Gaye, and smoothly danced around the room for the entirety of the cut. His plan was working beautifully.

◆◆◆

NICK LAY IN THE hospital bed and found, to his dull surprise, he could constantly sleep. At times, fleeting images of different fares he had driven floated through his head in a kind of regression back toward his first day. A blind jazz pianist, Irene sitting demurely in the back of the cab, a cab full of illegal immigrants from Oaxaca, the quiet little woman from El Salvador with the perfect breasts, tourists, and lonely night people all passed by in a slow parade.

At that particular moment, it was not a fare he was remembering but seagulls. He would notice the gulls around Los Angeles, eating from garbage bins behind pizza and fast food places. He liked gulls, the way they hovered and gathered together. They always seemed clean as well, unlike the pigeons he remembered in New York. Gulls had a diverse personality; they were both hunters and scavengers; they were fierce and yet gregarious. He remembered driving at dawn along La Brea and spotting a seagull flapping a wing ineffectually as it lay on its side in the gathering morning rush hour. Cars and trucks were passing perilously close as it struggled to make its way across the wide boulevard to the curb's comparative safety. Nick swung his cab around, drove close to the injured bird, opened his door, bent down, and picked it up. He remembered how surprisingly light it had been. With horns honking impatiently behind him, Nick reached around and dropped the gull onto the back seat. As he did so, the gull bit him on his ring finger, drawing a little blood. "Thanks a lot," Nick said.

Turning around, he drove back toward the yard. It was time to go in regardless. As he cruised down Washington Boulevard, the gull hopped to the top of the back seat and threw up a partially digested chicken wing. "Thanks again," Nick said. "You pull another stunt like that and I'm going to start the meter and make you pay." The bird regarded him balefully with its piercing eyes. Nick wasn't sure what to do with the gull. He had the idea to take it home and see if he could somehow help it recover. On the way into the yard, he stopped by his Camaro and thought to transfer the gull from cab to car. When he opened the back door of the cab, the gull, apparently fully recovered from whatever trauma it had, jumped out of the cab, and flew away. Nick watched it gracefully arc around and fly toward the rising sun. It was at that moment Nick became aware of a nurse taking his pulse.

He opened his eyes. As he did so, he wondered how long he had been in the hospital. He wasn't sure but thought it had been two days. A moment later, Dr. Trang came in. "Well, how you feeling today?"

"I'm not sure."

"I can understand that. You've been here four days and you're not getting better."

Nick just stared up at him and then asked, "No better?"

"Possibly worse. Have you ever had large doses of antibiotics before?"

"When I was injured in Vietnam, I had bad infections in my wounds and I was on strong stuff for a long time."

Dr. Trang regarded Nick from behind his glasses for a quiet moment and then asked, "Do you remember what they were?"

"I don't think so. There was more than one."

"We should switch to a newer drug. I recommend it, but as it has not been used as frequently, I can't guarantee it will work any better. What do you think?"

Nick's eyelids involuntarily closed as he tried to reach down inside himself to find an answer to a question he didn't actually care about one way or the other. Suddenly, an image of little Melissa toddling along the sands of Venice Beach came to mind. Nick savored the memory for a brief drifting moment, then opened his eyes. "Switch. Get me well and get me out of here." Trang nodded, turned to the nurse, and gave the orders.

Nick realized his personal quest for the killers was all but over. He had to take care of his daughter; he had to get back on track with his career. By telling the doctor to get him well, Nick instinctively knew he had made the first positive step in a long time. He had many more to make.

◆◆◆

NICK RECOVERED SLOWLY. As he drifted in and out of an odd dream state, he did a lot of quiet thinking. Five days later, he walked out of the hospital and went back to his apartment. He called the cab company and told Vern he'd be back to work soon but for the time being, he only wanted to drive four nights a week. Vern thought it was a good idea. Nick was afraid to bring it up but finally asked, "How about four-o-five?"

"They're going to fix it but who knows when they'll get around to it. It's a mess."

Nick hung up, moved the telephone a little closer, took a deep breath, and called Lillian. He had made a point of calling Melissa every seventh day when he took his one day off, but when he started driving seven nights a week, he had stopped the routine and called infrequently. When Lillian answered the telephone, Nick could feel the chill. "You're just being the worst sort of daddy. This little girl Melissa is the prettiest thing and you just sit out there in Los Angeles doing God knows what with all those crazy folk." The conversation continued going badly until Nick reluctantly mentioned he had been in the hospital with pneumonia and almost died. That brought out enough sympathy in the old woman to let him talk to Melissa.

Nick didn't recognize her. Her voice had changed a little and her vocabulary had grown. That was to be expected, but she talked to Nick as though she might speak to a clerk at the grocery. Her lack of true connection with him broke his heart and he vowed to get to Georgia soon.

He lay down on the bed, fell asleep for an hour, and then began making calls to publishers, news editors, and photojournalists he knew. It was time to get back to work. It was way past time. He didn't have much energy, but he kept at it. When the New York offices closed for the night and he could no longer contact anyone, Nick realized there was one important thing he had to accomplish, immediately. He went to the kitchen, stopped abruptly, leaned against the refrigerator for a moment, and wondered if he had the courage to maintain what he was going to initiate. Deciding, he methodically went around the kitchen and emptied the tequila and beer bottles into the sink. A few odd bottles of vodka and whiskey he seldom drank followed suit. Going to the refrigerator, he pulled out assorted bags of weed that were stuffed in various corners and compartments and emptied those into the garbage. Without them, the refrigerator was almost empty. He found an old peanut butter jar filled with seeds he had saved as he cleaned the marijuana. There were enough seeds to grow a forest. He removed the lid and poured those into the garbage bag, too. The seeds rattled and tinkled their way down over the empty bottles. In turn, the trash bag went into the Dumpster in the alley.

As the days passed, Nick was surprised he didn't crave either the marijuana or the booze. He expected he would, but he didn't. *Of course, nearly dying of pneumonia could do that to you,* Nick figured. But Nick knew it wouldn't be long before the demons would be back demanding their pacifiers.

✦✦✦

MOSE ARRANGED A MEETING between the Vegas buyer and Cranberry. The idea was simple. Louie, as Cranberry called Detective Lou Stabile, wanted to buy up to six kilos of cocaine. He would take no less than three kilos because it wasn't worth his while. Because Cranberry was able to set him up with the cocaine and be in on the cut if he had to reach out to other suppliers, it looked like a no-lose proposition to Cranberry. In fact, it was win-win. Cranberry grinned at what he thought was the big buyer and said, "We're gonna do some business, but I got to wait until my boys Jesse and Cal come back to town. Then there's gonna be more than enough to go around."

"Jesse and Cal, huh?" Stabile huffed. "Sounds like a couple of banditos if I ever heard."

"They're cool and they bring some fine white lady."

Stabile stood up and nodded to Mose. "You tell Mose here when they're around and you want to get together. I'll come to town and do the taste. If it checks out, we're all in business."

After Stabile and Mose left, Cranberry unscrewed the top on a small bottle of coke and tooted up. He realized he might just be on his way to a seriously profitable independent dealership. When his new suppliers Cal and Jesse completed their run from Juarez, he'd have something serious to talk about with this Louie character.

NICK CONTINUED CALLING CONTACTS in New York, London, and elsewhere on a daily basis. He also was beginning to find his way around to some of the editors in Los Angeles. Nothing broke for him and though he realized he was becoming a pest with his calls, he continued. Four nights a week he drove, but it was with a different rhythm, sensibility, and he limited himself to eight or nine hours a night.

One afternoon, he showed up at the yard earlier than usual and saw Clyde pull up to the pump and begin to service a good-looking cab that had arrived while Nick was in the hospital. Nick walked over to him. "Hi, Clyde."

"Hello, Nick. Good to see you back. Are you okay?"

"Better than four-o-five."

"Accidents happen," Clyde said in a quiet way and looked down as he pulled the nozzle out of the neck of the gas tank, replacing it in the pump.

"Clyde, I'm truly sorry I messed up our ride so totally. I feel like shit about it."

"Like I said, 'accidents happen,'" Clyde said as he popped open the hood.

A young man with a heavily freckled face and mop of curly red hair came over. "I'll finish up, Clyde, you can turn in your paperwork."

Clyde turned to Nick. "This is Jonathan. Jonathan is working with me driving four-two-one. He's studying acting during the day and driving nights."

Nick nodded his head, shook hands with Jonathan, and wished both he and Clyde well. He walked off feeling very much alone.

"Three-nine-four?"

"Three-nine-four," Nick answered.

"Pick up at one-four-one Rees Street, apartment five. That's off Trolley Way in Playa Del Rey. Going to the Port."

"Check." A ride to the airport from Playa Del Rey was not a big meter, but Nick thought it could turn into something good if he could snag a nice fare from there.

When he got near the address, he noticed Rees Street was actually a walkway common to the beach towns of Southern California.

Since he was unable to drive down, he gave one short tap on the horn to announce his arrival. He waited a few moments but no one came, so he got out of the cab and wandered down the walkway looking for the address. When he finally found the house, he squinted in the dark and tried to find some apartment numbers. He calculated apartment five must be in the back. Hoping no one would shoot him as a trespasser, he went between the two houses and was rewarded with the sight of some wooden stairs leading to a small balcony. The lights were on in the apartment and the door was open.

Number five was a sort of Rube Goldberg add-on to the back of a house that had been divided into apartments. Nick climbed the stairs and looked in. There were two large suitcases near the door and a variety of gym bags. A small, wiry-looking man emerged from the bedroom. He was dressed in a suit and tie and had a patina of sweat on his forehead. "Oh shit, you're here and I'm late. Take these bags down and I'll keep getting my stuff together."

As the man frantically scurried around the apartment doing an idiot check of drawers and cabinets, Nick studied the small place. There was only a bed and bureau in the tiny bedroom but there was a nice-sized window. While the man dropped odd items into paper bags, Nick peeked into the neat little bathroom and small kitchen area. Walking back into the living room, Nick guessed if you half broke your neck looking out the window, you could see some ocean. The thought pleased him. For the first time, he felt a strong motivation to move out from under the bad memories of his current home. *I remember this feeling*, Nick thought. *This is what happens when you start to get sober.*

"You leaving this place?" Nick asked.

"Yeah, only been here three months but I got a great job offer up in Seattle, new computer company starting up. They want me there tomorrow. The landlord is going to shit a big one with my jumping the lease but he's holding a month's deposit. That should help." The man stood in front of his paper bags, gym bags, and suitcases. "Well, I guess I'm ready. Only got an hour and fifteen minutes before the plane leaves. Think we can make it?"

"Sure. How much is this place?"

"Three ten a month. Not a bad deal. You want it? If the landlord goes for it, I want my deposit back. His name's Harv."

"Give me the guy's number."

"I've got it in my briefcase. I'll give it to you in the cab. Let's get out of here."

The next day, Nick gave Harv a call. "The prick ran out on me? Damn, this being a landlord is fucked. This guy a friend of yours?"

Nick covered pretty well. "He's not a friend. I just happened to hear about it and I need a place myself, soon."

"Shit, well, let me look at the apartment, see how he left the joint, make sure the fucker didn't trash it. If you check out, I'll see about letting you have it. I live just down the street. I don't know how that guy got away from me."

"He split in the middle of the night."

"I didn't like the guy anyway. Something weird about him, like he had a microscope for a dick."

"There's not much weird about me. I just work a lot outside and then sleep as much as I can. No cats, dogs, or fleas."

"You sound like an ideal tenant. We'll see. But it's got to be month to month. I got plans." Harv hung up. Nick grinned to himself. He liked the guy. He sounded like he was from the old neighborhood.

NICK HAD JUST GOTTEN to sleep after driving until 4:00 a.m. The telephone rang. Normally, he would have slept through it but being sober, though tired, the insistent ring snapped him out of his slumber. "Hello?"

"Nick?"

"It is."

"It's Philip, the Macaroni Man."

"Yo, Philip, what's happening?" Philip was a freelance photographer Nick had dubbed the "Macaroni Man" because Philip always traveled with boxes of macaroni and cheese to cook so he didn't have to eat in places he didn't like.

"What's happening with you, Nick, been in deep freeze or something?"

"Yeah, I guess."

"I happened to be up at Ken Dahlgren's office yesterday when your phone call came in and he refused to take it. They had wanted me to go on a truly cool assignment for them in a few weeks and I couldn't jump on it because I'm getting married."

"Congratulations, I guess. You didn't knock up some farmer's daughter, did you?"

"No, I knocked up a journalist. Can you believe it?"

"Sure."

"Just what I said I'd never marry. Anyway, I told Dahlgren they should send you. He said, 'No way.' So we get to arguing about it and I tell him you're the best hot-zone guy around, next to me of course. Finally, he says for you to call him. However, the final decision isn't his, at least not in your case. It's Blanchard. I'll try to give Blanchard a call for you as well and hopefully the prick doesn't hold grudges. But give it a try anyway, start with Dahlgren."

They talked awhile longer and when Nick hung up he felt both good and bad. He was happy to get the call but distressed at how frozen out of the industry he seemed to be. His reputation had begun to go sour when he'd had his binges, fights, and difficulties with people in authority, which ended with him walking away or getting fired. In addition, there was the fact he had withdrawn from the business for over a year. There was only one thing to do and that was to somehow get back in and show what he could accomplish, all over again. This time, however, he'd be better. He was almost certain he could stay sober, but there was something else as well. Very simply, he felt he could take better pictures. He wasn't exactly sure why, but the experiences of the last year had created an effect whereby he felt he could peer through a lens with an even deeper understanding of what mattered most.

With some anxiety, he placed the call to Dahlgren. When Dahlgren was doing reporting from out in the field, he and Nick had hung out some, smoked some dope together, and chased a few of the same women. Nick always was the one to score and he knew it distressed Dahlgren, but Dahlgren was such an overbearing geek. "Ken Dahlgren here."

"It's Nick Cullen."

"Well, well, Mr. Pussy Hound."

"That was a long time ago."

"That's right, I forgot, you're a married man. Still, knowing you, I can't believe you don't go out and get a little strange once in a while."

Nick wasn't going to bring it up but continuing the subject of his marriage had to end. "My wife was killed a year ago and I've been out of the ladies loop.

"Killed? She was killed?"

"Yes. If you don't mind, Ken, I'm going to pass on talking about it over the phone, I can tell you about it in person sometime. But, right now, I am ready to do some good work."

"Shit, Nick, I'm sorry."

Dahlgren gave up wisecracking and the two had a serious conversation. Nick left out the part about driving a cab, but did say he had been studying people and had some new notions on how to achieve really effective work. Finally, Nick got around to asking what the assignment was. He assumed it would be the Middle East—Sadat was in the State of Israel, giving them full recognition, thereby infuriating his Arab allies. The Shah of Iran was in Washington, DC, under heavy protest from several different groups. They were throwing tear gas at the guy. Nick didn't think peace could last into 1978. All of North Africa seemed like it could go up any second, so when Nick heard the answer, he was surprised.

"Afghanistan, pal. Blanchard has this theory things are going to break there. He wants someone to go in, build a background of photos, and wait for the big shift in gear. A kind of funky civil war is going on right now but Blanchard thinks the Russians might do something, an invasion maybe, and he wants to be first in."

"I want to be first in, too."

"Well, Blanchard is in London. I'll make the recommendation; he usually goes along with what I say. I can make the preliminary deal with you but it's not final until he says so and he won't review it until he gets back. That's just the way the fucker is. He'll be back in a couple weeks."

"I appreciate the vote of confidence."

"I don't necessarily have all the confidence in the world, Nick, so you won't mind if I don't stick my cock out all the way for you. I'm going to lowball you on the rate a little and that will help make up the cheap bastard's mind. But I'm recommending you for the job, subject to his approval. Get ready and don't fuck up."

Nick slowly replaced the telephone in the receiver and sat deep in thought. Deciding, he went out and started looking for cameras. He was in a hurry to get them but realized it would take time to make the proper selection of bodies and lenses. He collected literature on various possibilities. He also found himself looking into pawnshop windows to see what was being offered, partly in the vain hope of finding some of his stolen equipment. One night, he spotted a small Leica similar to the one he'd sold. He could use a good, small utility camera. The next morning, he went into the pawnshop and asked the owner about the price. It turned out to be a good deal, if the old camera was functioning properly. He went to the corner drugstore, bought a roll of film and returned to the pawnshop, handing over his ID and credit card so he could test it outside. Outside the shop, he quickly shot off the roll, doing focus tests on a sign in the store window and elsewhere. Two blocks away was a place that developed and made prints in one hour. It was with a sense of excitement that Nick went through the test prints and saw the images completely sharp all the way across. He went back to the shop and bought the camera. A few moments later, he got into his Camaro and looked down at his new purchase. Enthusiastically, Nick gently expelled some air from his mouth onto the camera lens. As the condensation from his breath coated the glass, he gently wiped the lens with his soft flannel shirt. He repeated the ritual, making a soft musical "ha" sound, and watched as the moisture from his breath misted the lens. He continued for some minutes until he was finally satisfied the lens was clear of any interference or blemish. Carefully placing it on the seat beside him, he stared down at it and experienced a feeling of peace.

CHAPTER TWENTY-TWO

J ESSE'S LONG MEDLEY OF drug popping was playing out in a cacophony of consequences; intermittent erections were the least of them. His mental state was skipping into high-level paranoia. The current drug buy in Juarez was not helping his mental equilibrium. He had stashed one of Chester's guns in Juarez and planned to retrieve it when next they arrived, thereby not having to take it back and forth across the border. He thought it a brilliant plan.

Raul, the Mexican supplier, sat behind a cheap Formica table in a small room at the rear of the Dos Saltamontes Cantina. Off to the sides, he was guarded by two sinister-looking enforcers there to protect, serve, and collect. Raul had dealt with the crazy Gringo and Tex-Mex sidekick before. He sold Jesse and Cal ever increasing larger amounts of drugs. He had profited, as had Cal and Jesse, but he knew the relationship would not continue. The gringo, Jesse, didn't look like he would be able to maintain any semblance of cool, and he figured it would be less than a year before the man was killed or in jail.

The door opened and Jesse jumped at the intrusion. A rotund man with a large face and body came into the room and sat beside Raul. "Who the fuck is this guy?" demanded Jesse.

Raul seemed pained by the question and explained, "This is Señor Hernandez. It is he who risks his life and the lives of his family to bring me the product from Columbia that you and others wish to buy. This man is a hero." Hernandez had a thin black mustache and when he laughed, which was not often, one could see his incisors capped with gold. He had the disadvantage of not speaking English and that added an interesting spin to the negotiation about to take place.

Jesse sat facing them, with Cal seated slightly behind and to the right of Jesse. Some conversing in Spanish was necessary to accommodate Hernandez. It caused a lot of tension and began to drive Jesse nuts. The more Spanish, the more amped Jesse got. He was afraid they were plotting to take away his money. With each sentence, he'd turn to Cal and ask, "What did they say?"

Cal would reply with something like, "It's cool, man, they didn't say anything important."

"I'm the judge of what's important and what isn't. Tell me what the fuck they said."

"Hey, you're making me look bad here. Why don't you just lighten up?" Cal would respond, getting upset.

"I'm making you look bad? You?" Jesse shouted. "Whose side are you on here?"

"I just want to get the deal done and get the fuck out of here. Let's do the deal, Jesse."

And so it would go.

As they sat in the hot, stuffy back room, tensions were strained and the Jesse/Cal show didn't put Raul and Hernandez at ease, either. Six kilos of cocaine wrapped in plastic lay on the table. In the past, their purchases were comparatively small, so Jesse would simply snort a sample to test its effectiveness. This amount posed more of a problem. He had no test kit and wouldn't have known how to use it, anyway. Jesse snorted a sample from the first bag and, after some tension-filled minutes, reluctantly pronounced it good. He asked Cal to snort from the second bag. Cal did a line, and as he felt his head lighten and objects begin to take on a sparkle, he pronounced it very good. That left the other four bricks untried, but both Jesse and Cal were too high to give it a fair test. The dealer from Columbia flashed his gold incisors and asked in Spanish, "You want us to test for you?" Everyone but Jesse roared with laughter.

After Cal reluctantly explained the joke, Jesse slowly pulled out his gun and laid it on the table before the dealers. The flanking bodyguards reached for their guns and Raul held up his hands to stop them. Jesse stared at the men. "I'm not fucking around here. I want to know if this is one hundred percent. So we wait and I'll test the next bag in an hour."

"Fine," Raul said and poured him, Hernandez, Cal, and Jesse short shots of mescal. They tossed them back and Raul and Hernandez stared back at Jesse. The room fell silent except for the macho music drifting in from the cantina. There was no question of who was in control. During the long silence, Raul studied the *gringo loco* and decided this was the last deal. If Jesse ever showed up again, he'd kill him, take the money he brought, and float his body down the Rio Grande.

Two hours later, Jesse and Cal snorted samples from the last two bags, and after an electric few minutes of waiting, Jesse grudgingly accepted the fact that they were good. The illogical part of Jesse wanted to discover the drugs fake, thus forcing a violent confrontation. But the cocaine turned out to be very, very good, so with that question behind them, Cal and Jesse had to wrestle with the next situation.

Getting their "buy" across the border was going to be a far bigger problem. Jesse never trusted the idea of taking the El Camino back and forth. That car would always attract unwanted attention from customs officials. On their last trips, he and Cal sat in the small back room watching "mules" grunting in discomfort as they inserted balloons filled with heroin up their rectums. Jesse figured they'd need a small army of men to cross the border, too many to control. There was simply too much cocaine. However, if he had fewer men conceal the drugs in their garments or luggage, they might easily be caught, or worse, escape with their purchase. Having someone skirt the border and wade across the Rio Grande was also dangerous. The "mules" could run away, or get caught by the Border Patrol. Jesse eyed Cal critically for a moment and thought it might be a good plan to have Cal carry it all, but suddenly that idea worried Jesse even more. Cal could just mosey off into the crowd and never be seen again, or if Cal didn't run off with the goods, he was almost certain to get caught. He had that look about him and the customs officers were sure to smell it. Between Jesse's increasing paranoia about Cal, his mule distrust, and his uncertainty of other options, he settled on the most outrageous plan. He'd carry the drugs across in a knapsack and take the gun, too. "There's not a man alive on that bridge can take this stash from me," exclaimed Jesse.

"Man, that's the most stupid fucking plan I ever heard," Cal railed. But Jesse wouldn't listen. His mind was made up. Jesse put the six kilos of cocaine inside the knapsack, placed a dirty shirt on top, stuck the pistol down the back of his pants, pulled his sheepskin vest over it, and prepared to set out for the border. Cal would go ahead, get the El Camino, and park it as close to the border exit as possible. Cal only protested to a point because he feared getting shot by Jesse if he complained too much. Still, Jesse was carrying his share of the investment and should he get caught, Cal would be flat broke. Well, not quite, Cal thought, because he would have the El Camino.

The thought of having the El Camino to himself put a little bounce in Cal's step as he walked across the Cordova Bridge. With his US driver's license and no bags, he was easily passed through. Forty minutes later, on a Sunday morning, when swarms of Mexicans and Americans moved back and forth, shopping and visiting relatives, Jesse crossed the Cordova Bridge on foot with his knapsack full of cocaine and a pistol in his pants.

In Jesse's line, the overworked US Customs officer glanced at Jesse who stood before him with a wide-pupil stare. On just about any other day, the Officer would have kicked Jesse out of line and had him searched. But they were down a man and the customs officer had to take a screaming piss. He didn't feel like hassling with the wild-eyed jerk jiggling before him. He glanced at his license, waved the man through, locked his gate, and went to the can.

Jesse quickly found Cal ready behind the wheel, and, once inside the El Camino, let out with a wild rebel yell. Turning to Cal, he said, "Compadre, we're going to Venice, Cal-i-fucking-fornia to see the Cranberry Man."

Cal shook his head and grinned in spite of himself. "Jesse, you got balls, balls the size of beer kegs."

"You got that right," Jesse gloated.

Dropping the shift into drive, Cal pressed the accelerator toward the Pacific Ocean and their big-time rendezvous.

DETECTIVE LOU STABILE WORKED his way through the crowded hallway of the Venice Police Station. It had been announced that construction would begin on a nearby site to build a modern police complex for the division. Stabile knew it would take years, and the crush of officers with little space to work would continue. More than anyone, Stabile resented the fact he didn't have a desk of his own. He was a private kind of guy and for good reason. He shuffled through some papers on the communal desktop and came across an "All-Points Bulletin" for a Cal Santiso and Jesse Carmody. It took a moment for it to click, but he remembered those being the first names mentioned by Cranberry. He studied the APB information. He calculated the odds the two men he was going to be dealing with were not the wanted men. *The odds are slim,* Stabile concluded. *Still, it's possible and the names are not uncommon.* As officers moved back and forth behind him, Stabile reasoned if the men he was going to buy from were also wanted for murder, rape, and grand theft, he might be setting up a bad situation for himself. Though their rap sheets didn't exactly read like drug dealers, Lou instinctively began to feel the wanted men were the same guys Cranberry was dealing with. Attached to the APB was an old memo stating Pearson was the point man on the case.

He put the bulletins back on the desk and started chewing on his lower lip as he continued to mull over the situation. This was something he could very well use to his advantage, or it could jump up and bite him on the ass. He'd have to think it through carefully. Meanwhile, he'd visit Pearson's office. Hopefully, Pearson wouldn't be around and he'd be able to take a look at Pearson's files in private.

Pearson's door was closed, so Lou knocked respectfully. When no answer came, he opened it and slipped inside. The place was a mess. Stacks of papers were everywhere. He avoided them, took a quick peek in the desk drawers, noticed Pearson's personal bottle of Irish whiskey, and then went straight to the filing cabinet. After some digging, he extracted the up-to-date information on Cal Santiso and Jesse Carmody. He read their long dance cards with interest, then removed a large envelope from the file and discovered Nick's creation: the collages of the likenesses of Cal and Jesse. It took Stabile a moment to comprehend it, but then he nodded his head at the ingeniousness of the process.

Jim Pearson walked in, saw Stabile with the file, and was immediately irritated. Lou started thinking fast. "You know something, Jim?" Stabile asked. "I think we might have a common interest in these guys. I believe they might be the same assholes we're looking to set up for a drug bust."

"You don't say," Pearson said. "You know, usually I like people to personally mention to me when they're going to come into my office and rifle through my files."

"Well, you know how we are in this shithole. No one has their own space except you and a couple of other guys. It's easy for us to forget our manners."

"Sure," Pearson said, waiting.

"I think these guys are involved in some big cocaine sales."

"They must be moving up fast then because those two couldn't be involved in anything but big fuck-ups," Pearson said, moving behind his desk, reclaiming his territory, and pulling the collages from Stabile's hands.

Stabile began to retreat. "Well, anyway, if you get new information, I'd like to know, because we're going to put a sting on them."

"Sure, but might I say, the same should go for you. Do you know where these guys are?"

"No, I don't. But if it is the same guys, when it starts getting set up, I don't want anything to get in its way."

"Oh, no, we mustn't get in the way of your sting. Drugs are king. I mean, these scumbags are only wanted for grand theft, rape, and murder. What's that, compared to a nice drug bust?"

"Hey, Jim, don't get bitter on me. The guy we're going after is a main shot caller. We'll all look good after this," Stabile said, walking toward the door. "By the way, I didn't drink any of the good Irish whiskey you keep filed away." Stabile slipped out the door with a grin, leaving Pearson feeling even more pissed off. He wanted to know more, but he didn't want to get all cozy with Stabile. To Pearson, Detective Lou Stabile had the look of an untrustworthy man, and most untrustworthy men stayed outside Jim Pearson's orbit because they could sense how he could read people. Just for the hell of it, Pearson thought, he'd make a call to Stabile's old station house and learn why they shipped the man to Venice. He had a feeling Stabile was walking with one foot off the tracks and one day might step off all the way. He may even get caught, but probably not. In all likelihood, Stabile would retire a very rich cop. There was too much money in narcotics. Murder was a cheaper business.

GETTING MOVED TOOK BOTH his consecutive days off, but Nick got situated into his new apartment. His rent was almost half what he had been paying and he wasn't sorry to leave the reminders of the brutal tragedy. The Salvation Army got the excess furniture and toys Melissa had outgrown. Nick went through all of Julianne's clothes and set aside several garments to save for Melissa.

The Venice Clinic received the rest for their fund-raising sale. He took a couple of Julianne's favorite remaining trinkets, books, and pictures and put them in a large box with the clothes he had selected. He thoroughly taped the box shut and wrote Melissa's name on it in bold print. The box was to be a personal time capsule to be given to Melissa at an appropriate age.

When he was completely moved into the new apartment, Nick felt a familiar insidious feeling creeping up on him. He wanted to have a drink and smoke a joint. The feeling came at him fast and hard. He nodded his head in recognition of the desire. To burn off the urge, he changed into some jogging clothes, went outside, and started at a light trot toward the beach. He didn't make the ninety yards to the sand before his breath came in deep gasps and he began to feel weak. He slowed to a walk and felt a purging sweat begin to drip from his forehead. After a few minutes, he was able to start jogging again.

PEARSON CALLED CAPTAIN AL Trotter at Stabile's old beat to ask why the Venice Station had inherited Stabile. Pearson and Captain Trotter had met at the Annual Detective's Convention in Reno and gotten along well over poker and drinks. Trotter explained, "It was one of those things where we thought something was going on, but couldn't be sure and he knew what we were thinking. We let it slip that maybe he should ask for a transfer. When he asked for it, we naturally didn't stand in his way; as a matter of fact, we encouraged it."

Pearson realized they had passed his station produce that was obviously going sour. "So you thought it would be better if we got him but didn't know anything, thought it might improve the reputation and integrity of our outfit."

"Hey, Jim, you know how these things go."

"Yes, I do, but I don't like the shuffle," Pearson replied as he let the line go dead.

Later that day, Pearson ran into Stabile's partner in the men's room. Arnold was a tall, very handsome man with a classic Nordic profile, who unfortunately had more profile than brains. He was a nice guy but not someone with whom you could effectively analyze a case; that's why the captain of the Venice station had stuck him with Stabile when he'd arrived. No one who had been around and had serious business to accomplish wanted Arnold for a partner. After some small talk about football standings, Pearson turned to Arnold and asked, "You ever hear of a couple perps called Jesse and Cal? I've put out an APB on them: Jesse Carmody and Cal Santiso?"

"No, what should I know about them?"

"Nothing, I guess. Just something I'm working on." Pearson zipped up and left the restroom with the curious question: Why Stabile hadn't confided in his partner they were going to do a sting that included two guys named Cal and Jesse?

NICK TOOK A MOMENT to study the light from the sun as it fell upon a bowl of fruit in the kitchen of his small apartment. He could smell the ocean breeze as it blew through the open door. Casually, he made himself a light breakfast of grapefruit, toasted bagel with cream cheese and raspberry jam, and a cup of coffee while he thought about how to spend the day. He decided to do something he had not done in the past year. He would completely take a day off. After breakfast, he went into the bedroom and tossed off his robe and stared at himself in the mirror. For the first time in a long while, he noticed his old scars from Vietnam. They had turned a pale pink, practically colorless. Then he studied his muscles where they had become thin and without their customary definition. He wasn't sure about his health and strength but he knew they weren't good. He had to get into shape and quickly. If his foreign assignment actually came through, it would be physically very demanding. Turning from the mirror, he suddenly laughed to himself as he remembered a situation he had witnessed years ago when he was working out at a Vic Tanny gym in New York. A pudgy-looking Irish guy came in with his beginning evaluation card, went to the instructor, and said, "I just signed up here and I gotta get in shape to take the cop's test. Their physical is supposed to be really fucking tough."

The hard-looking instructor peered down at the guy's huge beer belly and soft arms and confided with professional encouragement, "Sure, we can do that. We can get you into shape. When do you take the cop's test?"

"Tuesday," the man seriously replied.

Nick put on gym clothes and did some stretching and martial arts routines, stopping to rest when he had to. Putting on his sneakers, he trotted down the wooden steps, jogged down the long walkway, and started running along the strand by the beach. He didn't get very far before his body weakened and he had to slow to a walk, but it was a lot farther than the last time.

After he showered, he drove up to the LA County Museum of Art and walked around. In particular, he wanted to see the photographic exhibit the museum had recently assembled. It was a compilation of some of the great American photographic works of the last fifty years. He examined the works intently. Many of the pictures he had seen before, either in other exhibitions, books, or studied in class. The museum presented some Westons, which were not Nick's thing, despite Weston's great reputation. Seaweed on the sand was all right, but he preferred photographs of actual people, as in the works of Walker Evans or Robert Frank. It was one thing to advance the state of the art and the way one sees different images, but it was quite another to convey the human experience through powerful photographs of people caught up in incredible events of history. The trick was to have it seen from a slightly different perspective. Nick was never sure he had a personal perspective for his work, but he could feel the stirrings of it inside himself and he could hardly wait to get a camera back in his hands. From his time in the cab, he knew people and events simply presented themselves. You had to let it unfold and be ready when it was most clear. It was as though he were a pianist and had been sent to a Gulag for a year where there was no music. The time had come to play.

People were to be his new focus. He acknowledged that he had seen dozens of portraits in the back of his cab every night. He mused to himself, some were threatening or memorable for one reason or another and others faded off into the night like shadows. However, averaging once a week, one or two fares turned out to be "leapers." Had he taken a picture of every leaper that rode in the back of his cab and printed only the most compelling, he would have had a fantastic book of photographs. He realized that, as a photographer, he had been looking at and for the wrong things. Instead, what he had been focusing on through hundreds of nights had left him with acute frustration, a broken cab, and nearly destroyed health.

After the museum, he had an early dinner in Westwood and decided to see a movie. He was probably the only person in Los Angeles that hadn't seen the big new hit *Star Wars*. He left it that way and went to see *Looking for Mr. Goodbar*. The idea of a woman spending her nights searching for a man in the saloons of New York City appealed to him.

◈◈◈

DETECTIVE LOU STABILE PARKED the unmarked car in front of Cora's Coffee Shop on Ocean Avenue and when his partner Arnold obediently went in to buy their morning coffee, Stabile sauntered over to the exterior pay phone, dropped two dimes, and called Big TC. "I got a call from Cranberry. He says two guys called

Jesse and Cal are coming into LA with six kilos of coke and he's going to do the deal with me."

"Lou, now you're playing me true. We can do something with this," Big TC said. "Now, listen to what I'm sayin'..."

Three minutes later, as Arnold came out with their coffee and buns, Lou hung up, and walked to the car feeling good about everything. He and Big TC were of the same mind and together they had quickly created a beautiful hustle. They would let the Jesse and Cal guys present the coke to him and Cranberry. Lou could then bust Jesse, Cal, Cranberry, and Cranberry's crew. With the cocaine evidence in his possession, Stabile would then switch the bags containing Jesse and Cal's high-grade drugs for identical bags containing less than 10 percent cocaine obtained from Big TC himself. Stabile would turn the kilos of severely cut coke into the evidence locker to convict the dealers. The high-grade coke Stabile will have liberated would simply go to Big TC. In turn, Big TC would hand over $20,000 to Stabile. Stabile would then be a hero for the big drug bust, which included murderers, rapists, and hard-core drug dealers. He would also have $20,000, tax-free. Big TC would get approximately two hundred thousand dollars worth of cocaine and he would be rid of Cranberry who had wild and dangerous ambitions. As a bonus to all, the citizens of Los Angeles would feel good something was being done about murders and illegal drug sales. It would be a sweet deal all around—unless you were Cranberry, Cal, or Jesse.

◆◆◆

THE DAY WAS DARKENING when Nick walked into the yard. Several night drivers were standing around waiting for cabs. Nick hung out near the shack and for a while, Vern ignored him. With the wrecking of 405 and driving less frequently, Nick had lost some official favor.

"I've got two-three-three," Vern finally said. "That's the only cab for almost an hour. If you want to wait, I'll see what I can do."

"Geez, Vern, you ask me to switch some of my nights and now you want to load me into a tub of shit? I don't know," Nick half joked.

"If you want to wait, I'll get you something decent."

Nick decided to go. Standing in the yard for an hour was like waiting at a rental car dealer to switch from economy to midsize. For one night, it wasn't worth the time.

He got his trip sheet, serviced the cab, and left the yard. Oddly, the night was without clouds and no moon was discernible. As a result, it was getting dark quickly. The exception was that raging fires in Topanga Canyon brought a swirling veil of smoke over Los Angeles. Homes and acres of brush and trees were burning in the seasonal alternative to devastating floods and mudslides. When Nick squinted, his eyes could make out the deep red-and-orange glow of the fire burning out of control only eight miles away. *That's what the fires of hell must look like,* he thought.

Nick had wanted to simply play the airport and have a mellow night, but every time he turned up his radio he'd hear the call, "We need cabs." The dispatcher that had replaced Billy and followed Vern's shift was inexperienced and was unconsciously screwing Nick by giving him bad orders. Nick needed to bank as much money as he could over his last days of driving. When he finally purchased new cameras and lenses, they would be very expensive. He had sent two months' support money to Lillian so Melissa would be taken care of because he knew he wouldn't get paid on the photography assignment for at least two weeks, and by then he'd be in Afghanistan—he prayed he'd be in Afghanistan. Deep within himself he had a fear Blanchard might capriciously flick him off. The uncertainty wore at his nerves.

The new night dispatcher wasn't helping things and Nick wanted to ignore him, but occasionally he felt disloyal and he'd answer a call. He took an order for a pickup in a residential neighborhood in Culver City. He stopped in front of a small wood-frame house badly in need of paint and watched as a huge man came lumbering out. It wasn't until the man got into the cab that Nick noticed how very drunk he was. "Take me downtown, Hotel Figueroa," the man half shouted.

Nick wasn't happy about the condition of the guy or the destination, but he stepped down with his right foot and the old cab chugged toward the hotel. The drunk in the back slowly began to nod off and Nick feared he wouldn't be able to wake him when they got to the hotel. "Try to stay awake will you? We'll be there in just fifteen minutes."

"Don't fucking worry about it," the big man said. Nick watched as the man sprawled and tottered in the back seat and then passed out. As they neared the hotel, Nick came up with a good solution how to wake the sleeping giant: a very hard right turn on Figueroa. The trick was to go around the corner fast enough so the man would topple and hit his head on the window and yet not take the turn so hard the man's huge and no doubt hard head would break the glass. Nick swung a wide arc onto Fig at about thirty miles an hour. The big man slid sideways and, like an overladen ship in a storm, keeled over and cracked his skull on the window with a loud thud.

The man's eyes spun open in bewilderment, as he wondered where he was. He slowly caught on as Nick cruised up in front of the hotel.

Driving back along Adams Boulevard to take a shorter route to the airport, Nick peered out into the darkness at the depressed and dangerous space moving before him. Suddenly, a car with its headlights on bright appeared behind him and quickly raced up the lane alongside. It was a white Cadillac Seville with a gold radiator and matching gold wire wheels. The light changed to red and the two cars stopped parallel to one another. The muffler on the Seville was half blown and it grumbled noisily. Nick glanced into the window of the Seville, which had the dome light on softly illuminating the occupants. He noticed a young man dressed in a teal blue jacket with a pink shirt and a lot of gold chains. Closer to

Nick on the passenger's side was a woman with her eyes heavily made up and lips provocatively painted Chinese red in an arc that far outran the outline of her lips. She was wearing a fake fur jacket open in the front. She turned and stared at Nick and ran her tongue around her lips. Nick smiled at her so as not to be unappreciative and then looked back down the boulevard. The light changed to green and the pimp floored the Seville and the muffler roared like an abruptly awakened lion. Two-three-three lumbered forward in the Seville's wake. Just then, a medium-size brown mongrel dog ran out onto the street. The dog panicked at the bright lights and sound of the approaching Seville, turned around, and abruptly ran back in front of Nick. Nick slammed on the brakes, but his car hit the dog. He heard a headlight shatter and noticed it flare to a burnout. The dog flew about twenty feet and skidded to a stop on its side. Nick quickly got out and went to it. The dog was yelping with distress and what Nick took to be an accusatory pitch at getting hit. Upset, Nick bent over the dog, lightly put his hand on its side, and spoke gently to it. Suddenly, the dog surprised him, leapt to its feet, and ran off. Relieved, Nick watched it disappear into the night. He got up and went back to inspect the car. Apart from the broken right headlight, nothing seemed out of order. He kicked the broken glass from the headlight over to the side of the road, slid inside the cab, and decided to keep on driving. He could get through the night with just one headlight as long as the cops left him alone.

JESSE CARMODY CAREFULLY SPOONED a little over an ounce of cocaine into a plastic sandwich bag, rolled it up, and tied it shut. As an afterthought, he took a nice pinch out of the sliced-open kilo and snorted it. As he taped up the cut in the plastic, he spoke over his shoulder to Cal. "When we get in there, I do the deal. You just back me up, no sense both of us going back and forth on it."

Cal didn't care; he just wanted to get out of the fucking trailer where Jesse had kept them holed up in a paranoid fit of secrecy. "Let's get a beer before we head up."

"We got beer here," Jesse said.

"Yeah, but we got to get our heads open and get a little relaxed. Being stuck in here with you has made me fucking crazy, man."

"We'll see," Jesse said and went to stash the kilo of cocaine with the rest and then hide the large sample he'd bagged underneath the El Camino's front bumper.

Nick swung into the airport and noticed there were a lot of cabs for that late hour. "Gotten tough to make a buck out here," Nick said in frustration. Again, he silently prayed Blanchard would OK his assignment so he could leave. He knew there were a few planes coming in from international flights and decided to try his luck there. Parking the car, he got out and was cleaning the windshield when his turn came: a tall blond man carrying his bags arrived cabside. "I need a taxi, please," he said with a slight Scandinavian accent.

"Sure. Where you off to?"

"I must go to San Pedro."

"No problem," Nick said, placing the man's bags into the trunk. They drove along in silence for some time until they neared the Harbor Freeway. "Do you work on ships?" Nick asked, genuinely interested.

"No, I have a friend from my country Sweden who is a ship's captain and he sails out from San Pedro and Long Beach."

"So you're visiting."

"I am simply staying with my friend until he leaves with his ship and then I will be studying in Los Angeles."

"What will you study?" Nick wondered out loud, hoping he wasn't crowding the guy.

"I will be studying primal scream therapy."

"You could do well with that in Sweden," Nick said, putting on his entrepreneurial hat.

"Why would you say that?"

"Because Swedes have a reputation for repression, repressing their feelings that is, and if you professionally directed them to scream repression away you could become the primal scream guru of Scandinavia."

The budding therapist didn't find Nick's comment amusing so Nick let it go. Dense fog was drifting in along the coast and Nick had to peer carefully through the heavily pitted windshield. He missed the smashed headlight. Nick dropped the man off at a small, perfectly painted bungalow on Thirty-First Street, just off Pacific Avenue. After the man paid him and entered the bungalow, Nick remained outside the cab and took a moment to enjoy the fog and soft air, and to consider his next move.

He decided, since he was in San Pedro, he'd call in to keep the new and slightly manic dispatcher happy. It would be unlikely the dispatcher would have an order for him down there. That way, Nick reasoned, he could just deadhead back to the airport and hopefully grab another good fare. "Two-three-three."

"Two-three-three?"

"I just dropped in San Pedro, so I'm heading back to the port to see what I can pick off."

"Two-three-three, call me on the phone."

Whenever the dispatcher had a special and lucrative run, he would have the driver call him on the telephone, eliminating the danger of another driver or rival cab company stealing the order, but Nick was way out of position for those special orders. Maybe the dispatcher was going to have him get a medical package from a hospital or airport cargo and take it to Smith Klein Laboratories. The new man was probably trying to make up for jacking Nick around with the dead orders. A run to Smith Klein could be a very good deal because it was a long fare to Burbank with only a blood or tissue sample on the front seat and not a potentially annoying passenger with a lot of luggage.

Nick decided he would call it a night after whatever run the telephone call dictated. He didn't want to burn out and the old cab was giving him every possible notice it would much prefer being towed than running. Driving with one headlight was making Nick increasingly concerned as well. Glancing at his watch, he saw it was a quarter to one in the morning. He decided to find the nearest bar, all-night restaurant, or gas station that had a telephone, so he might use the bathroom and make the call.

The Crescent Lounge on Pacific Avenue was open. The sign was faded with flaking paint and lit by a solitary harsh spotlight. The joint had a dull entrance that made it look like one was walking into a cheap motel room. Inside, there was nothing inviting about the place save it was open with a bathroom and telephone.

As was his custom if he was going to use the bathroom, Nick purchased something to show respect. Not long ago it would have been a beer or shot of tequila, but this night, as it had been for many weeks, it would be ginger ale. Nick walked to the scarred wooden bar, along which were scattered a half-dozen men, and chose the most open spot. The place had an unpleasant smell as though it were never aired out, but Nick sensed there was more to it than that—the residual stale smoke and smell of the wooden bar soaked with years of soured beer were joined by another, even less inviting odor. After a few seconds, Nick identified it in his mind. It was insecticide. The place had been doused with Raid or something similar. Nick hated the smell and thought of leaving but realized how silly the notion would be considering he was only going to make a quick call and douse his thirst with a ginger ale.

At the bar, Nick checked things out with a brief glance right and left. For a moment, the guy on his right looked familiar. There was something about the large mop of black hair and his solid heavyset appearance that caught Nick's attention. Nick thought he might have seen him as another driver or even a passenger. He dismissed the thought. He didn't want to talk to anyone regardless. To the man's left was a half-drunk bottle of beer. *Someone is on the phone or in the john,* Nick thought. To Nick's left was an obese man in a red T-shirt. *Why would a fat guy like that wear a skintight red T-shirt?* Nick wondered to himself. Nick answered his own question, *The guy couldn't care less. He's just interested in the bourbon and beer in front of him.*

The barmaid came down his way. "What can I get you, honey?" She was short, with bleached blonde hair, and her large breasts that had been packed into an old-fashioned conical brassier gave her a definite fifties retro appearance and made her look noticeably uncomfortable. He was about to order the ginger ale when in the mirror over the back bar, he caught a full-frontal view of the guy on his right. Nick's mind went momentarily blank and, as though from the end of a long hallway, Nick heard himself ordering a Cuervo Gold in a rocks glass and a bottle of Dos Equis. Afraid to look around, he watched as the barmaid poured a heavy-handed drink into the glass then open the beer.

Nick was disoriented by the reflection of the man on his right and just as thrown by the fact he had ordered the tequila and beer. He hadn't had a drink in almost two months. He stared down at the light-yellow liquid. Even though he had drunk the beer from a bottle while driving the cab, Dos Equis was an amber-colored beer and he liked to see it in the glass. Unlike some beers, it tasted better from a glass.

A man emerging from the restroom hallway interrupted Nick's forced reverie on beer. Nick glanced at him and sensed a familiarity about him as well. Nick took in the cowboy boots, sheepskin vest, and Dallas Cowboys cap he wore. Nick returned his gaze to the top of the bar and a moment later was able to place him. A little light clicked on in Nick's head and a numb feeling worked its way up the back of his neck and the tips of his fingers began to tingle. The man came alongside Nick to claim his beer and join his partner.

The guy reached for the beer with his left hand. On his forearm was a tattoo of a black panther clawing its way toward his half-rolled-up sleeve. When the muscles underneath the inked skin tensed as the man picked up his beer bottle, the panther undulated. Nick was transfixed, like an owl tracking a snake on the road. "He was there," Nick barely heard the man say.

The jukebox was turned up loudly and Roy Orbison was singing his biggest hit "Pretty Woman." Nick did his best to block it out as he strained to listen to the two men.

"Look like we'll be goin' up?" asked the man with all the hair.

"Oh, yeah. The guy just showed up, wants to try the sample, just like the berry man said. Then we'll set the price and do the deal tomorrow night."

"How come we don't set the price and just do it?"

"It's a quality and security thing. That's the way it's done in the big leagues."

Nick reached for his tequila and upended it all into his mouth. The woman had so over-poured him it took three swallows to down it. He could feel it descend his throat and esophagus before burning its way out over the contours of his stomach. He almost coughed as the fumes caught in his lungs. *How did I ever drink this stuff?* he wondered.

The barmaid returned with his change. "Thanks. Want another tequila?" she asked.

"No," Nick said, not yet recovered from downing the drink. He was afraid to look to his right lest he find himself staring. As the tequila began to flood his body, he instinctively grabbed his beer and walked to the jukebox. He pretended to fish in his pockets for a quarter. Regardless, the Roy Orbison record flipped off and another dropped down. Johnny Cash singing "Folsom Prison" vibrated forth. Nick turned around, looked at the two men, and had to suppress a laugh. Suddenly, the whole thing seemed silly. A year of incessant driving, searching, and now here were two men who could very well be the killers. The bar was at least ten miles from the nearest places Nick had spent a year hunting. It all seemed too impossible, too bizarre, and possibly too difficult to accomplish anything. What could he do now?

Letting his eyes run around the room and then drop back on the two men, Nick decided they looked like the men he remembered. But were they? Suddenly, he was filled with doubt. Taking a slug of beer to flush away the saliva-sucking tequila, he studied the two as he walked slowly back to his place at the bar. The height seemed right on the one with the sheepskin vest, but the Hispanic-looking one seemed bigger. Nick strained to listen.

"We're gonna do good with this," said the man with the full black hair.

"We'd better. This is the big easy trade-up for us, but I don't like goin' up to that part of town. We've done our thing up there a plenty." The man suddenly became very aware of Nick's presence and quickly glanced over to see if Nick was listening. He watched as Nick stared into his empty tequila glass, briefly inspected the curious scar that ate its way into Nick's hairline, before turning back to his partner.

Nick kept staring at the empty glass in front of him until, suddenly, he grinned and poured the Dos Equis carefully into his glass and turned his back to the men. He slowly shook his head and thought again, *It couldn't be.* After a year of searching, to inadvertently stumble upon them in a dive in San Pedro didn't add up. He momentarily concluded he was mistaken. They didn't look precisely like he remembered the killers: the guy with the dark hair looked slightly different and the guy in the sheepskin leather vest had shorter hair than his remembered image. Nick's mind swirled under the tequila assault and the identification possibilities. So what if the man had a panther tattoo and was left-handed? Half the guys who get tattoos get a panther; it's the most popular one. The guy had shot Nick with his left hand because he'd been holding Nick's lens case with the other, so maybe he wasn't left-handed at all. Besides, just because the guy picked up the beer with his left hand didn't mean he was a left-handed killer. Nick pondered what to do. He didn't take long to conclude he would go to the phone, call the cops, and tell them there were two *possible* murder suspects in the bar and for them to come and take a look. That sounded like the plan to him. Nick turned to go to the phone, but the guy wearing the vest suddenly said, "Let's get out of here, we've only got twenty-five minutes. I don't want those boys gettin' nervous."

The two of them yanked back their barstools and walked toward the door. The barmaid came up to Nick and asked again, "You want another tequila?"

Nick shook his head, left the change from his ten, started to leave and then turned back to the woman. "Those guys look familiar. They come in here a lot?"

"I've never seen 'em before but I only been here a few nights."

Calmly, Nick turned and headed for the door as rapidly as possible. When he bolted out onto Pacific Avenue, they were gone. He had a moment of panic; they had slipped away. Suddenly, from around the corner, he heard the sound of an engine starting, a big engine. Nick turned and bolted toward his cab when he saw a maroon El Camino with a black shell pull around the corner. He knew it had to be them. Sliding into his cab, he snapped on the ignition. The old engine groaned in protest. Nick tapped the accelerator and it clattered to life. He had to punish the cab by flooring it to catch up. The pickup turned onto Twenty-First Street, easily climbed the hill, and made a right on Gaffey heading for the freeway.

Where Gaffey Street metamorphosed into the Harbor Freeway, the powerful El Camino easily accelerated to seventy-five in a matter of seconds. The freeway was empty except for a few trucks, but Nick was immediately left behind as he struggled to pick up speed.

He punched the accelerator. Gradually, he caught up close enough to feel he could stay with them, slowly dropped back, switched lanes, and was hopefully not noticed. A few minutes later, the El Camino swung off the Harbor Freeway, looped around, and took the 405 North toward Santa Monica with Nick in pursuit.

The familiar stretch of freeway and easy trail of the El Camino comforted Nick even though there was no way to anticipate what lay ahead. He felt for his knife in the bag, and though it was there to reassure him, he recognized how difficult it would be to carry out any sort of vengeance. He bitterly realized he had never run through the actual encounter in his plans. It was always just the search. Finding them had been the thing. He hadn't reckoned how he would behave once he had them in view. Yes, he had thousands of violent and explosive fantasies about killing the men, but they had always been an abstraction. This was different. This was real. He had to make something happen. Another thought came to mind, a logical one. *What if they weren't the killers? What if they were just two men who looked like them?* Nick considered and advised himself, *Let it unfold until it's clear.* Nick remembered he hadn't made the telephone call at the bar. He called the dispatcher on the CB. "Had a little personal problem. I'll fill you in later, but I'm going dark."

"Hope she's worth it, it was a good order," the dispatcher said, trying to keep it light.

"We'll see." Nick switched off his CB and concentrated on following from as far back as he could.

Ten minutes later, Nick's excitement rose as the El Camino pulled off the freeway onto Venice Boulevard and headed west. Nick cursed the yellow light on the roof of his cab and decided to start the meter so it would go out and the cab would be less conspicuous. He'd be his own customer.

The El Camino made its way down Venice Boulevard, turned right on Lincoln, then made a left onto a small side street. Nick dropped back, shut off his remaining headlight, and followed. The El Camino made its way west into Oakwood and suddenly stopped in front of a small apartment building. A block away, Nick decided to pull over and watch from there. Carmody and Santiso got out of the pickup and looked around before removing something from beneath the front bumper. They turned and walked back toward Nick. He reached into his bag, pulled out his knife, and opened it.

He wished he'd had a gun. The knife felt insignificant as the two men continued to walk up the sidewalk on the other side of the street. They turned into the walkway of a two-story apartment building and went inside. Again, Nick felt a tingling numbness from fear and anticipation. He got out of the cab, crossed to the apartment, and assessed the building from the front and sides in an attempt to determine exactly where in the building they might have gone. There were two apartments with bright lights on, both on the second floor. He studied them for a while and was rewarded with a momentary glimpse of Santiso's bulk crossing by one of the windows in the rear unit. Getting into his cab, Nick started it up and drove to where the El Camino was parked. He copied down the license plate number and studied the pickup. It had a lot of road dust on the body and gray break dust on the expensive mag wheels. Nick knew with a good wash and polish the machine would look incredible, but it was incongruous; the machine was so well put together and yet in such a grimy condition. Nick found a parking spot farther down the block on the same side of the street as the El Camino. He pulled in and waited.

STABILE SAT IN A stained and fraying stuffed chair casually watching Santiso and Carmody. In the apartment next door, Stabile's partner Arnold and two narcotics detail cops listened on headphones to the microphone in the lamp next to Stabile; another mike was placed in the small kitchen. In the corner of the room, Cranberry was seated and backed up by a huge punk in a lime-green jacket with two pistols stuffed in his belt. Cranberry didn't like doing business with guys like Stabile. He didn't know Stabile but had heard most of his life if you traffic with Italians, they'll take your business, and this guy looked Mafia all the way. Cranberry was branching out on his own and he didn't like the idea of working with a man who might take it all away, but for now this Stabile character was actually setting him up with the beginnings of his own dealership.

"So lay it on me," Stabile said, rubbing his hands together with eagerness.

Jesse turned and nodded to Cal. Jesse always made sure it was Cal who was carrying in case they got busted. Cal reached under his wide belt and pulled out the bag containing over an ounce of cocaine and handed it to Stabile. "It's good shit, like always," Cal said.

"I don't know you, man. There's never been an 'always' before this," Stabile countered.

"Well, we always, and I mean always, give good shit and a good deal," Jesse interjected. "Right, Cranberry?"

"That's why you motherfuckers is here, tonight," Cranberry said with conviction. Cranberry was going to enjoy this. He was to get $5,000 from Jesse and Cal for arranging the buy with Stabile and he was to get $5,000 from Stabile. Minus the $3,000 he had to pass on to Mose, the $7,000 balance was going to put him right.

Stabile got off the stuffed chair and made his way to the kitchen. There on a small Formica table was a testing kit. "Whoa, what's this?" Jesse asked, freaking a little.

"It's a testing kit, asshole. I'm going to see how good this is and then we'll arrive at a price. But I'll test what you bring up tomorrow, too, so don't pull any fool's play on me. You step on it and the deal is off, no matter what. This is just to see how real and how much."

"I thought when the Cranberry said you were going to test it you were going to snort it, like he does."

Stabile dumped the coke out onto the tabletop, scraped a couple of lines away, chopped it, and placed a crisp hundred alongside. Cranberry came over to the table. "I am the motherfucking white lady tester. This nose knows." He picked up the hundred, rolled it into a tight tube, and quickly snorted the lines. As he did so, Stabile got a good look at the round, maroon-colored growth on the man's jaw, just below his ear. It did indeed resemble a cranberry.

"Cranberry here tests it with his nose, but I'm doing the science thing, see," Stabile explained, as he dropped twenty milligrams of coke into a pale liquid test tube.

Cranberry walked around the room with his nose in the air, sniffing like he was scenting an animal. "This lady is the boss, Stabile. This shit do you fine in Vegas."

"We'll see." Observing the results, Stabile felt a little rush of adrenaline as the liquid gradually changed to a dark coffee brown. He kept his best poker face as the test showed it was over 90 percent pure cocaine. Taking the 10 percent out for the evidence locker, that still left 80 percent coke. *Big TC is gonna piss his pants with joy*, Stabile thought. A few seconds later, Stabile looked up and said, "Seventy-nine percent cocaine, twenty-one percent some other fucking shit. All in all, not too bad, but you're not going to get top dollar for this. We're talking eight hundred an ounce. Not a fucking nickel more." Cranberry began pacing the room, listening and grinning. He had made his deal regardless of price and was now simply on for the ride, but Cal and Jesse got tense.

"Cranberry was talking eleven hundred an ounce," Jesse said aggressively.

"That was for pure but this ain't near that. Eight hundred an ounce; fuck and you've got how much?"

"Six K's."

"Shit, man, that's about twelve pounds. You stand to make..." Stabile hesitated a minute, even though he knew the answer. "That's over a hundred forty-three thousand dollars. Hey, you've come a long way, baby." Stabile waited to see if Jesse or Cal would catch the fact that he shorted them over $10,000, but Jesse went the wrong way.

"Six K is more than twelve pounds and you fucking know it," Jesse blustered.

"How much more?" Stabile asked, enjoying himself.

"It's like, ounces more."

"Practically nothing, and this is some less than superior shit."

"You're sitting with a quarter million dollars' worth of blow, low wholesale price!" Jesse yelled.

"I'm sitting with an ounce of stepped-on coke and the money you're dreaming of is something you're gonna have to forget about, immediately." Stabile waited for effect. "Unless you can go somewhere else and pull that kind of dough down." He knew they couldn't, but he rode out their confusion and decided to give a little to insure they'd stick around. "Tell you what, after you go, I'll talk to Cranberry here and I'll talk to my partners in Vegas. If they say it's okay, we'll go a hundred fifty grand all in. That's if it all checks out like the sample; if it don't, you sell it someplace else. Go over to East LA and see how they do you."

"They do you to pieces," Cranberry offered.

Jesse remembered getting ripped off there only too well. The thought of $150,000 had his head spinning. He had hoped for over $200,000 but that was probably a fantasy in the air. This was reality, which equaled $145,000 after Cranberry's cut. He walked over to the table and started to scrape the remaining coke into the bag. "Hey, leave that shit there," Cranberry said loudly.

"You ain't paid for this with nothing but talk. So you'll get it all tomorrow. A hundred fifty grand, bring it."

"Man, you got to leave that shit, so Louie and me can take it to our brothers and they know we're talking true. We can't go asking them for the whole fucking treasury for some jive talk. They gotta party some to get in."

Jesse considered this. "I'll leave you half, but if you don't come up with the money, you owe me a grand, retail."

"Motherfucker, I don't owe you shit. This here is business and in business you got to give out samples," Cranberry blustered.

"Sample this, asshole," Jesse said pointing to his cock.

"Motherfucker, you..."

Stabile stood and held up his hands. "Cranberry, the man's got a point. You got eight hundred dollars' worth of coke there. So take half and you owe him four hundred. We don't have to get the whole fucking gang high to make a deal, just the guys who make the choice." Stabile turned to Jesse. "Go ahead, take half with you." Stabile saw Carmody hesitate. "Hey, man, we set the whole fucking thing up and I'll guarantee the four hundred."

Tensed all over, Jesse slowly moved toward Stabile. The man in the lime-green jacket slipped his hand on one of his guns. "What the fuck is going on here? You just cut me down from two hundred thousand to a hundred fifty, and now you're guaranteeing me only four hundred for this bag when I asked for a thousand dollars, and you think I'm not supposed to notice?"

"I didn't say you weren't supposed to notice. I'm saying you're not supposed to care."

In the next room, Stabile's partner Arnold and the cop with the recorder looked at one another suppressing grins and near giggles at Stabile's maneuvers around Carmody.

Stabile looked at Jesse as a schoolboy. "We're coming up with a hundred fifty fucking thousand dollars and you're busting my chops about this little bit of blow?"

Jesse stood with his hands on his narrow cowboy hips, his broad shoulders hunched forward, and his head cocked to the left, deep in thought; then he stared hard at Stabile. "We didn't come here for four hundred fucking dollars. We came for the deal. Do we have a deal?"

Cranberry looked at Stabile with confidence. He knew what he and his Las Vegas partners could do with six kilos of fine coke. It was a lot. Stepped on and spread around in little gram bottles, it would bring them back way over tenfold what they were paying. Stabile nodded to Cranberry that the deal was done and Cranberry turned to Jesse. "Don't worry, Jesse fucking James. This gonna be all right. Eleven o'clock tomorrow night, right here."

Jesse looked at them and then at the guy in the lime-green jacket. "Just the two of you. I'm not interested in meeting any of your friends or blood relatives, including this fucker with all the iron in his pants."

"The same goes for you fucking desperadoes," Stabile said.

Jesse handed the remaining dope to Cal, who slipped it under his wide belt. Stabile appreciated the exchange. After Cal and Jesse walked out, Cranberry turned to Stabile. "I can see why the Hollywood folk go for this shit so much. A man could fall in love with this. I mean this bitch is fine, so fine, I'll do another line." Cranberry laughed and bent over the table. Stabile grinned in return, sat back from the table, and let Cranberry snort away. Wiping off his nose, Cranberry stood up and looked seriously at Stabile. "Man, weren't those some dumb motherfuckers?" Cranberry broke his stern look and laughed uproariously.

"You don't want to be messing with those guys, Cranberry."

"Oh, I ain't gonna mess with them. You mess with them and somebody gonna die, maybe more than just somebody. Besides, them motherfuckers gonna come back and sell me some more bitchin' stuff at a motherfucking Woolworth's rate." No, thought Cranberry, he wasn't going to do those suppliers; if anyone was going to go down, it would be the man sitting at the table. The man he knew as "Louie" would be walking in with $150,000. The man said he had partners in Las Vegas, but as far as Cranberry could tell, Louie was all alone. In the drug business, being all alone was not a good thing.

AFTER ALMOST AN HOUR of waiting, he still didn't know what he was going to do. He didn't even know what to do with the knife, whether he should keep it in his pocket or in his bag, open or closed. When Nick saw Jesse and Cal coming toward their pickup, he grabbed the knife, opened it again, and stabbed it deep into the old seat to have it ready beside him.

Once inside the El Camino, Jesse looked at Cal and then gave out with a loud whoop. "A hundred fifty fucking thousand dollars, compadre." Cal grinned in spite of himself and tried to figure what half of $150,000 was minus the agreed upon 30 percent reinvestment in another run to Juarez.

"What are you going to do with your third? A third, man, that's about thirty-five thousand dollars!"

Cal suddenly got hot and turned to Jesse, "I don't get this third shit, man."

"Listen, compadre, a third is generous. It was my cousin we took that original dough from, my family blood. I been doing all the thinking and hustling and you been dragging your sorry ass along. I risked everything and carried that six kilos across the border on my fucking back. I think a third is generous, outright stampeding fucking generous, man."

"You just bring this up now? We were partners in this."

"'Were' is the right word, compadre, but you ain't been pulling your weight. Hell, if this was a normal scam, you'd just be getting ten or five percent, like the Cranberry man."

Whether from the tension in the meeting, or Jesse shorting him cash, or just his long-suffering repressed hatred of him, Cal flashed red in his brain and impulsively reached out, grabbed Jesse by his vest, and pulled him violently around to face him. At the same time, Jesse yanked the snub-nosed .38 out of his back holster and jabbed the muzzle up into Cal's armpit. "I'm offering you fifty thousand dollars cash minus the thirty-percent reinvestment, more money than your beaner brain has ever thought about, and you're giving me shit?"

Feeling the gun muzzle in his armpit, Cal slowly loosened his grip on Jesse. He knew Jesse would shoot him as fast as he cared to. But Cal's pride wasn't going to let it all end that quickly. "It isn't fair; you're giving only thirty-five thousand dollars. What about the hundred fifty thousand we're going to get? How does the thirty percent work out of that with you shorting me my half?"

"You don't know what it is and that's why I get more than you do. Besides, that original money we traded up belonged to my blood fucking relative, compadre, and that's why I'm taking it."

Cal relaxed his hands on Jesse's vest, pulled them back, and began to sulk. Jesse took the gun away but not before forcibly jabbing the nose of the barrel into Cal's armpit for effect. Cal winced in pain but didn't complain. Jesse placed the gun down by his crotch where he could get at it fast in case Cal decided he hadn't had enough. He turned back to Cal. "Just thank your lucky fucking stars you're in the outfit with a guy like me, or you'd be washing dishes in a Taco Bell." Jesse reached out and turned the key in the ignition, and the El Camino sprang to life.

It took Cal six seconds to think of a good retort. "They don't have dishes in Taco Bell. Everything's throwaway."

Jesse looked at him and snickered, "You dumbass fuck." Laughing, he pulled out into the street and drove away. Cal flushed with anger again but let it pass. As he relaxed with the now-familiar sound of the El Camino's powerful engine, the vision of Jesse killing him again came to Cal. He had a glimpse of Jesse standing over him with a gun, shooting him over and over, grinning the whole time. The vision frightened him, and Cal's mouth and jaw slowly went slack. He breathed shallowly and stared out through the grime-streaked windshield, silently whispering for Jesus to protect him.

Watching them leave, Nick flipped his meter so the roof light would not illuminate, left his one good headlight off, started up, and pulled away.

Jesse and Cal retraced their route back up Venice Boulevard, stopped at a Jack in the Box takeout window, then jumped onto the San Diego Freeway south.

Nick realized they were heading back toward San Pedro. He put on his one good headlight and lay well back, following. Twelve minutes later, they curved onto the Harbor Freeway, but before they got to San Pedro, they surprised Nick and whipped off onto the Pacific Coast Highway heading south into the Wilmington area. Nick floored the accelerator, barely managing to keep up.

Wilmington was a depressed little community, bracketed by the sprawling working man's city of Carson, oil refineries, and the less-attractive end of the seaport. Cal had a friend there with a trailer secretively parked in the back alley behind a run-down house. Cal's friend from his reformatory days worked as a second mate onboard a long-haul tuna boat and was often gone for weeks or months at a time. There was a bathroom nearby in a poorly converted garage that had never morphed into the little one-room cottage the original owner had envisioned before he died. The current owner of the house was a retired longshoreman and petty thief. For $130 a month, the owner illegally rented Santiso's friend rights to the parking space, an electrical outlet, and the dirty bathroom in the cottage. Unbeknownst to the owner, the neglected cottage now also sequestered six kilos of cocaine carefully hidden near the rafters.

Nick followed along, and in the sparse traffic, his cab became more and more conspicuous. Jesse finally noticed it. "I can't tell if that fucking cab is following us or not."

"A taxi ain't gonna bother us."

"Sometimes cops drive around in taxis and things like that, especially drug cops. Or it could be some of Cranberry's guys coming down to rip us off." Cal considered Jesse's statement and realized Jesse was indeed a smart guy. Jesse smirked and said, "Let's see what that guy's got under his hood before we turn." Jesse floored the El Camino, and the cranked-up engine and beefed-up transmission made the rear tires peel rubber. It quickly roared up to one hundred ten, hurtling down the Pacific Coast Highway and leaving the cab in the dampness of early morning. Nick saw them burn away from him and realized he'd been made. He stepped down on the accelerator but knew it was useless, catching them was impossible. Peering into the distance he noticed the brake lights flash as they braked and turned down a residential street over half a mile away.

When he arrived near the area, he impulsively turned down one of the blocks and saw nothing before him but parked cars, old houses, and apartments. He agonized over the loss and pounded the steering wheel in frustration. He had been so close. But maybe he still was. He calmed himself and began to methodically cruise the neighborhood.

Satisfied they were not being followed, Jesse drove down the alley where they had been staying, pulled the El Camino up snuggly to a termite-riddled fence by the trailer, and parked. Jesse got out and went into the trailer. With practiced irritation, Cal cleaned up Jesse's mess of paper, napkins, and cup from Jack in the Box and followed Jesse inside.

Nick cruised the first block and noticed as he came out on B Street there was nothing but the industrial harbor before him. He estimated they would have to be within a twenty-block radius, unless they had kept on going completely out of the area down into Long Beach. If that were the case, he'd lost them. The fact he had spotted them earlier that night in the Crescent Lounge gave him encouragement they were still around. He set about carefully scouting the area, carving it up, street by street, alley by alley.

JESSE LOOKED AROUND THE cramped little trailer and shook his head. "Man, your friend sure likes Jesus. Got these fucking Jesus pictures and statues all over the place."

"I like Jesus, too," Cal said quietly as he lit a small votive candle under a picture of the Virgin Mary.

"Gimme a fucking break. Your Jesus can't love you, or he wouldn't have made you so ugly." Jesse chuckled at his own joke. "This place has been fine for a hideout, but don't try making this home sweet fucking home." Jesse sat down on the bunk across from Cal's, pulled off his cowboy boots, and dropped them to the floor from shoulder height, one at a time. "We do the deal tomorrow night and then head over to Las Vegas, get us a nice room with one of them Jacuzzis. Then, compadre, we pull a couple of hundred-dollar hooker gals that can suck the chrome off a trailer hitch and get ourselves done until we're dry." Jesse grinned at Cal and knew he liked the idea. "Pass me that coke, compadre."

"You do too much of that shit," Cal mumbled.

"And you do too much whining. I'm gonna see a smile on your face tomorrow, though, when we drive away with that money." Jesse stuck his little finger in the bag and scooped out some coke with his long fingernail, snorting it into his right nostril. He repeated the ritual for the waiting left nostril and then sucked the remaining cocaine off his finger like the last spoonful of chocolate from a sundae. Jesse huffed in appreciation and a few small rocks of coke blew out his nose onto his blue jeans and rested there like tiny icebergs.

"See how you sleep now with all that blow packed in your nose," Cal said, popping open a warm beer. He jammed the remaining fries from Jack in the Box into his mouth and chugged the can of Bud. Removing Chester's .45 revolver from his back holster, he put it on the small shelf next to a plaster figurine of the Blessed Virgin. Pulling off his shoes, he slipped out of his black denims and crawled under the abused blanket. The narrow aisle between him and Jesse seemed even smaller than before, and Cal resolved when they got to Las Vegas, he would get his own room. He smiled at the thought of such luxury. Yes, he'd have his own room and his own women. Taking comfort in the possibility, he quickly began drifting off to sleep. In total disregard for Cal's need to sleep, Jesse turned on the cheap clock radio and roughly spun the dial until he found some country music. Cal hated country, but he was tired and sank further down toward sleep regardless of Merle Haggard's best efforts.

After two hours of hunting the area, Nick finally spotted the tail end of the El Camino sticking out nine inches from behind a rotting fence. Nick parked the cab around the corner, pulled his knife out of the seat, got out of the cab, and stealthily approached the darkened alley.

Jesse had his hands behind his head enjoying the lonely singing of Patsy Cline. He was trying to think what to do about Cal. If he kept him along, they could do another run to Juarez and begin a really serious trade-up, maybe make $500,000, certainly $200,000 or $300,000. But then, Cal would want his "fair share." Or he could simply give Cal the $50,000 minus Cranberry's hit and the 30-percent reinvestment from their current run. Hell, he'd been a good compadre in his own way. Give him the money and then just cut him loose, or take him along, it probably didn't make much difference. On the other hand, he could give him the money and then take it back, forever, in a remote area somewhere between Barstow and Las Vegas. He listened to Cal snoring next to him and began to like the last option best.

Nick stood some twenty feet into the alley close to a garage door, letting his eyes completely adjust to the light. As he peered down the alley at the square end of the El Camino, it stood out in sharp focus and a small section of the chrome bumper glistened. Keeping close to the garages and fences, Nick slowly crept forward.

A gnawing suspicion occurred to Jesse that maybe the cocaine wasn't still up by the rafters. The owner of the house could have gone in there and spotted it. He glanced over at Cal to tell him of his concern and quickly realized Cal could go in there while Jesse was sleeping and take the stash and El Camino for himself. Jesse sat up and knew full well he wanted that coke near him for the last day. He wanted to see it. He wanted it in his arms so he could protect it. He slipped out of bed, pulled on his boots, jammed his gun into his belt, stood up, and, bending over from the low ceiling, went to the trailer door and opened it. In response to Jesse's movement, Cal rolled his wide body over but remained deep asleep.

Outside, Nick was almost upon the trailer when he heard the door opening and caught the elongated shadow of Jesse Carmody on the ground. He quickly ducked behind a battered Dumpster, knelt, pressed himself against the neighbor's fence, and held his breath. From inside the neighbor's house came the deep, loud barking of a large dog.

Jesse cursed the dog and pulled open the gate giving him entry to the guest shack. After fumbling for the key, he opened the door and went inside. He threw the light switch, and a dusty forty-watt bulb eked forth dull illumination. Jesse peered up at the hiding place and was gratified to see the bags still wedged under the eve behind the rafters. With powerful agility, he jumped, caught a rafter with one hand, reached up with the other and pulled out two brown paper bags from under the eaves, each of which contained three kilos of cocaine. Dropping to the floor, he placed the bags on an old desk heaped high with nonfunctioning shipboard electronic gear. A quick glimpse into the paper bags satisfied Jesse all was well.

Recovering from his near encounter with Jesse, when Nick didn't hear anything, he stood up and quickly crossed in front of the Dumpster, peered around the corner, and caught full sight of the El Camino and the trailer. The trailer door was slightly ajar and Nick noticed the fence was also open. A moment later, Jesse came walking through the fence carrying two paper bags. Nick could have taken him right there, but a paralysis took hold of him and he pressed up against the fence, again, in the hope he wouldn't be discovered. Jesse turned in the direction of the barking dog and yelled, "Shut up!" Getting into the trailer, he pulled the thin aluminum door closed and locked it. The dog's barking continued, and a moment later Nick heard a muffled voice call out from within the house chastising the dog. Nick stood still. The dog knew he was there and again broke the momentary silence with three more forbidden barks. As he started to move, the dog began again until the owner obviously got out of bed and punished the dog. The dog, which had proudly been doing its duty, gave out with a short hurt yelp. Nick stood uneasily in the new silence.

Jesse lined the six bricks of coke across the top of his bunk, placed his pillow over them, tossed his gun down, sat back down, and again pulled off his boots. He stared over at Cal who was sleeping deeply, his mouth wide open. Jesse needed Cal with him for security, but Jesse thought, as soon as possible, the Tex-Mex had to go. If the cops ever got him and kept him around for a while, old Cal would tell them everything, especially if he got the idea Jesus was watching. Yep, Jesse could find a new compadre. He lay down and felt the lumpy bricks of coke under his pillow and took great comfort from their hard, rectangular presence.

Outside, Nick forced himself to take some deep breaths. The tequila and beer he'd drunk hours earlier had long since deserted, leaving him in a space below sober. He was alone on the planet. Gradually, he left the false security of the fence and, clutching his knife, walked carefully to the trailer door. In the dim light, he peered intently at the built-in lock securing the door. The lock was inexpensively made but still solid enough to keep him out, especially as the pale-green aluminum door molding showed he couldn't break the door inward but instead, the door opened only outward. Nick stood frozen for a moment and listened to the country music coming from inside, then he turned and carefully walked away. He left the alley, went to his cab, opened the door, got in, and sat down.

He stared off down the street, his eyes open and unblinking, because mostly he was staring inside his own head, and in there all reeled in confusion. Putting the knife back on the seat, he put the key in the ignition and then stopped. He waited and questioned. They couldn't be the killers, he kept telling himself, but he knew they were. If it had been one of them alone, he would have had serious doubts, but together, it had to be them. Still, some spiraling doubt lingered. He took his hand away from the ignition and sat rigidly behind the wheel, peering out the pitted windshield.

The lone streetlight a hundred feet away made the tiny holes in the glass sparkle like diamonds.

As Jesse lay on the cot, he impulsively reached down and played with his cock. He didn't feel like masturbating, he just wanted to feel reassured it hadn't forgotten what to do. He wasn't disappointed and his mind drifted to Las Vegas and beautiful women. As suddenly as the sex fantasy flew into his head, an alarming thought pushed the pleasure aside. He sat up, realizing his gun was not in a good position in case Cal got cute, or something else should happen. He reached to the foot of the bed where he had tossed it, brought it up near his eyes, and inspected it in the dull light. Satisfied, he slid it under his pillow by one of the kilos of coke. He felt better, having the gun and the stash all compactly near his head. He put his hands behind his neck, enjoyed the cocaine dancing around in his brain, his numb nose, the feeling of his nearly hard cock hanging out of his pants, and for the first time in twenty hours, he let his eyes close.

As thoughts raced through his mind, Nick grasped a few of them: go to a phone, call Pearson and tell him what was up, drive away, and forget it, after all, things were going well now, why ruin it or get himself killed? He was not in very good shape, and those were two tough guys he was contemplating confronting and they most certainly had guns. Contrapuntal to those practical thoughts ran the impulse to take the tire iron from the trunk and use it to pop the door to the trailer. The tire iron would probably work right the first time, or certainly by the second quick try. The men inside the trailer were probably sleeping, but they wouldn't be the moment the door was noisily popped open. He could enter the trailer, and if they didn't shoot him on entry, he could try and stab them with his knife or bludgeon them with the tire iron. It was not a good plan and he knew it. Regardless, it was time to make a decision. Deep within, he knew he could never live with himself if he let this moment pass. Taking action was the only way he could purge himself of the racking sense of guilt and anger that had dogged him for a year. It would have been one thing if he'd never found them, but they were less than seventy yards away. With his breath coming in deep, barely controlled gasps, he found himself getting out of the cab, going to the trunk, and removing the old tire iron. He stopped himself from closing the trunk lid, to save the sound. Walking down the alley with the tire iron in his left hand and opened knife in the other, his mind was briefly emptied of all thought and he strode perfectly through the moment. He got all the way to the trailer door with a warrior's grace, but was gradually overcome with a sense of uncertainty. Something had momentarily defeated him or given him the right impulse, he wasn't sure which. It wasn't so much that he had fear, because he did and knew it. The problem was that he lacked total conviction. He wasn't positive it was them and he wasn't sure that what he was contemplating doing was what the situation demanded. Slowly, he turned away and began walking back toward the cab when, like a flash from an old news photographer's Graflex, it came back to him, the awful tableau. Julianne on the floor, Melissa crying for him from her crib. There were three men. Rainey, for certain, the other two were the question. Finally, Nick couldn't hide the certainty from himself anymore.

As the vision persisted, Nick saw Jesse Carmody reach out with his left hand and shoot, and before the bullet slammed into his head, Nick noticed something else, something he had forgotten until that moment. Jesse was standing with one boot on his wife's hair. Julianne lay sprawled on the floor, her hair fanned out behind and above her head almost as in a fashion layout, and Jesse was standing on it with his left boot. As though in a trance, Nick found himself turning around and walking back to the trailer door. The dog began barking again as Nick stared at the dully glistening door lock. He carefully slipped the pry end of the tire iron between the door and trailer body, close to the lock. To quickly pry the lock was a two-handed job. Holding the tire iron in place, Nick stuck the blade of the open knife under his belt. He found that calm within himself again, like when he was taking a picture during a battle and tuned everything else out and peered through the confines of the lens toward his subject. Firmly grabbing the tire iron with both hands, he closed his eyes to further adjust to the coming darkness and braced himself.

Jesse suddenly found himself with his eyes wide open, staring at the ceiling. In addition to the radio, there was a sound. He couldn't identify it in the half dark, but it sounded like metal on metal. *Too much coke will make you paranoid*, Jesse thought, but still it could be some of Cranberry's men, or that Louie guy coming to rip him off. It could be anything. Jesse reached across the narrow isle and poked Cal a few times, hard. Cal began to stir. Jesse reached back and let his hand slide toward his gun. Suddenly, there was a loud wrenching sound and the trailer door flew open. The abrupt sound startled Jesse's cocaine-laced nerves and he inadvertently knocked his gun to the floor.

Nick leapt into the trailer. The tire iron caught on the doorway and was knocked from his hand. He made a near-fatal hesitation before he adjusted to the sight of the two men in their bunks and saw Jesse's alarming movement toward his gun lying on the floor. Jesse grabbed the gun, wrapped his fingers around the handle, and quickly flipped off the safety. Nick pulled the knife from his belt and sprung toward Jesse across the narrow space. Jesse rose and brought the gun around. Nick's knife would have gone into Jesse's heart had he not begun to sit up and turn to fire. Instead, the blade struck down into Jesse's shoulder socket and lodged there. Nick's knee landed on Jesse's arm, knocking the gun sideways. The gun went off. Awakened by Jesse and the commotion, Cal had groped his way onto his left elbow in time to receive the bullet from Jesse's gun. The bullet entered Cal's chest and nicked the aorta above the heart. Jesse hung onto the gun and tried to turn it toward Nick from under the arm pinned by Nick's knee. "Shoot the fucker, shoot the fucker!" Jesse yelled to Cal in a strained, almost impossibly loud voice.

Cal, unable to process the situation, stared at his bullet wound, having just had his nightmare of Jesse shooting him become a reality. Cal dully watched as Jesse, screaming in agony from the twisting blade in his shoulder socket, fought to turn the pistol toward Nick. Degree by degree, the gun turned inward toward Nick's belly and finally was in line with his side. Jesse had a brief moment of joy as he realized he had the right angle. Noticing what was happening, Nick pushed down harder with his knee at the man's arm and wiggled the knife farther down into his shoulder. Fearfully, Nick felt his body begin to fatigue, his hand slid down the knife handle and the top of the blade sliced deeply into his palm. Jesse fired his gun again and again and again, just barely missing Nick and putting three holes through the aluminum ceiling. Through his horrible agony, Jesse wailed again to Cal, "Shoot! Shoot the fucker!"

Gradually, Cal was pulled away from his trance and became all too aware of Jesse now barely gasping out the words, "Shoot the fucker, shoot the fucker." Cal awkwardly groped around on the small shelf, knocking the statue of the Blessed Virgin down onto his narrow bed as he gripped Chester's .45 revolver. Fumbling with the safety, he slowly brought it around to face the intruder. Nick saw Cal arc the large pistol around and point it at him. He knew there was nothing he could do. If he let go of the man struggling beneath him, Jesse would shoot him, and if he remained where he was, Cal would shoot him. Nick felt a strange calm as he accepted his fate and waited for the bullet. Feeling himself quickly fading away, Cal dazedly held the gun pointed at Nick's chest. "Shoot, you fucking asshole," Jesse snarled.

Jesse's last words stung Cal like another bullet, and for that and the thousands of other insults he had received, Cal sluggishly swung his gun off Nick and deliberately shot Jesse. The first shot hit Jesse in the tip of his jaw and spun his head to the side. The second blew in behind the ear. The sound of the .45 going off in the trailer was incredibly loud. Nick was splashed with blood and debris from Jesse's rupturing head. As the man's arms suddenly went limp, Nick lost his balance and fell face-to-face upon Jesse. Horrified, Nick rose up and turned to Cal, resigned to being shot himself. With the gun now extended toward Nick, Cal stared at him with glassy eyes and then the heavy gun dropped from his hand. Nick watched as the man reached down, grasped the cheap figurine of the Blessed Virgin, and pulled it to his blood soaked chest. Slowly, as though going to sleep, Cal Santiso lay down on his pillow and quietly died.

Nick slowly backed off Jesse's body and stood, tapping his head on the low ceiling. Blood flowed freely from his cut hand onto the soiled carpet runner. Smoke from the gunfire wafted eerily in the quiet air. With his ears ringing so loudly it made him dizzy, he backed toward the door, tripped over Jesse's boots, fell backward, and crashed into a cabinet and small butane cooking stove. Getting to his knees, he found himself staring at the picture of the Blessed Virgin with the flickering votive candle beneath it. Operating on instinct, Nick picked up the candle, bent down, and placed it under the hanging bedclothes. Reluctantly, at first but then with gathering eagerness, the blanket began to burn. Nick stood, went to the door, opened it, and carefully looked up and down the alley. There was no activity, except a few more lights were illuminated in the ramshackle houses, and for some reason the dog had stopped its incessant barking.

Stepping back into the trailer, Nick took a last look at the scene, and as the flame on the blanket began to grow, he turned on the butane stove and noticed with gratification that the pilot light was out. The butane gas hissed at him, and Nick turned and stepped down from the doorway into the late night air. Unperturbed by the rising flames, the cheap clock radio continued to send forth plaintive country music from within the trailer. Closing the door, Nick hustled down the alley dripping blood onto his clothes and the crusty blacktop. It wasn't until he got to his car that he remembered his knife was still sticking in Carmody's shoulder and the tire iron was somewhere on the floor. He reached into each pocket to find his keys and his hand brushed across the compact metal body of the Leica. He realized he was sorry about the knife, but he was more disappointed he hadn't taken a picture. Nick had a moment's hesitation, while he contemplated the photograph not taken. Then, he got into the cab and turned the key. The engine was reluctant at first, having been enjoying its respite in the cool foggy night, but finally and without much enthusiasm it coughed to life.

Blood continued to flow from the deep cut on his hand onto his clothes and now into the cab. When he had to stop for a light on Pacific Avenue, Nick looked at his face in the rearview mirror, and in the dim light saw Jesse's blood splashed everywhere. Inspecting his cut for the first time, he saw a deep three-inch gash on the pad of his right hand and, as though the visual observation were a signal, he began to notice the pain. He grabbed some of the airport paper towels from his bag and wrapped them as best he could around his cut. The light changed and, with his mind reeling from the night, he decided to return to his apartment, clean up, and think. He prayed the cops would leave him and the broken headlight alone.

Twenty-nine minutes later, Nick climbed the wooden steps to his door and a moment after found himself looking in the bathroom mirror at what appeared to be a madman. He scarcely recognized the person staring at him from the mirror with wide, wild eyes. His hair, face, and clothes were splattered with pieces of Jesse's head and smeared with blood, almost to the point of extinguishing the true color of his skin and clothing's fabric.

Examining the cut on his hand again, he confirmed it was severe. He'd have to go to the hospital, which meant it would be necessary to concoct a story. Nick began to think about it, trying out different possibilities. Stepping into the shower, he removed his clothes and washed the blood from his hair and body. His hand continued to bleed profusely. Not having any large bandages, he took a fresh athletic sock and secured it to his hand with black camera tape. He changed into fresh clothes as quickly as he could. Once dressed, he put the bloody clothes into a plastic bag, went outside up the walkway, and dropped them into the trunk of the cab along with the large, blood-stained towel. As he drove to the Marina Mercy Hospital, he continued to think of a plausible explanation for the cut. He decided on something uncomplicated and obvious.

Nick was concerned when Dr. Lombard walked in. He hoped the doctor wouldn't remember him, but he did. "Ah, you're the cab driver who rolled out of his own cab. I've told that story often," Dr. Lombard said, scratching his slicked-down hair before washing his hands.

"Glad you got some mileage out of it," Nick said.

The doctor put on gloves, then poked, separated, and peered into the wound. "How did you cut this hand so badly?"

"I was trying to pry open the lid on a can with a kitchen knife and my hand slid down."

"This is nasty. You're lucky you didn't sever any tendons," the doctor said, shooting Nick's wound with Novocain. A few minutes later the doctor began stitching. Nick didn't think Dr. Lombard believed him, but he didn't question further.

Nick declined the offer of painkillers, and forty minutes and twenty-eight stitches later, Nick stepped from emergency and walked toward his cab. He looked with some apprehension at his right hand, which poked out of a sling Lombard insisted he wear. It was completely padded and bandaged in bright white, impossible to keep from view. He would have to stick with the suspect story of opening the can with the knife.

Nick removed the sling and got in his cab. He was surprised how calm he felt. He had just killed two guys and wounded himself. Reaching over with his left hand to start the cab, Nick corrected himself. He hadn't killed the men, they had killed one another. Regardless, he had initiated it, and if he were caught it was clear he was to blame. He realized what he had been planning for the last year was done and he felt a quiet buzz enter all over his being.

He had two more things to accomplish before he could put the cab back in the yard. He turned down Washington toward the ocean and stopped at a Dumpster behind a convenience store. He placed the bag of bloody clothes inside the Dumpster, which was near full, and covered the bag with adjacent garbage. Back in the cab, he continued down Washington to the Venice Pier parking lot. Using his Windex spray bottle and the towel he brought from home, he cleaned the blood from the steering wheel, steering column, seat, and floor. He would have preferred to power-wash the interior, but he couldn't drive into the lot with a sopping interior and huge white bandage. That would draw suspicion. He cleaned the best he could with his left hand, and then, with a sense of finality, he threw the bloody towel into a garbage can, locked the cab, and slowly walked to the end of the long pier.

The pier ended in a large ring of waist-high cement. On one side, a few fishermen were trying their luck even though signs officially proclaimed the fish were not to be eaten because of contaminants. Nick found a spot to himself on the southeast side and stared out to sea. The first glow from the sun was beginning to declare itself through the moist air.

There was the rhythmic slap of small waves glassed off by the quiet air against the barnacle-encrusted pilings. As he clutched the railing, his mind was presented an objective view of himself on the pier, cleaning the car, throwing away the clothes, getting stitched, showering, and abruptly breaking into the trailer and attacking Jesse Carmody. The event suddenly seemed utterly preposterous. The stupidity, the near-comic end to his quest, which but for the most fickle of circumstances could have resulted in him being killed, suddenly struck him as funny. Nick started to laugh. At first, a repressed laugh, but then it broke out and grew until at last he was staggering along holding onto the railing, laughing wildly and uncontrollably. His laughter bounced off the cement walls, echoed, and multiplied. The few fishermen on the opposite side of the circle looked at him briefly, then turned back to their lines in the water. They had seen early morning lunatics on the pier before and didn't want to get involved.

Amid the laughter, Nick felt tears welling up in his eyes, and moments later he leaned on the rail and wept. He wept completely, with no restraint for a long time, until finally it passed and a deeply hidden peace rose from within.

CHAPTER TWENTY-THREE

W HEN NICK AWOKE AROUND eleven in the morning, his hand was throbbing, and as he looked at the awkward white bandage, the events of the previous night came back with a rush. Curiously, he didn't seem to feel much emotion one way or the other. It all seemed like a surreal memory, so bizarre; he felt disconnected from it. Most vivid was the kinetic recollection of Jesse Carmody writhing in fury and agony beneath him. He had one feeling of regret, or at least poignancy, and it was from the look in Cal Santiso's eyes before he died. Why Cal shot his partner and not him was a mystery. Now that Nick had escaped relatively unscathed, he considered the next possibility: Could he be caught? From his earlier years shooting crime scenes and talking to detectives in New York City, he knew any number of clues might lead back to him. He just hoped no one would find them. He had left his knife with his prints on it, but the fire should have destroyed them. If the police did put something together, he hoped enough time would elapse so he'd be out of the country before they could get to him. He could move around the world and work for years. He could bring Melissa to London and, well, he didn't really know what he could do. This was a new beginning, but the notion of Blanchard holding strings to his life filled Nick with dread. He needed to keep a positive flow going, so, he impulsively went and bought the two new cameras and seven lenses he had researched. It was as much as he could possibly afford and it wiped out most of his savings from the year of manic toil.

Driving back to his apartment, he suddenly had a curious thought. Had he not acquiesced to Vern's request and swapped the nights he was to drive, he never would have found the men. Had he not taken the old cab, or gone to the airport, or gotten the Swede going to San Pedro, or called the dispatcher, he never would have found the men. He realized that for a year, he had been studiously traversing the irregular galaxy of LA's streets, and despite his best efforts, it was by sheer happenstance he found the killers. When he stopped his car near his apartment, he tried sitting calmly for a while to see if he felt any different from the night before. Save for the haunting image of Cal Santiso's soulful dark eyes drifting off to infinity and the painful throbbing in his right hand, he couldn't tell.

NICK HAD THE NIGHT off. He treated himself to a Japanese dinner in Santa Monica and wandered the bookstores selecting a few that would hopefully accompany him on his assignment. He then went back to his apartment to lay low. He didn't want to tempt fate in any manner. Nick was tempted by the idea of a few beers, an innocent enough thought, but he fought back the impulse. Instead, he sat down at the kitchen table with his new cameras and opened a small bottle of black automotive touch-up paint he had purchased. With painstaking precision, he delicately painted out the white logos and brand names. He didn't want to advertise a product and he wanted the cameras to look as inconspicuous as possible. A few hours later, he examined the work. Apart from the very small focus and F-stop markings on the lenses, there was no visible color but black.

AT THE APPOINTED HOUR of 11:00 p.m., Stabile and Cranberry waited for Jesse and Cal to show; so too did Arnold and two cops in the adjoining apartment and backup police scattered around the neighborhood. At first they were patient. Stabile watched as Cranberry sat down, stretched out his long legs, and rested them on another chair. "How you like living with the name Cranberry? You must get some shit from the brothers, especially ones with names like Abdul and Mohammed."

Cranberry regarded Stabile for a moment and in the spirit of the evening decided to share. "Louie, I used to hate that name, but then one day, I actually saw a real cranberry." Getting up, he casually walked around the room. "It was Thanksgiving and we went to my grandma's house. I was ten years old and she had some uncooked cranberries. I picked one up and looked at it."

"You never saw a cranberry before?" Stabile smirked.

"Shit no. That's a white folk dish, mostly. I discovered it was hard, had a beautiful color, a strong flavor, and was used to dress up the best holiday dinner of the year. Since then, I didn't care, because a cranberry is a righteous thing."

"Yeah, I guess if they called you dingleberry, it wouldn't have been the same," Stabile offered.

"I heard that one before, motherfucker," Cranberry said, smiling tightly.

BY 3:30 A.M., CRANBERRY and Stabile had waited four and a half hours for Cal and Jesse. Cranberry kept pacing the claustrophobic room, crying out, "Goddamn," over and over, every time with a different inflection, each more creative than the last "Goddamn." The guy was wearing on Lou's nerves.

Inside the tiny apartment next door, Arnold and two policemen sat waiting quietly, taping, and prepared to call in the backup when the deal went down. But nothing was happening and the men were getting tired of wearing the headsets and listening to Cranberry complain.

Lou was especially frustrated with Cranberry because the man had no way of contacting Jesse and Cal. No one knew where they were. Possibly they had been driving to the apartment and spotted one of the undercover cars parked a couple blocks away. Possibly they had gotten drunk somewhere, or found a better offer. No possibility suited Stabile, and finally he threw up his hands and said, "I'm out of here. If those deadbeats ever show, give Mose a call and he'll get in touch. All I can say is, my boss in Vegas is going to be one pissed-off Capo. So you'd better start lining up something else and line it up fast."

"Maybe you scared 'em off with that lowball money shit you was pullin'. I could sell that shit to my granny for more than you were offerin," Cranberry countered.

"Hey, they walked out of here happy. You got a free half ounce of coke. All I got was a pain in the ass from sitting. Come on, let's go."

Stabile got up, picked up the gym bag intended for the six kilos, and went to the door. Cranberry reluctantly followed. Outside, Cranberry watched as Stabile walked to his undercover car. It was a new 1977 Buick Roadmaster. Stabile had thought it an appropriate set of wheels for a character from Las Vegas. He slid in behind the wheel, cursed his luck, and drove off. A few moments later, Cranberry followed in the candy-apple-colored Corvette. He had bartered it from a strung-out pro football player for an ounce of coke at three on a Sunday morning.

It was now 3:45 a.m., and Cranberry was hungry, upset, and itching to toot up. He had purposely remained clean while waiting for the delivery, but the hours had taken their toll. He drove to McDonald's on Lincoln Boulevard, and through the speaker he ordered himself a large Coke and Big Mac. Since no one was behind his car, he went to the trunk and removed a small brown bottle from its hiding place in an old pair of high-top sneakers. Leaning into the small trunk, he stuck his gold spoon into the bottle and took a few good snorts. Feeling better, he drove toward the pickup window. During the forty-foot drive to the window, the cocaine lit his brain and he suddenly had a thought. Stabile was ripping him off; so were Jesse and Cal. Stabile would save five grand and Jesse and Cal another five. All they had to do was wait until Cranberry tired of waiting and left. They were probably there right now, making the switch. They could all easily do the deal without him. *Shit,* he thought, *they had already made the motherfucking deal.* His brain shrieked at him, "Why hadn't you seen that coming?" Cranberry left a tired kid behind the takeout window holding a large Coke and Big Mac extended toward his car as he peeled rubber out of the parking lot.

Stabile had driven off and then swung around and followed the Corvette up to Lincoln Boulevard to make sure Cranberry was actually leaving. When Cranberry turned south on Lincoln Boulevard, Stabile was satisfied and drove back to the apartment. However, just to be extra cautious, he parked the undercover car down the alley behind the apartment. When he saw no one around, he went back upstairs to see Arnold and the two detectives. He gave the orders to release the police backup teams and prepare to leave. Arnold kept asking questions about what could have happened to Jesse Carmody and Cal Santiso, and Stabile reluctantly gave forth different notions but said he hoped Cal and Jesse would be back soon. Hell yes, Stabile hoped they'd be back, because he hated the notion of losing the bust, disappointing Big TC, and missing out on $20,000.

Cranberry parked down the block, quickly walked up the dark street, and quietly entered the apartment building. As he walked toward the stairs, he began to hear Stabile's voice. He knew it; he fucking knew it. He pulled out his chrome-plated Ruger, pushed off the safety, and with his long legs quietly took the stairs three at a time. His thought was to quickly waste all three of them and take everything.

Cranberry was on his way to the back apartment when he passed the open door to the adjoining unit. Arnold and Stabile were on their way out and the two uniformed cops were following them with the recording equipment in their hands. Cranberry glanced into the room and the four cops stared back at Cranberry. A tenth of a second later, Cranberry spun around and sped down the hall. Of the detectives, Stabile reacted first and thundered down the short hall after Cranberry who bounded down the stairs eight at a time. In a practiced move, Stabile yanked out his compact Beretta, snapped back the slide injecting a bullet, and flicked off the safety. Stabile knew he'd better kill Cranberry. He strained and heaved his considerable muscled bulk after the faster man. In the dim light, Stabile misjudged the distance from the end of the hallway to the top of the stairs by three-sixteenths of an inch, and his right foot went over the edge and slipped off the first step. As he pitched forward out of control, the fingers on his gun hand inadvertently tightened, and as he somersaulted down the stairs, he shot himself through the right knee.

It was a bad place to get hit. The other men were following closely and they half fell over him as Stabile continued to roll down to the last step. Panicked at the sound of the shot, the officers stopped on the stairs. They couldn't tell where the shot had come from and their detective was down, obviously shot by someone. They pointed their weapons over Stabile who lay writhing at the bottom step. A moment later, they heard the sound of the Corvette roaring away. Satisfied Cranberry was gone, they rushed down the remaining stairs to Stabile's side and peered at their wounded leader. It didn't take long for Stabile to go into shock from the pain and stupidity of the whole caper.

The detectives and Arnold dumped Stabile into a car and got him to the hospital in record time. After he was admitted, sedated, and sent to the operating room, Arnold took Stabile's keys and had the boys take him back to the apartment. With one circle around the block, they discovered the Roadmaster in the alley. Arnold got out and drove it back to the station. By the time he parked the big Buick, it was already after seven in the morning, and he was exhausted. He picked the gym bag off the front seat where Lou had left it. Just to make sure Stabile hadn't left any of his things in the car, Arnold took a look in the trunk. He noticed a gym bag identical to the one he was holding that Stabile had brought with him for the buy. Opening the bag in the trunk, he was surprised to see six kilos of what looked to be cocaine. For the life of him, Arnold couldn't think what it was doing there. It confused him, so he took the two bags into the station house, went to see his captain, and posed the mystery. The captain was having his morning coffee and Danish. He bit off a hunk of bear claw as Arnold unzipped the bags, one empty and one filled with six bricks of cut cocaine. The Captain peered intently at the contents for seven seconds and then said, "Hmmm."

It was then that Arnold thought he possibly should have talked to Stabile about it first.

CHAPTER TWENTY-FOUR

THE SHOOTING AND FIRE at the trailer in Wilmington took some time to piece together. Forensics at the Harbor Division spent a couple of serious days investigating and did a pretty good job, finally concluding Jesse Carmody and Cal Santiso had killed one another. Getting their identities took a little longer, but the fingerprints in the El Camino brought the whole business into line from Texas to Venice. What didn't add up was the knife they discovered stuck in Carmody's charred body. Nothing seemed to fit, unless Cal had stabbed Jesse, then gone to his bed, lay down, gotten shot, and then in turn had shot Jesse. A more plausible theory concluded there was a third person. But that person would have taken all the cocaine, but hadn't. So that theory made little sense in a practical view. Their final conclusion was that Cal had stabbed Jesse, the two had struggled, and then they'd shot one another. Although burned and subjected to a propane detonation, the cocaine had been well packaged and more or less stayed intact under the bloody pillow and Jesse's exploded head.

When he heard about the incident in Wilmington, Pearson was more than a little interested in the details. With Jesse and Cal dead, it looked like a case closed on the Thombridge-Cullen murder. He thought of informing Nick but decided to wait. There were still a lot of possibilities flying around about Jesse and Cal, especially considering what had happened with Stabile. It was Stabile who had the direct line on those guys, and now there was the trailer mayhem to consider. Just to check it out and piss the guy off a little, Jim picked up a box of See's Candy and paid Stabile a visit in the hospital.

Stabile looked ugly, with a bruised head, IV drip, and a leg bandaged like a tyrannosaurus had chewed it. Despite being under sedation, Stabile's eyes shifted nervously. When Pearson asked him about the night in question, Stabile ranted that Cranberry was a boss in a drug gang, had committed murder, grand theft, extortion, and drug racketeering, so Stabile wanted that man and wanted him badly. Pearson understood Stabile was just grandstanding and had his own agenda, but at the moment, Pearson didn't care. It turned out Stabile hadn't gotten the news about Jesse and Cal. When Pearson told him they were dead and cooked, he noticed Stabile seemed to go into shock and looked as though his own mother had died. Pearson knew then that Stabile had lost more than a drug sting.

When he left the hospital, he decided to take a ride to Wilmington and sniff around. After talking to the chief investigating officer, Pearson drove to the alley where the trailer had been. He patiently stared at the crime scene, which now had been released, an abandoned yellow police tape flapping listlessly on the ground. He talked to the owner of the house, got the scoop on who owned the trailer, and learned the man was on a tuna boat off the coast of Costa Rica. That was little or no help. There was a big, nasty-looking guy with a large nervous dog. The man looked like he had a lot to hide but Pearson didn't think it had anything to do with the trailer mayhem. Again, no help.

Pearson worked his way beyond the last house the Wilmington Police had questioned and went around the corner. A lot of detectives didn't like going into the field and tracking things down, but Pearson loved it. That's what he enjoyed most about the job, walking down some facts and in the process dropping in on all sorts of people. He'd questioned short-order cooks, psychiatrists, waiters, doctors, bums, jazz musicians, aircraft designers, and librarians. In this case, as he arrived at the corner house, he found a woman who weighed 350 pounds if she weighed a gram. A piece of outgoing mail said her name was Selma Godowsky. She had on one of those wraparound dresses designed for easy wearing, contractions and expansions. It had been some time since the dress had been washed and Pearson couldn't help but glance at some large food stains decorating the front. The stains were interestingly spaced around yards of Disney sky-blue fabric and Pearson thought they looked like tiny multicolored cloud formations. Reflexively, he offered her his card. He could see from the cluttered interior of the house that the woman had serious neighborhood history. He started by gently asking some questions about what she had heard on the night of the murders. Selma seemed pleased with the attention and happy to respond to questions. She answered in a surprisingly light and pretty voice. "I had my bedroom window open. I was smoking a cigarette. I don't like to smoke in the house, but late at night, I'm fearful of going outside. There was some yelling. One man yelling the same thing over and over. It sounded like 'hoot the mucker,' or 'toct the sucker,' goodness, I don't know what it was," she said, wiping her palms nervously on her dress.

"Shoot the fucker," Pearson offered, hoping he didn't offend the woman with his language.

She wasn't offended at all. She had been married to a tugboat captain. "Yes, that could have been it. Yes, I believe it was."

"Anything else?"

"Just the shots and then some minutes later, the explosion." Pearson nodded and waited through a long silence, just in case she had anything to add. She did. "And the cab."

"The cab?"

"Yes, there was a cab parked on the corner. When I heard the yelling and shooting, I wasn't sure of the direction and I looked farther out my window and there was an older cab parked on the corner."

"Do you remember the cab company or the color of the cab?"

"Oh, yes and I remember the cab number too, because I had quite a bit of time to look. I wrote it down. I was frightened and wasn't sure what was going on. I keep to myself and don't get involved with these new people. We've had a lot of shooting and bad gang business around here."

"I understand," Pearson gently prodded.

"Then, later, a man came around the corner, got in the cab, and drove away."

"Could you describe the man?"

"Well, it was fairly dark, but I believe I could." And she did, down to his boots.

NICK GOT UP EARLY, and as recommended he called Blanchard at 9:00 a.m., New York time. He was kept on hold while the secretary told her boss of the call. A moment later, she came on and told him Blanchard would call back at the end of the day. Nick didn't think it a good sign. Frustrated, he went for a run. After a time, he had to stop. His lungs and muscles were feeling better, but his cut hand began to protest loudly.

The day dragged by. He tried to sleep, but his mind was racing. He spent some time on the back steps watching two little girls playing in a makeshift sand box and worried about how he would relate to Melissa after his long absence. He concluded he'd just have to see how things went and not press it.

His bags were packed and resting by the door. His travel clothes were laid out on the bed. His cameras and lenses were in two newly purchased camera bags, and regardless of circumstances, he took some pride at seeing them on the kitchen table. He reached into one of the bags and removed the secondhand Leica, loaded some film, carefully cleaned the lens for the second time that day, and dropped it into his pocket. He was dressed for his last night of driving. In the morning, he had a ten o'clock flight to Atlanta. From there he'd go to Macon to see Melissa. Then, hopefully, it was back on a plane five days later to JFK, a quick jog into the city to have dinner with his dad, and then begin the journey to his assignment. If Blanchard didn't come through, it would just be the overdue visit to see his daughter and Dad, then back to LA, and the cab while he continued his efforts to get an assignment. If it came to that, he decided he'd go over to Sea Cabs and work with Billy.

When the call didn't come through by 6:00 p.m. New York time, the walls of the small apartment closed in and he went outside onto the porch and stared at the six degrees of ocean view. He fretted about why the prick Blanchard would keep him waiting until the last second for final confirmation. He grew increasingly fearful the guy would blow him off.

At 7:12 p.m. New York time, the telephone rang. Blanchard's secretary asked him to hold and Nick held everything, including his breath.

When Senior Vice President/Deputy Editor Peter Blanchard got on the phone, he got right to the point. "I let Philip Dahlgren damn near talk me into sending you. You were always a first-rate, ballsy, lunatic photographer, and because of that he said we'd get some very good, exciting stuff from you. On the other hand, you are possibly just a lunatic fuck-up and I may not get anything except a headache." Nick waited. Blanchard's equivocation had left him stunned and the fact he had said "*damn near* talk me into sending you" left Nick cold. For a moment, neither man said anything. "Are you comparatively sober now?'

"I'm totally sober and I'm not a lunatic—anymore."

"Really? Well, maybe you're the wrong person for the job. We need something big, and whether it heats up or not, Afghanistan is no easy gig. There's a lot of competitive press sniffing around for something to go down, but we're going to get the drop on them. That is, if whoever goes actually sends us back great stuff."

"You know I can do that."

"Yeah, and I know there are people out there who won't give me palpitations from long distance. I've got photographers beating on my door every day, wanting to go, anywhere, anytime; good guys, too."

"I'm the right person and I want it. My bags and cameras are by the front door."

"It's a ten-week assignment, a lot longer if we want it."

"As long as it takes," Nick said.

There was a long pause until Blanchard finally said, "I gotta warn you, they've got some great dope over there, heroin and, in particular, that Afghan hash."

"I'm not indulging."

"That's good. But if convenient, send me back some of that hash they've got." The editor laughed, but Nick knew he was serious. The senior VP could play around, but Nick couldn't. That was clear.

"I'll send you back some great pictures."

"That'll do just fine." And it was a done deal.

Nick returned to the porch, took some deep calming breaths, and relished the glare on his face from the setting sun. Half blinded by the light, he returned to the kitchen, and when his eyes adjusted to the comparative dimness, he dialed the phone. He impatiently waited the two long seconds it took to be connected to Macon, Georgia.

Lillian sounded pleased with Nick's announcements, but before putting Melissa on the phone and in preparation for Nick's visit, she was compelled to give warnings and instructions, all of which Nick intuitively knew. When Melissa answered, her voice sounded so beautiful to Nick, he was having trouble speaking. He just wanted to listen to what had become a little girl's lilting southern accent.

"Daddy?

"Yes?"

"Are you really old?"

"I'm so old, you'll have to carry me around."

"Okay," came the chipper reply. "I'll carry you all around and put you with my teddy bear."

◆◆◆

AFTER HE HUNG UP, Nick kept his hand on the receiver, reluctant to let go of the connection to Melissa. Something was going on inside him, and after a minute of staring at the silent phone, he identified it. He was happy. Opening the front door of his apartment, he jogged to the beach, across the sand, and stood silently at the water's edge for a long time. The waves were small and complimented the gentle onshore breeze and glow from the sun's last rays. His contentment was finally interrupted by the thought of what he had to do next. He turned and walked toward the landlord's door. After a loud "Hold on," his landlord appeared. Harv was a short round man in his early fifties with a carefully maintained California tan. "What happened to your hand?"

"I quit telling that story. It's embarrassing." Nick went on to decline the offer of a beer and gave Harv the news that he was leaving.

Harv didn't seem to care, and Nick was almost insulted. "Where you going?"

"Overseas for ten weeks, but when I do a great job, they'll let me rest a bit and send me off again."

"You've been a good tenant but I'm glad you're going. I'm gonna fix the joint up, extend the kitchen, bay window, hardwood floors, new plumbing, the works. I can jack up the rent." Harv extended his arms like he was showing a castle. "By the beach, ocean view, boys and girls." He turned to Nick. "You gotta love it. I'm playing the California game. If you want, come back in four months and I'll rent it to you again for two fifty more a month."

Nick shrugged. "Maybe, we'll see how it goes."

"You taking the Camaro?" Harv asked with interest.

"I found a place to stash it, in case."

"Fuck, sell it to me. I'll give you six hundred."

"It's rusted out and leaking transmission fluid," Nick confessed.

"I got eyes."

"What do you want it for?" Nick asked.

Harv moved closer to Nick and stared up at him. "Are you kidding? It's a fucking Camaro, not some Jap piece of shit. You ever look at the license plate holder? 'Butler Chevrolet, Newark.' I'm from fucking Newark. We're meant for each other. I'll go seven hundred. I'm gonna paint her candy-apple red and make her my bitch."

Nick laughed and felt his face break into the widest grin in a year.

✦✦✦

Vern gave Nick a good cab for his last run, 393. Nick reached into his pocket and pulled out his Leica and took Vern's picture. Uncharacteristically, Vern grinned broadly. With some embarrassment, the men told one another they had enjoyed working together. As he drove from the yard, Nick remembered 393 was the same cab in which Stepper had been murdered. He hoped it wouldn't bring him bad luck.

Nick decided to make a long night of it. He'd drive until six or seven, then drop off the cab, go to his apartment, get his bags, and head to the airport. He could sleep on the plane. He realized, with a touch of irony, he'd have to take a cab to LAX.

Shortly after Nick drove out, Pearson walked into the taxi yard and looked around. He had never been inside an actual cab company's facility. He stood studying it for some time. Looking out the dispatcher's window, Vern saw Pearson and recognized he was a cop. Vern had done a little time early in his life and still had a knee-jerk reaction when he saw the law. Vern told the two ladies taking orders he was going out back to have a smoke. He didn't want to talk to the man who was making his way toward the shack, and he had a personal rule never to get involved with any business drivers got into with the police.

Pearson cordially greeted the two ladies, flashed his badge, and said he had a request. One of the ladies ignored him completely, instantly understanding why Vern had slipped out the back door. However, the other woman liked any man in a jacket and tie and became very chatty. "Not a big deal," Pearson said. "I just want to know who was driving cab number two-three-three, four nights ago."

Had it been an identifiable driver from the cab number, she might have inadvertently lost the record. Had it been Vern, he would have told him the cab was "shopped," that night. But the woman didn't remember who had been driving it, as it was one of the old cabs that had no regular driver. She went to the file near the door, pulled the trip sheet from the folder, and handed it to Pearson. It wasn't until she was handing it to him that she noticed Nick Cullen's name. She liked Nick, but it was too late to take it back. Pearson took the trip sheet and stared at it for some time, without expression. Finally, he spoke. "Do you mind if I keep this? I'll get it back to you."

"Let me make a quick copy," she said, walking to the small half-burnt-out copy machine at the end of the room.

"When does Cullen come back in?"

"Usually, he doesn't come in until seven in the morning or after, though lately he's been coming in earlier. You never know with him."

"So he's out now?"

"Yes, you want us to call him?"

"No, that's all right. Thanks for the help," Pearson said, accepting the trip ticket. He walked out of the yard, got in his car, and drove toward home. He'd get Nick tomorrow on his way in to work. In the morning, Nick would be tired from driving all night. It would all work out well. Pearson liked the idea of making the arrest. The man had obviously gone around the bend, was out there, driving around in a cab with weapons, and could go off like a bomb at any moment. Next time, he could take out a customer even. Pearson didn't need to let any more characters go out and create problems, as he had with his son, Reginald Post, and others in his life. He remembered only too well the mad look in Nick's eyes when he'd trashed his desk. *Yeah*, Pearson thought. *Take crazy Nick back into the station and say to the boys, "By the way, I solved two major crimes with one bust and here is the sorry slob who is both victim and perp."* It had a nice ring, but Pearson took none of his customary pleasure in the thought.

✦✦✦

As Nick drove that night, everything seemed to take on a new freshness, a new clarity. Nick caught himself smiling at the thought of seeing Melissa. The smile would sometimes fade out of concern about seeing her after the year apart. He had purchased a few gifts and convinced himself all would be fine as long as Lillian didn't throw too many curves.

Alternating with thoughts of Melissa was the excitement of getting back to traveling and shooting pictures. There, too, he had some apprehension. It had been too long. However, not taking pictures for a year had served to reveal the connection between him and the artistic expression he would now try to accomplish. There was, as always, the specter of failure, but he had growing confidence he would find his way. Before, he was great at capturing the moment, but to his mind he was often missing the soul of the image. If he could better accomplish that, he could build a body of work that would result in expressing his vision of the pain and hope of the human condition. The idea was a simple and practical enough direction Nick felt comfortable with. He believed it could work as a new and creative beginning.

Around 1:00 a.m., Nick drove over to Sea Cabs to say goodbye to Billy. When Billy saw Nick step up to the office door, he took off his headset, handed it to a pleasingly trashy-looking young woman with beautifully shaped breasts, and said, "Try your luck at this for a few minutes."

Billy stepped outside and his eyes peered at Nick's bandaged hand. "How'd that happen?"

"Stupidity."

Billy nodded, fished into his pocket, pulled out a fresh joint, lit up, and passed it to Nick, who smiled and waved his hand as a soft rejection.

"I just came by to say thanks."

"You going somewhere?" Billy asked.

"I'm stepping away for a bit. See my daughter and stuff." Nick looked directly at Billy. "You were a big help to me. I owe you."

"You don't owe me anything," Billy said. "It was good working along with you."

"Why don't you go over to my cab and I'll take your picture."

"Why your cab?" Billy asked.

"I don't want any of these Sea Cabs in the shot. I want to remember you from our old company."

Billy grinned, went over, and leaned up against Nick's taxi. The light was insufficient, so Nick jumped into a parked Sea Cab, started it, switched on the headlights, and backed the cab into position so the lights shined on Billy at a good angle. Stepping out of the car, Nick moved around taking several shots. It was awkward with his bandaged hand, but he managed. Billy was relaxed in front of the camera. Encouraged, Nick took some of Billy taking a hit off the joint and some of him staring straight into the lens. Satisfied, Nick said, "Give me a card from this place and I'll send you some prints."

Ever the good company man, Billy pulled a card from his wallet and handed it to Nick. "Send them within the next month or two, because I won't be here after that."

Surprised, Nick asked, "Where you going?"

"Going into partnership in a garage and back to driving a tow truck. The cab thing is just about over for guys like us. There are more and more cabs on the street, they're going to put monitors out at the airport and have holding areas, it's finished for making decent money."

Nick looked down at the card, then put it in his pocket. "I'll get the pictures to you in a couple of weeks." He reached his hand out to shake Billy's and, remembering the wound, withdrew it. The two men looked at one another for an awkward moment, then gave one another a brief hug.

"Just as well you never found those guys," Billy said. "It could have been a mess."

Nick looked at Billy when suddenly the dispatcher called Nick's cab number.

"Three-nine-three?"

Nick leaned inside the cab and grabbed the mike. "Three-nine-three."

"What's your location?"

Nick didn't tell the dispatcher precisely where he was but informed him of the general area.

"Pick up Irene. Ride's going near Westwood."

"Check."

"What's she do, anyway?" Billy asked. "She always asked for you."

"She's a receptionist." Nick didn't think he had to share the true information with anyone. He felt protective of Irene. He got into 393 and started the engine. "See you around, Billy. Thanks again, for everything."

Just before two in the morning, Nick picked Irene up at the Airport Marina Hotel. She got in the cab and rode on in silence for a while as Nick drove toward her motel in West Los Angeles. Nick studied her for a moment in the mirror. Irene was usually quiet, but this night she seemed more pensive than usual. Nick found he had developed a true interest in her. She had an ever-present air of mystery. A large part of it was because of her profession. Her girl-next-door dresses and clean-looking face definitely gave her the advantage in the prostitution business. Nick thought about the many customers she must have met who were startled to see she was the working girl and not someone who had just come from a Bible meeting. "I'm thinking of going home for a while."

Nick was surprised by the confession and realized he didn't actually remember where she was from. "Where is home?"

"Washington. Seattle."

"Near where you want that house, on Waldon Island?" Nick recollected.

"The island is distant in time and space from Seattle, but it's not that far in miles," she said.

"Got it."

She hesitated a moment. "Lately, I've had the feeling I'm being watched. I don't know. I don't feel safe anymore. I'm thinking of going home for a while," she repeated. "What do you think?"

"I think if you're feeling a bit paranoid, you ought to go with your instincts. You could probably use a break, anyway. You've had a pretty good run, haven't you?"

"Yes, it's gone as planned. I think I can buy the house."

"Well, mission accomplished. Waldon Island, here you come."

"I don't know."

"Well, for what it's worth, this is my last night. Maybe you should make it yours, as well."

"You're not going to be around anymore?" She seemed genuinely disappointed.

"No, I'm off to some other things. I'll be leaving this job and Los Angeles for a while."

They rode on in silence. Nick took his bandaged hand from the steering wheel and drove with his left hand only. His right hand still throbbed painfully if he used it too much. It was healing slowly, but he would be able to have the stitches removed in Macon before he went overseas. After they pulled into the motel courtyard, Nick turned around. Irene leaned forward and pressed ten dollars into the palm of his left hand. "I'm going to keep thinking about what you were saying."

"Don't think about it too long," Nick said.

Irene looked at Nick for a moment and suddenly got terribly shy, gave a nervous little gasp, and said, "You may come upstairs with me for a little while, if you care to. Since you're leaving."

"I think I should keep on going," Nick said reflexively. She suddenly looked just a little sad but in a gentle way, and she put her head down, then looked up at him again with her hazel eyes, magnified by the round lenses in her glasses. Nick felt his chest rise as he took an involuntary breath. She remained where she was, timorously looking up at him from under her long eyelashes, and Nick could easily see why the guys fell for it and so did he. Nick could feel his head lighten as his blood rushed downward. He heard himself say, "Come on, I'll walk you up."

Inside the surprisingly large motel room, Irene turned to Nick shyly. "I'm sorry I don't have anything to offer but sodas. I don't drink."

"Me either, although I used to be pretty good at it." Nick paused for a moment. "Well, maybe I wasn't good at it at all. Water will be fine." He followed her with his eyes as she went into the kitchenette and got some cold water from the refrigerator. She brought it to him and Nick thanked her, then took a long drink. The water tasted great, refreshing. *Now what?* Nick wondered.

Irene didn't help. She simply stood there, smiling sweetly, and finally took the glass from him, went to the kitchen with a slight skip in her walk, and then just as quickly returned to Nick who stood immobile and uncertain. For fifty or sixty trips from the hotel near the airport to the motel in Westwood, she had been in the back of the cab, but now here she was, cavorting in a playful way right in front of him. "You may kiss me goodbye if you wish." She stood before him, hands clasped behind her back, and looking as though she would be disappointed if he didn't. He bent down and kissed her lightly on the lips, but the kiss easily grew in passion as her teeth gently bit his lips and her tongue flicked and darted around his mouth. He felt her well-formed body press against him and he knew he probably couldn't stop. Finally, she pulled away from him breathlessly. "Oh, are you going to make love to me?" she asked in an almost helpless but eager way. It was then that it hit him, the certain similarity between Irene and Julianne. It was the ability to look plain but womanly, in-command but elusive, downright intelligent and sexy all at the same time. Nick went to her and put his bandaged hand behind her back. With the other, he pulled out the clips holding back her hair, and it fell down and bounced softly off the frames of her glasses. Nick removed the glasses and her hazel-brown eyes went soft and abstract. "I should pay you."

"I'll do you for free, it being the last night and all."

"You've been paying me all along, I should pay you. It's fair."

"All right, I'll do you for fifty."

Nick was curious. "That sounds like a good rate."

"It's half." She paused for a moment, and then smiled shyly. "Without tip and extras."

Nick turned away and went over to a small table and counted out fifty dollars and set it down. As he did so, he said, "This is my last night and maybe I could be your last trick."

"Yes," he heard her say. "Possibly you will be." When he turned around, she had unbuttoned her dress and it was lowered to the top of her breasts. She clutched it with one hand and with the other she had lifted the dress up to just below her panties and showed her long shapely legs. Her breath was coming quickly and deeply and Nick watched her breasts rise and fall. He couldn't tell if she was truly aroused or acting. As Nick walked toward her, he thought it looked real enough, and suddenly he didn't care one way or the other.

A few minutes later, they were in her bed making love. He had decided to try and be patient and slow, but it had been a long time and Irene didn't help. She grabbed him and moved against him quickly, with a surprised expression Nick found unbelievably exciting, and all the while she chanted, "Oh Nicky, Nicky, Nicky." When he was involuntarily going up and over the edge of his control, he felt her pull him to her and moan, "Oh, Nicky, Nicky, we're free, we're free, I'm coming, I'm coming," and so did he.

As he walked down the stairs from her second-story motel room, he was aware of Irene's scent on him. There was no perfume, it was just Irene. He turned around and looked back up to her door. It had cost him fifty bucks, almost half a night's work, but Irene was worth whatever she got. "She's so good, it would be a wonder if the woman couldn't buy all of Waldon Island," Nick said to himself.

He wished her well.

◆ ◆ ◆

Ever since the Louie character had revealed himself to be a narc, Cranberry had been holed up with one of his lady friends by the name of Leticia. He was confused about who was doing what to whom and why. Finally, he called Mose at his home. "What the fuck is this shit? You set me up with some motherfucking narc."

"I don't know what you're talking about, brother."

"Nigga, don't 'brother' me. I almost got my fucking ass shot and busted over that shit."

"Where are you?" Mose asked. "We got to talk 'bout this."

"Man, if you say you don't know nothing, then I ain't talking to nobody till I figure out what the fuck is going on." Cranberry slammed down the phone.

Cranberry was right; he had a lot of thinking to do, but mostly he snorted a lot of coke and fretted for a few days more. Mose could have been stupid enough to set him up with a narc without knowing. The jails were full of guys who had been busted that way. It occurred to Cranberry he might have been deliberately set up by Mose, but why? If the deal was bogus, there was nothing in it for Mose, so then it could have been Big TC behind it, but once again, why? He knew the answer would come soon and it would either be the narcs or Big TC, or both. Either way, it was bad news.

Around 10:00 p.m., Leticia came back with her girlfriend from seeing *Kingdom of the Spiders*, starring William Shatner and Woody Strode. Cranberry had been holed up for days and knew he should have stayed that way, but after getting Leticia and her girlfriend high, he got restless. He left Leticia, her friend, and the security of the apartment, jumped into his Corvette, and drove over to his favorite bar in Inglewood to shake the dust off.

After last call, Cranberry was feeling better. He stepped out into the night and briskly walked around the corner toward his Corvette. There, he saw Mose sitting on the front fender, which sunk awkwardly under his massive weight. Cranberry wasn't sure whether to run, shoot, or slap a high five, but the answer came as he felt a gun pressed into his back. "Shhh," hissed a voice behind him, and a bony hand reached around and took the chrome-plated Ruger from his shoulder holster.

"You and I got a lot to talk about," Cranberry blustered at Mose.

Mose stood up and the Corvette's shock absorbers gratefully stretched upward. "There ain't gonna be a whole lot of talkin'," Mose said.

Big TC's Cadillac suddenly pulled up. The narrow-looking man with the bony fingers opened the back door and held it for Cranberry. Mose went around the other side so Cranberry wouldn't be tempted to scoot across the seat and leap out the other side. Mose had seen that one before.

At 2:50 a.m., Nick pulled up to the stand at American and observed two cabbies talking to a slightly built young man about eighteen years old. The kid had long black hair to his shoulders; his clothes were clean but worn thin. Nick could tell from the physical language of the trio that the young man wanted to go somewhere but neither driver wanted to take him. Nick was third up behind them, so he wandered over to see what was going on. He stared at the young man who looked back at him with a wide-eyed gentleness he found disarming. Nick tried to remember where he had seen that look before, and then it came to him. There were villages in Africa and India where he had seen people look at him that way. The villagers had an openness and honesty about them that was disarming to the world-weary. No matter how well intended you might feel, the perfect comfort and peace they had within themselves created a spiritual quality that somehow made an outsider feel corrupt. Nick learned the innocents were often hated for that very quality.

The young man tried again to explain his situation to the drivers. "She said to just take a cab and she would pay when I got there."

"Neither of you guys want to take him?" Nick asked.

"Hey, you know how it is. Any long fare with a kid like him, you get the money up front."

"Where are you going?" Nick asked.

The young man produced a small piece of paper with an address in the south part of Long Beach, a thirty-five minute ride with no traffic. "Miss Morrison said to just take a cab and she would pay when I got there."

Instinctively, Nick knew the young man was telling the truth. The only problem would be whether or not Miss Morrison was there to pay. He turned to the other drivers. "If you don't mind. I'll take him."

"You take him and you take the chance," said one of the drivers, and they walked away.

"Let's go," Nick said to the kid, and they walked back to his cab.

"My name is Dewey George. I'm an Aleut."

"My name is Nick Cullen. I'm a New Yorker," he said, going with the flow. He shook Dewey's hand and then placed his small canvas bag in the trunk. "What are you doing down here, Dewey?"

"I'm going to the anthropology department at the university to record the dialects of my language. I know all the dialects. They want to record them before they all die out."

"I see," Nick said and wondered what university, but Dewey kept on talking.

"They picked me because I can speak English well. I learned most of it from TV and the guys on the pipeline. I was like their mascot," Dewey said, getting in the cab. As they drove out Century Boulevard and dropped onto the San Diego Freeway heading south, Dewey stared out at the darkened buildings and kept repeating, "Wow," over and over again. "Where do all these people come from?"

"They've been coming here from all over the world for centuries."

There was a pause while the kid let that sink in, and then he asked, "What do they eat?"

Nick grinned at that. "Well, they eat food that comes from all over the world as well. You can't eat the fish you catch along the shore here and there is no game."

"You can't eat the fish?"

"No, they're poisoned from all the chemicals around here."

"Wow. I go out in my kayak and catch salmon. It's dangerous, you've got to know what you're doing, but I couldn't live without my salmon."

Nick knew when Dewey said he couldn't live without it, he meant he literally couldn't live without it.

"I made this ring," he said and leaned forward to show Nick a thick gold ring with a large green stone setting. "It took me all summer long to find the gold for the ring in the streams. I spent hours every day looking."

"I think it's beautiful, but you shouldn't show it around in Los Angeles too much. Just to friends when you have them."

"Will you be my friend?" Dewey asked.

"I would be happy to. I may be going away for a while, but I'll give you my number. I've got an answering service on it and will be checking in from time to time. If I'm not around, leave me a message and I promise I'll get back to you." They drove on while Dewey stared out into the night. Finally, Nick got around to asking the question he wanted to know as soon as he heard Dewey was hanging around the pipeline. "Did you run into a photographer up there by the name of Johnny Cox?"

"Yes, I met him," Dewey said, as though it were the most normal thing in the world to know someone in common four thousand miles away. "He came back and forth a few times. Was he your friend?"

"I knew him a little. I had heard he got the...a job shooting the pipeline construction." *It would have been a good gig,* Nick thought with added regret.

"He took some pictures of me," Dewey said.

"That's great." *Funny,* Nick thought. *That he would have wound up meeting Dewey George.* He wondered if it was an omen of some sort. Well, regardless, in a few hours or so, he would be off again to a new adventure. There was no sense looking back, but as he drove down the 405 and came upon the Harbor Freeway, Nick glanced over at the oil refineries that marked the beginning of Wilmington and thought of his actions some nights earlier. He remembered the sad eyes of Cal as he died and the powerful serpentine struggling of Jesse snarling beneath him. He shuddered with the memory. As he stared over in the direction of Wilmington, he couldn't help but wonder what the trailer looked like now. He knew he shouldn't go. He had done enough crime photography to understand not to return to a crime scene.

He and Dewey talked some more, and in a not too subtle way Nick tried to explain how Dewey should look out for himself in Los Angeles. Dewey seemed confused but grateful and quietly fearful of the information. A little while later, they woke up Miss Morrison and she paid Nick. "Watch out for my new friend, Dewey," he said and left.

On the way back, rather than take the freeway the entire trip, Nick drove through Long Beach and went across the Vincent Thomas Bridge into the Wilmington/San Pedro area. The bridge itself was rather pretty and gave some variety to the endless freeways. It was not very long but extremely high for the span and it showed a vast expanse of docks, storage areas, and harbor making it a welcomed change of scenery. He enjoyed going over the bridge and drove it whenever the occasion allowed. But this night, possibly there was something more to it. Against his better judgment, he found himself driving into Wilmington and turning down the alley where the chaos had taken place. The trailer was gone and so was the El Camino. Only some broken glass, fragments of burnt paper, and piles of dirty sodden trash left behind gave a hint of what had happened. Nick felt a moment of panic and had the irrational thought that maybe Jesse and Cal had survived and had hooked the trailer to the El Camino and were driving away across the country, free. He shook off the bizarre idea and knew the vehicles would be in the police impound lot. Where Jesse and Cal were was now a matter of speculation, but one thing he understood with a sense of finality: they were dead. He had seen Cal Santiso die and he had worn pieces of Jesse Carmody's brains on his face. They were dead. Curiously, he didn't derive any pleasure from the fact, but he did feel a certain calm. The demons were leaving and so was he. Dropping the cab into low gear, he drove down the alley.

It was almost four in the morning and Selma Godowsky had been up all night. She stood up slowly and let her blue dress out a notch as she had just finished eating the quart of strawberry ice cream and was ready to sleep till noon. Hearing a vehicle coming down the alley, she pulled aside the curtain. Cars either had to turn left or right at the end of the alley, and either way, she had a great view. She watched as Nick made a right turn around the corner under the streetlight. Selma made a note of the cab's number, then went and picked up Pearson's card by the telephone. She knew her call would probably wake him, but she was too excited to wait. After all, he had said, "Call anytime."

EZEKIEL CLEMMONS ROUSED HIMSELF from his cardboard home in the alley and decided to go for breakfast before the Department of Sanitation took it away. He limped the three and a half blocks to Ruby's Barbecue and went directly to the Dumpster in back. He paused momentarily as he considered whether he felt like gnawing remnants from chicken, beef, or pork bones. Something inside him said to go for the beef bones if he could find them. Grabbing the lid on the dumpster, he lifted it up and found himself staring down at a six-foot-three-and-a-half-inch brown man with four bullet holes in his chest. The man's legs were bent under him at the knees to accommodate his height in the five-foot Dumpster. The man was staring straight up, eyes wide open. Recovering from his initial shock, Ezekiel stared at the man's face and noticed a smooth round growth below the ear that looked like a cranberry. He studied the oddity for a moment, then began going through the man's pockets.

❖❖❖

NICK DROPPED INTO LAX on the way back from Wilmington. It was the best place to pick up a fare on his move through the Westside. He was having a good night and enjoyed doing the sweep around the long horseshoe curve and was rewarded by seeing a businessman standing alone at United. The man whose luggage had been lost was feeling frustrated. He was on his way downtown to the Hilton without as much as a toothbrush. At that hour, Nick usually would have just jumped onto the freeway, but feeling a little pity for the man and his lost luggage, Nick explained he could either take the freeway or the surface streets. The freeway cost two dollars more but the surface streets took a little longer. "Which way would you like to go?"

"Why does it take longer if it's cheaper?" the man asked.

"Because you're going faster on the freeway, but it's more miles, the other way is shorter but slower."

"But how can it be cheaper if it's slower?"

"It just is." Nick was sorry he had explained the options to the man. He wasn't going to miss this part of the public service job. As a matter of fact, he thought, he wasn't going to miss any of it. Nick turned onto the long ramp that led from Century Boulevard to the La Cienega split. He had been waiting for a decision from the man, and finally at the last minute, Nick called to the man in back, "This is it, the split, fast or slow, two dollars more or two dollars less."

"The freeway," the man said, surprising Nick.

When Nick dropped him off, he thought about bringing the cab back in, but he was hungry, and it was only three blocks to the Pantry Restaurant. Plus, back home, everything was out of the refrigerator with the door propped open and the plug pulled from the wall. He was ready to go.

He parked the cab and stepped into the restaurant. He liked the funky look of the place and the eclectic mix of workers, lawyers, and stockbrokers. He had eggs, bacon, hash browns, and coffee. The food was disappointing and ordinary, but he wouldn't be starving when he got on the plane.

Nick's luck continued as he made a quick pass of the hotels and caught a fare to the airport. When he dropped the two Japanese businessmen at JAL, he started out of the airport and noticed there were fares waiting on Continental and United. It was time for him to go in, so Nick passed them by. He had booked his last fare forever and found he was taken by a sense of excitement but also concern. He had some lingering self-doubt about leaving the cocoon of the cab, and whether he would do a good job with the assignment. It had been a long time. A lot had happened since he'd last gone forth with cameras hanging from his neck.

At 6:42 a.m., Nick drove into the yard and began servicing the cab. Pearson got there a little late and thought he might have missed Cullen and would have to find him at home. He parked the unmarked car outside the gate. Just as he stepped inside the yard he was gratified by the sight of Nick turning in his paperwork at the dispatcher's window. Pearson watched as Nick casually hung out at the window, apparently having a nice conversation. Pearson thought, *If it hadn't been for that fucking Stabile, he could have picked Cal and Jesse up with what he had on them. Then he wouldn't have to be hanging around a taxi yard waiting to take down some slob whose wife had been murdered.* Pearson shook his head in disgust with himself. He was getting soft. If he was going to keep walking around with his detective's badge, he'd have to not give a shit. That's what got him into trouble with Reginald Post and others. Although the killers had it coming, Nick Cullen had beaten one so hard he fled LA, then he'd stabbed at least one more, and possibly shot them both.

Then he'd torched their trailer. The man had gone off the deep end. Pearson blamed himself for not locking him up after he'd confessed to beating Morgan Rainey and trashed his office. If not arrested, he wondered where Nick would go from here? Probably break some guy's neck that didn't have the right fare.

Nick waved goodbye to the people in the shack. Favoring his bandaged hand, he placed the strap of his bag over his left shoulder and walked toward the street. A moment later, he noticed Pearson waiting for him and knew he'd been had. *Well, maybe not, we'll see,* Nick thought. He pulled up his courage and greeted Pearson. "You must have some news to come find me here. You catch those guys?"

"In a manner of speaking, we did." Pearson said, studying Nick. "What'd you do to your hand?"

"Cut it with a knife opening a can of beans."

"You must have really wanted those beans. Looks like it must have been serious."

"It's easy to cut yourself. I'm sure you've done it," Nick said quietly.

Suddenly, Pearson did a double take. Nick looked like a different guy than the one he'd been talking to for the past months. He cocked his head and looked at Nick more closely. Nick thought he was waiting for him to say something else, and Nick didn't mind, so he went for the bottom line. "What have you got for me?"

"You got anything you want to tell me?" Pearson hedged.

"When I've got something to tell, or ask, I usually go to your office. This is the first time you've visited me, so what's up?"

Pearson studied Nick for a while. Nick looked younger, and despite the fact the guy had just driven for thirteen hours, he looked rested. It threw Pearson to see Nick looking so well. He was used to seeing people go the other way. It was going to make the next conversation all the more difficult. Pearson reached over, pulled on Nick's shoulder, and led him out of the yard to the other side of the fence. "I'll tell you some good news. The men you believed murdered your wife, and you accurately described as having the first names of Cal and Jesse, were a couple of guys called Jesse Carmody and Cal Santiso."

"'Were?'" Nick covered.

Pearson looked at him shrewdly. "Yeah, 'were.' We had those guys set up on a drug sale. We were gonna bust them for that, which was cut and dried, and that would have let us keep them around for a long time while we worked them on some other cases. I had them for the murder of some poor slob who caught them raping his girlfriend, almost the same MO as your case. All that tied together nicely, and in addition, I had your description and partial prints from your place that would have implicated them in that case as well. All in all, we had those guys solid on that. There's other stuff coming in from around the country. Those guys would have been doing consecutive life terms."

"Sounds great," Nick said, suddenly feeling nauseous.

"Yeah, it would have been, but some character went into their trailer and stabbed one of them and somehow got them to shoot one another, or shot them both and made it look the other way. Then this character burned up their joint." Pearson paused and watched Nick for signs. There weren't any. Nick waited. "So, as it turns out, they pull the knife from this guy Carmody's barbecued shoulder joint, and guess what the initial on the blade is?" Pearson waited for a reply, but knew he wouldn't get one. "'N.' It was a fucking 'N.'" Pearson stepped back and cocked his head again, looking Nick up and down. A habit of his he'd found effective over the years. He wasn't above enjoying himself in an explanation, and so he went on. "Then, if that's not enough, we learn a cab was parked on the corner near where those assholes were living. The cab number was two-three-three. As it turns out, that was the same cab you were driving that night. A woman identified the man who ran away from the scene and jumped into that cab." Pearson couldn't help but crack a smile and shake his head in wonder. "Basically, she identified you!" He barely suppressed a chuckle and then went on, "We have some blood samples they later found in the alley. If we had you tested, my guess is the blood would be a perfect match from the cut you got opening your fucking beans." Pearson almost giggled. "Then, about four this morning, I get jacked up in my bed by a call from our key witness who informs me cab number three-nine-three just cruised by the crime scene. I'd bet five hundred to one, it's the same number as the cab you just turned in."

Nick didn't say anything, suddenly very aware of the irregular pattern of the hurricane fence pressing into his back.

"That was really impressive how you found them and then killed them both. How'd you do it?"

Nick just stared at Pearson.

"You know, that was really an asshole thing to do. All you had to do was drop a dime and call me."

Nick was having trouble keeping from saying something, so he leaned back against the fence and tried to appear casual.

"You fucking jerk. Those guys were bad, bad, bad. The fact you're alive is like a fucking miracle." Pearson angled his head, tossed it to the side, and cracked a few stiff vertebrae. Nick heard them pop.

Unexpectedly, Nick just didn't give a damn anymore. He'd done what he had to do and there was enough finality to it. He was ready for the next thing, regardless. "If you're going to charge me, charge me. Otherwise, I've got a plane to catch."

"Oh, really? Funny you'd just go off like that, leave a knife stuck in a guy, torch the place, and head out of town."

"You can think what you want. It's been a year and I haven't been accomplishing anything. I don't belong in this job anymore."

"Where were you planning on going?"

"First, I'm going to visit my daughter in Georgia, drop by New York to have dinner with my father, then go on assignment to Afghanistan. It's my first photographic assignment in almost two years and it's a good one. Then, when I come back to the States, I'll go to New York, see my old man again, and between us, we'll decide what to do about my daughter, him, me, everybody. Those are my plans." Nick hesitated before asking, "What are yours?"

"I'm gonna read you your rights." And he did. Nick listened to Pearson's exhortations routinely tumbling forth and felt strangely disconnected. It reminded him of a priest's blessing at communion. Pearson followed the litany with the hard line, "You're under arrest."

There was a long moment of silence as Nick waited to get cuffed. Instead, Pearson reached into his pocket, pulled out a pack of cigarettes, tapped one on the soft pack, and lit up. He looked down at the burning Lucky Strike and said, "Let's go over to the car." He used the short walk to take a couple more drags and think. As they neared Pearson's car, Nick again waited for him to throw away the cigarette and cuff him. Instead, Pearson turned to Nick and asked, "Afghanistan, huh?" Nick nodded. Pearson shook his head in wonder. "I read there are some tribes, or whatever they call themselves, shooting at one another. You could maybe get killed or something."

"It's been known to happen."

Pearson regarded the Lucky Strike and then, as a habit from his days in the Marine Corps, he carefully fieldstripped it by tearing the paper end to end and scattering the remaining tobacco to the breeze. He turned to Nick. "You know, I can either turn this information over to my eager new partner, or I can do the paperwork myself, which will be a pain in the ass. Which should it be?"

Nick looked at Pearson steadily. "I don't see why you should have to do all that work and I don't see why I should have to deal with someone I don't know either."

Pearson studied Nick for a moment and decided to bump against his credo and ride with his instincts. "I'll tell you what. I'm going to put my information on how you killed Carmody and Santiso into a trunk, along with everything else. If you ever get busted on another battery or homicide and say, 'Hey, I killed two people and assaulted another and that Pearson guy let me go,' I'll put a bullet in your head. Got that?" Pearson didn't wait for an answer. "You're bad news for someone like me, get me confused about what I'm supposed to do, what duty is. I'm the kind of guy likes to do his duty," Pearson said, flipping away the little rolled ball of paper from the Lucky.

Nick didn't like hearing Pearson's bad news complaint. Considering the circumstances, it seemed frivolous. Nick personally had enough bad news to last a lifetime. He was momentarily confused as to what was really going on, and so for some subconscious reason he came back with, "If you would have done your duty in the first place, we wouldn't be standing here."

That's when Pearson hit him. It was a short, very solid right from a strong man who outweighed Cullen by eighty-two pounds. The hard punch was to the rib cage, right atop where Nick's heart was beating fast. Not expecting it and standing flatfooted, the punch staggered Nick backward five feet. Regaining his balance, Nick gasped for breath. Pearson came after him, but this time with his finger pointed. "Hey, asshole, you want to get cuffed and come in with me?" Nick shook his head and sucked air into his pneumonia-damaged lungs. Pearson was breathing a little hard from the short exertion and suddenly he was sorry he had done it. He hadn't hit anybody for a long time and wasn't even sure why he got so pissed at Cullen. Maybe it was because he liked the guy. He put his hands on his hips and stared at Nick. "I did my work, Cullen. Now you go do yours. I'm going to check from time to time to see how you've been behaving yourself and what you're up to. If you're in any kind of new trouble, I'll suddenly rediscover my memory and the information. Anybody asks me, I'll tell them my old partner who had a triple bypass and died when it sprung a leak somehow misplaced it. Then, you're going to be one sorry fucking cab-driving photographer." Pearson had backed Nick almost to the chain-link fence.

Nick pulled up and stood his ground.

Pearson stopped, looked at Nick, and shook his head. "I feel sorry for you. Go to Afghanistan, go anywhere, but get the fuck out of Los Angeles." He turned and walked away.

Nick watched the big man saunter across the street to his unmarked car. Stepping away from the fence, with his good hand, Nick intuitively pulled out the Leica. As Pearson opened the door to the car and turned back toward Nick for a final look, Nick snapped his picture. Pearson nodded his head in grudging acceptance of the moment and got in his car. As Pearson drove away, Nick slipped the camera back into his pocket and routinely cocked it with his thumb to have it ready for the next picture, whatever it may be. He watched until Pearson's car disappeared into the distance, and gradually he became conscious of the rising morning sun warming his back.

EPILOGUE:

EARSON PUT DOWN THE magazine with the review of Nick Cullen's book. He remembered a few months after he had let him go free, Nick had sent him a postcard from Afghanistan. The card had one word on it: "Thanks." The next year, the Russians invaded. In protest, President Carter had the United States withdraw from the Olympic Games. Russia's war went on for nine years.

Five years after receiving the postcard, Pearson was still chasing killers. One rainy December day, he was going through the meager personal mail he received at the police headquarters, or anywhere for that matter, when he discovered a Christmas card in the form of a four-by-six black-and-white photograph. It was an interesting-looking picture of a girl about eight years old. She was nicely dressed, had long, thick dark hair, and a funny infectious smile. She was standing high on some monkey bars in Manhattan's Central Park. Behind her, tall apartment buildings reached upward, aesthetically complimenting the girl's raised arms. Pearson didn't recognize the girl, so he turned the card over. In large, legible writing it said, "Merry Christmas, from Melissa and Nick Cullen." That was the last Pearson heard of Nick until he saw the photo layout.

Pearson stood up in the small outhouse and pulled up his flannel-lined jeans. The cold continued to eat into him and he decided then and there to give up fishing. The current trip would be his last. Considering how much effort he had spent at the sport in his life, he was forced to acknowledge he was a mediocre fisherman. He had always thought as a detective, he would be great at it. You know, catching things, but the two had little relationship except possibly the patience factor.

It had been some time since he'd retired after twenty-eight years of service with the LAPD. Pearson remembered he had begun to actively plan the end to his police career after the death of his partner, and in particular, the charitable act of letting Nick Cullen go free. *It was pretty much the same thing now,* he thought. He'd been salmon fishing every season for years and he'd done more than enough freezing his ass off and hauling in fish. The expressions, "we caught 'em," "we murdered 'em," "we were killing 'em," now left him cold as seeing a murder victim's body. He was tired of watching the large fish flop around on the bottom of the boat, their brilliant eyes looking up like a wide-angle lens, all-seeing of the gray sky with big overweight guys crowding in, staring down at them with hungry grins. He realized he now felt sorry for them. They were beautiful. Certainly better-looking than the people he was acquainted with. Shaking from the early morning chill, he knew this was his last trip for salmon and he mumbled out loud, "Let the poor guys come up river and drop their loads. What am I stopping them for? Next time, I'm going to Hawaii to warm my sorry old ass in the sun."

Pearson took another look at the magazine with Nick Cullen's startling photographs and thrust it between his shirt and thermal underwear. "This one's a keeper," he said as he buttoned his shirt. "Besides, it'll help stop the wind chill and keep me warm."

Opening the door of the outhouse, he stiffly walked down the wet trail to where his friends were waiting to cast off. His old friend Harry had brought along his twelve-year-old grandson. That would put a break on some of the fun. The kid was obnoxious and caught more fish than he did. *But what the hell difference does it make?* Pearson thought.

Arriving dockside, he looked around at Harry, the twelve-year-old kid, and the cynical old river guide gathered by the boat. "I have a feeling I'm gonna have a good day," Pearson said.

His friend and the kid flouted his remark, but Pearson didn't care. He stepped into the skiff with a new assurance born of having just made a generous decision and feeling very good about an old one.

THE END